# THE PONZI

P. T. Dawkins

Greed is central to Dawkins' (The Analyst, 2011) second novel, which astutely paints an ugly portrait of the financial industry's seedy underbelly, complete with unscrupulous brokers, ruthless bosses and their relentless pursuit of financial gain. An engaging… tale about the power of greed.

Kirkus Reviews

I highly recommend reading The Ponzi by P.T. Dawkins. (It) is incredibly well- written, with subplots and vivid characters. This is one book you won't want to put down.

Paige Lovitt for Reader Views

The Ponzi is a novel that will engage and entertain readers. It is one of those books that make you want to give it to the next person you come across, with a "you have to read this." (5 Stars.)

Lit Amri for Readers' Favorite

This is a work of fiction. The characters, incidents, dialogues and some settings are products of the author's imagination and are not to be construed as real. Any resemblance to actual events or persons, living or dead, is entirely coincidental.

Copyright © 2013 P. T. Dawkins

All rights reserved. No part of this publication may be reproduced or transmitted in any form or by any means electronic, including photocopy, recording, or any information storage and retrieval system, without permission in writing from the copyright owner.

ISBN-10: 1481256475
EAN-13: 9781481256476

# Dedication

*To my family –*
*my core*

Also by P.T. Dawkins

*The Analyst*

## Acknowledgement

Most novels are written with some level of support and The Ponzi has been greatly enriched thanks to the valuable insight and contribution provided by Anne, Pat, Doug, Ruth and Sandy - and kudos to John for his help with my website www.ptdawkins.ca. They know who they are.

# Chapter 1

"Michael. It's Tommy Van Buren. I have an urgent matter to discuss with you, lad."

Michael Franklin Junior, son of Michael Franklin Senior - star stockbroker now retired - slid his hand down across his face as if he could wipe the intrusion away. An 'urgent' matter. Every client was the same. It was always urgent when it was *their* matter. He looked around the room. Every broker sat facing two black computer screens at identical fake hardwood desks, chipped and discolored after years of abuse, arranged in rows like an assembly line of financial advice, each monitor flashing different colored lights to the beat of the market. And since the market was open, all headsets were on. Most on the floor tried to speak in a somewhat subdued voice, not out of respect for their fellow workers but rather not to divulge any sense of market insight or information about any specific client. Depending on seniority, a broker might be closer or further away from the front entrance, the meeting room or the manager's office. It was well known that you were a rookie if you could hear the receptionist on the phone.

"I've been giving our *situation* a great deal of thought and, well, you know how far back your old man and I go. I'd never do anything but show complete respect to you both." He chuckled. "Hell, a fair degree of my net worth is because of your dad and his uncanny investment advice. Now there's a man that knows the markets."

Tommy couldn't see Michael, eyes closed, shaking his head slowly back and forth. On retirement, Michael's dad had given his book of business to his son, with promises to his clients that the Franklin magic would carry on from one generation to the next. But that was before the start of the bear market. Michael was so sick of hearing about his wonderful father whose shoes he apparently couldn't begin to fill.

"I don't want you to take this personally, son," Tommy said. "You're an honest enough citizen and, although I have no way of knowing, I suspect you're hard working. The fact is you're not making me any money. In the last year alone you've lost me 15%. At my age, I'm retired you know, I can't afford that."

As he'd listened, it occurred to Michael that each of his dad's clients seemed to have their own way of breaking the news to him.

"It just isn't like it used to be."

Michael Franklin Senior had retired at the peak of the market, riding off into the sunset like some sort of cowboy hero, having vanquished the outlaws for good. The market decline that had started shortly after he blew out the candles on the retirement cake had wiped out up to 30% of investor assets - so far. Like a true bear market, most people suffered losses.

Senior's former clients all blamed Michael. Senior did nothing to stop them.

"But Mr. Van Buren," Michael said now, "with all due respect to my father, he didn't advise you in the middle of the worst bear market since the crash of 1929. We've built a nice, solid portfolio for you of banks and utilities stocks. They're all paying a healthy dividend and longer term the prices will recover. I'm very confident of that. After we ride out this storm…"

Tommy didn't let the young broker finish.

"Michael, you've tried that story on me several times before," he said. "I'm not stupid, my boy, so let's not insult each other's intelligence, shall we? It's the bank stocks that have been hit the worst. For you to be referring to them using the word 'healthy' just confirms my fears that you don't understand things as well as you should in order to be responsible for my money. I'm not going to belabor the point. I called to tell you I'm moving my account. My new representative will be in touch shortly to transfer my assets."

Harry Lugarno was fifty-six years old, an age where on the street you were considered the exception, not the rule, to still be employed. Educated at North Seattle Community College, he had been part of the brokerage business his entire career, his first job in the back office pushing papers. He'd built his client list the old fashioned way, starting with a local Seattle phone book as his list of potential customers. Born in New York City, he and his immigrant parents moved to the Seattle area when he was two years old, in search of a better life. Harry had met Lucinda Americi at Tacoma High School and they recently celebrated their thirtieth anniversary. According to God's mysterious ways, Harry and Lucinda had not been blessed with children. For him, the office was part of his family. He had dark black eyebrows and black hair edged with grey. His brown eyes and warm smile had comforted both clients and staff alike for many years.

Sitting in his cracked and faded brown leather chair and monitoring his twenty-five brokers through his floor to ceiling glass walls, Harry saw the telltale signs - again. Young Michael had buried his face in his hands. If Lugarno was ever going to be promoted out of his position as manager of this insignificant office in the middle of a shopping mall, he needed every dollar of client assets. According to the monthly report showing his ranking against the thirty-five other offices in the Northwest region, his team of brokers was slipping. Michael was the worst, systematically scaring away his dad's list of blue-chip clients. Harry asked himself again, how long must he respect his former partner's wishes? Could Dad not see that his son was in over his head?

After the call ended, Harry watched as Michael rose and solemnly walked to the office to tell him what everyone already knew. Harry should have said no from the start. He knew it. This little charade was never going to work. But the former three-time broker-of-the-year had threatened to recommend to his clients that they move to another firm immediately – unless his son was given a sporting chance to prove himself. But look at him. Junior barely shaved, didn't smoke, had perfect posture and never swore. He looked more cut out to be a librarian than a broker. Harry knew that when people with money, most often older people, looked at Michael, he looked – well, young. Whatever bond the clients had with the old man wasn't standing up to the ravages of a bear market and their baby-faced advisor.

How long before you could call a 'sporting chance' a 'complete failure'?

As Michael approached his door, Harry thought something else was odd about the boy. Most of the other brokers would have tried to hide the fact that they'd lost an account, but Michael was too honest to pretend otherwise. There he was, still wearing the headset on his neatly trimmed black hair, chord dangling helplessly by his side.

"So you lost another one, hey Junior?" he said.

Michael grimaced. Harry still called him Junior. It had been appropriate, sort of, when he had worked with his dad in the office but he'd been on his own for over a year now. He was a professional, and deserved to be treated like one.

"Yes, Harry, Mr. Van Buren just told me he was moving his account but it's not like I lost it. He said I was costing him too much money – like a bear market is my fault. Why do they blame me, Harry? I just don't get it."

Harry sat behind his desk, the mahogany top obscured by blue and pink trade ticket confirmation slips, the *Wall Street*

*Journal,* and various other reports. In one corner was a memento, acquired at one of the many broker conferences, consisting of a large gold coin that had been attached to a small frame so that it could be spun with the flick of a finger. The base had the inscription, *Buy* or *Sell?* His youngest broker's father, over a stellar thirty-year career, had landed the Van Buren account along with a long list of other stable, premium clients. Junior was losing his dad's clients like socks.

"He said he had the highest degree of respect for my dad and he hated to do this to him," Michael said now. "To him? Come on, Harry, my dad's retired. Van Buren wasn't my father's account any longer; he was mine! Why can't people get their head around that?"

Knowing he was on stage now because the glass walls worked both ways, Harry looked down, pretending to arrange some papers on his desk. The young ones, the punks, they thought this business was easy, but he had been brought up in a working class family where, if you wanted something, you had to go earn it. He was known as being an immensely honest man in an industry where ethics were often called into question. Harry knew that, while he might be lacking in the formal education and degrees possessed by so many of today's brokers, he more than made up for it by his intuition and uncanny listening skills, his greatest strengths, both as broker and manager. Over the years his calm approach to all of the uncertainties of the markets had earned him the respect of everyone in the office. During one bear market, when head office demanded a 10% cut in staff, he pulled his team together and suggested that each of them take a 10% cut in salary and he, in turn, would personally take a 20% cut. While this was clearly outside the firm's policies, he successfully argued with a reluctant head of human resources that his people were an investment that became more valuable over many years. By not firing anyone, which would have required severance packages, the salary cuts actually generated greater financial savings.

In all the years afterword, Harry never lost one broker to a competitor's recruiting efforts.

"Well, Junior you got that part right at least," he said now. "He *was* your account. Look, son, you're not thinking right. It's not the client's job to see things your way. It's the other way around. I told you that you've got to get into their heads. When your dad was here, working to transition the customers to you, didn't he tell you about each client - their personalities - their hot buttons?"

It was true. His dad had said, over and over again, that you had to find where the client's greed lived and feed that animal until it burst. At the time, Michael had tried to hide the fact that he found it offensive to describe the client service method that way. He had studied hard about the proper way to advise customers on their investments. But hot buttons? Maybe that had been an appropriate expression in the old-school days. But today a broker had a fiduciary responsibility to uphold.

"Harry, my customers are being properly looked after," he argued. "The plans I have put in place are first rate. You even said as much."

Increasingly aware that everyone in the office was watching them now, that those closest could hear every word that was spoken, and no doubt would retell the conversation later in vivid detail, Lugarno saw his opening. Rising, he came around the desk, pushed some papers out of the way, sat on one corner with one leg still touching the floor and folded his arms. It took markets like this to tell if you had any stones. Senior had them, for sure. It didn't look like he gave any to his son.

"Yeah, Junior, I've heard your speech," he said, making no attempt to lower his voice. "But, you know, I've been in the business for a little while. Your dad and I started together over at the Main Street branch, and I've learned a thing or two over the years. One thing I know is that you can't buy groceries with a financial plan. A budget won't pay for a kid's college education.

Clients want one thing and one thing only – to make money. The sooner you figure that out the better off we'll both be."

"Come on, no one's making any money for anyone in this market. You know that."

Harry surveyed his protégé. Even his nails were perfectly manicured.

"OK Junior," he said, "fair enough. People lose accounts when the market turns bad. That's where prospecting for new business comes in. Remember me saying that? How many times? You got to keep planting the seeds in the garden so a new batch of crops comes up. Last I checked all your accounts came from your dad. You haven't opened one, not one, on your own. So, tell me about that. The way you're going, once you piss off the rest of Daddy's business, you're going to be out on your ass. You know this, as well as I do."

"Give me a break, Harry," Michael demanded, pointing to the stream of shoppers strolling by the glass doors of Milne, Ohara, Grady Investments, all seemingly oblivious to the opportunity to enter, open an account and get rich by buying stocks and bonds from what its employees called MOGI. "How the heck am I supposed to get new clients in a shopping mall? Just look out there, will you?"

There were children holding their mothers' hands, teenage couples dressed in ripped jeans and texting on smart phones, and older people sitting on the benches watching the world go by. A toddler was in a rage, pounding his fists on the floor. His frantic mother tried to rein him in with one hand, the other holding a stroller with her second child. Although the glass was supposed to be soundproof to protect client confidentiality, the muted screams were clearly audible.

It was a conversation they'd had before and, in truth, Harry couldn't disagree. He ran his smoke-stained fingers through a noticeably receding hairline. Thirty years in the industry, riding a roller coaster of client emotions mixed with market turmoil, had left its mark. He was the top producing broker before Franklin Senior and, for that achievement, they had made him a manager. He had long since realized that he missed the days when all he had to deal with was clients.

At 5' 10", Harry's 240 pounds were spread evenly over his face, hands and in his belly. His blood pressure was up and the doctor had warned him about diabetes. For a number of years, he'd thought about working out but now, what was the point? Besides, he was too busy and this was a critical time in his career. He could feel his momentum slipping away, watching other younger managers get assigned to more prestigious offices. Franklin Senior had been smart when he decided to retire after the head office moved their branch into a shopping center where people were more interested in buying shoes than securities.

Harry just wanted to finish his career in a way that would provide for him and his wife for the rest of their lives. Since his greatest skill was dealing with people, even better than generating commissions, he'd been an office manager for fifteen of the thirty years he had worked at the firm. Management didn't make the same lofty incomes as the producers, and now, to top it off, his wife was showing signs of serious arthritis that would only lead to increasing medical bills. Harry knew that in the competitive world of chasing dollars, he was not considered a hard charger. There had been numerous opportunities for promotion to other, larger branches and it wasn't lost on Harry that he was not considered for even one. Everyone assumed that a man with his reputation and respect would be expected to quietly finish his life's work on his own schedule.

No, the fact was that Michael, a clear failure if there ever was one, was dragging everyone, including Harry, down to his level. Harry loved the old man like a brother, but this had gone far enough. If Dad wasn't willing to face facts, that was his problem, not Harry's. He'd often thought that if he shamed the kid enough, he would quit and solve his problems. That way Senior wouldn't blame Harry. He had tried before but there was no harm in trying again. He held up both hands to signal stop.

"Look, Junior," he said, and this time he lowered his voice, "this business isn't for everyone. Some people are cut out for it and some aren't. Just because your dad was good - and he was one of the best I've ever seen - doesn't mean you're going to be good too. But hey, you're smart and God knows honest, and you work pretty hard so I'm sure there's a place in the world for you. I'll make this easy. Your dad convinced me that giving you his book was a good idea. But here it is, a year later, and you've got nothing to show for it. In fact, you've got less than nothing. Your dad won't continue to make you do this if you say you don't want to. No harm done - you tried, but it didn't work out, and now it's time to move on to something else. You just march in here and quit, call me an asshole if you want, worst boss in the world, and we'll move on."

Michael could feel the creeping warmth in his face and neck. Lugarno had hinted about this before but he had never actually said it straight out like he was now. The thought of being coerced to relinquish what his father had taken his whole career to build, setting yet another vivid example that he would just never be as good at anything as the old man, was not something he could face. It was one thing to try but not make the grade. It was something entirely worse to take his father's success and let it drown along with his own long record of failures. Worse than that, he'd have to tell Jennifer. They'd been dating for two years and any time he wanted to discuss their future, she always brushed him off. He didn't dare add another negative - like giving up what he had always told her was a lucrative job - to an already delicate situation.

"No way, Harry," he said. "Not a chance. I will not quit. You watch - just watch me go. I'm going to blow all of you away."

That was, Harry reflected bitterly, just what they all should be worried about.

Michael paused, and it was clear that he was struggling to find the right words.

"The fact of the matter is, Harry, I can't quit - not ever," he said finally. "You know it and so do I. If you want me out of here, you'll have to fire me."

And Michael knew that as long as his father was alive, that could never happen.

## Chapter 2

Saturday was always a good day for ice cream.

Mr. Anthony Carrantino, sole proprietor of "Seattle's best Italian ice-cream," a dark haired man dressed in a white tee shirt with matching apron and chef's hat, leaned out the aluminum sliding window of his white panel truck to wipe the colored pictures of his various products with a towel so that they were as appealing as possible. There was still a bit of dew on the grass from the cool late August night air, but the forecast was warm and sunny - summer's last treat before the little ones went back to school. Soon, the sound of laughter and dogs barking would accompany the view of Mt. Rainier, 100 miles to the south. When the clouds parted, everyone would say, 'The Mountain is out.'

Tino had circled the park with the carnival music playing to let everyone know that he would be parked at his usual spot, right off the main entrance where they could be tempted by the irresistible images of cones, sundaes, shakes, floats and ice cream sandwiches, even though most of them weren't truly 'Italian'. He had been selling ice cream here for thirty-five years now and had seen toddlers that could barely hold their cones grow up to be adults who, in turn, bought from his truck for their own children. Loving kids as he did, he couldn't imagine doing any other kind of job.

Now, however, catching sight of a familiar figure, he frowned. It was the gelato girl again. She didn't come by his truck every Saturday but it seemed like lately, it was more often. She was always alone, looking behind her as if someone were following, and Tino was pretty sure he knew why since, even though she always spoke to the ground when placing her order, he could still see the bruises. And she always ordered the gelato, the coldest ice cream he had. He knew she didn't order the gelato to eat; it was to reduce the swelling on her face. On a bad day, once the soothing ice had melted and the contents discarded, she would come back for a second treatment. Embarrassed and still offering him only a view of the top of her head, she would laugh and say, "Well, I most certainly have an appetite today now, don't I?"

But he knew.

His best business came from those who, arriving at the park, considered a chocolate covered vanilla cone as part of the ritual of beginning their day. Then, when everyone started heading home, they'd say that they were hot, hungry and thirsty after a day in the sun, and a banana split smoothie, a concoction for which he was famous in the Seattle area, would really hit the spot. As much as he liked the revenue, he enjoyed the relative peace between the busy times; it gave a man time to think. And, he was sorry to say, he'd thought about the gelato girl a lot lately, trying to imagine what kind of person she was, where she was from, and who had done this to her.

Since she seemed too old to be living at home, he had concluded that it must be a boyfriend or even a husband. But all he really knew about her was that she was of medium height and had beautiful black hair. The details of her features eluded him, in part because she rarely looked up at him. But there was something extraordinarily appealing about her, perhaps because her voice reminded him of his mother's when she used to sing lullabies to him at bedtime.

And she was a victim. He would grit his teeth when he tried to imagine what kind of man would do this to such an innocent flower. He knew that answer, too. He'd seen his father hit his mother so many times and, when he was old enough to complain, had learned to retreat when his father said he'd get the same thing. It was a matter of respect, his dad would explain guiltily after the immediate crisis had passed, that there were things his son would never understand, that back in the home country, this was the way it was.

His mother, God bless her soul, would defend the man when Tino told her that, when he was big and strong enough - maybe at fourteen - he would make the man pay. She would say that, underneath, his father was a loving man but that he had been raised in a different time and place, and that there was enough violence in their home already. Tino would always agree, but inside he vowed somehow, someday he would even the score.

However, the old bastard had died before Tino had had the chance to teach him the consequences of his actions.

Today, when he thought of her, he was aware of a sense of urgency. The summer was coming to a close. What would the gelato girl do if she came looking for his medicinal treats only to find that he had driven his white truck to San Diego for the winter business? He had thought many times that he should say something to her, to try to help her. But time was running out. Today, perhaps, was the day. He kissed the cross that always hung from his neck, asking Jesus for the strength to do the right thing.

As she got closer to his van, looking down as usual, Tino said, "Good morning, missy! What will it be today?"

"Um, good morning, Mr. Carrantino," she said. "I'll have a large gelato cup, please."

"How many times I have to say you? Please! Call me Tino or Tony but not Mister. You make me feel the old man. You tell me your name, too."

"Angela." It was difficult for Tino to tell, but he thought that she smiled when she said it.

As he opened up the stainless steel lid over the arm-deep bin that kept all of his treats cold, he fished around as if he needed to look to find where the gelato cups were. In fact, since Angela had started arriving at his truck, he always kept at least one in reserve towards the side of the bin just in case, telling the other customers that he was sold out.

"Miss Angela, not to worry" he called over his shoulder. "It's in here somewhere. Ah, here it is, one large gelato cup, way down at the bottom. Don't get no colder."

She reached up to put the money on the counter and waited with her hand open, as she had done so many times before. It was as if she was accepting Holy Communion from her priest.

"Miss Angela, I think there's a problem."

Without thinking, she instinctively glanced up and, for what seemed like an eternity, looked the vendor in the eye, exposing her entire face. She quickly looked back down but it was too late. Mr. Carrantino sucked air between his teeth.

"Sweet mother of Jesus," he muttered.

Later he would realize how quickly the moment of truth had come to him. He had to make a split second choice. He could have just given her the ice cream and been done with it - until the next time, and the time after that. But it was as if another force, a marionette pulling the strings, was controlling him now.

"So, there, Angela, you had another fall, eh? Need to be more careful, young woman. Your nose - is it broke? You want me to call the 911 to take you to the hospital?"

"Oh, you know Mr. Carrantino," she said, again speaking to the ground. "I'm just a bit clumsy. I can't - don't need to - go to the hospital. Could I please have my gelato cup now and I'll be on my way?"

Tino knew that his moment was at hand.

"Yes Miss Angela, I got the cup right here. In fact, let me get another one. I think you're going to need them today. And, there will be no charge. But I have to tell you a quick story. When I was a young boy in Italy, my dad had the temper of tempers. He'd have a bad day at the shipyard, get liquored up and then come home to take it out on my mother. I will never forget the sound of his fist hitting her face. I was too little to do anything. Lucky for him, he died before I got older because I would have looked after that myself. But missy, I used to see my mother the next day. She'd spend hours trying to cover it all up with her makeup. But she couldn't. I remember her face. Like it was yesterday or, like what I just saw from you."

"Mr. Carrantino, please!"

"No, sorry, this ain't my business but I've gone this far now and I'm going to finish. I'm going to tell you; men like that, they are cowards. They may say they're sorry and it will never happen again, until the next time and the next. And then, one time, you don't wake up. You know what I'm saying?"

He could see her, holding her breath, trying to suppress the tears. And so, not wanting to hurt her more or cause a scene, he reached into his cash box, lifted up the tray and grabbed the piece of paper he'd been holding back for so long.

"OK, look there, Angela, I don't mean to make you feel worse, but I'm going to give you a piece of paper. It's got a number. You call that number and you talk to the man who answers. He's a guy that knows a guy who can give you some... advice - to ah - help you deal with your clumsiness. Tell him the ice-cream man gave it to you. I don't even know whose number it is but, these people, they can help you. I know they can. You call them - before it's too late."

She grabbed the slip of paper and the gelato and walked quickly away.

Under his breath, the ice cream man said

"God bless you missy. God bless us all."

## Chapter 3

"What in Christ's name are you doing to me, boy?" Michael's father demanded. "What took you so long to answer the phone? Are you asleep over there?"

Back at his desk, Michael saw the line light up to indicate that an outside call was coming in and when he saw who it was, his first impulse had been to let it ring. He knew that Harry counted the seconds it took for his brokers to answer their phones, and after the lecture he'd just gotten about prospecting, knew he had to pick it up. But... of all the people he didn't want to talk to right now, it was his father. He imagined him, in his den, sitting absolutely upright at his leather-top desk retirement present, dressed in a suit and tie, although now that he was fully on the shelf, he allowed the knot to be loosened and the top button undone, tapping away on his computer, checking stock quotes and market news like he'd never left.

"Yeah, hi Dad, good morning to you too," he said listlessly. "What's up?"

"What's up? Is that all you have to say for yourself? I think you know very well what's up. I received a very disturbing phone call this morning from perhaps my oldest and dearest friend in the world who was near tears. He kept apologizing, over and over but he said he had no choice. I told him I thoroughly understood but, Michael, the damage is done. You have single-handedly hurt a friendship that spans over forty years. What the hell are you doing? That's the third one this month."

Michael Franklin Senior, at fifty-eight years of age, had a full head of hair that without regular applications of coloring would be completely white. Knowing that the brokerage business is a young man's game, he started coloring early in his career and decided that even though he no longer worked, looking young was always the better choice. He also went to the gym four times a week to satisfy his insatiable desire to cheat time. His eyes were the color of a robin's egg, but the crow's feet framing them told so much of the truth that he had seriously considered cosmetic surgery. He also colored a neatly trimmed moustache.

As far as Michael was concerned, the man was always on the attack.

His life had been defined by his work, which bordered on obsession in terms of being seen as successful while, in actuality, his insecurity permeated every aspect of his life - not just his work, but his business and personal relationships. His favorite motto was "I never lose twice." Everyone assumed that was what happened to his marriage. At the time the split became public Michael Senior translated it into getting rid of baggage and claimed to anyone who would listen, that he was better off without the "old ball and chain."

Senior had been born into a family of seven brothers and sisters, his father a mid-western farmer going back many generations. For whatever reason, from the time that he was seventeen, as he would tell the story, Michael's father wanted to abandon the farm and go out and make his own name. It was a decision that wasn't well received by his family, which added to his constant desire to prove himself. At university, he had tried several majors but, with no guidance or experience, moved from one to another, although always certain that, whatever he did, he wanted to make money, and plenty of it.

Junior considered his options. He could hang up. He could say he had to go to a meeting. Or he could scan the news wire for a potential breaking story that required his immediate attention. But he knew he would have to have this conversation eventually. It was probably better to get it over with and not let his dad think up too many more lines of attack.

"Mr. Van Buren *did* call me this morning," he admitted, "and yes he is moving his account. You have no idea how disappointed I am. Don't get mad at me. Do you think I am trying to lose accounts? Like I'm going out of my way to damage your life-long friendships?"

"Well, if you want to know what I really think, you'd start by losing that tone of voice and showing me proper respect."

Michael knew there was no point responding. The old man was going to take his pound of flesh, like he always did. After an awkward silence, his father continued.

"All right then, I will consider your silence as an apology. I accept. Now, tell me what happened."

Tell him what happened, like he'd been in a car accident or something? Like there had been some definable, short-term problem that his ever-knowing, ever-blowing father could wave his magic wand and solve? How about a bear market, dad? How about the worst bear market since the depression? How was the old man going to solve that?

"What happened?" he repeated bitterly. "Your life-long friend, Van Buren called me and fired me - some friend."

"Do NOT criticize one of my closest associates for making such a difficult decision. This isn't HIS fault. It's yours. Maybe that's the problem here. You are just not willing to be held accountable for your actions. Tell me what he said."

Michael shook his head again. He should have hung up. He knew full well that his father had likely spent an hour this morning on the phone with his old buddy before Michael even knew what was coming down. But he had to get Michael to say the words to ensure that his level of discomfort was maximized – and to show he was still in control.

"He said he wasn't happy with the performance of his account, and that since he was retired, he couldn't afford to lose any money, and that it just wasn't like it was when you were his broker."

Junior couldn't see the smile break out on his father's face. Of course it was better when Senior ran the book of business.

"Well, what did you say to him?" he demanded. "How did you counter his arguments? There are a million things you could have told him. What did you come up with?"

Dad knew the answer. It didn't change, nor did his son's approach to managing client money. He had been well schooled in the finer aspects of modern portfolio theory and applied it to all of his accounts in a disciplined and consistent fashion, but no approach worked in this market. So why did his dad want to have the debate again? It was the same discussion, over and over.

"I explained to him what I've been explaining to all of my clients. Their portfolios are well diversified, populated with highly conservative, dividend-paying stocks that will recover well when the market does. There's nothing I can do about the market."

Michael Junior could hear the swivel chair creak through the phone. His dad was leaning forward, going on the offensive - again.

"Are you kidding? There's nothing you can do? Why the hell do you think they have brokers? You just spend all day hiding behind all that portfolio theory crap you learned in school. It's the *stocks* you buy that matter. The stocks you have been buying, saying they are conservative and dividend paying is nonsense. You've been buying the banks! Do you watch the news? With the asset-backed commercial paper scandal, all of Wall Street's most solid financial institutions are sinking into quicksand. Bear Stearns - gone. Merrill Lynch - sold. Those lovely dividends are all going to be cut. But you've been buying them like a lost sheep."

Michael Junior had heard about enough.

"Look, Dad, times have changed. Nowadays you *have* to make sure you have a fully diversified portfolio. It isn't like it was when you used to be able to buy a few hot tips and ride it out. Not all the banks are in financial difficulty. The diversification will make sure that my clients will be OK."

"Michael, when the tide goes out, all boats float lower. Haven't you learned anything from me?"

"Look, OK, you were a great broker - in your time. You've taught me a lot but even you have to agree that I have to find my own way, my own style. You said that. You aren't giving me any credit for anything. By the way, did I mention that this is one of the worst bear markets since the 30's?"

As soon as the words were out of his mouth, Michael cringed. He knew what was coming.

"Oh *really?* You ever hear of October 19, 1987? Black Monday? Now there was a tough market, I'll tell you. That one took everything I had to survive and protect my clients' assets. But I did it. How many customers do you think I lost, Michael? Eh? How many?"

Michael knew the answer and kicked himself for setting up the old man's podium, yet again.

"Not ONE, Michael. I actually grew my book. My existing clients were so happy with my expertise they recommended me to their friends! I added value. You don't. It's pretty easy to understand."

"OK, Dad, you're the best, always were, always will be. If conservative, dividend-paying stocks aren't the right thing to buy, what would *you* do?"

Michael realized he was raising his voice and that several of the other brokers had turned to watch the show.

"Food, Michael! Buy the stocks of companies that make and sell food. No matter how bad Wall Street gets, people still have to eat."

Michael dropped his forehead into one of his palms. It was one of the old-timers' favorite sayings. It sounded so simple. 'People still needed to eat.' Well, people still needed banks, too. In a down economy, the food stocks would suffer just like all the others. Consumers would shift their purchases towards lower-priced, lower margin products. The food company earnings would decline, sometimes by a lot. But the way Senior said it, it was the most obvious strategy in the universe and anyone that missed it was an idiot. It was an idea that would sell. Michael had to admit, his father could sell sand in the desert.

Michael Franklin Senior looked at the picture in the corner of his desk and considered the boy. All of the coaching, the guidance, the training appeared to be having zero impact. Maybe he should have made him pay his own way through university. It wasn't a complicated business; he'd gone over it with him a hundred times. So what was the problem? He thought about his own path to success. As Michael Senior approached graduation he'd attended a job fair put on by a major Wall Street brokerage firm and had been immensely impressed by the smoothness and professionalism of the presenters, who went on and on about how a stockbroker's role was one of giving back to society, of helping every client achieve the common goal that everyone shared - achieving independent financial wealth. When one of the senior brokers had pulled him aside and explained that it wasn't just the clients that got wealthy, that a broker who was smart, diligent, worked hard and was a little lucky, would likely make more money than they ever dreamed, Senior was hooked. "You know what, boy?" Senior said now. "I've been thinking. I know I wanted you to get into this business. I probably pushed you a bit. I got so much satisfaction over the years, both professionally and monetarily. I guess I just figured it would be right for everyone. Yes, I will admit to wanting to have my son follow in my footsteps. Maybe I'm asking too much. Maybe this business was never right for you. Maybe you should pack it in. I thought giving you my book of business would be a good idea, but clearly that's not the case."

There was no one who could work a room better than Franklin Senior. He greeted a new person for the first time by looking them directly in the eyes and shaking their hand with both of his. He took courses about remembering people's names through word association, another trait that was admired by his peers. He would read each issue of *The Economist* cover to cover, not because he understood all of it, but just so he could say that he did. Over the years, he became an expert at asking people to talk about themselves, listening carefully and appearing genuinely interested in their stories. In order to build relationships with some clients he joined the local church, although he thought God was basically a crutch for those who had less drive than he. He knew the only way to succeed in life was through your own efforts.

This was the part of the conversation that made Michael seethe. Senior knew it would. It was a test. The day that the boy agreed, that he was in over his head and just didn't have what it took, was the day to get out. It was a tough way to motivate, he knew. At some point though, the lad needed to show he had a little piss and vinegar.

When the line went dead, meaning Michael had hung up on him, Michael Franklin Senior smiled.

## Chapter 4

Saturday and Sunday mornings were almost always worse than Friday and Saturday nights.

Twenty-eight year old Angela Messina had been born in a barn in Iowa when her mother went out to milk the cows and miscalculated her daughter's arrival time. She grew up being told that the farm, which had been in her family for generations, was her future. In this day and age of the Internet, glossy magazines and television, however, she dreamed of what it was like 'on the outside', with the result that, when she came of age, she applied to the University of Washington in Seattle. Her parents were stunned by her traitorous act. Their threats of no money wilted when she received a scholarship and found a part-time job in the university library. She earned her degree in teaching and wanted to dedicate her life to helping others learn how to learn. At school, she met her future husband, an aspiring investment banker whose eyes were as bright as the rising sun. When they began talking, Angela was intrigued by the man who was able to overcome the adversity of growing up in a broken home - his father was jailed for public intoxication and spousal abuse - and put himself through university, working two jobs while in school - just as she had. They started dating and were married after eighteen months in a simple wedding, which featured expressions of love and vows to honor and respect, "till death do us part." He made a point of promising, as early as their second date, that the one thing his future wife could be sure of was that he would never lay a hand on her.

The apple, as it turned out, hadn't fallen very far from the tree.

Her parents, back on the farm in Iowa, weren't thrilled about her choice for a spouse, and weren't shy about telling her, her mother in particular being all too fond of saying that, "There's something about the boy." And Angela had been suitably indignant. After all, they were just farmers, closed-minded and envious because she'd found a man with an education, who could do something more with his life than shovel horse manure out of the stables. That they refused to come to the wedding in Seattle, saying it was a bad year for crop prices, and that they couldn't afford the drive from Iowa, or the time away from their chores, had been fine with her at the time. But now, although she hadn't spoken or written to either of them in over two years, she desperately wished she could contact them, to tell them the horror story her life had become, a life where every phone bill was examined, every letter opened by a man who justified his invasion of her privacy by saying that he was just trying, 'to protect her interests,' whatever that meant. When she asked him if he didn't trust her he would just smile and say, "It's all the other men out there that I don't trust."

He kept her under strict control, calling the house four, five or even six times per day, and refusing to allow her to work, saying that was a man's job. This was the beginning of the friction in their marriage. Without any income - he had quickly 'merged' her savings account into his - she couldn't afford a car or even a cell phone. He did allow her a computer, with Internet access, to order groceries that were delivered. Recently, he had begun to talk about their trying to start a family. Angela, as always after a bad night with her husband, went out to see the ice cream man to apply the cool balm of the gelato. Above all, she never wanted him to catch her trying to reduce the swelling - it made him angry, at first saying "Stop being melodramatic, it wasn't that bad." Then, when he grabbed her hand away from her face to see the extent of the damage, he blamed her, saying she had put him up to it - had deliberately made him mad so she could give him a guilt trip.

She had managed to get him to agree to her volunteering at the library within walking distance down the road. She'd also learned to be a master of the Internet, erasing any trace of websites she'd visited about wife-abuse, leaving your husband and how to protect yourself during a fit of violence. Instead, she would leave a trail of pages visited about baking, knitting and how to plan for having a child. He didn't think she knew that he checked her computer - while she was in the bath or busy in the kitchen. She had learned, through the Internet, that there were three stages to the violence but she desperately wanted to believe that her situation was different. What was happening was temporary. It was caused by his stress at work and it would go away as his career and their financial situation improved.

This morning he slept in, as he did every Saturday, allowing her time to get to the park and back. Hearing him get out of bed, Angela could only hope that the gelato had once again worked its magic, and when he appeared on the stairs, she greeted him as though nothing was wrong, that their marriage was, when he wasn't beating her at least, the honeymoon he claimed it to be.

"Where the hell were you this morning?" he demanded. "I woke up for a piss at nine and you weren't in bed. A guy would have a hard time getting lucky in this house. Where'd you go?"

Unshaven and disheveled, he was wearing only pajama bottoms, and for a moment she experienced a flashback of the body she had once been attracted to.

Angela never understood, until it happened the first time, that when he stared at her like that, his eyes seemed to be burning a hole in her head. It was as if they became fuses burning down to their stub, before the explosion. Now she was caught in an impossible position. If she admitted to going out, she'd have to tell him why and where she might have gone so early on a Saturday morning. On the other hand, if she said she didn't go out, what proof did he have?

"Well, I didn't go anywhere. I've been right here looking up recipes for breakfast," she told him.

"Listen you stupid bitch, who do you think you're talking to?" he said between clenched teeth. "I'm not some dumb-ass off the farm like you are. Tell me where the fuck you went right now... or else."

Later, when she played the scene back in her mind, she realized that she had just become a stage two victim. She remembered saying, screaming actually, that she'd had enough; the words erupting like water from a cracked pipe. He couldn't treat her like this, she told him. She was his wife, not some slave just sitting there to cook his meals, clean his house and let him fuck her when he was in the mood.

It was the f-word that set him off this time. She tried to run away but he was too strong. She tried to defend herself, scraping her nails along his face, drawing blood, and remembered him saying, "You ungrateful, slut. I'm going to teach you a lesson." She also remembered his hands around her neck. The last thing she'd thought was, "Is this how I'm going to die?" And then she must have blacked out. She didn't know for how long, but when she came to, she was lying on the floor. Her ribs hurt and her neck felt as though it was on fire. She managed to get to her hands and knees but tried not to inhale. The pain was too intense.

As she became more aware of her surroundings, she heard another sound, a whimpering in the corner of the room and had seen that her husband was lying on the floor in a fetal position, clutching his knees and rocking back and forth. His eyes were closed and the sound he was making was like that of a wounded animal. As she struggled to get to her feet, he opened his eyes and cried,

"OH MY GOD, oh my God, oh Jesus, oh, what have I done? I thought I'd killed you."

"No, no," she gasped as he rose and came toward her. "Go away, don't touch me... please. No more."

"I'm so... SORRY. Oh, Ange what can I do? What can I say? Let me help you, please!"

She needed to lie down on the couch and she pushed his hands away.

"I - I need to lie down," she told him. "Please, just leave me alone."

As the full level of shame flooded his mind, he realized that what she had asked was probably the best thing. He had so much he wanted to say, he was horrified, but she needed to rest. He would go out for a drive, leaving her to the quiet of an empty house. By the time he returned, she would feel better. Then they could talk. He would even buy her flowers.

Everything would be OK.

"I'll go to Starbucks and get us some coffee," he told her. "That will make you feel better. I'll be back soon."

Watching him go, the skin on her neck throbbing, Angela was suddenly aware of the change in the way she felt about him. She didn't want to be with this person any longer. She wanted him out of her life.

There was something terrifying about her thoughts.

## Chapter 5

The message light on his phone was blinking bright orange as Michael sat down at his workstation. Before he had decided whether to answer it or not, being in no mood to lose any more clients that day, Ivan Diversky, the now number three ranked broker in the office but "moving to the number one spot soon enough," as he let people know on a regular basis, appeared beside his desk.

"Hey man, we just watched you get reamed," he said, grinning. "Hard to watch but must be harder for you to take - right up the ass, huh?"

Ivan told everyone, including Michael, that he was their friend, which like everything else he said or did, was blatantly self-serving. The others called him Ivan the Terrible.

"Thanks for caring about my business, Ivan," Michael said, "but I didn't get reamed. Harry and I were just talking about how to handle one of my accounts that's being a bit difficult, that's all."

Ivan Diversky was only twenty-six, but he dressed like a highly successful broker who had been in the business for many years. He wore $3,000 suits, had three platinum cards and was always quick-witted. His advice, always freely given even when not requested, was rarely supported by either fact or experience. Born and raised in Los Angeles, he had dreamed, as nearly everyone in LA did, of becoming an actor, certain that his outgoing, aggressive behavior was just what movie producers were looking for. After scraping through UCLA as a drama major who was more interested in partying than attending classes, he started a job as a waiter in Sammy's Oyster Bed, a popular bar frequented by successful stockbrokers. One night he peppered one of the regulars with questions about how to get into the business, and how you could learn about the markets. The broker, amused by the advances from a food server, gave Ivan his card and said to call him. It was the opening Ivan needed, and he never forgot the lesson about the importance of business cards. He also never understood the point of marriage; his motto being, "Why buy the cow when you can get the milk for free." At 6' 1" tall and weighing 195 pounds, he kept his wavy black hair on the long side, with a neatly trimmed moustache and sideburns that were cut to a downward sloping V. His favorite saying, when he was with the boys was, "Never love a stock because it won't suck your cock," a motto that he changed for clients to, "…because it won't love you back." He was often seen, coffee in hand, standing at a co-worker's station 'comparing notes' as he called it while, in fact, trying to steal each broker's best investment ideas to use with his clients. By not doing his own research, he had more time to prospect for new business. Everyone knew about his tactics. If, for example, you went to the washroom, it was an unwritten rule not to leave papers on your desk.

"Give me a break, Michael," he said now. "You're not talking to some fresh out of school rookie here. Another one of your dad's clients just shucked you, didn't they? Hey, man, that really sucks. I feel very badly for you. How many is that now? Your father must be shitting a brick."

Ivan had trouble keeping a straight face while offering his condolences. This kid had no chance, zero, of making it. It still rubbed his ass the wrong way that when Senior packed it in, Michael got every single one of his dad's accounts, totaling almost $25 million. As the story went, Senior had told the clients that he'd teach his son everything he needed to know. Ivan thought the book should have come to him - they were, after all, clients of the firm, not the man. To give them to a complete rookie was not only the worst form of nepotism but was also clearly a mistake based entirely on office politics. Hello, anybody thinking about the clients' best interest? If Ivan had gotten the accounts, the clients would be happier. It also would have made him the number one ranked broker overnight. Being number one was important.

"Hey look Mike," he said now. "It's almost two o'clock. Let's go have a late lunch - on me - and talk about old times. A couple of beers would do you some good."

Michael looked at his adversarial friend, and then back at his desk. If he said no, Ivan still wasn't likely to go away, and a beer *would* be good. Besides, he wasn't going to get any more work done today with the market down 150.

The one good thing about being inside the mall was there were a seemingly endless variety of places to eat, from the fast food linoleum tables, to the more expensive variety that actually gave you a menu. But Michael knew which one they'd be going to. The hostess there had great lungs, as Ivan called them, and they were always on display. Her name tag read Kitty and after she'd rubbed Ivan's back as he sat down, and told him how wonderful it was to see him again, he'd give her a tip just for seating them, after which she'd giggle her thanks and walk away in her silver hot pants and high heels.

This time, as usual, she delivered the beers without Ivan having to ask and while Michael held his to his forehead, Ivan said, "Tell the waitress to give us the best you've got, Kitty. Surprise us."

"Kitty's got the high beams on today, eh Mike?" he said as she went swaying off again. "God, I love this place."

It was the beginning of the sort of monologue that Michael always figured was part of Ivan's success. The guy could talk forever. And that was OK because it meant that all Michael had to do was to listen and nod his head now and then. The one-way conversation rambled from the Seahawks, to the market, to the hot new secretary and to the damn clients that didn't understand how to invest during a bear market.

"You know, Mike, the clients are their own worst enemy," he said, having decided that it was time to float that proposal he'd been thinking about. Why not? The kid was just staring at him like a deer in the headlights. "If they'd just listen to us, all of the time, we'd all be better off. And speaking of clients, I've been thinking about you. You've been put into an almost impossible situation and, frankly, I have a hard time just sitting idly by and watching you get lashed all the time. We all had to start somewhere and no one is stepping up to help you. One thing's for sure. Our boss isn't doing anything to help you out. He's just sitting there counting the days until retirement. He doesn't care about the business anymore and he especially doesn't care about you."

Michael listened but could never believe the fantasy world Ivan seemed to live in. Did Ivan believe his own BS? Did he think Michael was that naive not to recognize what he was doing? Did he think Michael would be swept away by his sudden apparent compassion?

"So, listen," Ivan was saying. "I have an idea, a mutually beneficial idea that I'd like to float by you. Do you mind?"

Michael had been hoping Ivan wouldn't go there again, but what had he been thinking? Ivan was Ivan. He was never going to change. Better just to let him blow his hot air.

"The way I see it, the problem you're having is like a bad handoff, like a broken play in football. Your dad was the quarterback and he had the ball, and he called the play and handed it off to you, the halfback, before you were ready. You see it in the NFL all the time. The halfback's got to have his hands and arms in just the right position to take the ball. That, in itself, takes hours and hour of practice - to be ready to take the ball. You haven't had enough training for that yet and what we have on our hands is a fumble. The ball's on the ground and the other team's trying to recover it. We can't let them do that. Do you see where I'm going with this, Mikey?"

For a moment, Michael admired the creativity of his co-worker. He wanted to ask him why 'we' couldn't let them do that. Where did the 'we' come from? This must have been Ivan's seventh or eighth attempt to get him to give up his dad's accounts, only temporarily, of course, until he got his feet under him, but the football analogy was a fresh approach.

"Yeah, Ivan," he said, "I see where you're going. I saw where you were going the last time you asked me and the time before that. The answer's still the same and I'm betting you could even recite it back to me by now."

Ivan held a half-eaten wing over his plate, wiped his mouth with the back of his other hand and licked his fingers. Why couldn't this kid get it through his head?

"You know, I have to say, we are all under a lot of stress these days. I'm not sure I appreciate your tone there, Junior. I am trying to help you. Don't look a gift horse in the mouth."

Michael sighed.

"OK, Ivan, no offense intended. But you've got to admit that we've had this conversation before. And my response is still going to be the same."

It was Michael's greatest frustration. If people would just leave him alone and stop putting so much pressure on him, he could do this. He knew he could. He just needed more time.

Meanwhile, Ivan was clearly tiring of the game.

"Yeah... you're right there Mikey," he said. "I probably could recite your response. And you know why? Because, it is an old, worn-out excuse. I want to keep this friendly but I'm going to be honest with you - for your own good. It's time for you to have a reality check. Just for a moment, you need to look at things from a different perspective and, if you don't mind me saying, stop being so selfish. When one hockey player hogs the puck the team doesn't score, unless your name is Gretzky. Everyone, and I mean everyone in the office, has been giving you the benefit of the doubt. But it's been a year now and you aren't rising to the occasion. When you lose an account, it doesn't just hurt you, it hurts us all. You are bringing the whole office down to your level. I have tried to talk to you, to offer you some help, many, many times. Instead, you just sit there, arms folded, and throw it back in my face."

Michael had heard enough.

"Ivan, you said you wanted this to be friendly. Fine with me but, to do that, you need to stop now with the sermon. Don't lecture me. Don't ask anything from me. I'm not interested."

Ivan had to hand one thing to him. Michael was a stubborn SOB that was for sure.

"Well, Mikey," he said, "I'll tell you this much. I for one have had enough. If you aren't willing to partner with me on what's left of your dad's book, then I'm walking into Lugarno's office and demanding that he make me the senior advisor on the accounts, until you're more qualified to fly solo. Don't get me wrong. This isn't some blatant money-grab - you'll get everything back. You can thank me later."

Kitty appeared again and, with only a brief glance at Michael, asked Ivan if the wings were everything he'd ever wanted. She knew where her bread was buttered.

"So, you're threatening me now - for my own good of course," Michael said, throwing his napkin on his plate of untouched food. "Nice touch Ivan." And to Kitty, "Just get me my check, please. Here's my Visa."

After a feeble attempt to indicate his willingness to pay, there was no further conversation. Ivan continued to eat his wings, and even the chopped carrot sticks and celery, as if nothing had happened, until Kitty appeared, frowning, to tell Michael that his credit card had been refused.

The laughter from across the table was immediate and so loud that it hurt Michael's ears.

"There, you SEE?" Ivan said. "I told you that you needed my help. Oh my God, that is classic. Don't worry there, Mikey, I got your back. I always did. I said I was buying anyway. Stick around and finish your wings - you've hardly touched them."

Michael quickly rose to leave.

"All right, suit yourself." Ivan said, grinning. "But just remember, my offer's still on the table. I AM going to see the boss, whether you like it or not."

Michael, who had started for the door, stopped and raised his middle finger towards his lunch partner. The mall was in that period between lunch and dinner where it was quiet. Michael ambled along, his pride still stinging. He didn't want to go back to his workstation while the market was still open because everyone would be there, and knowing Ivan, he'd likely be sending a broadcast text message about Michael's declined credit card. No, he'd wander around the mall until around four-thirty, after the market was closed, when most of the other brokers would have headed out to meet with clients. He needed to gather his thoughts and create his version of the story that he would share with Jennifer.

When he arrived back at his desk, there was another blinking message light. He thought about just deleting it without listening - say he never received it - some sort of technology glitch - but he would have to deal with whoever it was and their issue sooner or later.

Would it be another client firing him? He kept reminding himself - he knew that the only reliable way to make money in the market was to own solid dividend paying stocks like banks and insurance companies and just be patient. He wasn't sure, but he thought that Warren Buffet, one of the richest men in the world, would approve. So worrying about what the market did on a daily basis was a waste of time.

It was exactly the opposite approach to his dad, whose clients, hearing his professional sounding voice, like a big city newscaster - would salivate over his latest market insight, news tip or otherwise transaction-worthy idea. Not all the ideas worked out - most of them didn't - but the frequent handholding, the thing Junior hated most about the job, was his dad's greatest skill. During his so-called 'training period', he'd watched his father spend all day on the phone, spouting off the odd news headline to show how 'in-touch' he was with the market, but do little or no analysis to support his recommendations. He often told clients that Wall Street research was clearly biased by the potential for lucrative investment banking fees so he didn't use it. Sometimes the clients would come up with their own ideas and he would always applaud them for their insight. Hey, if the client wanted to do a trade, do the trade.

It was what Junior hated most about the business. All of the studies had shown that his dad's approach didn't build long-term wealth and, therefore, was clearly not in the clients' best interest. And yet, Dad had become broker of the year multiple times by simply telling his clients what they wanted to hear and blaming any poor results on the vagaries of the market. It was nothing short of a complete sham.

Falling into his chair, he grabbed his headset and punched in his code only to hear Jennifer's message that his father wanted to buy them dinner that night. "He said it was important so I accepted," she added. "Try to get home early. The reservation's at six."

It was, conceivably, the worst news Michael had heard all day.

## Chapter 6

Breathing, even slightly, still made Angela wince. A rib must have been damaged in the fall. Lying on the couch, she found herself thinking about her playground days when someone had sneaked up behind her when she was standing on the merry-go-round and jerked it just enough to cause her to bounce off the thick metal bars that were supposed to be a safety feature. She tried to recall if this was what she had felt like as she lay in the dusty brown dirt, worn down by years of laughing children. No one was laughing now.

Looking around the den, she remembered, when the agent was showing them this house, being the least excited by this dark room with its old cedar walls and a speckled ceiling. Her first thought then had been whether hours of scrubbing could put a dent in the years of grime that had nestled comfortably into every seam of the wood. As she was surveying the 'pit' as she came to call it, she had caught the look in her husband's eyes as he strolled over to the hand-built stone fireplace and caressed it as if a newborn child. Years of fireplace smoke had left its mark. The inside, the hearth and even the stone itself were irrevocably tattooed with soot.

"Yes," the agent added, "I thought you would like this. The fireplace is one of the key features of the house. You won't find anything like it elsewhere."

She had wondered then if the whole house-buying process was a hint about the kind of person she had really married. She didn't remember how many other houses they had gone through. Some of them were beautiful, and could, with a woman's touch, have become fantastic. But he hadn't seemed interested in any of them. He was going through the motions. They would only pick the house that he wanted and he wasn't going to change his mind. Could she or should she have picked up on the clue?

But here she was, in the pit. It was like a dungeon, her pain like shackles. The room wasn't warm and, in truth, she'd done nothing to it. She had tried, but anything bright, cheery or otherwise uplifting was engulfed by the ever-present smell of old, including the bookcase filled with musty volumes that had been left behind by the previous owner. Even the couch she was lying on was wrong. It was brown cracked leather and uncomfortable except for one end where the seat would extend into a recliner, his recliner. The smell of spilled, stale beer that had fallen into its crevices after he fell asleep was always there.

She would like to burn everything in this room. Actually she would like to burn down the entire house.

The smell of the salty grease hit her before the door even opened. His version of breakfast, from a fast food place, the oil from the 'genuine home fries' having permeated the cheap paper coating and the large piece of fried meat coupled with an overdone, and now cold, egg made her want to retch.

"Hi honey!" he greeted her. "I'm back! I got us a nice breakfast and some fresh coffee. Have a bit of that. It will perk you up."

He looked around the room as if some invisible audience, having caught the joke, was laughing.

"Ha, perk you up. Get it? That's funny."

He looked down at her motionless figure.

"Oh dear, are you still not feeling well? Here, let me help you up."

The coffee was the strongest smell in the room now and it massaged the lining of her nostrils. Maybe a bit of that might help. But when she put the cup to her mouth, the heat made her bruised lip hurt so much that she cried out.

"You OK?" he asked, frowning.

In that moment, she would later realize, she learned something about herself that would change things forever. What she should have said was, "You idiot! You just beat the shit out of me, my ribs are probably broken, my lips fattened and who knows what else? How dare you stand there like everything is OK?! Get the hell out of my house and don't come back!"

But she didn't. Instead, she said, "No, it's OK. The coffee's just a bit hot."

In that moment, she understood. At this point in time, she was defenseless, just as she had been on the farm when she first tested the waters about leaving for an education. She could never win that argument with a direct approach. So, what had she done? She'd planned, used her wits. And in the end, she'd got exactly what she had wanted. For the first time it dawned on her. She had the skills to get out of this mess, but clearly a direct approach not only wouldn't work, it would put her life in danger. She must not upset him again. She thought she could even smell alcohol on his breath. Was it from last night or today? She was pretty sure that the fast food joint hadn't added booze to the menu. Did he carry a little bottle of courage in his glove compartment? Whatever, she was weak, injured and in no position to defend herself. If he 'went off' again, this time he might truly kill her.

She wasn't sure how quickly she went to sleep or how long she'd been out. For a minute, as she woke, she wondered where she was. She never slept on the couch. Alarmed, as she tried to quickly get up, the sharp pain in her ribs reminded her. As she looked around, she was startled again to see that her husband had pulled up a chair close to her and had been looking at her.

Slowly pulling herself up, she noticed that he'd eaten her breakfast too.

"You know, you're so beautiful when you sleep," he told her. "I've been watching you, thinking about… so much. Can we talk now? Are you feeling better?"

She sat up straighter and looked around the room. The lights were off and it must have been much later in the day because the sun had moved to the other side of the house, making an already dark room even gloomier.

"Before we do that, I'm thinking that I may have broken a rib," she told him. "I can hardly breathe. Maybe I should go see a doctor."

He frowned at that idea. They both knew why. People didn't break ribs walking around the house. There would be questions.

"Oh, wow, really?" he exclaimed. "I saw you fall. It didn't look that bad. Maybe we should just wait until tomorrow morning. Besides, you have no idea how difficult this has all been for me. I had to have a couple of beers to calm my nerves, and I shouldn't be driving for at least an hour. After that, if you're still feeling rotten, I'll take you. I promise. But right now I have a million things to say to you."

"OK," she said in a resigned voice, leaning back into the couch and exhaling slowly as though blowing smoke into the air. "Talk."

"I have so much to say that I don't know where to start," he began. "First, I want you to know that I love you with all my heart. I've tried for hours now to make sense of what happened here this morning. I think I have a bit, but I will get to that in a minute. I know that I haven't been the man to you that I should have been. I feel like the lowest piece of dirt that ever existed. I know what you must be thinking of me."

She thought about how wrong he was because he had absolutely no idea of what she was thinking right now.

"And honey, I am very, very sorry." he went on. "I just can't believe that this is happening to us. I know it's mostly my fault and I'm going to make you a promise right now. What happened today will never, ever happen again. I'm going to change. You'll see. I know I have a bad temper - I'm just going to have to learn to count to three. I'm just so stupidly jealous. I have to learn to get over that but, when I met you, you were like, the best thing that ever came into my life. The thought of you with another man drives me insane."

She looked at him, silent and expressionless, aware that she was making him uncomfortable.

"You said this was 'mostly' your fault. What did you mean by that?"

He ran his fingers through his hair.

"Well, it's like this. You know how I am, or at least how I was, but I'm going to change. You'll see. But, this morning, when you started fighting me - all I was doing was asking where you were. It was like you attacked me. I was surprised. I wasn't expecting that. So, I know... I shouldn't have gotten rough with you but can't you see? It was partly your fault?"

"My fault!" she exclaimed. "I probably have a broken rib, and it was *my* fault."

He looked at the ceiling and sighed. Clearly this wasn't going like he wanted it to.

"You fell on the table," he told her. "I didn't break your rib." And then, as she arched her eyebrows, "Oh, shit, honey! That's not what I meant to say. SHIT! This is hard."

She only stared, arms crossed, with nothing to say.

"Oh my God, honey, I know you're mad - furious probably, but don't do this to me. You are everything. I am begging you to forgive me. If I didn't have you in my life, I just don't know. Well, I mean, I don't want to say it but I'd probably kill myself. That's how much you mean to me."

As she listened, she realized she was on the receiving end of a carefully planned script. The ace of spades, the threat of suicide, was his trump card. How pathetic. But then a flood of awareness engulfed her. His speech sounded familiar because she'd read it before on the Battered Women's Society's web page. His behavior, the anger, jealousy, control, belittling, it all fitted a norm, a pattern that had been well documented through a litany of broken bones and bruises. It was a classic three step pattern: first was the need to control all aspects of her life; second, flying into a rage when she tried to stick up for herself; and lastly the remorse filled with apologies and promises to change. It was a cycle that would repeat itself, and each time the severity of his attacks would grow.

Despite her attempts not to show any emotion, she began to sob.

"I'm sorry Ange," he said, stroking her hair. "I shouldn't have said that stuff about suicide. It's OK. We're going to work this out, you and me. It will be all better. I promise."

Her tears had little to do with his confessional. It was when she remembered the part about repetition of the cycle. A true abuser would never change. He would be nice to her now, more careful of his behavior, but for how long? And the violence in the next cycle would be worse. After what she had just gone through, she wasn't sure she would survive another episode.

And she also cried because, for the first time in their short marriage, she experienced a feeling she'd never truly felt before. For the first time, she clearly understood that she was deeply afraid.

## CHAPTER 7

The deal was so close, he could taste it.

Skip Williams, Managing Director of retail client services, Northwest Region, of Fifty States Investments, was working late Friday night, as he would be all day Saturday and Sunday. There was a lot to do before the market opened on Monday. Since the target acquisition was in his region, he'd been integrally involved, with all of the higher-ups from the New York head office, in the discussions, negotiations and, now the announcement and transition plan. He knew this was a once-in-a-career opportunity and, so far it was going amazingly well. No doubt, the voracity of the bear was a catalyst to get the three founders of MOGI, who owned 90% of the private company shares, to finally agree, but Skip was able to take a large part of the credit for convincing them to come on board. He explained to the owners that the world had changed. If nothing else, the cost of regulatory compliance and increasingly sophisticated technology was now both unavoidable and ill affordable for a smaller firm. Don't even talk about the investment required in new risk management systems! The larger integrated companies that offered clients a total financial solution were eating the smaller privately owned firms, eroding their stature along with market share. His final point put the discussions over the top; the founding partners needed to get their value out now before competitive forces eroded it further. Each owner, realizing they would make millions on the transaction, felt a sense of guilt and expressed concern over the future of their long-time, loyal employees. Skip again saved the day, arguing that by selling out now to the bigger, younger, more aggressive firm, the future of their clients, and their employees would be in good hands. Ultimately there would be more unemployment if they didn't sell. That line of reasoning certainly made the owners feel better. They all signed an agreement not to compete for three years. Essentially, they were retiring.

Skip knew it was all bullshit, even the part about keeping the three former owners on as strategic planning partners. When the deal was announced, his first job was to secure the higher production brokers and lose the deadwood. In either case, he had to help convince MOGI's clients to stay on with a new broker and a world-class firm. The consultants had reviewed every account worth over $1 million, every office and every broker in terms of efficiency and profitability. Although the opening message to all MOGI employees on Monday would be, "We're all on the same team - together we are bigger, better and stronger," they had identified the brokers that were likely to be targeted by the competitors when the news broke - because unexpected events unsettled everyone. The top salespeople needed careful attention - 'hugging' it was called - and a budget to satisfy their demands for financial guarantees had been created and approved by the board. The brokers who were on the 'maybe' list were singled out and depending on their responses during their individual informational interviews, would be reassigned to a smaller office or just terminated. The employees that clearly weren't going to make it had also been identified and would immediately be let go. In the short run, Skip knew that getting rid of the unproductive brokers was more important to him personally. Even though the higher-ups talked about 'long-term strategic benefits', once the first financial statements came out - only three months after the deal closed - he would be evaluated on the short-term profitability. Acquisitions were about money and this was his chance to shine.

Head office would be watching carefully. Skip would be assessed by the timeliness of the implementation of the consultant's recommendations, and the management of the funds set aside for severance and retention bonuses. If he could spend less than the budgeted amount to keep the people they wanted and lose the people they didn't, it would be an important feather in his cap.

It was a glorious time in his career.

It was unusual, although not unheard of, that Harry Lugarno and the other office managers at MOGI would be summoned by the President Ohara for an 'important meeting' at the fanciest hotel in Seattle, on a Friday night, with only a few hours notice. But the message was very clear. This would be the most pivotal meeting in the history of the company. Attendance was mandatory. Harry had been to one of the hotel's numerous conference rooms on the second floor many times for broker lunches, company presentations and dog and pony shows. Each of the rooms was named after a prominent state. If a Louisville-based company were discussing its most recent acquisition, the meeting would most likely be in the Kentucky room. He wandered around the floor looking for 'Alternate Room A' until he was finally directed to the basement, which puzzled him. With all of the beautiful, well designed rooms they could be using, their President had chosen a non-descript, hard-to-find venue that was likely a freshly-painted storage facility that hotel management had decided was a way to bring in additional revenue. There were no windows, of course, the ceiling was pockmarked with small, round recessed lights, seemingly placed at random locations, and the tables and chairs were positioned to ensure non-conformity to any prescribed pattern.

For this occasion, the armless metal chairs had been draped with a white cloth covering and at each seat was positioned a professional-printed name card for each attendee. At the front of the room was a podium and, behind it, a large projection screen. In his entire career Harry had never met in a basement for any reason, much less an important corporate gathering of senior management. After he had shaken hands with some of his partners from the regional branches, he poured himself a glass of ice water and picked out three red candies from the bowl in the middle of the table. Each year the candies got smaller, he thought. Why even bother to have them?

He was disappointed that the chair with his name in front of it had its back to the podium, meaning he would have to turn his neck in order to watch. As he glanced around the room, he noticed that President Ohara was quietly chatting with a well-dressed, confident looking man at a table near the podium. Then Harry understood; this was another consultant of some sort that would 'reenergize' their corporate strategy - again. That meant another round of cost cutting measures. The consultant had clearly chosen the location to send a clear signal; companies that made money rented rooms with windows. Those that didn't - didn't.

The other regional managers were surprisingly punctual and soon every chair was filled. Apparently, the rarity of the time and place for the invitation and the short notice had intrigued all those on the invite list. Everyone seemed to suspect that something was up, and wanted to find out what it meant to them.

"Everyone please take your seats," President Ohara called out, perhaps too loudly given the size of the room. Harry noticed the microphone behind the podium and, in the far back corner, a man working the electronics. Hardly necessary, Harry thought. They could all hear. Save the money and open the bar for a bit.

"Ladies and gentlemen," the president began, "let me begin by thanking you for disrupting your busy schedules to come to this meeting. It is Friday night, it's been a busy week and you are all deserving of a rest, both tonight and this weekend, to enjoy time with family and friends."

He stopped to take a sip of water and turn the page of notes he was reading from.

"Unfortunately, as you will soon understand, that isn't going to be possible this weekend. Your company is entering the most important period of its history. As you know, Milne, Ohara, Grady Investments was started by me and my two partners based on little more than scribbles on a napkin, following a rather long and intense luncheon."

He chuckled slightly and his audience, picking up on the cue, followed suit. Many, however, glanced at their neighbors. Their weekend off was "not going to be possible." What was that about?

"But our history is just that, history - interesting to ponder but, by itself, ineffective at moving forward in this dynamic world we live in. Good lord, look at the changes we've witnessed over the years. The only thing that seems predictable these days is that the frequency and magnitude of innovation and yes, volatility seems to be growing."

He stopped for another sip of water. He'd worked on that last line for almost half an hour last night in front of his bathroom mirror and it had, he thought, come out quite well.

"Yes, change is everywhere," he continued. "In order for a company like ours to help our clients continue to grow and prosper, we too must be willing to take a good hard look within and make the decisions, sometimes difficult, to adapt and grow with the future."

Harry's neck was getting sore from the awkward position he was sitting in. He almost looked away - he could listen to the rest of it - when he noticed the consultant, an athletically built fellow, slowly stand and survey the room, beaming before approaching the podium even though Ohara was clearly not finished. It was impossible for President Ohara not to notice the intrusion and his eyes moved from his prepared speech to the approaching figure.

"But ah yes, enough of my carrying on, today isn't about me standing up here harping on history. It is about our future. Ladies and gentlemen, allow me to introduce you to Mr. Skip Williams, Managing Director of retail client services, Northwest Region of Fifty States Investments who will take over from here."

After shaking Skip's hand, he retrieved the rest of his pile of notes. Perhaps, Harry thought, it was just as well his presentation had got the hook. But the important thing was that Skip was now in charge and, at a nod from him to the electronics guy sitting at the back, a screen dropped down behind the podium, and he began to speak, his voice magnified by a small microphone attacked to the lapel of his suit.

"Thank you, Jim, so very much," he began. "I can't tell you how pleased and honored I am to be standing in front of you today. I can say with the utmost confidence on behalf of all the employees of Fifty States that we are nothing short of thrilled that you'll be joining our team. We all know that your history of client service, coupled with our leading expertise in providing the products and services that the average American family needs, is going to make us a force to be reckoned with in the northwestern United States."

Harry turned and looked at the others at his table who were each looking at one another with a puzzled expression. This was not the usual cost-cutting-tighten-your-belt-to-face-the-rough-times-ahead presentation and the man now comfortably standing at the podium was no consultant. Moving off to the side of the screen, Skip pointed at the shiny white piece of canvas and said:

"Ladies and Gentlemen, I give you Fifty States MOGI Limited, the greatest team ever assembled in the Pacific Northwest."

The instant that he said, "Northwest," the lights started to dim and the screen flickered to life, bearing the words Metropolitan Conference Consultants Inc. Another message followed:

> **STRICTLY CONFIDENTIAL**
>
> *Any persons wishing to view or otherwise partake in this presentation should understand that all subject matter and discussions are strictly confidential. Your participation in this event constitutes an agreement, by you, that you will not repeat, share or otherwise transmit any part of the information learned without the express, written permission from senior management. Persons unwilling or unable to comply with these requirements are asked to leave the room immediately. Failure to abide by these rules for any reason could result in termination and prosecution under the Securities and Exchange Act of 1933.*

"Lawyers!" Skip said, grinning. "You can't go to the can anymore without a lawyer."

On schedule, there was polite laughter from the room.

Then, the screen went dark and the room quiet. Slowly, an image started to appear on the screen. It was that of a man with a hint of grey hair, looking down at his hands, grasped warmly together in his lap. Off to one side could clearly be seen a picture in a desktop frame of a smiling woman and three children.

"Why do I use Fifty States?" the man said. "Well, growing up, I played a lot of sports. And I came to truly understand the power of being on the winning team. Fifty States is a winning company. It's as simple as that. I want the Fifty States team to be looking after my family. I will accept only the best."

Harry remembered the commercial from watching the U.S. Open golf tournament that summer. He remembered being impressed and had made a mental note at the time to tell President Ohara that they should do something like that.

Next to appear was another video, this time leading off with the company's name and logo. In the background, soft violin music gave way to bass, then flutes, and then trumpets and horns in a loud crescendo as the next full page image appeared.

## WELCOME TO THE TEAM!!

Harry turned his head back to face the others at the table who, like him, stared with mouths open. They'd all talked about it before, even joked that their carnival show would someday be sold to the Ringling Bros. and Barnum & Bailey Circus. President Ohara had said he would never sell out. He could not work for someone else, and it was his full intention to die at his desk.

But something had clearly changed. And although everyone in the room was trying to catch his eye, the die-at-his-desk president was making a determined effort not to look at them. But they all knew. Their firm was being sold. The founding partners had cashed in.

As Skip stepped down from the podium, each manager looked at another knowing their future would never be the same. There was a culture, a new enthusiasm to this firm that was different. Harry quickly surveyed the eyes of his fellow managers at his table. The room was eerily quiet because people didn't know what to say. Within seconds of the presentation ending, the doors opened and a team of food servers placed cutlery, forks, knives, salt and pepper shakers and a basket of bread on the table. A chef wearing a starched white hat began to ladle a clear soup filled with pieces of lobster and crab into their bowls, a delicacy that was followed by beautiful filet-mignon steaks covered in béarnaise sauce along with roast potatoes and asparagus spears peppered with sliced almonds. By the time the wine was poured, everyone was smiling. This was a feast. Whatever this new firm was about, they knew how to eat. Skip, their new boss, was going from table to table, giving high fives and shaking hands.

He seemed, somehow to know everyone's name. At precisely eight-thirty, after the chocolate mousse had been consumed Skip moved to the podium again.

"All right, ladies and gentlemen," he said. "I hope you enjoyed our little welcome dinner. Let's give it up for the servers, huh?"

A spontaneous applause filled the room even though none of the waiters and waitresses remained; having been told to leave and finish clearing the tables after their meeting was over.

"Sorry folks," the new boss said. "It would be great to extend the party but, fact is, we have work to do. Come Monday morning when the announcement is made, we want to hit the ground running. You, as office managers, are critical to the successful implementation of our new strategy and corporate vision. We will reconvene here tomorrow morning at eight where a full breakfast will be served and I will introduce you to your new regional managers who have already spent more time than you know working to ensure that our business combination is as successful and profitable as it can be. Please don't be late; we have a lot to do. Unfortunately, given the short time available, I'm going to have to ask you all to come in on Sunday as well - at noon, to accommodate those who want to observe their faith. Please head on home - don't drink and drive - and we'll see you back here in about twelve hours."

Don't drink and drive, Harry thought. There had only been enough wine opened for a half-glass each. He had hoped, over coffee, that maybe there would be some after-dinner brandy, when everyone at his table, everyone in the room stood to leave.

"Oh right, one other thing. No pillow talk. It is very important that you keep all of this to yourself until Monday morning when the official announcement comes out."

It was at that point that Harry knew that the party was really over.

## Chapter 8

Angela knew it wasn't the pain in her ribs that kept her up all night.

No, the cause of her insomnia was the conversation she was going to have on Monday morning after her husband left for work. She wasn't really sure what she was doing and she could only hope that the ice-cream man was really trying to help her. But would the telephone number he gave her even work? Who would answer the phone? What would she say?

When her husband got up, shaved and showered, she pretended to be asleep, buying herself some time since he usually didn't call to check on her until ten which meant that she'd have a full two hours to get dressed and head towards the park where there still existed a rare payphone. After equipping herself with three dollars in change, she reached into her pillowcase where she'd been storing the treasure she hoped she would never use.

It was the piece of paper with the phone number on it.

She grabbed her heaviest coat because even though it was only 50 degrees - a warm day in the Seattle area for October - the wind off the water could suck the warmth out of you in no time. And it was grey. She didn't know how long she'd be standing outside.

As she locked the front door behind her, she found herself wondering what the hell she was doing. This wasn't going to work.

Why should she trust her fate in a man who sells ice-cream? But what other option did she have? If she were to go for help at one of those places that advertised on TV, he would most certainly find out - and that prospect frightened her even more. She could find a way back to Iowa; she had enough money for a bus ticket, hidden inside a Tampax box - she knew he would never look in there - but he would somehow come looking for her.

She breathed easier when, reaching the entrance to the park, she saw there were very few people milling around and that the payphone was still there. And, although it had been vandalized, there was a dial tone. Not giving herself time for second thoughts, she dialed the number. When it rang two, three, four, and then five times, she began to wonder what she had been thinking. Did she really believe that an ice-cream man was going to be her pathway to joy and freedom? She started to pull the handset away from her ear to put it back on the cradle when she heard someone say, "Wha' do ya want?" in a deep, raspy voice.

"Oh, dear, I'm terribly sorry," she said. "I must have the wrong number."

"Waj you dial?" And when she told him, he said "Naw. You got it right. Now what do you want?"

At first she couldn't think of what to say. There were so many thoughts racing through her mind. Where did she start? Who was she talking to anyway? How much could she - would she - reveal to this perfect stranger?

"I want help," she said finally. "Mr. - Mr. Carratino gave me this number, He - he said that I should call. He's the ice-cream man at the park."

"I know who he is. Why you callin' *me?*"

Whoever it was she was talking to wasn't making this, whatever this was, very easy. She didn't want to say too much but she didn't want him to think she wasn't genuinely interested in whatever it was that he might be able to do for her. Clearly, she was running out of choices.

"Well, a few months ago I was, um, talking to Mr. Carrantino - and he gave me this number and said that you might be able to help me with my ... problem."

Again, there was another awkward silence. She thought she could hear him flipping sheets of paper.

"You da' gelato girl, ain't you?" the man said. "Tino said you'd call."

She inhaled sharply with the sudden exposure of who she was and the fact that the ice cream man had said something to this stranger. What had he said? What did he know? What could he know?

Slowly, like a child caught in a lie, she said, "Yes, I am. That's me."

The voice on the other end didn't hesitate this time.

"OK, we doan talk here. I'm a guy, but not *the* guy. We need to meet."

"In person?" Angela blurted out. Suddenly she felt as though she had been stripped naked. She heard a chuckle and then he said, "Doan know of no udder way."

Angela felt as though she were on a precipice. If she went too far, too fast, she would go over the edge, engulfed in tears.

"But don't you want to hear about... my problem?" she said.

"NO! Not over the phone. You meet me tomorrow, where you usually meet Tino."

And then, abruptly, the line went dead.

## Chapter 9

Jennifer never stopped thinking, planning or assessing risk. To let down your guard, even for a second, could prove fatal. 'Dad', as he requested she call him, had arranged an impromptu dinner and, as asked, she relayed the message to Michael. Two things were clear. This was not going to be a social occasion, and he was going to make some sort of announcement. The man always had to put on a show, with himself as center stage. And Michael wasn't going to be happy about it, whatever it was.

At twenty-eight, she was born and educated in New York City. Never married - who needed the baggage? She conducted many relationships of various lengths and intensities, depending on her read of the situation at hand. At 5' 8", her commitment to fitness gave her a body that made men stop and stare. Her smooth blonde hair just reached the top of her broad shoulders. She wore little jewelry, except for gold studs in her ears. She often wore pin-striped shirts with an extra button undone. Her breasts pulled against her remaining buttons. The product of an upbringing fraught with fighting followed by a messy divorce, Jennifer had learned the hard way to always be on her guard, using her superior street smarts and intuition as a weapon. The lies and counter-lies of her upbringing made her distrust any form of structure. She knew the only way to survive was to rely on her own instincts, even if that meant going around the law. Her morals having gone by the wayside a long time ago, she had no hesitation about using her sexual prowess to her advantage whenever necessary. Most men were easily manipulated fools.

Now, as she surveyed herself in the mirror on the outside of the front hall closet, she was certain that the cream silk blouse and purple skirt were perfect for her father-in-law's favorite Italian restaurant. She knew that Michael's dad was attracted to her - probably physically. He'd even confided, after a couple of scotches, that meeting Jennifer showed that, "Michael was finally getting his life in order." And, with Michael taking over his father's book of business, the outlook for her, in this strange city on the other side of the country, had never been better.

While Michael's growth was a positive for her, she was coming to fear that it might take much longer than she had planned to recreate what she'd had before - Wall Street-sized money and the advantages that came with it. Money was the only source of security and always would be. Still, she reminded herself, her last encounter had been close, far too close for comfort. It had taken all her cunning to get out without repercussions, but in the end, the Russian was deported, the kid was promoted and she got out of town. She was and always would be a survivor.

And, as far as living conditions were concerned, she was sitting pretty. The house was more than adequate, designed for the just-starting-out couple. The kitchen, eating area and den all blended together and a small gas fireplace with artificial used, red brick gave the room a sense of luxury. The hardwood was new and the walls painted an off-white. On the whole, it was nice enough and would have to do for now, even though it was rented. She might have left a few things in Manhattan, but not her expectations of the good life. Michael, in the role of struggling young broker, would be fine for a while but it was starting to look like he wouldn't be able to follow in daddy's shoes. Christ, he was even taking the bus to work to save on gas. What broker with any chutzpah takes the bus? Clients wanted successful brokers and successful brokers didn't use public transit. He got a full book of business handed to him a year ago and was just letting it slip away.

She'd keep her powder dry for a bit longer but, deep down, she knew she would, eventually, have to take control. After all, her options had been narrowed a bit. She was barred from working in the securities industry for life - a fact that she hadn't seen fit to share with Michael. He didn't need to know her real name, Sandy Allen, either. It had been relatively easy to create the new identity in Seattle. In order to bargain her way to a reduced penalty before she left New York for good, she had to plead guilty to being a part of a large insider trading scheme, and a felony was a felony. She knew any employment application, which required her social security number and a background check, would be denied once her real name and her police record were discovered. That was why she couldn't take on a job.

In her new world, she held herself out to have a subtle confidence mixed with innocence. She avoided raising her voice in public at all costs but she never lost sight of the fact that, in order to succeed in this life, a woman had to be direct, aggressive and a fighter. You could never, ever lose sight of that fact.

She was careful about reaming Michael out for his lack of financial success. He was enamored with her beauty and had said, several times, that he couldn't believe he had found a girl like her, which was the truth. But she could only push things so hard. He'd bought the "I don't want to talk about my difficult past" line, and that was a good thing. Most other guys would have pushed harder. Even he would eventually point out that her volunteering work, which she never actually did, wasn't helping pay the bills and hint that perhaps she could bring some money in herself. It was what struggling young couples did.

Ugh. She could make ten times his greatest effort if she felt like it, and, perhaps, she would. It would be more difficult though with the new set of 'rules' she had to work with. How were you supposed to score goals if you weren't allowed on the ice? She'd have to find a new path. One thing was clear. Michael, left on his own, would fail but she didn't want to show too much of her hand - not yet anyway. For her to take too much control over his career would reveal that she knew far more than she was letting on and raise too many questions. To him, she was just a pretty woman. It was best to leave it that way for a while.

She turned as she heard Michael put his key into the front door lock. He was a bit late. His father would be at the restaurant by now, at his table, enjoying a drink and schmoozing the owner. For him and the proprietor, it was a mutual stroking exercise that could last for some time. But she also knew that Senior didn't like to be kept waiting.

"Oh no, Jennifer," he said when he saw that she was dressed to go out. "I have had the worst day. I am not going to eat with my dad, not tonight. You should have made up some excuse."

Jennifer stood up and started for the door. Michael had probably steeled up the courage all the way home to give her his flimsy ultimatum.

"Well, he's probably already at the restaurant waiting for us. Embarrass yourself if you want, but not me. I'll give him your regrets. Besides, he said it was important. I, at least, am interested in finding out why."

They argued about it all the way to the restaurant in their ten-year old compact car with sporadic rust spots and tires that looked fit for a go-cart. The bumper sticker from the previous owner read "Honk if you love Jesus," but because he thought it might be bad luck, Michael refused to take it off.

"Jen, how many times have I told you?" he said as she pulled down the sun visor and proceeded to check her makeup. "You can't just let my father run my - our - lives. He can't just call up like that, on such short notice, and think we have no other plans."

"Look sweet cheeks," she told him, "you might as well save your protests for your father. He said it was extremely important that we meet him for dinner tonight. It's not my fault that he gave us such short notice. He wouldn't take no for an answer."

Michael stared at the cars. Why couldn't the world just give him a break? First he'd lost the biggest account he had left. His slimy co-worker was trying to steal the rest of them, probably right behind his back. His credit card was over the limit again. And now he had to go to a crusty restaurant that smelled like old leather and try to look interested as his father recounted his, "When I was in the business" stories for the millionth time. But he knew his dad, and he knew that when he insisted that was the end of it. Even Jennifer, as compelling as she was, couldn't hold a candle to Michael Franklin Senior.

For Junior, it seemed as if his entire life was a comparison. His father had been the captain of the local high school football team thirty-six years ago, and several of his long-standing clients were former teammates. Michael, who had grown up in the same town and gone to the same school, had had to walk by the picture of his dad in the Alumni All-star area every day on his way to class. The new electronic scoreboard at one end of the field had a sign posted next to it, which read, '*With deepest gratitude to Michael Franklin, '72.*' Junior had tried out for the football team and was cut before the first game. He could still hear his father's words.

"You know, son, I'll go to my grave trying to figure out why you and football didn't take to each other."

Like football was the only thing in the world. He sucked at it. OK dad? Get over it.

Senior graduated dean's list from Stanford University. Michael graduated with a C average from Clatsop Community College. Because his dad put so much pressure on him to study English, it wasn't worth fighting him. It was bad enough that he hadn't got in to Stanford. He hated English. If he'd taken the sciences, like he wanted to, he'd have done much better. In spite of his age, Senior still carried a six handicap at the Puget Country Club. Michael hated golf. The last time they played together, and it would be the last, Michael's father had stormed off the course after Michael, in frustration, had thrown his club down the fairway after a bad shot.

Senior's favorite restaurant was Sostanza Trattoria because of its view of Lake Washington from the waterside patio, which Michael could never understand because they always went at night and sat inside. His favorite dish was the house specialty of pappardelle with ground veal, Portobello mushrooms, and a light wine sauce. Franklin Senior had booked his usual table, a bottle of fine Chianti had been opened, decanted and allowed to breathe for two hours before he and his guests arrived. He'd been a regular patron for over twenty years and, when he retired, he received the honor of having his favorite table declared as *Mr. Franklin's office.*

Senior savored eating. Even when he had been working, he'd admonished those who succumbed to the lure of fast food. A meal was meant to be enjoyed leisurely, over at least a couple of hours. If the business was such that there just wasn't enough time, he'd skip lunch altogether rather than "choke it down." Now that he was retired, he had lots of time for meals. Single, he rarely cooked for himself so he had established a wide array of eateries within an hour's drive from the center of Seattle. His little black book of names resembled that of a man with a list of mistresses.

As Michael and Jennifer walked in, they saw Senior at his table, holding up a glass of the Chianti to the closest light bulb. Everyone knew there were lots of remarkable wines available from the west coast. but his father always insisted that it was important to drink the appropriate wine that matched the food. To Michael wine was wine. But at least dad was paying. He surely didn't want to try and use his plastic in front of the old man.

Franklin Senior rose, kissed Jennifer on the cheek, and shook his son's hand with both of his, as if they were clients. As always, he wore a suit and tie. It was an old habit and one of the many lessons he had tried, unsuccessfully, to instill in his son. You just never knew when you might run into a client.

No wonder this man was so successful, Jennifer thought, his face oozed trust and confidence. She looked at her boyfriend's features. Maybe, but it would take a lot of time.

"Let's get the menus," Michael said. "I'm starving."

His dad might be able to disrupt their lives with short-notice dinner invitations but Michael could still control the clock. The last thing he wanted was a three-hour bonding session. Left unmanaged, his dad would allow the meal to go all night. Once they'd eaten, it would give Michael the opening to skip dessert (trying to watch my weight you know) or the after-dinner brandy in a snifter (really tired dad, long day, just want to go home and sleep. You know how it is in markets like this). But the restaurant owner knew better than to bring the menus before Mr. Franklin asked for them.

"Relax, son," his father said. "I'm sure you've had a hard day. Have a drink to steady the nerves."

Senior looked at his son and wondered where he'd gone wrong. The boy had no manners, none whatsoever, and it showed in everything he did and said. Who'd taught him to be so rude as to try to hurry a dinner, where he was the guest, and his father was paying? Why didn't he like to spend time with his own father? He seemed almost uncomfortable.

Whatever the reason, it was probably the fault of his whore of a mother. Not that it mattered. Senior was here for a reason. Once again he was going to step in and deal with his son's inadequacies.

Michael watched his dad. It was all, always, so predictable. Leaning forward over the table, just to make sure no other conversations could be had, Senior started his usual diatribe about the weather, his week (it was always about his week first), and then random news items that appealed to his sense of curiosity. Michael stared at the older man and tried to pretend he was somewhere else, while Jennifer showed an extraordinary level of interest, nodding her head and smiling whenever appropriate until finally his father paused.

"Michael, son," he remarked, "you look tired, very tired. How are you doing, really? I have to say that I'm a bit worried about you."

Michael shrugged and said that it was just a very tough time in the markets. He was sure his dad would understand that bear markets were hard on everyone. He immediately grimaced after his last sentence was out of his mouth, because he'd just opened the door to the story of the '87 market and how his father had miraculously survived.

"Well yes, actually, I do know how hard it is going for you," Senior said. "Since you are as tired as you say you are, I'll hurry along our conversation to get to the main event. I'm sure there will be lots to discuss after I reveal why I invited you for dinner. Jennifer, I hope you don't mind if we hog the dinner conversation to discuss business."

Jennifer smiled politely. What, she wondered, was the old man up to?

"Frankly," he went on, "it looks like one of the most exciting periods of my life will be starting. I've been a bit listless over the last year so I have made some decisions that I am completely thrilled with and I'm sure, you will be too. Michael, I hope you don't mind that I've included your future life-partner to hear my announcement since you are in this together."

That was another thing. 'Future life-partner.' There were always the hints, often not so subtle, that it was time for Michael to ask for her hand. Truth was, although his father didn't know it, he had sort of suggested it several times only to be quickly put off by Jennifer saying it was too early for her. Michael didn't dream of telling his father that he had tried and failed at that too. Why give him something else to lecture him about? Besides, in the marriage department, at least, his father had not precisely been an overwhelming success. But that was beside the point now. If he really had something important to say, Michael knew he'd better listen.

"OK, here goes nothing," Senior said. "As you know, I got a call from Tommy Van Buren this morning. He was most upset and apologetic but thought that he had to do something. We've been friends for so long that he felt he owed it to me, or I should say to both of us, Michael, to stay with the program for as long as he could. But, he finally had to capitulate, very reluctantly I might add."

Jennifer's eyes shot up. Michael had said nothing to her about this. So he'd lost another one of his dad's accounts.

Michael frowned. He knew now, that he never, ever, should have agreed to take his dad's business. What had looked like a good idea at the time had become his worst nightmare. Maybe he should just give the rest of his book to Ivan and be done with it.

"By my count, that's four of my best clients in just a year, Michael," Senior was saying now. "In rough numbers, you've lost 30% of the assets I left in your control. Now, don't get me wrong, I know what a bear is like. I've probably told you about what happened after October 19, 1987. But this is different, son. It isn't normal to have such high turnover, in any market."

Michael just barely resisted the impulse to get up and leave. Being reamed out like this for the second time in one day, and this time in front of Jennifer, was a little too much.

"I've been watching you, son," he was saying now, "proud as any dad could be, as you took over the wheel of the ship."

Proud? He'd never been proud of anything Michael had tried to do! Michael was now rubbing the back of his neck and staring at the table.

"Are you listening to me, son," Senior said. "This is important."

It was like he was still a kid. His father never accepted the fact that he was a man, his own man. And now he was nagging him. Maybe next would be to tell him to sit up straight.

"Dad, please, I'm tired. Can we just order?"

Senior thought about Michael's childhood. Maybe it was because, after the whore left, his father had decided to go a bit easier on his son. He did, after all, feel guilty. He knew he shouldn't, but he did. And he wanted to spend more time with his son, but his business franchise just wouldn't allow it. Regardless, Michael Junior should pay him the respect he had coming, tired or not. He ignored the plea.

"I will continue, then, and Michael, I think it would be in your best interest to sit up straight and pay attention. Because what I have to say affects you. Now, where was I? Ah, yes. I think, son, that even you would agree that there's a lot more to learn about this business than meets the eye. And you haven't really been given a fair shake. In hindsight, I couldn't have picked a worse time to retire."

Michael sat up straighter. He was in no mood for another sermon about his posture.

"Look Dad," he said, "I appreciate your concern but I'm doing just fine. Yes, I've lost some business - that's to be expected - but that's because the clients you left me are largely most comfortable with someone their age. And the market has sucked. Put those together and boom. What you don't see is the number of solid relationships I've developed with the rest of the people you used to serve. I've completed full financial plans for every single one of them and they are happy about that."

His dad looked at Jennifer and then back to Michael. When Senior had last spoken with Harry Lugarno, to tell him about his idea, the office manager had said that Michael was bragging all over the office about creating financial plans. It was clear evidence that the kid really was out in left field.

"Full financial plans. Michael I've told you that when the market is going down and clients are losing money, what they want is comforting, not more exact calculations on just how much money they are losing. How many lunches have you bought in the last month? That's the secret. Buy them a drink and listen to their stories. Show them that you are as pained by what's happening to them as they are."

Michael sighed and looked past his dad at the small bronze figurine hanging from the wall. There was a single cobweb thread running from the nose to the outstretched hand.

"Look, Dad, I don't want to be rude but can we not talk about work anymore? Let's just have a nice dinner, OK? I *really* don't want to go over this again. How you ran your business is old school. Times have changed and so have the methods for client service."

Jennifer looked like someone watching a tennis match. Senior paused a moment, looked at the table, and then back to Michael.

"Yes, you're probably right," he said. "This isn't the time to rekindle old debates. You're convinced of your position and so am I. At least you stand up for what you believe in. Like father, like son, no?"

He chuckled to himself as he straightened his knife and fork.

"Of course, my position has the benefit of having a proven track record. But, Michael, you just used a very insightful phrase – *Old School.* You're absolutely right. The clients I left you are old school, used to old school servicing. If the market were going up, they'd probably be more receptive to the changes your methods entail. But, when they're losing money - and this isn't just any money we are talking about here - it is the money they need to live on for the rest of their days - it's normal for them to revert back to what they know and trust."

Michael drained his water glass, wishing it were something stronger. His father had the most irritating and painful way of lecturing possible. Nothing was ever direct, but everything supported his point of view in one way or another. It was like death by a thousand cuts.

"But theories don't matter and I didn't ask you here to get into a debate," he went on. "I've given something a lot of thought and, frankly, as a result of our little chat just now, I'm more convinced than ever that this is the right step. This dinner is meant to be a celebration of an important event in my life. I'm very excited."

He had Michael's full attention now. What the hell was going on? Had the old man found another woman? That would be all he needed, some stranger cutting into his inheritance.

"OK, Dad," he said, "we're all ears. What's your big announcement?"

Senior smiled, folded his arms and leaned back from the table.

"Tommy Van Buren wasn't the only person I spoke with. I also talked to Harry Lugarno. As you know, he's probably my oldest friend and I respect his judgment as well as my own. He said he had given your situation a great deal of thought, Michael, and in his opinion, you were dealt a bad hand. Almost to the day that I handed over the reins, the market started going sour. At a time when my book of clients should have been getting service and consolation from someone they knew and were comfortable with, they got a new, young face who, in effect, was speaking a different language. The fact that you are my son wasn't enough. It was too much change too fast and that's what is making them most uncomfortable. If you think about it, it's a wonder they all didn't leave. Kudos to you, Michael."

Michael all but held his breath. He hoped to God his father wasn't going where he thought he was.

"All right, I won't keep you in suspense any longer. Harry has asked me, and I have agreed, to come out of retirement, effective Monday, and to be your partner again, at least until the market settles. Our first mission will be to win back each and every one of the clients that have strayed - this time for good."

Later, in the parking lot, when Michael closed Jen's door and walked around to his side of the car, the moment of peace he experienced was like that of driving through a bridge underpass in the heavy rain. When he opened the door, the sound of the storm came back full blast.

"... and, oh my god! Why don't you just go out of your way to embarrass the living shit out of me?" she was saying. "You had to make a scene. You know how much I hate that. Your father was just trying to help you. What the hell is wrong with you Michael?"

It took all the willpower he could muster to keep quiet. He knew that if he talked now, he would say things that he would later regret. This relationship was delicate enough as it was. Putting the key in the ignition, he backed the car out of the restaurant parking lot.

"So you just get up and leave? Throwing your napkin in your dad's face was a nice touch. The man was there trying to save your ass and that's how you thank him."

Michael couldn't hold it in any longer. First it had been his boss, then the old man, and now Jennifer.

"Save my ass!" he exclaimed. "Is that what you think was going on? Well then you're not as all knowing as I thought. There was one thing, and only one thing, going on at that table as it always has been and will be until he drinks his last bottle of Chianti. All he wants to do is prove that he was more successful than I am. It's worse now that he retired. The only reason he cares about me is because if I fail, it reflects on him. His old friends are calling him up and complaining that they're losing money. Well come on - it's a bear market, hello? Instead of defending me he says, 'Oh, don't worry, I'll step in and save the day'. I mean, after all, what choice does he have? He has to play golf with the old farts every weekend."

"Stop right there Michael!" she told him, when he paused to take a breath. "I think you've said enough."

Michael thought better of driving on the interstate, tense as he was. He chose the back route to their house, which should have been more peaceful, but with the overhanging willow trees blocking the streetlights, it was eerily dark and uncomfortably quiet.

His mind wandered to fill the awkward void. Meeting Jennifer had been one of those random, unexpected good things that seemed to just happen to people now and then. He had been swimming at the Y when he'd seen her. She was slim and fit and her gleaming shoulder-length blonde hair waved gracefully as she walked, her red bathing suit clinging to every part of her. She was, truly, the most classically beautiful girl he had ever seen, with the cheekbones of a model. He must have been staring because she looked right back at him and smiled. She wasn't shy, this girl.

Afterwards they'd had coffee, and she'd told him that she was new in town, having just moved out of New York City to escape the hustle and bustle, and that she'd come to Seattle to establish new roots, a new life. As their relationship intensified, he learned that she was a 'survivor of a bad relationship.' But she didn't like to talk about it. She'd say "Why dwell on the past? You can't change it, you can only learn from it. Why tarnish my life by thinking of what's past?"

Thinking about what happened at dinner, Jennifer knew that Michael clearly thought this was just another fight but she systematically evaluated the steps, the options, and the risk vs. return of each choice. She could raise the stakes if she wanted to. What the hell. Why not go for it? The life of the 'young couple trying to make ends meet' was getting old, fast. She decided she'd just stay quiet, even when they went to bed - she wouldn't even say goodnight. Let him stew in it. Most guys couldn't stand it. It would build up the pressure. Tomorrow morning would be step one. She'd say she had been working on her own strategy to help him - them - but it was too early. She fully understood Michael's troubles with his dad but what was the harm in partnering up with him, for a little while anyway? If nothing else, Michael wouldn't lose any more accounts while his dad was on the 'reactivated' list and she needed that money to fund her 'strategy.'

Eventually, Jen would sell him on the new design that was going to make them both very wealthy - rich beyond their dreams - but she couldn't risk scaring him away since, apparently, he possessed an unfortunate degree of ethical thinking. But, she knew he was the right candidate. He was failing at his job, estranged from his father and, just to make it interesting, facing the prospect of losing his potential fiancé. He would have to go for it. If there was one thing she believed, she knew that most people could be sold anything once you located their hot buttons.

And then she'd be back in the game!

## Chapter 10

When Angela arrived at the park, she wasn't sure who she was supposed to meet and where. The man she had spoken to on the phone had said something about where she and Mr. Carrantino would see each other, and so she had taken a seat on a bench not far from where he parked his truck. The wind was up today and the park was basically deserted. The only person she could see this early was a young man, dressed in blue jeans and a leather jacket, his black hair slicked back, talking on his cell phone, his cigarette bobbing with each word. He looked more like a character out of the movie *Grease* than someone who could help her with her problem. As he was about to pass her, he clicked the phone closed saying, "Ya, I got it" and sat down on the other end of the bench, apparently absorbed in admiring the smoke he was exhaling in a thin stream. Just then, the air was filled with the sound of a flock of geese flying in perfect formation, announcing to all of Seattle that they were headed to a warmer climate before the snows started.

"There goes the geese, headed south for the winter," the stranger said. "Just like Tino."

It took a second for the meaning of the sentence to register, but when it did, Angela said, "But you can't be…"

The boy, for he was little more than that, held up his hand.

"Too much talking, gelato girl. I'm just a guy. I know the number of another guy. That's all."

Angela looked at him, surprised and frustrated.

"But, you said..."

The hand went up again.

"I said nothin'. Now I'm going to get up and leave, right? And I'm gonna forget my phone - leave it sitting right here on the bench. After I leave, and you don't watch me, right, when you can't see me no more, you notice I left my phone. You pick it up, open it and push the send button. You understand?"

When she nodded, eyes wide, he jumped up without another word and strolled off. After five minutes, Angela, feeling as though she were part of a spy movie, slid her hand along the bench, picked up the cell phone and pressed 'Send.' The voice she heard sounded as though it had been eroded for years by cigar smoke and cheap bourbon.

"Look, gelato girl," the man said. "You been goin' to see Tino to put something cold on ya face, a face that looks like a used punching bag. You gots to go see him - ya wonders why you don't just go to your refrigerator and get some ice - because ya boyfriend might see ya. How'm I doin' so far?"

Shamed, she said, "Yes, you are on the right track."

"Yeah, I tought so. They're all the same, these guys. An' now, the ice-cream truck is gone for the winter, just when you need it most because the beatins is getin' worse."

As if to remind her of the truth, her stomach muscles gripped so tight that she gasped.

"OK, don't get all gushy on me," the man told her. "This is a business phone call, you understand?"

She wiped her nose on her sleeve and inhaled deeply.

"I just want him to stop, that's all. Can you make him stop Mr...?"

"I don't have no name. I don't exist and you never talked to me, not once, not ever. Understood?"

"Oh, yes, well of course. But please answer my question. Can you make him stop? How do you do that?"

The laughter through the handset made her pull the phone away but she quickly put it back, pressing hard against the side of her head.

"Gelato girl, you listen good. These guys, I spit on their graves, they's the lowest form of scum they is. But, we all know the 'ting that you don't want to. They don't stop. They hit you up good, then they have to hit you up more the next time, and the next time. An what's a gelato girl like you gonna do? Run away? He'd hunt you. He's watching you, all the time. Lady, we know how the game goes. We seen it lots of times - too many. Soon enough, if you don't do something, we'll be reading about you in the paper. You understand what I'm sayin' to ya?"

Her shoulders sagged under the weight of her existence. She was embarrassed to realize that someone she had never met knew her history.

"Can you make him stop?" she whispered. "Please."

He laughed again, but not as long or as loud this time.

"Look, gelato girl, this ain't no marriage counselor you talking to. Yeah, I know a guy can make him stop. But I tell you this, when the guy is done, this bottom-feeding piece of garbage won't never touch you again, not ever. You understand what I'm saying to ya?"

At first she didn't. She started to form another question in her mind when the reality of what he had just said to her sunk in.

"What? Oh my God, are you saying? You're not going to... hurt him are you?"

"I'm not sayin' nothing," he interrupted her. "But it seems to me some body goin' to get hurt here. You goes away and think about it and you call me back when you's ready... that's if you make it that far."

Hanging up the handset as if it was diseased, she started shaking so hard that she had to grab the side or the bench. And then, as instructed, she left the phone where she found it and walked away.

## Chapter 11

Jennifer decided to stay in bed Saturday morning to create the impression that their fight the night before had upset her so much that she hadn't been able to sleep. Normally, even on a Saturday, she'd be up with the sun, on the Internet looking for market news, a habit she picked up after years on Wall Street. She looked at Michael, still sleeping next to her. This would be a big day for him. She'd decided to introduce her plan to him in steps because he could only take so much so fast. But she was now sure of two things; it was time to move towards the next stage of the game she was about to be playing, and he was the chosen pawn.

The first thought Michael had as he came back to awareness was the presence of someone next to him in the bed, which, at seven-thirty in the morning, was a first. Jen was still asleep and that had never happened before. He lay still and held his breath, and was comforted by the steady but subtle rise and fall of the sheets next to him.

Thinking about their fight had kept him awake until sometime after midnight. He tried to look at things from her point of view. She'd come to Seattle from New York City where something bad, something she wouldn't tell him about, had happened. So, from her perspective, Michael reasoned, she had escaped to a place that was almost as far away as she could go and still remain in the country. What would someone like that be looking for? Depending on the circumstances, she might be hesitant to make a full commitment to a new relationship. That would explain why she often told Michael that, although she loved him, she truly did, it was too early for her to consider anything like an engagement. She hoped Michael could understand but would accept his decision to move on if he had to. And because Jennifer was the most beautiful, dynamic captivating woman he'd ever even spoken to, he'd wait for as long as he had to.

He imagined the other thing that had to be on her mind, because it was on everyone's, was security - financial security. She'd said that she was fortunate enough to leave with her savings but since she hadn't been able to find a job after almost a year of trying, she was cutting into her security. When Michael had suggested that he help her out until she got on her feet, she had reluctantly accepted. He was proud when she took the joint credit card from him, not realizing that by wanting to appear as the provider, he'd grabbed a double-edged sword. This had been made amply clear to him when, after his lunch with Ivan, the card had been declined. For most normal couples there'd be a serious discussion. Did she really need to spend $100 on another pair of shoes? In this case, he couldn't. After all, he'd practically begged to become her sole provider. To challenge her spending habits now would be a tacit admission that he couldn't.

He was screwed. If he pushed too hard, she'd just remind him that the leading cause of break-up in young couples was money.

Their romance had all happened so fast that sometimes it seemed to him that she had materialized out of nowhere. After University, Michael had roamed between temporary jobs, completely unsure of what he wanted to do. Even though he was still living at home, his father had seemed to be OK with it. He had learned growing up that his mother had hooked up with a surfing instructor she met while they were on vacation outside San

Diego, and it was clear by now that she had found a new life, one that didn't include him or his dad. She'd even forgotten Michael's last birthday. Still, Michael assumed his dad was the cause of the divorce. All he had ever known was a father totally focused on his work. Maybe if the man had spent a little more time on his wife than the stock market...

A soft moan interrupted his thoughts. Jennifer was waking up. His mind raced. Was she still mad? Had she slept well? Would she, at least, talk to him now? He was ready to apologize for having dragged her into the confrontation at dinner. But couldn't she see how important it was to him to prove himself - to everyone - especially his dad? His problems had nothing to do with her. He loved her so much. He imagined that she must be terribly upset; being exposed to someone else's family baggage is never pleasant.

Jennifer had been alert for about a half hour, and although she didn't want to turn her head, she knew he was both awake and staring at her. The element of surprise, her waking up next to him, would work well. She made several small noises, turned a bit, struggled to lift her head off the pillow and laid it back down.

"What time is it?" Her voice was somewhat muffled by the goose down bed covering.

Michael sounded like he was speaking to someone who had just taken a fall.

"Oh, hi there sweetie. Are you OK? Did you get any sleep last night? I'm sure I didn't. Listen honey..."

"Geez, Michael, give a girl a chance to wake up, will you?" she said, keeping it playful, friendly, pushing herself up against the pillows in a way that gave maximum exposure of her breasts under the sheer silk of her nightgown.

"All right then, boyfriend-of-mine," she said, running one hand through her hair, "what have you got to say for yourself?"

Michael could see that her smile, while still intact, had cringed up at one corner and she now had her arms folded across her breasts. She'd asked him the question he had been expecting, and he had his answer all prepared, having first concluded that if he explained everything that was on his mind it would overwhelm her. Best just to keep it simple; he loved her with all his heart and he only wanted to succeed on his own so they could get on with their own lives and get married. And the most important thing he had to say, as much as he didn't want to, was that he would agree to his father's plan - for a while.

Jennifer listened and adjusted her own presentation as Michael spoke, delighted that he was apparently making it easier for her. Still, she didn't want to move too fast.

"My father always used to say that if you slept on a problem, it usually wasn't so bad the next morning," she said, smiling broadly in a congratulatory sort of way. "Wow Michael, you've come a long way in twelve hours. I'm proud of you. And I know how hard it is for you to turn the other cheek with your dad but I'm totally impressed with your wisdom. It may not be what you want to do but, short term, it's the right answer. What's that expression? 'He who fights and runs away, lives to fight another day.'"

She slapped her hand down on the bed sheets between them in confirmation of a job well done. Now was the perfect time to slowly unveil her plan. The hairs on her arm felt as though they were standing erect and, at times like this she became exceptionally... well, true power over money was sexual.

## Chapter 12

After the disturbing events in the park, Angela walked back to her house while she replayed the conversation over and over thinking surely she had misunderstood. But what the man said - "This ain't no marriage counselor. I know a guy can make him stop but you don't want to know how" - had sounded very sinister. Surely to God that was just for effect. He'd said "He won't touch you ever again" but how could he be sure? Is this what people in her situation did? Could anyone, ever, get that ruthless? No matter what happened, she knew she could never become desperate enough to... In her heart of hearts, she knew that violence didn't stop violence; it just made it worse. If this was what the ice-cream man had in mind, then she would rise above. There had to be a better way.

After the first block, she was starting to breathe easier, and she found herself thinking about, practically speaking, how she should proceed. What was the better way? She thought back to one of the lessons her mother had taught her. "You catch more flies with honey than vinegar" she used to say. That was it. She and her husband were going through a rough passage. That was all. And she *did* know how to start to make him feel better. After all, the way to a man's heart was through his stomach. She would prepare a nice dinner, and to that end, she changed directions and went to the grocery store. Being without a car, she usually ordered online. But it was a crisp day and the sun was out, so it was a great time for a walk. It was thirty minutes to the store, but it would do her good.

When she arrived back home, after having been gone two hours, there were three messages waiting for her, all from her husband, wanting to know where she was, the first two delivered in increasingly impatient tones, and the last in a voice she knew all too well...

> *"See! This is what I'm fucking talking about. You drive me insane and then it's my fucking fault when I get mad. When I want to talk to you, you should be home! I don't know where the hell you are but don't bother calling me back. I just wanted to see how your day was going but now I really don't give a shit."*

**END OF NEW MESSAGES**

She called his office immediately, only to be told that he would be in meetings for the rest of the day. Sighing, she started cleaning up around the house in preparation for the dinner which she hoped might reconcile him to the fact that she had taken the unusual step of actually going to the grocery store. But she knew from past experience that he was likely to come home in a rage, even though she left several messages with his increasingly impatient secretary throughout the day. And it was only with difficulty that she kept herself from thinking about what the man on the phone had suggested.

She started to sauté the green onions mixed with tarragon for the sauce at around six, in order to fill the house with the scent of fresh cooking, and having purchased two beautiful salmon fillets, just off the boat, she decided to bake them in white wine and lemon. She would start the wild rice, which would take about thirty minutes, as soon as he walked in the door. The Bocconcini salad was waiting in the fridge, and a bottle of Californian chardonnay had been chilling several hours.

By seven, he had not arrived. Neither had he called to say that he would be late. Was this, she wondered, his way of punishing her because she hadn't been home at exactly the time he wanted her to be? And yet, knowing that when he did appear he would expect dinner to be waiting for him, she cooked the rice and poached the salmon - and waited. By eight, when she finally heard his car in the driveway, she was fuming. This was his childish way of revenge and he'd ruined a dinner that she'd spent the better part of the day planning and preparing. As he walked in the room, his tie askew, he bounced slightly off of the door and she knew that he had been drinking. And when she told him that dinner was ready, he laughed. It was not a pleasant sound.

"I wasn't sure you'd be home," he told her, hanging his jacket on the back of the chair. "You've been gone the whole fucking day, haven't you? Oh, I got your messages. Covering your tracks, weren't you? Want to tell me where you were calling from and who you were with?"

"I just went out for a walk," she told him. "It was a beautiful day. And then I decided it was high time we had a special home-cooked meal so I walked to the grocery store. It's a bit overdone, I'm afraid. I was expecting you home sooner. But let's not worry about that now."

When she put the plate down in front of him, she could smell the alcohol on his breath.

"Oh, I see. I come home a little late from work and that's a problem. You fuck off *all morning* but that's OK. Is that how this goes? You're not the problem, I am. Is that it?"

She looked at his eyes - one seemed to be slightly closed. How much had he had to drink?

"Did you go to the bar again after work?" she asked him, deciding to be upfront about it. "You know you aren't supposed to drive that way. You might hurt someone."

He slammed his hands on the table.

"Look bitch, don't you dare start lecturing me. Why did you go out this morning? Where did you go? Why did I have a shit day at work wondering whether you were walking up and down the street fucking all of the neighbors? Huh?"

Angela knew she was taking a risk by revealing her true feelings, especially since he'd been drinking, but enough was enough.

"You have no right to say something so vulgar to me. I've spent my entire day thinking about you and planning and preparing a nice meal - nothing more. Getting mad at me is ridiculous."

He looked down as if noticing the food in front of him for the first time.

"You cooked this?" he demanded. "It looks like it just came out of the garbage. And why the fuck did you buy salmon that smells as though it was caught three weeks ago?"

And then, looking her straight in the eye, he flipped the plate over with such violence that the rice spattered all over the table.

"I work too hard to eat shit," he said, and grabbing his jacket added, "I'm going to get some real food. Don't wait up."

"You shouldn't be driving," she began, pointing her finger at him, only to have him grab her wrist and twist it.

"DON'T YOU FUCKING TELL ME WHAT TO DO YOU WHORE!" he shouted spraying spittle all over her face. "That's right, bitch. Try to get away from me. I can hurt you real bad. You remember that!"

The unexpected pain had bought tears to her eyes, which as the door slammed behind him turned into uncontrollable sobs.

Angela wasn't sure how long she'd sat at the table in front of her plate of food, now cold, and his lying in a scattered mess. She had the urge to get up, clean everything off, do the dishes and retire in front of the TV with a warm cup of cocoa like she always did. She'd pretend, as she always did, that this nightmare, which was her life, was only a dream. But this time she forced herself to remain seated, looking at the mess, and think.

She looked at her plate, pretty basic white with a soft blue flowery trim. They were a clandestine wedding gift from her mother, after her father had refused to have any further contact with her and that two-bit excuse for a husband she supposedly married. Any marriage ceremony that wasn't performed in Our Lady of Mary Church of Martinstown wasn't, in her father's eyes, sanctified by the lord God.

She desperately wanted to call her mother, to tell her the truth about her life and ask her for help. But she knew she couldn't. At the very least, it would be a full admission that what she had done was wrong, that she should have listened to her parents. She would be expected to return home to the farm, try to rebuild her life, get married to one of her high school sweethearts, and start pumping out children. But she knew she couldn't do that. She had made her decision to leave, and that was one of the most important days of her life. Besides, she wasn't sure she was prepared to forgive the man who had carried her as a baby, taught her how to ride a bike and drive a car and, for as long as she could remember, expressed the unequivocal love that can only exist between a father and a daughter. He had, after all, turned on her, so fast and with so much conviction that it made her wonder if one of her fundamental beliefs was nothing but a sham.

There was, obviously, a greater threat than humiliation. Her husband, if that's what she could bear to think of him as being right now, was insanely jealous, with a fuse that could explode in a heartbeat. He watched and monitored her every move - perhaps more than she knew. Even if she did manage to call home unobserved, if her father answered, he would just hang up and she didn't know if she could bear such an outright rejection. She thought about running away, maybe even just showing up at home. If she was clever with her 'allowance', she could save up enough for bus fare. But there was always the risk that they wouldn't take her back and, if they did, he'd come looking for her. She couldn't live with the thought that her mistake could bring harm to her parents. She'd already ruined one life - hers, and to compound that situation was unthinkable.

No, the feeling she had in her stomach wasn't because she hadn't eaten. She was alone, and she would have to figure this out by herself. She thought about the man on the phone. It was very clear what he had in mind; she wasn't going to kid herself. Was that really her only avenue left?

She wasn't sure how long she wanted to stay up. He'd be drunk, for certain and would want to talk and if she somehow got to sleep and then he woke her up, the night would be ruined. By eleven her eyes were heavy and she knew she needed to get to bed.

She didn't hear his car, or the front door open, or even him come into the bedroom, but something woke her and, startled, she saw him standing at the foot of the bed.

"Wake up," he said. "We need to talk."

He walked around the end of the bed to her side, catching himself for balance. She couldn't see his face but watched as he moved slowly, struggling to keep from falling. He sat down on the bed, almost on top of her legs, and although she quickly moved away, he leaned so close to her that she was overwhelmed by the smell of alcohol and cheap perfume. He'd been to the strip club again.

He leaned further forward, caught himself with one hand on the bed board, and started trying to kiss her neck. When she realized his intentions, she pushed herself up and away.

"I'm not sure what you have in mind but we aren't going to 'talk' like that," she told him.

"No, I got it figured all out," he said, pushing himself up. "Our problem is we don't fuck enough."

She looked at him, arms crossed. She could now make out, in the moonlight that flooded the window, the disheveled hair and thought perhaps one of his eyes was almost closed. Whatever happened tonight, he would not remember it tomorrow. In the meantime, she would have to put up with something disgusting. The thought of it suddenly infuriated her.

"Is that what one of your stripper friends told you?"

He momentarily sat up straighter, surprised by the question. A broad smile spread across his face,

"Fuckin' right!"

He moved closer to her on the bed and started to unbuckle his belt. The sound was unmistakable. And the thought of him touching her was unbearable.

"We are *not* making love tonight," she told him. "No way. You've had far too much to drink and I'm too tired."

In spite of his inability to stand up easily, his belt was undone and, after a struggle he was able to step out of his pants. And then he was naked and had thrown himself - or fallen - beside her.

She threw the sheet off and started to get up. Later, she would remember that it was the speed of his movement that surprised her the most as he grabbed her and forced one of his legs between hers.

"Oh my God!" she cried. "What are you doing?! Stop it! I'll scream!"

Now, as the full realization of what was happening sunk in, she started to shriek as loud as she could. Someone, somewhere, help her. Maybe someone passing by on the street would hear and call the police.

"Holy shit, you're LOUD!" he shouted, and grabbing a pillow, pressed it down on her face.

Instantly, it was dark, quieter - almost peaceful. She could tell that he was saying something, ranting, raving wild now with anger, but her ears were covered as well. He was no longer trying to have sex with her. She was able to free both arms to try to pull the pillow but he was pressing with such force, she couldn't move her head. And then a new reality engulfed her. It was a sensation she hadn't felt in years, when she was a child playing the game with her friends about who could hold their breath the longest, under water in the pond. She remembered that she always won. But in that game, when the pain in your chest and the faintness from lack of air seemed unbearable, you could come back to the surface, look around, to see if anyone had beaten you.

She had tried to come to the surface two times, maybe three, but couldn't budge. Her final, desperate attempt, like an animal caught in a trap, helped her to summon strength she didn't know she had, and she flailed with her arms and legs, clawing with her fingers at anything she could find. She had one final push left in her. That was all.

As she started to lose consciousness, she sensed his weight falling off to one side and felt the cool air on her face as the pillow pressure was relieved, if just for a second. Instinctively, a rush of air filled her lungs. Then, it was dark.

She didn't know how long she'd been out but she woke with a jerk, her entire body in a spasm of recoil. She took inventory at the speed of thought, sorting through her senses one by one. The pain in her lungs made her think she'd had a heart attack. But, she was breathing. Then she became aware of his snoring, loud, like a power saw. In the faint light from outside, she could still make out his features, the stench of his sweat mixed with stale alcohol, and the smell of urine. The images started streaming back to her, uncontrollably. Had he realized what he was doing and stopped? Had he felt her body start to become lifeless and worry that he had killed her? Or had he just passed out?

Now afraid, horrified, she knew that she had to get away, from this man, this bed. Sitting up, she untangled herself from him, ran to the bathroom and locked the door. He had tried to rape her! And he might come after her again. She found a small pair of nail scissors, grasped it in her hand as if it was her passport to safety, and sat in the bathtub, arms holding her knees to her chest. There would be no more sleep tonight. To lose her vigilance now could mean her death. If he did break in, she would stand and hide behind the shower curtains. If even just for a moment, it might give her the element of surprise, and at the least it might cost him the sight of one of his eyes.

When she awoke, she was furious with herself for having fallen asleep. There was no longer the sound of snoring coming from the bedroom. The only thing she could hear was the sound of traffic, heavy enough to make her certain that people were going to work.

Was he still in the house? She strained to hear every sound.

Cracking the door open, she saw that the bedroom was empty, sheets and blankets tangled, the clothes that he had worn the night before on the floor. And because the house was silent, she crept downstairs and found that his car was no longer in the driveway. So he had gone to work, hangover and all, probably with no memory of what he had tried to do to her the night before.

Opening one of the kitchen drawers, she reached in the back and brought out the slip of paper the ice cream man had given her months before.

Bringing the phone over to the kitchen table, she sat down and dialed.

## Chapter 13

Harry never worked Saturdays.

Yet here he was, back in the bowels of the hotel. The scene, compared to last night's love fest, had changed. Half of the round tables used to seat everyone as they dined on steak and béarnaise the previous evening were gone, as was the podium and the audio-video equipment. Instead, at one end of the room was a longer table with various steam warming trays containing scrambled eggs, bacon, ham, sausages and home fries. Next to that was the lighter fare made up of yoghurts, cereals and fruits. On the other end of the table stood the large coffee urn with over-sized white ceramic mugs, emblazoned with the Fifty States logo. Towards the back of the room was what was left of the round tables, where you were meant to eat your breakfast and then leave. On the other side of the room were another series of long tables, decorated with chairs pigeon-toed into groups of two. In front of each set of chairs were stacks of inch thick binders, each with an office name printed on the front. Behind those tables a number of men in suits and ties were waiting, hands clasped in front of them. Harry's first thought was that the people that worked at Fifty States all dressed to look like Skip.

As other men filtered in, Skip, in a suit and tie, freshly shaved and showered, was at the ready. Smiling, he shook each man's hand again, correctly reciting their first name as if welcoming them to his home. Harry had thought that Skip's ability to remember each manager's name last night was a trick supported by a quick, clandestine glance at the placard in front of each seat. But no, apparently the man had committed each of his new employee's monikers to memory. It was very impressive - and somewhat unsettling.

"Welcome back!" he said to each of them, adding with each handshake, "Grab some chow and then come back over there to the long tables. As I warned you last night, this is a working breakfast. We have a lot of ground to cover so please start going through your office analysis right away. One of our transition managers will sit next to you and help you understand what you are looking at."

After Skip released his hand, Harry looked at the food table and then the ominous binders. He couldn't imagine how anyone could create so much information about a brokerage office. Deciding that breakfast could wait, he went to the coffee dispenser and filled a mug with steaming black liquid. As he started to look for the book with his office's name, one of the men standing in waiting, separated from the pack.

"Good morning, Harry," he said, handing him his binder and extending his hand. "I'm Roger Mayfirst, a member of the Fifty States transition team. No breakfast, huh? You're a man of my own heart. They say it's the most important meal of the day. I say it puts me to sleep. All I need is a cup of black coffee and I'm good to go. *Carpe Diem*, I say. Have a seat and we can get started." It was, Harry thought, impressive. Apparently all these stick figures had memorized the names of all the office managers.

Roger smiled to himself. It was uncanny. In all the takeovers he'd ever participated in, even though none of these people had likely ever gone through the depth of analysis they were about to, the managers with the weaker offices and thus more likely to face reorganization, seemed to be aware of that fact. Managers of the strong offices had breakfast. Those that knew they were faltering just grabbed coffee and got to work.

"OK," Roger said, "let's see what we've got here."

The entire Fifty States team had spent most of the previous week going through each and every book, page by page, coached by Skip as to the appropriate message to be left. To convey any message other than what was carefully planned, would likely result in termination. As Skip had said to his TM team several times, "If there are any questions about our message to each office manager, however small, ask them now."

Whenever he recited this mantra, he did not smile and there was a reason. One of his favorite expressions was "You never get a second chance to make a first impression".

"Harry, this is an analysis that we do on all of our Fifty States branch offices" Roger said, opening the book to the first page as though Harry were a child and they were about to read a story from Grimm's fairy tales, "and we discuss them quarterly with the branch managers. It is quite quantitative; formulaic really, because over time we've discovered that in spite of geographic and demographic differences, each and every branch can be measured using identical criteria. That doesn't mean that every branch is supposed to generate the same amount of revenue - far from it - but when you measure the results in terms of profitability, all branches are on a level playing field."

As Roger turned the pages, Harry nodded to indicate that he had grasped the concept that was being explained. Little more than this seemed to be expected of him.

"Our in-house analytics team is the best in the country, no question about it," Roger continued. "It's a huge competitive advantage for us. What you are looking at is a summary page of your entire branch. The pages that follow break down the same analysis by broker. Overhead costs are allocated to each individual as if they were running their own business, which, of course, they really are. In our world each broker shares equally in these costs - including your compensation by the way. Some firms allocate these costs based on revenue but we say every broker has to pull their weight. If an office costs X dollars a month to run, and there aren't enough brokers able to generate an economic return after considering their share of costs, then either the broker needs to be replaced, or the manager, or the office closed. Pretty simple. Very effective."

Harry continued to nod his head, desperately searching the page of charts for some indication of what was to come. As he did, he saw Roger look up to see that Skip had approached them.

"No breakfast for these two - just get right to work," he said approvingly. "Gotta like that! Any questions, Harry?"

"Not yet, Skip," Harry said, "but all this is very impressive."

Skip slapped him on the shoulder and, smiling, strolled away. Some of the other office managers, who had overheard the conversation, pushed their unfinished breakfast away and moved over to the analysis table.

"OK," Roger continued as he turned the page, "let's roll up our sleeves. This page here shows the profitability of your office, measured on a per-square-foot basis after deducting overhead allocations and a charge for the capital cost of your company. We then compared your results - this is on an apples-to-apples basis remember - with all of the other offices."

Roger pointed at a spot on a bar graph, and Harry, whose office was clearly at the bottom, took a deep breath.

"Well," he said forcing a smile, "that doesn't look very good, does it?"

"That's just one measurement, Harry," Roger said. "At some point we can talk about your views of having an office inside a shopping mall but we'll get to that."

Harry wondered. Was someone finally going to listen to him about what a handicap his office's location represented?

"Here's another chart which measures what we call potential profitability based on a fairly complex formula including client assets, the timeframe those assets have been with the firm, that sort of thing. Look what happens!"

As Roger turned the page Harry's office now vaulted up the charts to appear in the first quartile.

"So, of course, this is the kind of thing that interests us most. When we apply our management information systems to your company, boom - everyone makes more money. Let's drill down a bit more."

"Next, we do the identical analysis individually," he said, turning the page. "Fact is, we start broker by broker and then build up into the combined package. The next seventy-five pages contain three sheets of profitability analysis of each of the twenty-five brokers in your office. But I think this page we're looking at here tells the story. Look at this chart."

Harry saw a bar chart with the names of each of his brokers next to some calculated number, sorted by largest to smallest. At the top of the chart were the familiar names he would have expected. Michael Franklin's name was at the bottom.

"Now, look at the potential profitability chart," Roger continued.

The order changed. Many of the names had slipped down suggesting, Harry thought, that however they calculated this, most of his leading brokers couldn't be any more profitable than they were. Now, however, Michael Franklin's name topped the list.

"So, you have lots of reading to do, Harry," Roger continued, "but the one broker you have that kind of shouted out to us was this fellow Michael Franklin. Let's turn to his analysis beginning on page fifty six."

As he turned to the page, Harry noticed that, not only did Roger have the page number memorized there were several hand-written notes in the margin. Pointing to a chart entitled "Total Client Assets" with a line that was clearly moving lower over time, he said,

"Of course, we never like to see assets leaving the firm but, when we did some more homework, the story became clear. Michael is Michael Junior. We were scratching our heads trying to understand how a guy so new to the business could have amassed such a large book of assets and then we got it. Dad gave it to him. That kind of thing isn't allowed in our company because the assets belong to the firm, not one of its employees. But, no matter, when it happened you weren't operating under our rules."

Roger leaned back and considered Harry.

"Based on our analysis, Harry, you've got a hole in the dike and you'd better get something in there quick to stop the leak. Your broker with the best potential profitability is achieving the worst - and the assets are leaving the firm. As we go through our transition, we'll want you to put this situation front and center. You can't take these books with you, but why don't you pour yourself another cup of coffee and have a closer look."

As Harry rose, he saw some of the other managers watching him, and hoped that there was nothing in his expression that hinted at the fact that his coffee was now sitting like fermented acid in his stomach.

## Chapter 14

"Yeah, who's callin?"

Angela wasn't ready for the phone to be answered on the first ring. It was the young man's voice again. "Oh, yes, hi... it's me... the, uh, gelato girl."

She was even less prepared for the force of the voice that came back to her.

"Gelato girl! This your home phone? Hang up, now. Go to the park. One hour."

Now that she had taken the first step, all she wanted was for it to be over. She tried to busy herself, finishing dishes, fluffing pillows, but she couldn't take her eyes off the clock, which several times, she had been sure, had stopped.

As the time approached, she put on her heavy jacket and hurried to the park as quickly as she could without drawing attention to herself. She was unhappy to see that the young man was not waiting for her. Was she supposed to call him again from the payphone? Or should she just sit and wait for him? Then, she noticed it. On the bench, right at the spot that she had been sitting before was a silver flip case cell phone. She looked around. The young courier was nowhere to be found but had obviously left the phone that would connect her with the other man with the raspy voice. When she pushed the send button, the familiar speaker was waiting.

"Yeah," he said. "That you?"

She had practiced what she said next all morning and she knew if she didn't say it now, she never would.

"Yes Mr... yes, it's me, the gelato girl. I would like to, well I need to talk to you about... the next step."

The quickness and precision of the voice on the other end of the line was surprising and somehow comforting. She had the sensation that she was in a car repair shop, the mysterious noise having been quickly diagnosed by the expertly trained mechanic and the solution to the problem being described as easier, and less expensive, to fix than she had imagined. The man asked her for her husband's full name, the type and color of his car, the license plate number, where he worked, his normal hours and whether he ever drove after drinking.

"Yes, he does that, all the time," she said.

"That's not too safe," the raspy voice said reflectively. "Guy could get hurt."

"Now, gelato girl," the man said after he had elicited the name of her husband's favorite bar, the fact that he nearly always went there Fridays after work and, surprisingly enough, the code to their garage door opener, "this guy I know, dat can help you, he doan work for free, you understan? You got the money for dis?"

It was, she thought, as impersonal as though they were discussing a mail order. But the trouble was, she didn't have any money of her own and she was not sure how or where she could get some.

"How much money do I need?" she asked hesitantly.

"Fifty grand." The reply was quick, accurate and definite.

She felt as though someone had struck her in the stomach.

"But - but that's a lot of money. I don't have that. Where in God's name…"

"Fifty, take it or leave it," he interrupted her. "The guy, he's givin' you a deal, cuz he likes ya."

She took a deep breath "But where am I…"

"Go look at his life insurance. Look for stuff under employee benefits. Just about everyone gets that when they work these days. 'Cept me of course." He chuckled at his own joke. "You may be surprised. Then you call me back - as quick as you can. Understood? Today's Tuesday. Maybe the guy will be ready by Friday night. I gotta do a little 'homework.' You go do that right now, OK? And, gelato girl, you call from the park, see? Don't you never call my guy from your house again. Got it? Not ever."

And with that, the line went dead.

Back inside the house, she moved quickly, like a cat burglar, going into 'the drawer' where he always put all of his paperwork, haunted by the sense that she was violating someone's innermost privacy and trust as she went through the rambled stash of envelopes. She carefully put everything back in its place, because he checked everything. He must never learn that she had looked through his papers. Finally, she found a glossy brochure with the name Parsnip Life Insurance with the subtitle, "Exclusive Program for Employees of Global Investment Banking Inc." Opening it, she ran her finger down the page until she came to words that jumped out at her.

| Basic life | - | $2,000,000 |
| Accidental death | - | $4,000,000 |
| Beneficiary | - | Angela Messina |

It took a moment to sink in. That was more money than she ever dreamed of. And she was the sole beneficiary. That selection must have been made when he first started the job, during happier times for their marriage. She wondered if he would have made the same choice today.

Carefully placing the folder back into the exact position, she closed the drawer, replaced the desk chair just where she had found it, and hurried to get her coat. If this was going to be done, it had to be before she had a chance to change her mind.

## Chapter 15

The next morning, Harry decided that he might as well take advantage of the fancy breakfast that had been laid on. He wasn't sure why the managers needed to be back a second day and he hoped this wasn't one of those firms that liked to take advantage of weekends for meetings, since the market was closed. Besides, he'd gone through all of their material and understood all their fancy charts and graphs that indicated, among other things, that his branch was in a lousy location and needed to be moved. He'd been telling his own bosses that since shortly after they opened it; thank goodness that now there was someone to listen. And yes, Michael Franklin Junior *was* a problem, but Harry was glad that the new management, with all of its piss and vinegar, could now deal with Franklin Senior who, at the very hint that his son might face *adversity*, would threaten to move his accounts elsewhere. What had the guy said yesterday? The accounts belong to the firm, not the broker. The professional looking analysis confirmed what Harry already knew; Michael was like a dead, leafless limb sticking out on an otherwise healthy tree. For the good of the trunk and the rest of the branches, he needed to be pruned.

The set up in the basement meeting room had been changed again. The warm serving trays offering a full breakfast were replaced by bowls full of muffins and croissants. The stacks of binders were gone and the room, which now accommodated only four small tables, seemed colder and empty. Harry noticed there were fewer people standing around. He wondered if his clock had somehow screwed up, making him early. Even Skip hadn't arrived yet.

"Ah, Mr. Lugarno, good morning," a woman with rich black hair and eyebrows, dressed in a tailored business suit, addressed him. "Thank you for coming in. My name is Margaret Beech and I'm the head of human resources at Fifty States. Please - pour yourself a coffee, take a muffin and join me over at the table."

Harry noticed that the large coffee mugs with corporate logos had been replaced by smaller plain white ones. The coffee urn was smaller too. So that was it. There would be fewer meetings today, all focused on those managers with 'difficult' branches, setting plans in place to improve profitability. He reminded himself that he welcomed the change.

"All right then, all set are we?" Margaret said when he joined her at one of the tables. "Let's get started."

As Harry pulled the top off the muffin - that was always the best part - he wondered what they were going to 'get started' on and why, whatever it was, it couldn't have waited until Monday.

"You know, Margaret," he said, "I'm impressed that your firm has probably come to the same conclusion about my branch that I did several years ago. Finally..."

"Mr. Lugarno - or can I call you Harry?" she interrupted him, "it's probably best at this point if you let me do the talking."

Startled at her change in tone, Harry dropped part of his muffin in his lap and surreptitiously brushed it to the floor.

"There's no easy way to do this, so let me just get to the point," she continued briskly. "As a result of the extensive analysis you saw yesterday, management has decided to close your branch."

Harry had to stifle a smile. This was faster and better than he thought.

"The majority of your people will be offered positions at our nearest location," she assured him. "There is enough space and we hope, with this branch being only fifteen miles away from their old one, the move won't put too much strain on their commutes."

Harry felt a rush of excitement. He had driven by his former competitor's office, much newer and far more professional looking than his, many times. He wondered where his office would be and if he would have a window.

"You people don't waste any time, do you?" he said, grinning.

"No, we don't," Margaret agreed, sliding a manila envelope across the table. Harry knew what was coming. They'd have to fire all of the support staff. That was how these corporate takeovers made their money. It was too bad though. He thought the last receptionist was one of the cutest ones ever.

"OK," he said, reaching his hands towards the folder. "Let's see what the damage is."

"There will, unfortunately, be some 'dislocations' as a result of closing the branch," Margaret told him, before he had a chance to look at the papers inside. "Six in total. I have personally prepared termination letters for each."

Harry looked at her uncomprehendingly. There was only four support staff in his small office.

"Six?" he said. "We only have four administrative people."

Only then did he look down and find himself staring at his own name.

"I regret to inform you Mr. Lugarno that we will not be offering you a position with Fifty States."

Harry looked at her, then the letter, then back to her.

"You're firing me!" he exclaimed, "after all this time? I've been with this firm for my whole career! Maybe since before you were born! You can't just throw me out on the street like that! What the hell am I going to do?"

The look of pity that briefly crossed her face confirmed to him that this was real. It was actually happening.

"I can assure you Mr. - Harry - that these decisions are not made lightly," she said. "We realize we are dealing with people's lives. Our severance and outplacement packages are the best in class."

Harry was caught up in a kaleidoscope of emotions from which anger predominated. He ruffled the sheet in his hand in disgust. One thing was for God damn sure. This bitch was not going to make him cry.

"Well you can be sure I'll be showing this to a lawyer" he said, tossing the sheet onto the table.

"Yes, of course Harry," she said calmly. "You are entirely within your rights to seek legal advice. That's why these offers don't expire for two weeks. Difficult as this all is, we try to be as accommodating as possible."

She cleared her throat before proceeding.

"Actually, Harry, your offer is slightly different from the others. As the branch manager, we'd like you to stay on for a month to help us wind up the location. To begin with, we thought that you, being their leader, might want to break the news to your people. If not, we understand, but we wanted to give you the chance. In circumstances like this…"

"Yeah, that's right," Harry interrupted her. "You can cut my heart out if you like but I won't let you do that to my people."

For the first time since she had broken the news, he felt empowered. He could still make decisions, and this was one he was damn well going to make.

"Of course, Harry. I suspected that a man of your integrity and professionalism would choose that course," she said. "As you know, the stock market opens for trading at 9:30 a.m. tomorrow but the shares of Fifty States will be halted until news of the acquisition can be disseminated. The press release is scheduled to come out at ten so we would suggest that you have your chats starting around eight-thirty. Just so you know, I will be in your office at seven to support you."

Harry realized that their conversation was coming to a close. What else was there to say? He started to push his chair away from the table but stopped himself.

"Wait a minute," he said tapping his index finger on the file folder. "You said there were six people getting it. I only have four support staff and then there is me. Who is the sixth person?"

Margaret nodded her head in agreement.

"Yes, Harry, you're right. That's another reason why we thought you'd want to break the news. Other than your support staff, the other person who we won't be offering a position to is Michael Franklin."

Harry nearly fell off his chair.

"What?! Holy shit, you should have asked me about that one! His old man is going to flip out!"

She smiled again, this time noticeably weakly.

"As I said," she told him, "these are never easy decisions."

Harry found himself wondering if she really knew how difficult this was going to be.

## Chapter 16

"Angie, I promise you sweetheart, I'm going to go get help. This time I really mean it."

When Angela's husband came home, it was with his predictable after-beating behavior. The flowers he brought her were wilting - likely bought at the convenience store - and there was the usual blubbering about how sorry he was that he couldn't control his temper. He always came up with the same reasons. He was, after all, a man and it was difficult for him to put up with a woman who challenged his authority. She was a strong, intelligent female and when he felt like he couldn't get a word in edgewise, sometimes that drove him over the edge. He knew. He pleaded with her, that that was no excuse, no excuse at all. He would make it better if it was the last thing he ever did.

This time Angela tried hard to remember how she had acted in the many situations like this before. When he had said in the past that he would even attend anger management sessions, she offered to go with him. Of course, that wasn't possible since he never actually went to one.

"Sweetheart," he said holding both of her hands from across the table and looking solemnly into her eyes. "I have a demon inside me that I have to conquer. I *am* going to change. I know I've said that to you before but this time will be different."

After exchanging the final "I love you," a few corroborative tears and a long kiss that she just barely managed to endure, he made a sacred vow that this would never - ever - happen again. Everything was all right now, he assured her. All the violence was in the past.

The remainder of the week went by smoothly. He even tried to make love to Angela who alerted him to the fact it was the wrong time of month. By Thursday evening, however, she was becoming concerned. He had made no mention of going to the bar on the way home from work on Friday, a ritual that was as entrenched as their marriage vows. On Friday morning, she made a point of getting up early to make his favorite breakfast, steak and eggs. Later she would wonder if, subconsciously, she had knowingly prepared the last meal for a condemned man headed to the execution chamber.

"What's this about?" he said coming into the kitchen. "Honey, you should have told me. I have an important meeting that I can't be late for. Oh this smells so good. I'll just take a bite of steak now. But wrap it up and save it, for sure."

As he started to head for the door, she grabbed his arm. She hadn't wanted to bring the topic up, but it was now or never.

"Honey, will you be going to the bar tonight after work?" she asked him.

There was a long pause during which she was afraid she knew that he was considering the Brownie points he might earn if this week he were to come straight home.

"Actually, you know what?" he said. "I think I'll skip the bar tonight and come straight home. Maybe we can go out to dinner."

It was the worst thing he could have said and her greatest fear. The voice on the phone had said Friday night, after her husband went to the bar, would be a good night. He had actually used the word "excellent."

"No, honey, don't," she protested. "I want you to go to the bar just like you always do."

She knew now that this was high-risk territory, signaled by the tell-tale look in his eyes confirming that the juices of jealously were starting to flood into his brain. She jumped up and grabbed both of his hands. It was, she knew, time for the performance of her life.

"No, I'm sorry, that didn't come out right. Listen, I've been thinking about this, about us, all week. We need to go back to our normal lives as quickly as possible. You don't - we don't want the solving of our issues to become our main focus. It is, and should be, ancillary to our core; our love and our marriage. I've known, for a long time, how important your Friday nights with the boys are to you. You work hard all week under incredible stress. You need the release. A man needs the time to be with other men."

As she spoke, his eyes had narrowed. He was listening - carefully - to every word, which was unsettling in itself since he hardly ever listened to her. Finally he smiled, but it seemed to be a painful process.

"Oh, I see what's going on," he said, widening his eyes. "Just trying to keep me out of the house so BOB can come over, huh?"

She laughed as though he had made a joke and brushed her hair behind her ear.

"Oh crap, you caught me!" she exclaimed, assuming the role she had played when they were first married and there had been something to joke about. "Not just Bob, but ten of his friends."

She caught her breath in relief when he answered her in kind.

"My you ARE a busy girl, aren't you? Oh, Angela, seriously, you're a wonderful wife, so understanding and considerate. I'll take you up on your offer. I'm not sure what I did to deserve someone like you, but God bless the angels." He kissed her on the forehead. "Don't wait up. I love you."

She flashed a broad smile. He left without giving her a chance to tell him she loved him too.

And that, she decided, was just as well.

## Chapter 17

Monday was going to be a new start. Michael and Jennifer had 'made up'.

After Saturday morning, when they had told one another exactly how they felt, it was as though they had turned a page, and started fresh. And that night they'd celebrated by going out to dinner. Jen had even ordered a bottle of Champagne.

Now, as he rode the bus to the mall, Michael wasn't sure if his father would show up to launch his new-joint partner idea or not. Throwing the napkin in the old man's face had been pretty rude, for sure. But Jennifer was right, he told himself. She usually was, after all. He could use his dad's help to get through these turbulent markets. Once a client left, taking their assets with them, Michael knew it was for good and he couldn't afford any more of that. As a consequence, he had his apology to his father practiced and ready for delivery. The most important thing he needed to convey was he was wrong about many things - about how to manage clients in a bear market, how to prospect for new business and, most importantly, how to show proper respect to a man he owed everything to. Jennifer had given him that line. He knew his father really didn't need to have his tires pumped up any more than they already were, but in this case it was the right thing to do.

Meanwhile, Skip waited in Harry Lugarno's office and watched the clock as Harry read the newspaper. Here it was, eight-thirty and only a few of his brokers had arrived. The ones that had were standing around chatting, discussing the latest Seahawks' game. The flagrant lack of a sense of urgency reaffirmed to Skip that they were making the right call; shut down this remodeled shoe store, strip the valuable assets and brokers and move to a part of town where they at least looked like they knew what they were doing.

Of the offices that would be acquired in the announcement to be made public in about two hours, Skip had chosen this branch specifically to attend the launch of the new partnership. It had a decent asset base that needed to be nurtured through the pending change so that none of the money moved to a competitor. He certainly couldn't rely on this Lugarno fellow to convey the right sense of enthusiasm, even on a good day, but much less so since he hadn't made the cut. According to Margaret, he had acted very professionally yesterday when he got the news, fully agreed that he should be 'at the helm' to help 'his people' through the transition. But Skip had been around long enough to know that in spite of Harry's apparent sincerity, no one could deliver the sermon like he could.

He'd start at nine after Harry introduced him, instructing all of the brokers to stay off their phones, that this was highly confidential information he was about to share and perhaps the best day of their careers. Of course the regulators knew that, too, and the shares of Fifty States would not open for trading until long after the news had been fully disseminated. Even if one of the sharper brokers could figure out how to make some money on the inside information, he wouldn't be able to. Skip knew that the simple tactic of letting the brokers in on the secret, if only a few minutes before launch, would give them the sense that he both respected and, more importantly, trusted them. Of course, each of his transition managers who were sitting in their own target branches had been instructed to disclose the exact same script at the same time. Shortly after giving them the news, the screen would be rolled out and the promotional video started. Afterwards, Skip would stroll around the floor with his lapel microphone, extolling the virtues of a new, powerful team and answering any questions. He knew that, as soon as the announcement hit the wires, the branch's phone bank would light up, with clandestine offers made in a hushed tone from competing office managers trying to build their own asset base. "Let's go down the street for a bite," they'd say. "We have a program here you might not be aware of. I think you'd be interested. What have you got to lose? You're changing companies anyway."

Good luck to them. By ten, Skip knew he'd have the entire office eating out of his hands and, of course, lunch would be served in the office today, courtesy of the new firm, attended by a handful of brokers - their new partners - from their new branch. That apparent generosity would prevent any of his new brokers from dining with the competition.

No, Skip knew that even though the body count would be modest, this branch needed TLC. He had convinced Margaret to join him. He would rally everyone around the flag while the deadweight was cut loose. While he was singing the song, she'd be in the windowless meeting room, working her own form of magic.

Michael whistled as he walked briskly from the bus to the front door of the mall. He didn't see his father's green Jaguar convertible - his retirement gift to himself - although he looked a bit ridiculous driving around on a warm summer day with his reflective sunglasses as if he was cruising for girls. Just as well, Michael thought. Apologies were easier over the phone rather than face-to-face. As he came in the door, however, there were few surprises. The receptionist never came in much before the market opened, and she always said Mondays were never a good day for her anyway. In the office, the usual crew were standing around chatting, Starbucks in hand. As Michael sat down at his workstation and fired up his computer, he noticed that Harry already had people in his office, door closed, a man and a woman, both professional looking, the man looking out at the floor. 'Here we go again', Michael thought, 'another remodeling.'

As Michael's computer came to life, he checked the clock and saw that it was quarter to nine. The bus had been a bit late but there was plenty of time to check the electronic services for any late-breaking news. He'd already read the paper on the bus but he knew that his father would have been scouring Bloomberg for an hour by now. Did his father really think the clients would care that the price of copper futures are dramatically higher? Of course not - Michael was on to the old man's game. By having a piece of current information, however irrelevant, he was demonstrating that he lived, ate and breathed the markets. Michael knew it was a ploy that he wouldn't stoop to use himself. Still, he needed to be ready because his dad had embarrassed him several times before by both revealing the piece of extraneous news and then wondering out loud, since his son was clearly unaware, what rock Michael had been living under.

At nine, Michael was ready to start his day. He would deliver one genuine, heartfelt apology followed by a call to an appreciative Jen, but as he started to put his headset on, the door to Harry's office opened and the veteran manager walked onto the floor followed by the well-dressed man and woman.

"Everyone off the phone, please, right now," he said. "You'll call them back. We're having a meeting."

Michael heard a few grumbles, not so much he thought since Harry was interrupting important business - it was, after all, Monday morning - but because they knew they would all have to listen, and then live through, another one of Harry's 'initiatives.'

"I'd like to introduce you all to Mr. Skip Williams, Senior Manager with Fifty States Investments and his partner Margaret..." Harry paused. He'd forgotten her last name.

"Beech" the woman told him, smiling, obviously at ease, more so, Michael wondered than Harry himself.

"Today," Harry continued, "is the most important day in the history of our firm. At around nine thirty-five, you're going to see an announcement revealing that we have entered into a new, strategic business partnership with Fifty States Investments. We are all very excited by the prospects of our new alliance and believe that this will position us in a wonderfully competitive way for the years to come. And now, Skip, the floor is yours."

Harry noticed, as the video started on the screen that had been quickly set up by some audio-visual people who seemingly appeared out of nowhere, that it was exactly the same as the one he watched on Friday night. For a moment, he was caught up again by the thrill of the announcement, until he remembered what he kept trying to forget; whatever trails the new firm would follow, it would be without him.

As the presentation came to a close, the applause was awkwardly loud, probably, Harry thought, a result of the anxiety that new, unexpected information brings coupled with the feel-good message Skip had so expertly delivered. The final slide certainly had captured their attention; under the new management regime, they should all expect a healthy increase in their paychecks. Harry knew, of course, that this would only happen if each of the brokers generated more business and he suspected that the statement, "Everyone makes more" was true because, if you didn't, you'd be gone. He smiled to himself wondering if Skip would be willing to add the words "assuming you're still here."

His smile faded when he looked at Michael who, like all of the other brokers, was clearly excited by the news. For his sputtering franchise in particular, Junior probably thought the new firm with its increased marketing support and range of products was a godsend. Harry imagined that Michael's dream would include a greater appreciation of his modern way of doing business with clients that were twice his age.

But, Harry sighed; Michael's dream was soon to become a nightmare. Seeing that Skip was now at the other end of the room entertaining questions, strategically positioned as far away from Michael as possible, Harry walked up behind the young broker and put his hand on his shoulder. When Michael turned, a shit-eating grin on his face, Harry created his own grin as well. Truly, this was a great day - for someone.

"Michael, come over here with me for a minute, will you?" he said. "We need to chat. And, uh, grab your jacket."

Michael was a bit surprised at first; he wanted to hear every answer to every question but he understood. There still was the matter of his father's offer for help and, given their long-term friendship he wasn't at all surprised that dad had spoken to Harry directly. That explained why his dad hadn't shown up. With the new firm, his father's assistance would no longer be required. It wasn't necessary in the first place, Michael reminded himself; he was only placating Jennifer. But, still, the old man had stature and even the new firm had to respect his history. Harry had probably explained things to Skip, suggested they go with it for a few months and then maybe throw the old man another, smaller retirement party when it was clear to everyone that Michael was good on his own.

Michael didn't even try to suppress his smile as he followed Harry to the conference room. He'd had his share of arguments with the old boss, but this time his wisdom and sensitivity would prove invaluable. He was somewhat surprised, when Harry opened the door to the room, to see the woman from Harry's office sitting, waiting for them. But perhaps it was only natural that a new firm would want to be in on whatever was being discussed.

After introductions, Margaret looked at the younger man's eager face and confirmed to herself that Harry had not divulged the purpose of their meeting. It was a good sign. The manager, notwithstanding that he knew he was being terminated, was cooperating, being, in fact, highly professional. The discussions would go more smoothly. She leaned slightly forward towards Michael, both hands on the table gently clasped together.

Being this close to Margaret now, Michael noticed that she was impeccably dressed, her dark black hair wound in a bun and the wide collars of her crisp, cream blouse flowing over her jacket lapels. She began by handing Michael her business card and assuring him, in the friendliest way possible, that he should feel free to contact her, as head of human resources, at any time. Although he was not sure why someone like her should become involved in something he and Harry could easily handle, he thanked her. There would be a lot to learn about how the new firm did business. He could see that now.

"Fifty States Investments, as you probably know by now, is a highly successful firm," she began. "Sales and profitability have grown at an impressive rate for over five years. The key ingredient to these results has been an almost impeccable implementation of our acquisition strategy. Smaller firms, after coming under the Fifty States' umbrella have flourished."

Michael was nodding his head, yes, of course, that's why he was excited. He quickly turned to look at Harry's face and was a bit bewildered that he didn't appear to be as enthusiastic.

"Unfortunately, Michael, there is a more somber side to our successful strategy," she continued. "When we make these acquisitions, we do an incredible amount of analysis, identifying costs that could be trimmed and assets better deployed."

At the word 'somber', Michael lost his smile and tilted his head slightly.

"After completing our analysis on your branch, I'm sorry to have to tell you that we will not be able to offer you a position with the new firm."

As she had done so many times, Margaret was quiet now, allowing her message to sink in. Like most of them seemed to do, Michael dropped his head toward the desk. He looked left, and then right and finally his eyes found Harry's.

"You're... firing me?"

Harry found it difficult to meet his eyes. Soon enough, Michael would learn that they were in the same boat.

"But Harry... you can't... I mean my accounts. What will happen to my accounts?"

"Well, technically, Michael" Margaret said crisply, "the accounts aren't yours - they are the property of the firm. And they have obviously all been acquired as a result of this transaction."

Michael's mind quickly flashed back to Friday night's dinner.

"Oh Jesus, no, Harry. This is going to be a big problem - huge. I just agreed to let my dad partner up with me again for a few months to help get through this market we're in. He should be here at any minute." And then to Margaret, "You don't know my dad! He'll FLIP out. These are my accounts. He gave them to me. You CAN'T fire me. My dad will move every single penny to the competition."

Margaret didn't respond. As they had practiced, it was time for Harry to step in. Harry, in turn, considered the irony of the situation. All this time, since the day Franklin Senior retired, Junior had done nothing but say the business was now his and his alone. He didn't need his father. Now, backed against the wall, he couldn't wait to play the 'dad' card.

"Michael, both Skip and I have already spoken with your father, last night at his home. He won't be coming in here."

"What? You told my dad that I was being... Holy shit Harry, are you serious? You stabbed me in the back at the same time you betrayed your oldest friend? How the hell could you do that? You bastard!"

Margaret and Harry had debated who would take the reins when the conversation got more aggressive, as it undoubtedly would, and he had convinced her that his intimate knowledge of the players trumped any training she might have. He'd fired people before. This was personal.

"Michael, I'm only going to say one thing to you and then I'm leaving because you and Margaret have a lot to talk about," he said in a low, steady voice. "I spoke with your dad for over two hours last night. He's bitterly disappointed but he understands. He's not mad. He gets it. This is business and sometimes business sucks. I am sure you will land on your feet and I'd be more than happy to give you a great reference. I know you're upset, and I can only hope that over time you'll cool off."

What Harry didn't reveal was that Michael Senior had accepted Skip's offer for a highly confidential, short-term consulting contract to help in the transition of his former accounts. That was business between father and son, if Senior were ever cruel enough to disclose it. The courier package with the paperwork was probably arriving as they spoke. These people thought of everything. With Senior as a temporary employee, the accounts weren't going anywhere.

"Margaret has some things to go over with you now. You listen carefully. Call me after if you want to chat. Let me know if I can help - in any way - I mean it, son."

Harry opened the door to leave and the sound of Skip extolling the virtues of the new firm could still be heard. The door closed behind him with a hollow click.

## Chapter 18

Michael had never taken the bus home at this time of morning. Since rush hour was over they only ran every half-hour, but because the extra time would give him a chance to polish his story for Jennifer, he didn't really mind. He'd been fired, canned, sacked! It wasn't something he'd ever imaged happening to him. By the large reflective glass doors that led into the mall, an older balding man, unshaven and dressed in frayed blue overalls, was sweeping up yesterday's cigarette butts left by smokers who, having now been banished from practicing their habit inside the mall, felt completely entitled to take one last, long drag as they entered the building. Through those doors and down the corner to the right was a place full of excited people with a new lease on life, eagerly anticipating a news wire announcement that would have them commandeer their phones calling clients, friends and family with the happy news.

Michael sighed. It was a place he would never enter again.

His thoughts turned to Jennifer. They had finally solved their biggest source of disagreement - how to handle his father. And because the resolution they had reached had seemed to change her somehow, he imagined she'd been far more worried than he knew about their finances. And why not? A lifelong relationship required a steady income and for the first time, the fact that he could join forces with his father had made it seem possible that he could start to make a decent living at last. But, now, that fantasy had been blown to bits. Money probably wasn't her only concern. She was assessing his family relationships as well. When you got married, you joined a new band of relatives. His constant bickering with his father had to be of some concern to her as well as the unknown whereabouts of his mother.

He would show this woman, through his hard work and complete devotion, that he was the right man. He would earn her love. His termination would be their greatest test because he feared now more than ever before that the most beautiful, captivating woman he had ever dreamed of meeting would walk out of his life.

The roar of the bus startled him. Behind the huge tinted glass windows, sporting rear view mirrors the size of someone's head, the doors whooshed open as the man in the raised seat gave Michael a nod. He imagined the operator had seen it before; young people in their suits taking the bus back home in the morning. Michael must have been fired. At least the driver had found steady work.

What struck him most, however, was that, unlike the interior crowded with a variety of business types he had ridden to work with, this time only a quarter of the seats were taken, mostly by the elderly, along with a couple of teenage girls probably having skipped school and giggling as they relayed their adventure through their smartphones. There was even a young man in sunglasses with a Seeing Eye dog. Michael wondered how he would ever know which stop to get off. For a moment at least, Michael thought his problems weren't so bad.

Soon though, Michael came back to his immediate issue, which was how he would tell Jennifer what had happened. He knew that her first reaction would be one of shock and he would have to deal with that as best he could. He'd already been thinking about what he would put in his resume, and he'd ask her to get involved. With her New York experience, they could put together a document that would have employers lining up. The experience of managing his father's book combined with his state-of-the-art training would be an attractive package indeed. She didn't need to worry one bit. Yes, when she asked, he would agree to allow his father to help him find a new job - maybe even use his contacts - as distasteful a prospect as that was.

He knew he would do anything to keep this woman.

Another thought started to creep in and he tried hard to push it away. What, after all, had he really accomplished? He hadn't started out like the other young brokers, pounding the street, attending endless seminars and playing countless rounds of golf trying to build his book of business. No, his franchise had begun with a gift from his retiring father. What an enormous advantage! What had he done with it? Nothing - just frustrated several former clients to move their business elsewhere. No wonder the new firm hadn't offered him a job.

As he walked up the steps to his house, even the gardener eyed him suspiciously, probably wondering if he'd forgotten something. He inhaled deeply and opened the door to find her sitting on their living room sofa, legs crossed, reading a magazine. Seeing Michael, she threw the magazine on the table.

"Ah, the wounded warrior returns home."

It took Michael a second to understand her.

"Jen, what? You know? How did you find out?"

"Your father called me after you left this morning. He said I might want to stay around," she added, "seeing that you weren't going to be having a great day."

The heat instantly rose to Michael's face.

"My FATHER CALLED YOU! Jesus Christ! What the hell did he think he was doing! This is something very personal, between you and me. He had no right. Why the hell can't he just leave us alone?"

She didn't respond and just patted the sofa next to her.

"Sit down, right here, and tell me about it. Don't worry about your father. He was just trying to help."

"NO, he wasn't! He's just an arrogant meddling prick who..."

"MICHAEL!"

He talked. And she seemed to be listening intently as he moved from the events of the morning to his plans for the future. There was nothing to worry about. He would start working on his resume that afternoon. He still had his PDA with all of his contact numbers and he would be tearing the phone lines apart in no time.

Jennifer watched his lips move but her thoughts were elsewhere. This was all happening faster than she had planned but sometimes opportunity knocked when you least expected it and, at the moment, it was banging down the door. She listened to his feeble description of how he would 'pound the pavement' in search of a new, better job. It was a ridiculous idea, she knew, because he hadn't been able to do anything like that - not even land one new account - when he was actually employed. Now that he was on the street, the only sounds he'd be hearing would be doors slamming in his face.

She had a sense of comfort that, with Franklin Senior involved, the necessary funding of 'Plan P' would be there for the taking and would give her time to get Michael on board. The important new pressure point - time - would, she hoped, be enough to convince him that her way was the right way and, for their future, the only way. She realized that Michael had finished his dissertation into the benefits of hard work. She knew that no one got rich by working hard - they had to work smart.

Now, she would have to go get the money - but not to worry. She knew how to do that too.

"What kind of package did they give you? If the pricks try to go light, I know an excellent lawyer."

Michael hadn't looked that closely at the letter but remembered something about six months. Jennifer seemed to grab at that number.

"All right, Michael, let's consider the facts. You have six months of income left - six months. That may seem like a lot now but you wait - it's going to disappear very fast, and then what?"

"Jen, don't worry, the first thing I am going to do is go right after my dad's accounts - as soon as I'm with another firm."

His naiveté was starting to piss her off.

"Oh, Michael, come on. Give your head a shake. Your dad's accounts were firing you. If you think that Fifty States is just going to sit there and let you take them back, then you're a fool. I will guarantee that every single one of them has already been personally contacted, schmoozed like never before and sold, sold, sold. These people aren't going anywhere."

Michael was grimacing. Winning back his dad's accounts was an important part of his plan.

"Well, like you said, with the new partnership - that he suggested by the way - the accounts wouldn't likely move. With his help, I can bring them with me."

"Michael, wake up. Do you know what your dad said to me this morning? He said it was probably for the best. The firing would force you to find a new career, one more 'suitable.' Your dad's offer to partner up with you, which, let's recall you threw back in his face, was a desperate move on his part to save face with his friends in the hope that maybe the market would turn or you'd wake up and finally figure out what you were doing. Now, with the takeover, he is off the hook. Can't you see that?"

His feelings for his father hadn't been good for a while but now Michael was beginning to realize that Jennifer had a point. Regardless of the reason for Michael's 'failure', which he still didn't believe it was, it was clear now that dear old dad was just looking out for himself - at the time of Michael's greatest need.

"Well then, I'll just go out and find new accounts."

"Michael, you don't have a JOB. What is the first thing that the firms you apply to will want to know? What is your book of business and how much do you think you can bring with you?

Answer? Zero. OK then how about a reference from your former employer? They'll say, 'Well, we liked him so much he was one of the first guys we fired.' Come on Michael, you really, REALLY need to smarten up."

Her words were direct and a new sense of reality was creeping in like moss in an uncared-for lawn. He now had everything riding on this. He would prove to Jennifer, his father, those bastards at Fifty States and, most importantly, to himself that he could do this. Inside, he knew he had no choice. To do otherwise was to admit complete failure. And he knew his relationship with Jennifer was probably on the line too. Who wanted to marry a failure?

"Jennifer, I can do this. And I will. If you've ever trusted me on anything, trust me now."

She had him, of course, and it was time to light the fuse. She could use the time to prepare for her launch.

"OK Michael. Fine. I trust you. But let's agree on one thing. You've got three months - not six. I don't want to wake up broke. If after three months you still have no job and no accounts, then you agree to try things my way. Will you agree to that?"

Try things her way? What way? As much as Michael didn't appreciate the ultimatum and thought that perhaps this woman, rather than putting a gun to his head, could be a bit more supportive, he hadn't been aware that she had some strategy of her own.

"While you're working on your plan, I'll be working on mine," she told him. "If you succeed, then we put mine away. If not, then it's my turn. Deal?"

She stuck out her hand to seal the transaction, and after a pause, Michael grasped it.

"Deal," he said, feeling as though he was clutching a lifeline but not sure where it would take him.

## Chapter 19

"Mr. Franklin it's Andrew Millcroft. I'm a reporter with *The Seattle Reporter*. I was wondering if I could talk to you about the recent takeover of MOGI by Fifty States."

Michael had flinched when the phone rang and he'd carefully leaned over to scan the call display, exhaling when he didn't recognize the number. Now was not the time to speak with his father - or rather, listen to his lectures. He hoped there would always be little time for that. The voice at the other end of the line was calm and friendly but Michael was instantly concerned and he wasn't sure why.

"Uh, I'm not so sure that would be a good idea. What exactly do you want to talk about?"

"Mr. Franklin - can I call you Michael? - I am writing a human interest story about the big, heartless Wall Street sharks that come into local communities, take over some of our finest firms by throwing their cash around, and then completely disrupt the lives of some of Seattle's unsuspecting citizens, all in the supposed name of progress. Really, Michael, that's all BS. They're only interested in squeezing the last nickel out of every possible financial transaction with no regard for the lives they have impaired, sometimes permanently."

Michael was quiet for a moment as he digested the reporter's words.

At one point, Andrew had been in Michael's shoes and the takeover that dislodged him ended his career in finance, a job he lived for. He would never forgive or forget what one of the big New York firms had done to him. He would seize any opportunity he had to show to the unsuspecting public the ruthlessness of these people.

"Uh yes," Michael said. "But why are you calling me?"

Now it was the reporter's turn to pause. He reminded himself that there would be all kinds of emotions running through Michael's head at a time like this so he needed to approach slowly and carefully.

"I'm calling," he said, choosing his words carefully, "because I am aware of the fact that shortly after the takeover was announced, you were shown the door. Let me express my sincere condolences for that. It's that sort of behavior that has me particularly angry. They didn't even give you a chance. That just isn't right."

Michael was puzzled by the statement. Only Jennifer and his father were aware of his departure, and he was pretty sure neither would want to talk about it. But now some newspaper reporter knew all about his business. He didn't even have time to lament in private. It was embarrassing. His face was starting to burn.

"Holy shit, Andrew!" he exclaimed. "What is it about this, this fiasco? My termination is the worst kept secret in town. All I wanted to do was go home and sulk for a little while. I feel like I'm sitting on a street corner with no clothes on. How did you find out?"

Andrew was tapping a pencil on his desk as he spoke into his headset. The din of other reporters' voices searching for stories could be heard in the background. He needed Michael on side in order to get the story past the publisher. Michael had said he only wanted to sulk in private. Perhaps a better understanding of what was going on behind his back might loosen his lips a bit.

"Well, Michael, normally I don't reveal my sources but, in your case I will," he said in the tone of someone making a huge concession. "I learned you were fired shortly after you did. I got a call from Skip Williams, spelling it all out for me. I asked him why he was telling me all that and he said, 'You know how it is. I scratch your back, you scratch mine. I'm giving you an exclusive on this story and all I ask is that, in whatever you write, you present a balanced analysis from all sides.' So the guy was basically trying to bribe me into putting a positive spin on the takeover, saying things like having a larger firm in the market would help to both create and secure jobs and the added competition would lower the cost of investment management services to the local investment community. Let me be clear, Michael. I don't like these people and I hate what they do to lives for the sake of profits. The industry doesn't need to be cutthroat but they make it that way. I want to take advantage of the opportunity to tell the story about what a takeover really feels like to some people. Maybe there are a few ethical, compassionate souls still left out there and public opinion will drive these pirates back to Manhattan. So, what do you say? Will you help me?"

Michael had never spoken to a reporter before and the power he felt at being able to tell his story to the public provided him with an agreeable moment. But then it occurred to him that anything he said would be in print for all to see, and he had to wonder if broadcasting to the world would hurt his chances at finding another job and, more importantly, of winning new clients. He had agreed on the three-month deadline that Jennifer had proposed. Why dig a deeper hole than he was already in?

"I don't know, Andrew. I mean, yes I'm mad at them but is helping you write an article bad-mouthing them going to do anything? Won't any future employer think badly of me?"

"Michael, I tell you what? I won't use your name. I'll talk about a former employee who asked not to be named. People might suspect it is you, but Fifty States has a long history of going into smaller towns and ripping their soul out. So, it likely could be anybody."

That sounded better. He could be part of criticizing the firm without being identified. It gave him a feeling of power - something he hadn't felt for some time. So, he agreed to the interview.

Andrew started, as he always did with the easy questions. Did Michael enjoy working for the old firm? How was he faring during the bear market? What investment strategies was he employing? Michael particularly liked the last question because it gave him the opportunity to outline his technique of buying shares of conservative, dividend paying companies. No one believed in it but him. He knew, ultimately he'd be successful.

"Michael, did you have any idea that your position with the company was ever in jeopardy? Or did they just sneak up and whack you without any warning?"

He started to say that, no, he had no warning whatsoever but he knew that wasn't really true. Most of his clients weren't happy and several of his father's accounts had defected. And he and Harry had had more than one 'chat.' As the questions continued, he kept worrying that if somehow, someone figured out that he was the unnamed person in the story, it might come back to haunt him in a job interview. If he said that he wasn't aware that his position with the firm was tenuous, then was he admitting to being completely naive? If he said that he was aware, then what did he do about it? Apparently, not enough.

"Uh, I guess I'd have to say yes and no to that one."

Andrew let it ride. In all his years, no one he interviewed had ever admitted to being aware that their job was in trouble.

"How about your manager? Did he give you any support? Or did he throw you under the bus to save his own bacon?"

In truth, Michael had thought that perhaps Harry could have done more but he didn't really know. Harry himself was getting closer to the end of his own career and what would've been wrong with him thinking of his own safety first? In spite of everything that had happened, even the public humiliation of being called out by Harry to the meeting room while the rest of the office regaled in their new found partnership, Michael had managed to cling onto the belief that all along Harry really had wanted him to succeed. After all, his former boss was one of his dad's oldest friends.

"Well, I'm not sure how much influence Harry, I mean my former boss, had in the decision. I got the impression that Fifty States management came in and took complete control. I heard a rumor that the first anyone had heard of anything was two days before the announcement. That wouldn't have given them a lot of time to solicit the existing managers for their input. They must have gone through the company's numbers using their own approach without regard to the person in question."

"Yes, I understand," the reporter replied. "That often happens with these big companies. It's about cash, not compassion. Just one more question, Michael and we'll wrap this up. It's going very well. How did your father take the news? I know that the two of you used to work closely together and that you took over his book of business. Did he try to stick up for you?"

The question took Michael by surprise.

"Whoa there, Andrew," he said sharply. "That's a pretty personal thing to ask. You said this was going to be an anonymous article. If you talk about a father-son team and about me taking over his business, everyone will know exactly who you're talking about. I told you that you had to leave my name out of it and if I answer that question and people put two and two together, it's not only going to make it harder for me to find a job, it would embarrass the hell out of him."

Andrew wasn't going to back down. This was a critical part of his angle. These big money machines didn't just rip out the hearts of individuals; they destroyed families too.

"Michael, don't worry. I will write it in such a way so that no one will be able to identify you. There are lots of examples where sons or daughters take over their parent's book."

Michael wasn't too sensitive to nuances, but he sensed that perhaps this wasn't going to be as simple as he had thought, and certainly more dangerous to his interests.

"You know what?" he said. "The more I think about it, maybe this article isn't such a good idea after all. It doesn't seem to be like what you said it would be. I think you've got some sort of score to settle with Fifty States. That's your business. If this article goes out, I think there is a big chance it will embarrass and hurt some good people who don't deserve it. This phone call is over and you do NOT have my permission to write your story."

"Michael, come on," Andrew persisted. "Who are you trying to protect? I told you that this Skip guy called me and tried to sugarcoat everything. He said to me that there was only one loser who had to go. Who do you think he was calling a loser? He said they were doing you a favor by forcing you to make a career change because you clearly weren't cut out for this industry. He called firing you a 'clean and fair kill.' A KILL, Michael! Why would you be protecting this prick?"

The warmth was returning to Michael's face and neck.

"Look Andrew, I don't care about him. After what you've said, I'm glad I'm not working there."

"Then who could possibly be hurt by exposing the truth about these people?"

Michael started to raise his voice.

"Hey, Andrew, listen to me. Why don't you go look in the mirror? You say you're all worried about people's feelings. How do you think my dad's going to feel if everyone knows the article is about his son, who has done nothing but disappoint him, like he isn't floored enough already?"

Andrew waited a moment before responding. He wanted this to sink in.

"You're worried about your father Michael? Really? Did you know that Skip called him on the Friday night before the announcement and offered him a temporary job to help convince his old accounts to stay with the new firm? Did you know that he accepted the offer? Skip wouldn't tell me for how much. He just said 'above market rates.' Your father knew you were being fired well before you did. Did he warn you? Try to soften the blow? Who threw whom under the bus, Michael? This article is your one chance to correct a lot of wrong. I won't publish it if you tell me not to. But I think you're a fool if you don't let me."

## Chapter 20

## THE SEATTLE REPORTER

*"What Price Progress?"*

By Andrew Millcroft
—— *Staff* ——

*Records from the earliest civilizations show that not long after man moved from being a simple hunter and gatherer to a specie that had some control over food and shelter, the role of philosophers came into existence. Even in their earliest form, these thinkers urged their fellow man to focus on his individual spirituality to try to understand why we are here, to achieve self-awareness, and in the process overcome his desire to acquire wealth, which the philosophers claimed was the path to ruin. In modern day terms, these visionaries might have said that one should never fall in love with money because it truly is the root of all evil.*

*The United States is still one of the predominant examples of free enterprise in the world, based on the importance of three aims alone; to maximize profits, to improve asset values and to satisfy 'The market'. Money is the ultimate measure of success or failure, with the richest receiving the greatest accolades and admiration. How is it, we all ask ourselves, that some people seem born with the knack, the ability to see dollar signs when most others don't?*

*These are the people that run the world, that shape our society and dictate, to a large extent, the future. We are envious and we wish, somehow and someday, we could be more like them.*

*Or do we? More importantly, should we?*

*Hidden in the dark crevices of the fabric of our capitalistic society are those left behind, often indiscriminately, as the money making machine relentlessly marches on. This is called progress, but what price does it exact? Who are these people in our rear view mirror? And what if, heaven forbid, someday we might become one of them, watching as the smokestack on the engine pulling our hopes and dreams to the land of success continues to chug relentlessly forward, leaving us cast on the tracks behind, bruised, our thoughts and feelings in total disarray.*

*Allow me to present a real-life example of my point, which speaks volumes louder than any words this author might wax. The reader might have noticed a large headline in the business section of our paper: "Local Firm MOGI Acquired by Fifty States." In the article, President Ohara was quoted as saying "MOGI has a rich tradition serving clients in the Seattle area and we are thrilled to have formed a partnership that will allow us to provide an expanded line-up of products and services. Fifty States is committed to being 'best in class' when it comes to serving our clients, wherever in the country they might reside. This community has my personal promise that our new firm will continue to earn their business, each and every day."*

*Makes you want to put hand over heart, doesn't it? Looking deeper into the interview, however, there is little in the way of any discussion about the dark side of takeovers. Some people always lose their jobs when an acquisition occurs. But when this reporter spoke with the Fifty States representative, Skip Williams, responses to some pretty specific questions were fuzzy and ambiguous. If nothing else, these companies, which will always have to answer to the court of public opinion, don't like to discuss the dirty laundry created by their actions. Everything is 'new.' There is momentum. Why focus on the past?*

Through a variety of sources, I have been able to determine the following: the back-office head count will be slashed, as much of the book-keeping will move to super computers in New York. There will be some combining of office space wherever both Fifty States and MOGI have branches in close proximity, causing an increase in the unemployment lines of support staff but, for the most part, severance packages - in the immediate future - will be the exception rather than the rule. When questioned, President Ohara simply replied, "We value the contribution made by every MOGI employee and it will take us time to configure the new team optimally."

In other words, this firm has decided to keep its machete hidden behind its back until public attention moves on to the next topic du jour. Smart really. A bit more expensive to keep unwanted payroll running, but a savvy move nonetheless.

This brings me to the point of this article. Not everyone was given a stay of execution. The school motto of Dartmouth College in New Hampshire is Vox Clamantis in Deserto or, *A Voice Cries in the Wilderness.* There is one such individual who wasn't even invited to the welcoming cocktail party and who, suddenly and without warning, finds him or herself on the outside. In exchange for sharing their story, this individual has requested anonymity, a demand that will be gladly honored. And before the reader starts to argue, "Wait a minute. Why single out just one employee? You just said that the new company was taking its time to assess everyone. What could be wrong with that?" The answer has nothing to do with numbers, although surely there are more to come, but rather the way in which the employee was let go. Senior management at Fifty States, when discussing the acquisition with this reporter, spoke proudly of the efficiency of the transaction, even referring to one termination as a 'clean kill'. The terminology used is both offensive and disturbing. Here is *a former employee who, having had his dreams for the future crushed, is offered a severance package as though it were the prize from a safari hunt. And what about the others involved, friends or relatives that might also have been hurt or embarrassed? This reporter has learned that the bulk of the severed employee's book of business was inherited from his or her father. After finishing a long and illustrious career in the industry, dad saw a way to put his feet up while, at the same time giving his child a head start by transferring his client list to his heir apparent. Judging by the timing, the protégé was just getting going when the axe fell. In a bizarre twist of fate, the father was approached by Fifty States and offered a financial retainer to help ensure that his former clients didn't drift away during the transition. "It's done all the time," Fifty States Senior Manager Skip Williams snorted. "It's part of the business."*

*Pitting father and child against each other in a terrible conflict of interest is part of the business? How does child sheepishly explain to father, 'I'm sorry dad, I guess I just wasn't good enough?' How does father ever explain to child that the young one's termination led to a temporary source of income for the dad?*

*How indeed? This clean kill doesn't seem so to this writer, who feels morally obligated to warn clients of Fifty States that the trimming isn't over and it seems almost certain that future terminations will be done without regard to honor, dignity or family.*

*If that is the ultimate price of progress then we are losing our battle of money vs. morality, of business vs. ethical behavior. The ultimate cost of this defeat is yet to be understood, but when it is, God help us all.*

Skip Williams threw the newspaper down on the table in disgust.

"What a load of crap," he said.

## Chapter 21

"You talked to WHOM about WHAT?" Jennifer exclaimed.

Michael never thought that she might have a reaction to the fact that he actually spoke to the reporter. He'd been careful. He'd considered the pros and cons. And the fact that he had considered his father's feelings went right out the window when the reporter, Andrew, revealed that good old dad had sold out to the very people that mercilessly fired his son. That was the thing that had tipped him over the edge. He didn't really care about his father's feelings now.

None of that had anything to do with Jen who, sitting at her usual spot these days, at the kitchen table with papers spread out in orderly disarray, glared at him. What was her issue?

"It's not a big deal, Jen. I talked to a reporter - from *The Seattle Reporter*. Somehow he found out about me being fired, and he has some sort of axe to grind about these big New York companies that come in and terminate everyone. I don't think he really wanted to talk about me so much as he wanted to make his point. In fact I made him promise not to use my name in the article."

Jennifer was sitting with her arms folded now. The look on her face had not changed, and it was one that made the hair on the back of his neck stand up.

"Michael, how many hours have I been putting into our new business plan?" she demanded. "This will be a complicated thing to get started and a positive public perception will be absolutely critical. Besides, don't you know that you can't trust these people? They'll twist the truth any way they want as long as it suits their purpose. They don't really give a shit who gets hurt in the process."

She hadn't forgotten the outright lies, the stretching of the truth, and the twisting of the facts by the New York papers. If it hadn't been for her, the Feds never would have nailed the Russian for insider trading. And what had she got in return? She was barred from working in the securities business for life. OK, maybe she understood that. The authorities had to be able to show their competence - even though they had none. She could have, and would have, stayed in the Big Apple if it hadn't been for the press. She had managed to hide a bit of coin and even if she couldn't work in the business, she could still trade her personal account. Her years of 'networking' would have ensured that many profitable investment opportunities came her way - before the general public was aware of what was going on. But after what the press had done to her, she had become an outcast. She'd had to leave - to go as far away as possible - and start over, even though she'd been born and raised in New York and what was left of her family was still there. She even had to give up her NAME, for God's sake! Who had the right to do that to a person? She'd left years, YEARS of hard work behind. All thanks to the fucking press.

Michael couldn't understand why Jen would be so sensitive about a newspaper article. But he was no fool and, by the way, there was another point to be made here.

"Look Jen, I don't know why you're bothered by all this but I'm not naive. I didn't just get off the boat. I talked to the reporter, asked him a bunch of questions and came to a well-reasoned decision. He won't be using any names. So, no harm, no foul."

He started to add that, while he appreciated all of the work she was doing on her idea for a new business for the two of them, he still had time, plenty of time actually, to find a position at another brokerage firm and pick up his career where he left off. They had an agreement and he was sure that they would never even get to her idea since he would be back in the saddle in no time. The look on her face made him hold that thought back, however. Probably she didn't believe that he could do it, but he was determined to prove to her, his father and to himself that he could. If he was sure of anything, it was that.

"Just so you know, I was worried that somehow my identity would get out and it would embarrass my father," he said in a conciliatory voice. "I told the reporter that. Do you know what he said? Are you ready for this? Apparently dear old dad isn't too worried about his son. Fifty States offered him a temporary position, a *paid* position I might add, to try to keep as many of his old clients with the new firm as possible. And he took it. You know what else? They came to whatever agreement before the news broke. So my own father *knew* they were going to let me go. Did he warn me? Give me something to cushion the blow? No. That was when I said, 'Screw him! I don't care if people figure out that the article is about me and he gets embarrassed.'"

Jen continued to stare at him... calculating.

"Look Michael, I'm not going to go into great detail, and we've never talked about what happened to me in New York, but the press absolutely screwed me. They took things out of context and ruined my reputation and that is why I'm here. You cannot trust these people - ever."

"Jen, this reporter has a bone to pick and a point he's trying to make. Have you lost sight of the fact that they fired me? These kinds of people have no heart and if this guy Andrew can call people's attention to that, then that is a good thing. He wants to help me. And, by the way that seems like more than anyone else around here does."

Jen had to catch herself. No one was trying to help him? It boggled her mind that he was so clueless. But then it occurred to her to wonder why this reporter was really offering assistance. What did he care about an inexperienced and underachieving stock jockey? There could be only one reason and it wasn't benevolence. He clearly needed Michael in order to write the article. Michael had said that he had a 'bone to pick' with Fifty States. What if Michael had read the guy right? This reporter, Andrew, would owe them one, thanks to Michael's help. For whatever reason this fellow Andrew hated Fifty States and, most importantly, might just represent a potentially valuable marketing tool that could help launch their new business at a level she could only dream about achieving herself. She uncrossed her arms.

"You know what Michael?" she said, "Maybe you have a point. Whether you are able to restart your franchise before our deadline or we start up my new business idea, we are going to need some friends. This guy might be of some use after all. Please agree with me that I have a lot more experience at this than you do. If we are going to get into bed with this guy, the relationship has to be managed very carefully. I want to meet Andrew and make sure he really is on our side. You set it up. But you have to agree with me. No more talking to the press without running it by me first. Can we at least agree on that?"

Michael realized he was still standing in his front hallway. What had just happened? In one breath Jen had been haranguing him for talking to the press and now she wanted to meet the guy and become friends. There were times when he wasn't sure he fully understood his future wife at all. Perhaps it was just because she was a woman. Whatever, it felt good to win his point.

"Yeah, sure Jen," he told her, "whatever you say."

## CHAPTER 22

*Dear Mr. Franklin. Thank you for your application to join Thoroughbred Securities Inc. in the position of retail sales. After careful consideration of your resume, we regret to inform you that we will not be in a position to offer you an interview at this time. We do wish you, however, all the best in your future endeavors.*

Michael threw the letter onto the pine desk. It, and an older reclining office chair, filled the small office that he shared with all of the other clients at Royal Futures, the Seattle area's leading outplacement firm. As he had been instructed, he signed into the shared computer, entered his account number and password and logged the result. It was critical, he'd been told, to keep an accurate record of all correspondence with potential employers. His summary screen was clear:

| | |
|---|---|
| Number of inquiry letters sent | - 97 |
| Number of responses | - 29 |
| Follow ups * | - 00 |
| Interviews granted | - 00 |
| Job offers received | - 00 |

* Follow ups indicate informational discussions that could include coffee, lunch or impromptu conversations at conferences or other types of non-employment related meetings.

Michael questioned the value of keeping such an extensive list of rejection letters and suspected the company combined the results of all of their clients, put it into a professional looking slide format and used it as part of their presentations documenting the vast extent of their current market research. "It's a tough market out there," they would say, "and we have the most up-to-date data to prove it."

Michael didn't harbor a grudge against the headhunting firm. They were only doing what they were supposed to and besides; it was a welcome retreat from Jennifer's scrutiny. And the firm made everything look professional; there was a receptionist who had the list of all current 'clients', each with their own personalized voice mailbox. They even made up business cards, very professional looking, although, unless the recipient had been living under a rock, when they saw the name of the firm, they knew what it meant. The firm's mantra when you walked in the door for your first meeting with your counselor was, "Your job now is to find a job." But they had also told him that, in this market, it could take a year. They asked him if he'd ever considered employment in other industries. The answer was a clear "no" and, no he wouldn't consider going back to school.

As he had agreed to do whenever he received correspondence, he dialed his home number to bring Jennifer up-to-date. His index finger hit the button slowly. He didn't see the point. It was always the same news. But, she had demanded that he did, constantly reminding him that they were in this together and that she was deeply interested in his progress, good or bad. This time, it took a full five rings for her to answer.

"Good morning," she said in her usual voice, always cheerful, seemingly without a care. It was always "good morning" or "good" whatever time of day it was, without even knowing who was calling. It could be some horrible person or someone with dreadful news but her first greeting was always a welcome to their day. This time she added that she was sorry it had taken her so long to answer and then, as usual, said, "How's it going?"

"One contact," he said, aware that he sounded robotic. "No interview offered, no follow up suggested, just another PFO."

Michael had heard the term in the office before the takeover was announced and he remembered laughing until his stomach muscles hurt. Please Fuck Off. They didn't like him using the expression in the outplacement office.

"Well, that's OK, honey. You've got a lot more irons in the fire. I'm sure a positive response is out there."

She was so pleasant, cheery, like what he was going through wasn't really happening. He'd asked her about it and she was quick to reply.

"Look Michael, we don't need two long faces around here. What's the point of that?"

To Michael, it seemed as if everyone had gotten the happy drug but him.

"Besides, you haven't asked why it took so long for me to come to the phone. Go ahead, ask me."

Michael thought he knew the answer but played along.

"OK, shoot."

"Well, I was downstairs by the printer. I've been working on my - our - marketing brochure and I have to say, it looks outstanding - very, very professional. I've found a firm that will bind it for only $10.00 each. I'm quite pleased."

Michael wasn't in the mood. It seemed like Jennifer had found some hobby that kept her occupied while one of them at least was looking for work. Now she was going to spend $10.00 to have it, whatever it was, professionally bound. It sounded to him like a complete waste of her time and his money.

"Professionally bound?! Come on Jen, we can't afford that. Like I know you're trying to help with whatever it is you're doing but don't you think we should maybe save our nickels? This is looking like it will take longer than I expected."

Not as long as that, Jennifer thought. She knew that Michael was highly unlikely to find a job as a broker. Firms were firing people - not hiring. Clients were upset because no one was making money in the market. Michael had nothing to offer to a prospective employer, not a single account. But she knew she had to let him try - and fail. His full capitulation that he wasn't going to find work - in time - and a keen sense of remorse and even desperation, were critical elements to bring him onside.

She lowered her voice an octave.

"Michael, do I need to remind you of our agreement? You have three months and we're halfway through that. You've written a great resume and sent out lots of letters. Good for you. You are doing everything you can and I'm proud of you. And I'm more positive that you're going to land an interview than you are - any day now."

Michael looked around the small office at a poster on the wall. It was a picture of some sort of marathon runner with the caption, "The harder I work, the luckier I get."

"Look Jen, I'm sure your book, whatever it is about, looks great. All I'm saying is, don't go spending a lot of money until I find another job, OK?"

"No Michael, it's not OK," she was telling him. "We have an agreement and I am going to hold you to it. In spite of everything you've done, all of the hours researching and writing resumes and cover letters, you're still coming up empty. I told you - you obviously don't believe me but you will see - that I have another plan, a great strategy for managing people's money, which will blow both you and them away. I've been working very hard too while you're in your outplacement. You have six more weeks and then it is my turn. And I *will* be ready."

Michael had heard her song before but still didn't have the first clue what she was talking about. He raised his voice and waved his hands towards the computer terminal.

"Fine! Fine, Jen. You've got a better idea. Let's hear it. Just let me know what it is and I'll hurry home right now."

She found herself wanting to tell him just what she did think, but she also knew a good deal about self-control. It wouldn't be productive to play her anger card until the right time.

"I'm not ready yet, Michael," she forced herself to say in an even voice. "When the time comes, I will be. But let me give you two things to think about. The first is, during times of strife, people want someone to lead them to a better place - like Moses parting the Red Sea. We're in that space right now, and doing nothing about it. Secondly, and this is the important one, everything to do with money is based on trust and perceptions. When you used to bring home a paycheck - what was that? It was nothing but a piece of paper with numbers on it. And you were able to use those numbers to buy things, like food and clothes, because the person that accepted them perceived that they, in turn could give them to someone else in exchange for something they wanted. Think about it, Michael; it's like a game. Everything about money is based on what people believe. In itself, it has no value."

Michael didn't move. He had no idea how to respond. For the first time, he was worried that the stress of his being fired was getting to her. Money has no value?

"All right then," he said. "Thanks for that Jen. I have to go to my group meeting where we compare how pitiful we are at finding work. I'll see you tonight."

Jennifer laughed.

"Yeah Michael," she told him, "you don't get it yet but think about it. You will!"

## Chapter 23

Angela barely heard the knocking.

The person on the other side of the front door had chosen not to use the doorbell, perhaps thinking that pressing the button at four o'clock on a Saturday morning would be an unwelcome intrusion, which, of course, was the truth for all such visits conducted by State Trooper Officer Arnold King.

Angela had been sitting up in bed since three. Even at his worst, her husband had managed to make it home by two and, given the fact that this time he had offered not to go to the bar at all, he should have been home earlier. The truth was that Angela was facing the fact that she had put certain events in motion that would mean she must be prepared to give the performance of a lifetime. If what she thought had happened had, someone would be contacting her, although she did not know who or how. Now, hearing the knock on the door, she was afraid that she would raise suspicion if she answered it too quickly. Surely, at this time of night she should be asleep. Or should she? After all, her husband hadn't come home She should be wide awake, worrying. Wouldn't whoever it was want to know why she hadn't called the authorities? It was, she realized, important to decide on a story. She could say that her husband often went out with his friends on Friday night, which was the truth. Sometimes, being the solid citizen that he was, he would take a cab to a local motel rather than drive home. He didn't just take the cab home because... he didn't want to wake her up. He was that kind of man, oozing with consideration.

The truth was, she didn't know where her husband was or whether the man with the raspy voice on the other end of the phone had done what he implied - but never said outright - he would do. She had no way of knowing if the play had started. Was the man who surely was going to kill her, still alive?

The knock on the door was repeated, louder this time.

Not bothering to make any attempt to improve her appearance since it was natural that she should look tousled, she wrapped her robe loosely around herself, and without releasing the chain, opened the door a crack and peered out. The police officer, dressed in a starched blue uniform, showed his badge, introduced himself as sergeant something or other and asked if he could come in. As she tried to undo the chain clasp, her hands were visibly shaking. She wasn't acting.

As the officer came in the door, he removed his wide, stiff brim hat out of respect. His patent leather black boots seemed to have laces climbing halfway up his legs. Should she offer him coffee? No, Angela, dear God, this wasn't a social visit! As she showed him to the living room sofa, she quietly asked,

"What is it?"

Although she was trying to remain composed, she could hear her voice - high, anxious and cracking - like that of a nervous teenager.

"Why are you here? Is something wrong?"

"Mrs. Messina, I'm with the 107th Unit Highway Patrol," the officer said as they sat down facing one another. "I retrieved your address from the license plate of a badly damaged vehicle. Does the owner of a black BMW 325i live here? His name is John Messina."

"Yes," Angela replied softly. She held her hands together tightly in her lap and hoped that she looked sufficiently concerned. "Is my husband in trouble?" she asked, this time adding a quiver to her voice.

"There has been an accident, Mrs. Messina," the officer said, "a terrible accident. Sometime around one this morning the driver of this vehicle must have been travelling at a very high rate of speed on I-5. We don't have all of the details yet - the highway is still closed and we are trying to gather as many facts as we can. But it is clear that the driver of the car lost control, hit a guardrail and flipped several times."

On cue, Angela buried her face into both of her hands.

"Oh no!" she cried. "Oh, dear God, no!"

The tears, which came from the greatest sense of relief after years of life-threatening persecution, seemed to come pouring from her very soul. Surely the officer would not be able to distinguish the difference between the reaction to a horrible tragedy and one of the happiest days of her life.

After what she thought was an appropriate period of time, Angela stopped crying and lay on the sofa, looking absently across the room.

"Mrs. Messina," the officer said, "I realize this is a very disturbing time for you but I do need to ask you some questions. Can I get you something, some water perhaps?"

Sitting up, Angela shielded her eyes in the tissues she pulled from the pocket of her robe while quietly, but efficiently, the officer began to ask his questions. When had she last seen her husband? Had she spoken to him at work that day? Did he usually come straight home from work? Had there been any trouble between them recently?

Thrusting both hands into her lap, she said "why are you asking me all these questions?" Angela cried. "What's happened to my husband?"

"With the impact, the gas tank must have ruptured because the car was completely engulfed in flames," he explained. "The driver... well, we are having a difficult time identifying him or her. Do you know for a fact that your husband was out in the car last night? I don't want to hold out false hope but given the condition of the... accident scene we can't, at this time, confirm that it was, in fact, your husband in the car. It could have been stolen. He might have loaned it to someone."

Angela hadn't considered this possibility. The realization that, as a result of her actions, a completely innocent person might have been killed made her entire body shake.

"Oh, my God, officer!" she cried. "You made me think that he must be dead or terribly hurt and now you say that maybe it wasn't him at all!"

"Yes, well Mrs. Messina, these things are never easy for anyone," the officer told her. "I'm just trying to gather as many facts as I can. We won't be able to officially identify the... victim until later today. I'll go now. Here is my card. Please call me immediately if you hear or think of anything."

He started to get up but paused.

"I am also going to need to ask you the name of your husband's dentist."

With the realization of why the officer wanted this information, a full comprehension of what had happened swept over Angela. They really couldn't be sure who it was. Had these horrible people made a mistake? Was it possible that her husband might walk through the door? If he did, she would be in even greater danger than she was before and would live the rest of her life knowing that because of her an innocent person had been killed.

And then where would she get $50,000?

This time, as Angela fell face-down onto the couch, her wails were real and uncontrollable.

Officer King made a mental note. Now that he had presented the grief-stricken woman with the faintest of hopes that her husband might still be alive, she almost seemed to be crying harder.

## Chapter 24

"He just wouldn't take no for an answer," the receptionist from the outplacement office later explained. She had forwarded a call to Michael from a man who hadn't called before but assured her that what he had to say was important to Michael's future. Normally, she screened out these types of inquiries but she knew - everyone in the office knew - that since Michael joined them, he hadn't had so much as a nibble. Beggars can't be choosers, right?

Michael knew this call could be from no one but his dad, checking up to see how his day was going and, in his own way, to remind him that he was still a failure.

The voice was not his father's, but it was equally unwelcome.

"Junior! Hey man, how they hangin'? You still alive?"

Michael hadn't thought much about any of his former co-workers since he left. It was, he had decided, better to just put the whole exprcicncc out of his mind.

"Oh, hi there, Ivan," he said now. "How are you doing? How are things going at the new firm?"

Michael bit his lower lip. He wanted to know but he clearly should have chosen someone else to ask.

"Junior, you won't believe it!" Ivan exclaimed. "It's amazing here. We moved out of that shithole in the mall to a real office downtown and now business just walks through the door. They've given us so many products to sell. Do you know why ETF's are better than stocks? Well I sure didn't but I do now. And commissions? It's like shooting fish in a barrel. It was too bad they didn't give you a shot - even you could build a book here."

Michael cast his thoughts back to the so-called lunch with Ivan that he walked out of. The guy was an arrogant prick then and it sounded like he'd gotten worse.

"They toasted Harry about a month after they nailed you. You could see it. He knew. He kinda walked around the office with a glazed look in his eyes. Just as well, I say. The guy couldn't talk a cat out of a tree. Some leader."

Michael could feel the warmth move from his stomach, to the back of his neck and to his face. While Harry wasn't a close friend, he was someone to be respected. It was terrible to trash-talk someone who was facing adversity. If Michael was having a hard time finding work, he couldn't imagine what Harry, twenty-five years his senior, was going through. He was about to tell Ivan that wasn't called for but he bit his tongue and waited. Presumably Ivan had something to tell him unless he had simply called to gloat.

"You still there, Junior? Hello?"

"Yes, Ivan, I am still here. Why did you call me?"

"Whoa there, partner, let's exercise a little professional courtesy here. We're both in the trenches together."

Michael remained quiet.

"Yeah, OK, that's how it is, huh? Fine, I'll get to the point. I need to ask you a favor, well OK, not a favor I just want to test your memory. Did you know that I was given four of your father's clients after you left?" He chuckled. "I guess I was going to get them one way or the other. Well, one of them is Mr. Mulvaney, who's now eighty-seven, and, what do you know? He's been diagnosed with Alzheimer's and can't remember shit. He had this intricate plan in his head about putting all of his money into a trust for his kids, giving his wife survivorship rights and that kind of stuff, but he didn't write it down. His wife now has power of attorney but she is of no use either - he didn't tell her. She'll do what I say but I don't want to screw it up and give everything to the dog. Do you remember what his plan was?"

As Michael listened, images of this fast-talking greasy-haired broker filled his mind. He hadn't liked him before their awful lunch and he sure didn't now. But he was still a professional and a client or at least a former client was in need. Truth was, Mr. Mulvaney hadn't shared the details of his plan with Michael either.

"Ivan, as always you've got that special soft touch with people. I can't help you. Why don't you call my dad? If anyone would know, he would."

Yes, Ivan, call the same dad who only called Michael to rub it in.

"Thanks for that keen insight, Einstein. I just got off the phone with him. You're a bitter family, you two. He said, 'my son is so smart - says he has all the answers - why don't you call him?' Then he goes on like he's looking for a shoulder to cry on. You never call him. That's the thanks he gets. Geez Michael, the guy's getting old. You could at least give him a shout."

"Ivan, my relationship with my father is none of your..."

"It sounds like he didn't take your firing too well, either. What is it, ten in the morning? The old coot sounded like he was already into the sauce."

Ivan's tone had changed from sarcastic to as cutting as the blades in a Cuisinart. Michael had heard it before. His face was burning.

"Ivan, I don't know what the hell you think you're doing," he said, "but I'll be hanging up now."

"By the way, Junior, I wanted to tell you one more thing. Mulvaney, before he went senile, told me he was *very* pleased with his new broker, you know what I mean? Said his old broker didn't know his ass from third base - his words, not mine. After you were gone, I was able to talk Van Buren into moving back - with me. See Michael, you should have listened at our lunch. You'd still be working here. You let your ego get in the way and see where it got you? By the way, how's that cute little girlfriend of yours? Has she dumped you yet? I have to hand it to you, that chick has one fine ass. Tell her to come see me if she wants a man who can hold a job."

By now Michael was breathing through clenched teeth.

"Oh, and by the way," Ivan continued. "Skip Williams of Fifty States was in our office today and made a point of coming by my desk to say that, if I was ever talking to you, that he really enjoyed that little article you fed that dipshit reporter. Said he hoped you were happy and felt a real sense of revenge. He also said he hoped you enjoyed wherever it was you were moving to because you would never find another job in this town if he had anything to say about it."

Michael slammed the handset down with a force that made the receptionist look up in concern. She was even more alarmed when she saw his face.

After Ivan's call, the bus ride home was so mind-numbing that Michael had almost missed his stop. His face was still burning. Was Ivan right? Should Michael have taken him up on his offer? He didn't want to share that thought with Jennifer because second-guessing himself would be admitting that he was a failure. Their relationship was fragile as it was.

"Guess no job offers again, hey boyfriend?" Jennifer called to him when he got home. "How about just packing it in and come over to the dark side. We're wasting valuable time."

Sitting at the kitchen table, her hair in a bun, dressed in a baggy t-shirt that said New York Knickerbockers, she was typing away so fast and furious that she barely looked up as Michael approached her.

"Come on Michael, look at you," she said, glancing over her shoulder when he remained silent. "Every day you come home looking like your dog died."

When he told her about Ivan's call, her first impulse was to be furious, but as he went on and on, she began to think that perhaps Ivan had done her a favor. It might be that if she played the right strings, she could accelerate her plan.

"Can you believe the nerve of that bastard," Michael concluded, "calling me up and saying things like that?"

Jennifer looked at him. He was upset and, as she well knew, emotions created opportunity.

"Look, Michael. I think maybe the time has come for you to step up and start acting like a man. Whining about a phone call from a clear deadbeat isn't going to get you - or us - anywhere. As long as you let guys like that drag you down, you're going nowhere. Don't you see what they're doing? They are making themselves the winner and you the loser."

Michael did a double take. The woman he wanted to marry - and hoped she felt the same - just called him a loser.

"Hey, thanks for that Jen," he said. "Glad to see there is someone I can go to with my problems. Really helps a lot."

It was clear that Jennifer didn't like the tone of voice.

"Michael, you may not like it but it's time you faced the music. There are bullies everywhere. You need to learn to stand up to them and stop running away. You got a bad phone call from the big ogre, Aw. Man up. He's called me three times asking mc out."

Michael, who had been slumped in a kitchen chair across from her, leaped to his feet.

"WHAT! He's called you! You didn't tell me that. Why would he call you - three times?! Why didn't you just tell him to leave you alone?"

She smiled.

"I did, Michael," she said. "Some men just don't give up. Maybe that's why he's got a job and you don't."

Michael rubbed his face with both hands.

"Holy shit" he shouted! "You think this is funny! He called you!? What did you say to him? You must have said something to lead him on."

"OK, look, Michael, I get it about you and all your troubles, about you wanting to prove yourself. But you've got to get a grip. When we were at the restaurant with your dad, you acted like the most immature asshole I've ever seen. For Christ's sakes, you almost knocked over the waiter with the drinks. If you want to be treated like an adult, start acting like one."

His mind was reeling. He'd tried to forget about that. How was bringing up that little bit of dirty laundry going to help? He knew if he kept talking, he'd soon be yelling and he might say a few things that he regretted. Jennifer could be *such* a, a what, a traitor.

Everyone was against him. No one was giving him a chance. Realizing that he hadn't responded to her, he chose his words very, very carefully.

"Look, Jennifer," he said, "the last thing I want is to get into a fight with you. But, hopefully, you know how important it is for me, for us, that I establish myself in my career. My father lied to me. If he wasn't going to give me his book for good then he never should have done it in the first place; I'd probably have been better off starting from scratch."

Eyes narrowed, nostrils flaring, Jennifer went for the final play.

"I am so-fucking-sick of you making excuses," she told him. "It's not your fault that you pissed away half of your father's accounts? Why the hell do you think they fired you Michael? They kept the people that were going to make them money! What would you have done if it had been your money? The reason you have nothing to show for the last two years is that you've achieved nothing.

You haven't opened up one new bloody account on your own, not one! Hey, honey, guess what? The credit card is maxed out again and the electricity company is threatening to cut off power unless we pay them on time. Does that sound like achievement? You should have welcomed your father back with open arms but it's too late now."

He looked away from her. She'd never spoken to him like this before. He counted to three again. He was not going to talk about this with her any longer. Speaking to the floor, he said,

"There's a lot you don't understand about the brokerage business, Jennifer. That's all I'm going to say. If you did, you might be able to see things more my way."

"Michael, do not patronize me! We're not done with this. You know what pisses me off the most? You won't let anyone help you. You're going to flush your life right down the toilet and for what? You have no idea how much I know about the brokerage business. Do you? Don't say shit you don't know."

His eyes were closed. He listened to the air quietly go through his nose and felt his chest slowly rising and falling.

A long period of time passed. The silence was deafening. But Jennifer knew she had to wait. She had won the argument but needed him to see that.

He looked up at her and sighed deeply, trying to make light of it all.

"OK, so now what do you want to talk about?"

She leaned forward and grabbed his hands between hers. Now was the time for empathy, for real concern.

"Michael," she said quietly, "I know what I want to talk about - our future. It's time."

## Chapter 25

"It's time? What do you mean, Jen? Time for what?"

Jen had been practicing her delivery. Admittedly, today was a bit earlier than she had planned the 'launch', as she liked to call it, but - she smiled to herself - strike while the iron's hot.

"Michael, look at me. It's time to put my plan into effect. I need to explain it to you but after I do, your life - and ours - will never be the same."

Michael held up one hand to stop her.

"Wait a minute, Jen," he told her. "We just had a fight, that's all. That doesn't mean I'm going to give up finding a job. Besides, I still have time left on our agreement. I've got a lot of feelers out there. You can't just throw away all of the work I've done."

Jennifer looked at her future partner in crime - or not. It would be better, easier and faster if he came on board, but if he didn't then he didn't. Throw away all his hard work? He must be kidding. It had resulted in virtually nothing and the best thing to do with trash was take it out before it started to smell. But she had decided a while ago to start with a soft approach and hopefully not have to use the hammer. The boy, after all could prove to be very useful.

"Actually Michael you're running out of time. I just want to tell you about…"

"No, Jen! I know you have some sort of plan but don't you get it? This is about me, proving to you and everyone else that I can look after myself. If I just go ahead with your plan, whatever it is, I will have admitted that everyone was right, that I really am a failure. Don't get me wrong, I really appreciate your offer to help but I *have* to figure this out on my own."

He had interrupted her. She could feel the hairs on her arm standing up. It was time to turn the thumbscrews a bit.

"Michael, we've had this conversation how many times? I've listened to you, respected your wishes and supported you. It's my turn now. Please don't interrupt me again. You owe it to me to at least listen to what I have to say."

She folded her arms across her substantial breasts and looked out the window at the sunlit afternoon. It was a beautiful day out there. Could she create the same atmosphere inside? She waited quietly for his apology.

"Sorry. It's just that..."

When she turned back to stare at him, Michael held up both hands in surrender.

"OK," he said. "OK. I'll listen."

Jennifer had decided that there needed to be three steps. The first was to make Michael understand that he was being a fool; he didn't need to do everything himself and some of life's greatest successes came to those who recognized their shortcomings and partnered with people whose skills complemented their own. It was an interesting thought - of course she didn't believe it for one minute. She'd lived her life - survived really - by ensuring that she never allowed herself to rely on anyone.

"Please do, because I have been thinking about this for months, years even," she told him. "This is very, very important Michael. Do you understand?"

That was part of the second step - to make sure he realized that the stakes at this table were high. Soon she'd show him just how high. But that had to come later, at just the right moment.

The third step was to get him to agree to something he didn't fully understand so that later if he tried to back out, she would play the "But you agreed!" card. She wouldn't allow details or facts to interrupt their progress.

But first she needed to start by changing the mood to a more positive note.

"Let me make a few things clear," she began. "First, I am not trying to 'bail you out' or take away your opportunity to prove yourself. Not at all."

A good opportunity, she thought, to salt the meal with uncertainty.

"And if you don't believe me, then maybe you don't know me as well as I thought. Maybe we should be having some *other* kind of discussion."

She waited to make sure that the fact that she had stressed "other" would sink in, that he had been warned. He chose not to speak - a wise move she thought.

"I am a businesswoman, or at least I was. I am going to explain a business opportunity to you, one that we will run together. While there are no guarantees in life, I am as confident as I can be that it will be very successful. But let's be clear here. The success of our new enterprise rests largely on you. If you somehow think that partnering with me is a form of capitulation, then you need to wake up. The best, most successful business people are that way because they have included strategic partners on their team. I am asking you to run with the ball. I'm not going to do it for you. This venture will be a success largely as a result of your hard work. Think of it this way. You've tried to find a job the traditional way and in these markets there's little to no chance that you'll succeed. So it comes down to this. All you actually want, really, is to find a job. Who cares where it comes from? I have created a job for you. Now it's up to you to succeed at it."

She watched his face closely as the thought soaked in.

"Let's both accept the elephant in the room," she continued when he began to stroke his chin, the very absurd image of the thoughtful man he considered himself to be. "There is one reason, and one reason only why you haven't been able to find a job. You know what it is and so do I. Beating your head against the wall in denial isn't going to help. The good news is it has nothing to do with your skills, or background, or honesty or work ethic."

Again she waited. She wanted him to believe that she thought it wasn't his fault.

"You have no assets, Michael! Those pricks that took over your firm stripped them away from you. In this market, no one is willing to pay you while you generate no revenue until you rebuild your book."

She thought it was clever, if she said so herself, that she was able to shift the conversation from Michael's failures to blaming everything on a bad market. Michael was nodding his head now. He'd been telling himself that for months; it wasn't him, it was the market. She grabbed both of his hands.

"Michael," she whispered, "we can build our own business - just the two of us. You are the client expert and I have the investment management experience. We, as a team, will be unbeatable."

A broad smile came across Michael's face. He had never considered anything like this before. It was brilliant!

Jennifer recognized the smile. Step one was complete.

"So, you mean we start up an investment management firm? Just the two of us? How does that work? I have no idea how to do that."

Funny how his mind could go from defensive to accepting, in milliseconds, she thought. That probably explained why Michael hadn't achieved more in his life. If you spend all day second-guessing yourself, you'll never get anywhere. It was time to raise the ante.

"Michael, there's something else you must understand. Our success, whether we get there or not, is going to largely be based on trust," she went on, confident now. She had thrown out the line and the sucker had taken the hook. "While I might be concerned about your selling abilities, I am going to trust that you can handle that part of the business. And although you might not know as much about managing money as I do, you will have to trust me. Do you see how important this is? Everything in life is based on trust. Our relationship - our future... It can be no other way."

Michael exhaled deeply.

"Jen, my God, of course I trust you. I love you!"

It was exactly what she had wanted him to say. So now it was time for the third step.

"Right, but I know what you're thinking. If the problem is the bear market, how are we going to be able to get anyone to give us their money to manage?"

Michael smiled and quietly nodded his head. From the coffee table, Jennifer produced a yellow pad and a pen.

"Come sit next to me. I'm going to show you how we're going to get rich. Then you can tell Ivan to shove it up his ass."

Michael slid over on the couch so that their legs were touching. He could smell her perfume.

"Don't get any ideas there, killer," she warned him, smiling seductively. "We're working."

Jennifer proceeded to draw a large blank chart, the vertical axis marked by a dollar sign and the bottom axis marked by the word 'time.'

"You see," she said, "there are three widely known and accepted ways investors analyze the markets. There are the guys that use fundamental analysis - you know, go in and try to understand a company's business, predict how much money they will make and then guess how the market will value those earnings.

Analysts all over Wall Street are doing that - have been for years. But the problem is..."

She drew a zigzagging line from left to right across the graph.

"Sometimes that way of looking at the market makes money and sometimes it doesn't"

Michael made an indistinct sound that was meant to demonstrate that he understood. And she could tell from the way he was leaning against her shoulder, staring at the pad of paper that he was absolutely absorbed in what she was explaining to him.

"Then there's the next group - the quants," she went on. "These guys are like propeller heads - they just build computer models that take into account numbers that are known. They don't believe in trying to predict anything. They say their way works better because they only deal with facts. But..."

She drew another zigzagging line across the chart that didn't coincide with the first line and added, "That way doesn't work consistently either."

Michael continued to nod his head. He was a fundamentalist for sure but he was aware that quantitative analysts had quite a following on the market.

"And then there's the third group - the technical analysts. These guys are weird ducks - almost cult-like. But they believe that the most accurate predictor of a stock's future price is what it has done in the past. They spend all day reading historic price charts looking for head and shoulders patterns, resistance, break outs, you name it. They call them 'lines of happiness.'"

She drew a third jagged line that did not coincide with the other two.

"But, same problem," she said. "Sometimes it works and sometimes it doesn't."

Michael continued to nod his head. She did know a thing or two about the markets. He thought 'head and shoulders' was a shampoo.

"So, Michael, the problem is, which discipline does an investor follow and when? That's always been the issue. But what if there was a way to know? What if you could shift gears between fundamental, quant and technical at just the right time?"

As she spoke, she circled the highest most points of each of the three lines. Michael nodded his head emphatically now. Yes indeed, if someone could figure out how to do that, they'd make a fortune.

"Michael," she said, cupping his chin in her hand and turning his head to face her. "I've figured it out. I have that way."

Michael's studies were extensive. For Jennifer to think that she could pull out a pad of paper and draw a few crooked lines on it in order to demonstrate how they could 'beat the market' was ridiculous and almost offensive. After all, she was speaking to someone who was highly trained in the intricacies of the Efficient Market Hypothesis, which statistically proved that what she was proposing she could do was impossible. But that fact alone made him wonder. She was either underestimating his many hours of training - that wouldn't be a surprise, most people did - or overestimating her own capabilities. The possibility that she truly believed in what she had just articulated was more unsettling. It would be very difficult to explain EMH to someone who'd never heard of it. But he couldn't flatly dismiss her plan either. She was, after all, just trying to help and the least he could do was to pretend to go along with it.

But had this really been what she'd spent all that time working on while he was trying to find work? How do you nicely tell a person - especially someone you deeply love - they had completely wasted their time? Still pretending to listen to her ramble on, he came up with a good deflection, one that was virtually unarguable and would avoid getting into an academic debate.

"This all sounds very interesting, Jen," he said when she paused to take a breath, "but I think there have been quite a few people who have tried to come up with the magic formula and it has probably worked better for some than others. Whatever, let's say that your plan works. We will be rich; you're right about that. But I see a problem, and it's a big one. People will be interested to hear your story but the next two questions will be 'How long have you been managing money' and 'how much in the way of assets do you presently have?' When the answers are 'just started' and 'zero', we're not going to be in any better shape than if I just kept pounding the pavement. You said it yourself. Without any assets, we're sunk."

Michael had watched as Ivan, Harry and even his father flatly rejected the concept that the best way to invest was by enlisting a process that was both academically legitimate and scientifically back-tested. They probably thought of themselves as legendary sea captains who could sail the ocean of managed money without so much as a compass. Michael had long since promised himself that he would never stoop to such nonsense.

Jennifer was quiet for a moment. He didn't believe in her methodology. That was both clear and unsurprising. It was interesting, though, that he apparently wasn't going to take her to task on it. She'd have been ready for that - hell, she was ready for anything. She knew what she was saying was bullshit, but that was of little consequence. The pitch, whether he bought into it or not, was meant for their future, unsophisticated clients who would want to believe that it worked. Still, she had to maintain the appearance that she, at least, believed that her 'management style' was both legitimate and effective. The time would come to discuss that in more detail. By raising the issue that they had no money to manage, Michael had actually moved the discussion along. Slowly and systematically, she had to pull him over the line.

"You're a smart guy!" she exclaimed. "In about two seconds, you've exposed the Achilles heel of my plan. My investment management technique does work but it must be done using a large sum of money. There is quite a bit of trading required in order to shift disciplines and with a small amount of money the excess returns get eaten up by transaction costs."

Michael was amazed to hear her talk the talk. Was it possible that he had underestimated her? But how could she possibly be this experienced? And if she was, there must be a lot about her past that she hadn't told him. But he knew from experience that to press her too hard about that 'past' would be to invite a lot of anger.

"All right," he said. "Let's presume your new technique actually works. For the record, there'd be more than one academic that said it wasn't possible. Having said that, how much is this 'large sum of money' you're talking about?"

Jennifer considered that there would be a number in Michael's head that would seem daunting but not impossible to accumulate. She knew that the book of business that had been transferred to him from his father was about $40 million. Not record setting by any standards but pretty large for such a small branch. Of course, the right answer was 'as much as we can get.'

"We need to get about $100 million, minimum."

Michael didn't mean to burst out laughing but in his mind he was expecting something closer to $1 million.

"What? Oh my God, Jen that is really, really funny. You're saying that all we need is someone to drop $100 million bucks in our lap and all our problems will be solved. I don't know why I didn't think of that. Thank you so much."

From the way she was biting her lower lip, he knew he had pissed her off but, Jesus, come on. His grin started to fade as she looked up and down his face as if something needed to be brushed away.

"Actually, Michael, that's the easy part," Jennifer said patiently. "Here, let me show you. How much money have you got in your wallet?"

Michael reached into his back pocket, quite eager now to continue along with the game - for a while anyway.

"Uh, let's see. I've got fifty bucks - two twenties and two fives."

She reached out her hand, her eyes having narrowed.

"I'm your new investment manager. What kind of return do you think would be good in this market?"

"Christ, any kind of return would be good these days," he said wearily. "But, OK, I'll play along. Ten percent. I want a ten percent return."

"Oh, I can do better than that, much better," she told him smiling.

Taking the two five dollar bills, and handing them back to him, she said, "I just earned you 20%. Here's your cash distribution."

Had the stress of all this uncertainty about their financial future sent her over the edge, Michael found himself wondering?

"No you didn't," he explained. "You just gave me some of my own money back. You didn't earn anything."

Her smile broadened even further.

"Yes, but Michael, what if you didn't know that? What if you thought I'd actually earned it?"

He looked at her, the lines across his forehead bulging as the realization of what she was proposing sank in like spring snow melting into the warming grasses. He had hoped that Jennifer was just confused but now he was starting to fear the worst.

"Well, Jen, you can't do that," he protested. "That would be not telling the truth. It's at least unethical and at worst illegal."

As he threw the two bills down on the table, she leaned closer to him.

"Michael," she said in a low voice, "do you remember the other day when I talked about what money really was? I said that everything having to do with money is based on trust and perceptions, that it was all like a game, that in itself it has no value."

It came to Michael quite suddenly, with a force that took his breath away, that maybe - just maybe - she was right.

"Are you saying that, since money in itself, has no value, it would be OK to lie to people?"

As soon as the word 'lie' passed his lips, he wanted to grab it with both hands and stuff it back in his mouth. Jennifer took full advantage. She had learned some time ago how to flare her nostrils on command.

"Michael, unless I am missing something, you just called me a liar," she said, speaking very slowly. "Please tell me I'm wrong because if the answer is yes, it's been nice knowing you."

He rubbed his eyes. How could someone not tell the truth and be anything other than a liar?

"No, Jen, not at all. But look. If you tell someone that you did something that you didn't really do, that's not honest, is it?"

She could see the beads of sweat forming on his forehead and was reassured that their conversation was proceeding according to plan.

"OK, then let's try this," she suggested. "Supposing there was another person that joined our little group and he came in with $50 too. Suppose I took the $10 from him and gave it to you. Now I would not be giving you your own money back. Are you happier with that?"

Michael's hands were shaking now that he could see where she was going.

"Jen, I uh think I understand what you are getting at now," he said hoarsely. "There is a name for this type of thing. It's called Ponzi. Do you know what I'm talking about?"

"I certainly do, darling," she told him, "The great Charles Ponzi, one of the best investors of all time."

"Jennifer, if I am not mistaken, he was convicted of fraud."

This was a hurdle that she knew she had to cross. It would, of course, be easier to operate without him, but she'd like to have him on board because between the two of them they could probably raise more money faster. But she knew, if she couldn't close the deal here and now, she'd go somewhere else. There were a good many other suckers out there. But she'd worked for this and the moment was at hand. She had to take what he had given her and what she knew about him and make him see things as if they were to his advantage. Of course, this was the requirement for all Ponzi schemes, and she was giving him the honor of being her first official victim!

"Michael, let me get a few things straight with you," she said. "You've just scoffed at my having said that money is just a matter of perception. And you make it sound like what I am proposing is some sort of crime. Well, if it is, then every public company that offers a dividend re-investment option is breaking the law too. Think about what they do. They say, rather than you receiving an actual cash dividend payment, they'll give you the option to reinvest in more common shares at a discount. These things called DRIPs are hugely popular with old people - who don't know what they are doing. So, what happens? The shareholder that should have received a cash payment gets what? More paper! Then, if the company goes tits up what are the poor shareholders left with? How do worthless paper and no cash sound? So, if you think what I am proposing is somehow criminal, explain to me why DRIPs aren't equally as offensive and liable to prosecution."

Michael was not going to be swayed. He didn't understand why this woman he thought he knew was going down a path he couldn't imagine.

"It's not the same... at all," he told her. "Dividends come from profits that a company actually earns. You want to use other people's money..."

"Michael, what does a frigging bank do? They take other people's money and then lend it to someone else. And they earn their profit by charging the guy who borrowed it more in interest than they pay the guy who gave it to them. But it's not their money! People use other people's money in business all the time."

Michael had to admit to himself that what she was saying might be worth thinking about.

"All I am talking about, if you would give me the chance, is to use people's money for a while, until we get up to $100 million in assets. Then I can start using my system, which, by the way, will do better than 20%, that's for sure. So, think of this as a short-term loan to help us get started. That's all."

He wasn't sure when the idea came to him but he breathed a sigh of relief. He wasn't going to win this debate as long as he used her terminology. It felt a bit awkward to use his father as an excuse after all he had said about him but it would be a line of reasoning that she couldn't touch. Truth was, he was running out of intellectual ammunition.

"Jennifer, let's say I agree with everything you've said so far," he parried. "The problem is that the vast majority of people out there wouldn't see what you've described as anything other than a Ponzi scheme. At worst, we'd both go to jail. At best, we would both be disgraced. Maybe you're OK with that risk but I'm not. Think of what it would do to my father. He and I may not agree on how to succeed in the brokerage business and, I suppose, many other things but one thing is for sure. We both know that this business of managing other people's money is based on integrity. Like I said, Dad and I may not always see eye to eye but if there is one thing I've been able to rely on my entire life, it's that my father is an honest man - sometimes brutally so - in his work relationships, friendships everything. His word was and always will be his bond. Hell, I doubt he even cheats at golf. I've already embarrassed him enough by getting fired. But if people knew that I was part of some unethical scheme that I went into because finding a job was too hard, my disgrace would ruin his reputation forever. I may not always like the man, but he *is* my father and I love him. I won't do that to him for anyone, even you."

Michael was breathing hard and the perspiration had soaked through the back of his shirt. He didn't want it to come down to something like this with Jennifer, not ever and he worried with that last line of his, she might walk away and never see him again. When he finally found the courage to look into her eyes, he was surprised to see that she was smiling.

"So you think you've got this all figured out, that life is fair and good people are honest, do you?" she said. "Dear old dad stands like a statue in the center of town with the inscription, 'Here goes an honest man.' Is that it Michael? Have I got that right?"

Michael wasn't sure where she was going with this, but it didn't matter because, apparently, it was a rhetorical question.

"OK, look," she went on, getting up. "I'm going to go out now to get some more supplies to prepare my marketing package. While I'm gone, do me a favor, will you? Call your dad and say this to him. Say that you and I were talking, and I told you that you needed to call him to learn the truth about your mother, once and for all. Tell him I said that if he didn't tell you, I would. Then, I'll come back and see if you're looking at the world any differently."

"Jen, wait!" he cried. "What are you talking about? What's my mother got to do with all this?"

She turned and walked briskly towards the door. This fish was all but in the boat.

"Just call him, Michael," she said. "That's all. Just call."

## Chapter 26

Senior picked up the phone on the first ring, almost as if he'd been expecting the call and said, "Franklin here."

"Yeah, hi Dad, it's Michael. I, uh, have a question I need to ask you."

As soon as Jennifer had left the house, leaving her parting shot ringing behind her, Michael had decided that he might as well call his father and be done with it. If she knew something about his mother that he didn't know, the playing field between them was far from as level as he wanted it to be. He just came right out with it.

"She said that, did she?" his father said reflectively…"that you needed to learn the truth - about your mother?"

He was stalling. It wasn't like him to ever refrain from expressing his opinion.

"Well, that's unfortunate," he went on. "Not the question per se - oh, what the hell, I've been meaning to have this conversation with you for quite a while. I guess there's no time like the present."

"Dad!" Michael said impatiently, "will you get on with it? What is this big frigging secret about my mother that everyone seems to know but me?"

As he spoke, Michael realized he had never said anything that aggressive to his father before. He clenched his fists waiting for the violent response. It didn't come.

"All right then, son, about your mother...Perhaps she wasn't exactly the sort of person I allowed you to think of her as being. I've never told you the true story, but she left me when you were three years old. Did you know that son? She left me!"

Michael wanted to say that, given the fact that his father had been an inconsiderate egomaniac for as long as he could remember, he was amazed that she hadn't gone sooner. Be careful dad, this is my mother you are talking about now.

"Dad, whatever your big secret is about Mom, you don't need to drag her down to your level," he said.

He could imagine his father's face tightening and waited for the eruption that, once again, didn't come.

"Drag her down to my level... right. Michael, with all due respect, there are some things you need to know. Your mother made me swear never to tell you - told me that some things are just better left unsaid - but that has all changed now, hasn't it? I'm not going to fight with you. I've thought about our relationship a lot over the years. We both know I haven't been the best dad in the world. I guess I thought my job was to provide and then the fathering part would come later. But it never did, did it? All these years I just hoped that you could learn to be more like me. But I guess blood's thicker than water."

Whose blood? Michael wanted to say, but the words stuck in his throat. What did that mean?

"Your mother left me and all these years you've assumed it was because I'm a bad man," his father went on, "a man who spent too much time at work, with my clients, and at the golf course. I guess that's true, too, but it isn't why your mother left. At least it's not the whole story."

Michael had never heard his father's voice shake before.

"OK, Dad, it's OK. Just tell me your story."

"While I was out at a fundraiser in San Francisco, your mother was up here being busy herself, with some guy. I don't know his name. The thing is, she managed to get herself knocked up. I remember being so excited. Our first child! I was stupid. If I'd done the math, I could have figured it out. She's Catholic; did you know that? She doesn't believe in abortion, but why couldn't she have just told me the truth? We could have put you up for adoption."

There was a long pause during which Michael's heart seemed to stop. What was this man telling him? That he was not his father?

"After you were born, there were too many things that didn't make sense," his dad went on, "but I just ignored them. My whole family and hers had blonde hair - yours is black. Everyone had some shade of green eyes, and yours are blue. You're left-handed, even though no one else on either side is. Finally, much later, I guess her conscience got to her. Ha, that's a joke. She told me around your second birthday. You were my pride and joy and, I don't know, I guess when I found out, something snapped. We managed to stay together for a year after that but it wasn't a marriage any more. We didn't even talk. One day, I woke up and she'd gone, leaving me some bullshit note about how this was for the best. You can't imagine how hard that was. I remember going into your bedroom. You were lying there, sleeping so peacefully. But I made up my mind. It wasn't your fault. I vowed that I would do the best I could, even though I knew that wasn't going to be good enough."

Suddenly Michael was overwhelmed with a great sense of grief. Whether it was for him or his father or for the woman who had been capable of leaving a little boy behind, he could not tell.

"Your mother didn't just leave me; she left you, too, because she knew that someday you would learn the truth," the older man went on. "She didn't want to have to face you. I've been telling you that I hardly ever hear from her. That's not true either.

She calls me every year, on your birthday, for an update. She uses some sort of unlisted number so I could never track her down even if I wanted to. But Michael, you need to understand something."

He paused and a moment passed during which neither of them seemed to breathe.

"I'm not your real father, and I have no idea who is."

When Jennifer returned from her errands, she found Michael still sitting by the telephone, his face expressionless. He did not look up when she bent to stroke his hair and ask if he was okay. She had thought that when Michael learned the truth, it would be the final step towards eliminating his reservations towards her plan. But now, searching his face like a road map, looking for a hint of the package of emotions that were set to erupt, she found nothing; no anger, no trace of fear or bewilderment, just a blank sheet of paper.

"How did you know?" Michael whispered to her. Jennifer had been prepared for an onslaught, a ferocious attack over keeping something so close and personal from him. Her defense would have been that his father had made her swear on a stack of bibles - not that she'd ever seen the inside of a church - and that Michael knew what a powerful, forceful man he was. But there was none of that.

"I, well, I called him at his home and just asked him," she said. "I thought maybe you were adopted - a lot of parents don't tell their children that. I must have caught him by surprise because he told me everything. It wasn't such a strange thing for me to do. After all, you and he look nothing alike; you have different hair, eyes, nose, even your ears. The first time I met him I just kept comparing you two. I don't know Michael. That's just my way. I want to know about people that are close to me and I'm not afraid to ask. I guess it's some sort of defense mechanism."

When Michael did not respond, she added

"Do you want to talk about it? Are you all right?"

He sat up straighter and ran his hand across his forehead.

"What's there to talk about, Jen? I feel like my insides have been stolen from me and I'm just learning about it. First, I do a terrible job at a business I've always wanted to be good at. Did you figure that out, too? I went into it because of dear old dad, wanting me to carry the banner of his success forward. How could I say no to that? How could I disappoint the man I've always looked up to, when he entrusted me with the one thing that defined his entire life? And, I didn't get it at the time, but I do now. I was in a terribly vulnerable position. You're right, Jen. In that business it's only about the money - always. So, of course I got fired. Harry Lugarno should have done it a long time ago but he didn't, out of respect for my dad. I wonder if he knows the truth."

Jennifer had moved over to the table and was rubbing Michael's shoulder.

"I don't think so, honey. I'm pretty sure I was the only one."

Michael nodded his head again.

"Yeah, I've got to hand it to you, you're good."

Jennifer shrugged modestly.

"I'm learning Jen, about people and how brutal they can be. Ivan, he's like a shark - smells a little blood in the water and then attacks, my business, my pride, even the woman that I love."

Jennifer started to protest that such a thing wasn't even remotely possible, but Michael raised his hand.

"No, let me finish. You see it's like the very foundations of my life arc being systematically destroyed - one by one - like the ocean where the waves just keep crashing against the rocks. They eventually get pulverized."

Jennifer remained quiet.

"Today I find out that my very own father, a man whose level of success I dreamed so many times of just coming close to, and thus finally earning his respect, has been lying to me my entire life. I wanted to be like him Jen. Now, I find out that he is nothing more than a caretaker. I have a real father out there somewhere, a man I'll probably never even meet."

As Michael spoke, he had been staring out the window, but now he turned to face her.

"And then you came along, the most beautiful, gracious, inspiring woman I've ever met. I remember thinking that first time in the YMCA that I was beyond lucky that you even spoke to me. I never thought that there would be any question about your ethics. But Jen, your investment scheme won't work and the way you want to raise money is illegal. I know that."

He sat back and stretched his shoulder blades.

"So, here I am Jen. In the space of a few short months, I've lost everything I believed in, wanted or trusted. I might as well be dead. I think I feel that way, anyway."

She considered him. He was at the lowest point she'd ever seen, which meant that he had hit his maximum state of vulnerability and susceptibility. But that was not, in itself, enough. It was important that he endorse her plan, to actually believe that it was the right path for them to travel on.

"I think you're right, Michael," she said. "What's the expression? Life's a bitch and then you die."

"Yeah, I suppose that's right, isn't it?" His voice, she noted, was without inflection.

Jennifer moved closer to him. All her planning and preparation had now come to an unexpected but massively opportunistic crossroad. It was time, as they said at the poker table, to go all in.

"Michael, I think it's time you learned the true story about that past that I never want to discuss, you know, my escape from New York. Hopefully, after you do, you'll have a better understanding of where I am coming from."

He waved his hand in capitulation.

"Sure, whatever," Michael said. "I don't really have anything to lose, do I?"

"But it's good news," she told him, "by the end of the story anyway. I've told you that I left New York under difficult circumstances but I never explained to you what those were. I was engaged, Michael, to a man I thought I loved - an analyst named David Heart. I thought he loved me too. But, as it turns out, he was just a calculating predator who turned out to be jealous of my expertise when it came to finances. I was just sitting at my desk one day - my job was institutional equity sales - when the phone rings and some guy I'd never heard of called Alexei Baikov calls me and said he wants to buy $5 million worth of his company's stock. I didn't think anything of it at the time. Hey, a trade is a trade and that was going to be a nice commission for sure. So I did the trade. That's my job, right? The next thing I know this Alexei guy is indicted for insider trading and David, the man I loved, is covering his backside and saying I had something to do with it. Nice, huh? I guess I dodged a bullet with him, anyway. We were engaged! You really learn about a person when things turn for the worse. Anyway, in the end, the Baikov guy gets busted, and David Heart gets a promotion! Guess what happens to me? I get fired."

Michael stared at her, clearly astonished by this unexpected revelation.

"But Jen, why didn't you call the police on this David guy?" he demanded.

"It was like he created all this evidence against me. Before I knew anything the police were on his side. I had no choice. I just had to leave. Remember the adage: he who fights and runs away lives to fight another day. Well, that's exactly what I did."

Suddenly, an uncomfortable stream of thoughts went flashing through Michael's mind like a shallow river bounding off flat rocks. He had been completely, totally focused on his own problems - at the same time that he had been telling himself that he was working for the two of them. Here was a woman whose life had been deliberately, coldly desiccated and all he could think about was his own ego and his jealousy of his own father's success. He had told her, and he had believed it, that he loved her and now he realized he had been a fraud. True love meant caring more about the problems of your partner than your own.

"Jen, I uh, oh my God I don't know what to say. I didn't... I mean I can't believe."

She put a finger to his lips.

"Hush Michael, you don't need to say anything. My past is my past. I've been waiting for the right time to tell you and I guess this was it."

"But Jen, I never would have known. You're so strong, so confident. Here I am feeling all sorry for myself and, my God, look at what you've had to go through. I feel... guilty."

"Michael, that's my point, don't you see?" she told him. "We all have to go through tough times in this life - no one is exempt. The thing that separates us is what we learn from adversity."

Sandy Allen had chosen her new name - Jennifer - from a billboard as she traveled on Amtrak from New York towards Seattle and her new life. She wanted to give Michael enough of her story so that if it ever came up or, God forbid he ever researched her past, it was close enough to the truth. Of course, the real story was that she had been convicted of insider trading along with the Russian who was working in the United States illegally and subsequently deported. The Feds hadn't been as clever as Sandy. In exchange for her testimony that put Baikov away for good, she was barred from employment in the securities industry for life, narrowly avoiding serving jail time. As for David Heart, he was justifiably promoted for blowing the whistle on the entire scheme.

That had been a close call, for sure. But here she was, on her feet again and poised for her next adventure. This time she wasn't going to work for anyone but herself. She wondered if Michael had ever wondered why she didn't find a job when the fact was that for her to give a perspective employer her social security number would mean opening up a whole can of worms.

"Jennifer, you've faced way tougher things than I have and look at you," Michael marveled. "You've come out on top!"

"Not yet," she told him. "But I just want to be certain that, before we go any further, you understand that the world is unfair and that it doesn't owe you or me a thing. Even if it did, it wouldn't honor the debt. So, you have to be a survivor, Michael - we both do. Think about it. If you and I work together - just the two of us - we'll never have to answer to anyone. We can't be fired, no one can stab us in the back or try to steal our business and we will be very, very successful. I know a lot about the markets, far more than I've let on. My whole job was working with these institutional investors managing billions of dollars. I've watched you run your father's book of business, and I can tell you that there is nothing wrong with your approach - as far as it goes. But here's the thing. If you combine your work ethic and intuition with what I have learned about the 'real' stock market, we will be an unstoppable force. I am as sure of that as anything I've ever been in my life. And yes, we have to tell a little white lie in order to get started but that's all it is. Is there anyone who has to go to the bank to try to get a loan to start a new business that hasn't stretched their projections a bit? I am as uncomfortable with it as you but it's a necessary evil. Once we're up and running, everything will be on the up and up. And I can tell you for 100% sure that my investment model works. I know you think it doesn't but just you wait and see."

She could tell just by looking at him now that he had been completely won over. At his lowest point ever in his life, God had sent an angel.

"So, what do you say, partner?" she said, extending her hand. "Do we have a deal?"

The smile on Michael's face exploded and his eyes seemed to light up the room as he shook hands.

"You're one hell of a negotiator there, Miss Jennifer!" he exclaimed. "Yes, we have a deal. Hey, what are you doing?"

"I'm taking my clothes off, Michael, and I suggest you do the same," she said, grinning. "And hurry. All this negotiating has made me incredibly horny. First order of business is we consummate this new venture properly."

## Chapter 27

"All right, Jen, how do we do this?"

It was the following morning and Michael was in pajamas sitting at the kitchen table, his hair looking as though it had been arranged with salad forks. Bacon was sizzling on the stove and he had just poured himself a cup of steaming hot coffee. Yesterday's love-making had continued for the rest of the afternoon and evening, the locale moving from the kitchen, to the couch to the bedroom and even, at one point, the shower. Now, understandably, they were both very hungry.

"I hope you're asking me about our new business venture," Jen said, laughing, "because I want to talk about real business, not monkey business, even though you're really good at that." She carried the plates of scrambled eggs with cheese, bacon, toast and some sliced fruit to the table. The smell filled the room.

"Oh, my God, does that look good!" Michael exclaimed, grabbing a strip of bacon. "I am starving!"

Jennifer was a contented woman in more ways than one. In less than twenty-four hours, an expected showdown with unpredictable results had turned into a fait accompli. Michael seemed fully onboard and ready to go, which was very important because, she suspected, the implementation of their plan would concern him. There were a few more hurdles to jump in this marathon.

Jennifer moved her plate to one side and started to speak. The time was now and she could eat later.

"Listen," she said. "We're about to join the fraternity of a great global tradition. I'm going to start by explaining the theory of raising our necessary start-up money, and then we'll get into specifics."

Michael seemed eager, ready to learn and quite content to munch bacon and listen.

"What you need to know about is something called the 'theory of the mind.' The good news for us is that there are lots of gullible people out there. They tend to believe in things that, on the surface appear too good to be true, because they *want* to. As it turns out, there are widely recognized personalities that make the kind of people we're after more likely to let us manage their money. There are four parts to gullibility, and the astute person, if they only watch and listen, can easily identify them. You have to recognize your environment. You have to assess the personality of the person. And by asking a few simple questions, you have to find out how much the target knows. Oh, yes, and you have to always consider the state of mind of your prospective victim. A meeting with a successful type-A businessman, dressed in a suit, in the popular corporate luncheonette with no alcohol requires an entirely different approach than a business encounter with a single woman, who is both tipsy and obviously attracted to you, and couldn't spell stock market if her life depended on it. As a bonus, if the target has some deep-seated burning desire that consumes their day-to-day thoughts, it can make the difference between success and failure. So, the idea is that we identify these people and prospect them. We're going to tell them what they want to hear. If someone says they want a 10% return, we'll say we can do 15%. If they say they don't want to pay any taxes, we'll say 'no problem. All of our accounts are registered offshore in tax-free countries. 'You see what I mean?"

Michael was listening carefully. The use of the words 'target' and 'victim' were making him uneasy. Now it was his turn to push his plate away.

"Jennifer, I just want to remind you. What you are talking about is entirely against the law."

She ignored the comment.

"I know it sounds a bit crass," she admitted, "but, to be successful at this, we have to follow a process, which, by the way, has been proven effective over many years. It's like fishing. First, we have to know exactly the type of fish we are after. Then we need to know the perfect lure. And finally we have to go catch it. These fish aren't going to come on board by themselves. Our first few clients will be the key to the start up. After we get the core group enlisted, word of mouth will take over and the business will come to us. We won't need to do any prospecting. You just wait and see. Oh, and by the way Michael, at some point, word of our success is going to get back to your former office. In fact, we are going to go after that shithead Ivan directly. By the time we are done, we will have *all* of your dad's accounts back. But when you're contacted by anyone in the business who knows you were fired, you tell them that being fired couldn't have happened at a better time because you were in the process of starting up your own money management firm and your severance package gave you the necessary capital to launch. You and I have been working for months getting ready and I came from Wall Street with the investment management formula."

Michael looked as though he couldn't believe what he was hearing.

"Do you really believe we could do that to Ivan?" he asked her. "Really?"

"Trust me," she told him, taking some files off the windowsill. "By the time we're done with your friend Ivan, he'll be on his hands and knees begging to join us. And the answer will be 'Fuck off.'"

Michael nodded his head and sighed. The dream of revenge, as pleasing as it was, was interrupted, again, by a far deeper feeling. He kept trying to remind himself that this was all just a temporary measure to get their business up and running. No one would get hurt. But he was losing the argument with himself.

"Jennifer, you know, isn't there another way to do this?" he said now. "I mean this whole 'targeting' thing is deliberately taking advantage of people. I thought we were just going to tell people about our new company - give them a brochure or something like that - and they'd give us their money. What you're talking about goes way beyond that. It's all based on lying - telling them what they want to hear. Why can't we just tell the truth; you have a new investment management technique that works really well but we need startup capital?"

Jennifer slapped her hands on the table.

"Michael... you said you were on board. Don't get cold feet on me now. If you don't like what I've told you so far, just wait until I tell you about our first target."

Michael frowned. Jennifer had sounded good yesterday, but now, when he stripped away the thin veneer of her words, it put a different perspective on things. And, love or not, he wasn't going to let this woman have him completely turn his back on everything he believed in.

"Look Jen, don't get me wrong. I really appreciate everything you're trying to do for us. I am excited as I can be about our new money management business. But, when people hear your story, about how you've perfected your technique to pick stocks, the money will come in and you can earn the returns you say you can. That way we don't have to lie. I mean, what's the hurry? It might take a little more time going about this the right way but then at least we won't be completely misrepresenting the truth."

"You want to talk about lying?" She spat out the words. "You're going back on your promise. We have a deal, remember?"

"But what you want to do isn't just some white lie. It is unethical and illegal. A person's integrity may not mean that much to you but it does to me."

He was being very careful not to say that he was questioning her ethics and integrity even though he knew he was.

"I've made up my mind," he told her with as much defiance as he could muster. "I'm not going to go through with this Ponzi idea. It is against the law and I don't want to go to jail."

Michael had never seen the look on Jen's face before. And she was actually shaking with what appeared to be nearly uncontrollable rage.

"All right then, Junior" she said, "have it your way. But I have to tell you that I'm feeling a bit used. We had a deal last night, a deal that we shook on. You're worried about integrity? Why don't you go look in the mirror? You're worried about using people? You didn't seem to have any problem using me all over the house last night. Maybe your dad is right about you. You get close to being successful but just when you're right at that point to put you over the line, you can't pull the trigger."

She started to organize the papers back into the file folder.

"It's *you* that lacks integrity. It's you that uses people. And it's you that doesn't have the balls to win."

File in hand, she rose from the table.

"That's three strikes Michael, and where I come from it's three strikes and you're out."

When she disappeared into the bedroom and slammed the door, Michael put his head in his hands and stared despairingly at the cold eggs on his plate. It was, he thought, probably better to let her cool off so that they could reach some sort of middle ground together. He loved this woman and he believed with all of his heart that she loved him back. Right now he'd clean up here and then he'd go to the bedroom and see how she was doing. She might even have gone back to bed.

The warmth from the dishwater felt soothing on his hands. He imagined him and Jen, in their own house with a dog and a back yard, their business flourishing. Their dream was so close. All they were disagreeing on was one minor point. She wanted to move fast which unfortunately required telling a lie, the biggest he would ever tell in his life. Her way would mean a life filled with self-doubt and shame. If they just took more time, everything could be on the up and up. Why couldn't she see that?

The dishes were done and he was wiping his hands on a towel as he turned to see Jennifer standing in the kitchen doorway, dressed with a carry-on suitcase in hand.

"Jen, what are you..."

"I don't know what you think of me," she interrupted him, "and I really don't understand the fact that, when every single other person in your life has lied to you, cheated you and turned their back, you won't allow the one person who believes in you and has the power to change your life, to do so. I don't know if you realize that I'm serious when I say I am. If you were listening, you'll remember that I told you that I am going through with this, with you or without you. It's pretty clear now that you made that decision for me - it will be without you. I can't have you looking over my shoulder, so I have to leave Seattle and find another place to live. It would have been nice, me and you, but I guess that's not going to be."

She started to walk towards the front door. She had no intention of leaving, at least not without giving it another try. Michael's capitulation had all been going too smoothly anyway. Now, at least, she knew that he had the sort of integrity that she would be wise to keep her eye on - if, in fact, he gave in now.

"I'll come back to get the rest of my things later," she added.

Michael exploded out of the kitchen, grabbing the small suitcase out of her hand.

"What! Jen! NO! Wait. You can't."

The tears started to stream from his eyes and the sentences that followed were short, disrupted, and incoherent. It was pitiful, really, but necessary. She'd made enough of an investment in time not to give up on him yet. She allowed him to lead her to the couch with only a minimum of resistance.

"Look Michael," she said wearily "you've made it clear. You've got your point of view and I've got mine, and neither one of us is going to change. That's fine, that's the way it goes."

Through his sobs, Jennifer could barely make out what he was trying to say.

"I... can't... lose... you're... all I've got...*please*... don't."

"This is a waste of time," she told him briskly. "Just suck it up."

She grabbed the tissue box from the side table and handed it to him. The frequency of his convulsions declined as he blew his nose and wiped his eyes. Jen waited before delivering the final, killing blow.

"Do you have something to say to me Michael? I don't want some long song and dance. Tell me right now, and this will absolutely be the last time we ever have this conversation. Do you understand? And I am not kidding."

She sounded like a judge asking a jury for their final verdict.

"Are you in or not?"

"In," he said. She could scarcely hear the word and so she made him repeat it.

Finally.

She was in the driver's seat now.

## Chapter 28

The terrible truth was he wasn't strong enough to fight her.

They didn't speak about it again that day. Jen went to another room after Michael asked her if he could sleep on her ultimatum, and she reluctantly agreed, having decided that Michael's recent behavior had actually increased his value to her plan. Yes, she could go to another town and start over but, after his total breakdown, he would be a more than willing accomplice. There were some activities ahead that the weak of heart would find troubling.

At the kitchen table the next morning, coffee in hand, he agreed, but only after making her reiterate her promise that the deception would be short-lived and that, as soon as they built their assets to the minimum required size, they would launch her investment computer program and start running a solid, profitable - and ethical business. No one would be the wiser about the methods used to reach 'launch size', and, in fact, investors would be more than happy with their returns. The concept that the faster they raised the money the shorter the time they'd be operating a Ponzi scheme became his sole focus. He embraced it completely and professed himself eager to learn as fast as he could.

"All right Jen, let's get this over with," he said, doing his best to smile as Jen reached into her folder and pulled out a page torn from the local newspaper.

"We've lost a day so that doesn't give us much time to train you but that will have to work," she said. "The reception is in two days and you need to attend."

Michael was taken aback when he saw "Obituaries" at the top of the page, but he didn't say anything. She was the leader now for better or for worse.

"Remember when I told you that there were recognizable personalities that were more likely to be gullible?" Jen asked him. "Well, think of it as though we're prospecting Snow White's seven dwarfs. The first one might well be called 'Bashful' but you'll need to go find out."

In the middle of the page, one of the notices had been circled using a red marker. Michael read it slowly as the realization of what Jennifer might be contemplating sunk in. After he finished, he looked up, frowning.

"You've got to be kidding," he said. "Do we really need to sink this low?"

"Come on, Michael," she said impatiently. "What did you see? What did you learn?"

Michael looked down into his now cold coffee but took a sip anyway.

"I see a terrible tragedy - a poor young widow - they probably hadn't even been married very long - loses her husband in a terrible car accident and...Look, you can't be thinking of doing something like this, can you?"

Jennifer continued.

"You didn't read it carefully enough. What I see is a young woman who has likely inherited a lot of money. Look at the dead husband - he was a rising investment banking superstar. Guys like that make lots of coin and, more importantly, probably signed up for the greatest corporate life insurance amount available.

The cost would have meant nothing to him so why not go for the max? His widow could know a lot about running her own money but given what the guy did for a living I'd bet not. Relationships where both people are money smart don't do so well. So, here she is, wealthy and suddenly without anyone to look after her richness. Since she doesn't know, she'll be shy about bringing it up - afraid she's going to make a mistake. She'll be polite to a fault when you first speak with her because it would appear rude to seem untrustworthy. But she will be worried - very worried about her future... and that's where you come in."

Michael scratched his head and pushed his chair back from the table.

"Wow, you're serious about this, aren't you? I'm supposed to walk up to a perfect stranger and start chatting. When and where would you suggest I do that?"

"Well, that should be pretty obvious," she told him. "The widow wanted a memorial reception, which had to be delayed for some reason. But, according to the paper, it is coming up soon at the Puget Golf and Country Club. That's a very big venue because there will be a ton of people; investment bankers come out in droves when one of their own goes down. They like to take inventory about who didn't make it so they can badmouth him or her behind their back later. But not everyone knows everyone, so you'll be able to blend in without being noticed. Ever see the movie *Wedding Crashers*? You'll be a memorial crasher."

Michael's stomach was starting to make noises but he didn't think it was because of something he ate.

"Oh, I get it. I'm going to walk up to a poor widow at her greatest time of sorrow and say 'Hey there, are you rich now?'"

Jennifer looked up from her papers and frowned.

"Michael, fuck off. This feels like a good one and you have a lot to practice before you go in. Now pay attention. You're going to remain in the background until most of the people there have gone through the receiving line. Look at her, but you almost want her eyes to find yours. What you need to do very early on, once you start talking to her, is to assess her personality. If it turns out that she isn't what I thought she would be, then you hightail it out of there. But here are the clues you'll be looking for to confirm that we have a live one. It's a good sign if she seems embarrassed by her lack of knowledge about money. If she appears submissive at all, that's even better because she's likely a dependent type that needs to be taken care of. She'll cover up her lack of understanding by saying she needs to find someone she can give her full trust to. Also, make sure you check whether there is a friend or relative in the background that could step in. Given her age, that might be less likely. Eventually, what you are going to do is to satisfy her fear of uncertainty by presenting her with an overly simplistic explanation."

Michael's enthusiasm was quickly waning.

"Are we really going to take a poor, defenseless widow's money? Are you serious?"

"Yes Michael I'm dead serious," she said, all business now and clearly in no mood to quibble. "And by the way we aren't taking her money, we are borrowing it. I told you, you have to look at things from the target's point of view. You will likely be lifting a huge weight off of this woman's shoulders, an angel sent to help her at her time of greatest need. You will be, in every sense of the word, helping her. And, by the way, if you really think that I have the capacity to be so cruel, then why do you keep saying you love me?"

Michael didn't respond to that question because it had already occurred to him several times during the past few days, only to tell himself that it was unthinkable. This *was* borrowing. And it was only temporary. He decided to challenge her with a more obvious issue.

"Let's get real, Jennifer," he said. "Do you really believe that this widow, who doesn't know me from a hole in the wall, is going to just say, 'Well, you look like a nice guy. Here, take all my money.'"

Jennifer shook her head in disgust.

"No, Michael, I am teaching you things one step at a time because it is important that you get all this. You won't gain her trust after only one meeting any more than you're likely to get lucky on a first date! This one will likely take a number of approaches but we'll do as many as it takes - until we get her money. But pay attention and let me explain how this works. What you need to do in order to bring in business is put yourself in her shoes. There are a lot of people out there that tend to believe in things that, on the surface appear silly or can't be supported by facts. I mean think about it. People love magicians even though they know what is happening isn't real. That's what we are Michael, magicians. We have to make people believe in us by tailoring each pitch to the unique circumstances of each target. I'll explain more about that to you later. In each case, we will use an explanation that seems to make sense on some level even though under closer scrutiny it wouldn't. In effect, we are going to get each new client to deceive themselves in whatever way they choose."

She leaned back in her chair. Michael was no different than any of the people they were going to scam. His own gullibility was confirmed when he fully accepted her story about coming from New York but not wanting to talk about it. He was infatuated with her and would tell himself whatever lies he needed to. Ultimately, he would come to fully accept that the model she created would work, just as he already believed that taking people's money would be temporary. It was a wonderful example of him using self-deception to avoid questioning her.

Also, in the case of the widow, she didn't reveal to Michael that one of her options was to get the woman to fall in love with him. Even though that might take a good deal of manipulation on her part, it was, she knew, definitely doable. Then the money would flow like butter on a hot sidewalk.

"OK, I'm the widow and you are you," she said. "Let's practice. What is your opening line?"

## Chapter 29

Angela, having never been a widow before, wasn't sure how she was supposed to act.

Once the police had confirmed, using dental records, that it was indeed her husband who had been driving the car that fateful night, she had felt an enormous sense of relief. The accident was all over the newspapers along with a glowing obituary outlining the many corporate and social milestones achieved by the late John Messina, graduate of Princeton University, captain of the football team, head of the United Way campaign for the greater Seattle area, rising investment banking star and beloved husband of Angela Messina.

And wife beater.

Angela didn't bother telling her own parents, especially her father, who had written her off when she decided to marry. She wouldn't give them the pleasure of knowing that she was now single again.

Her greatest challenge was demonstrating the right balance between remorse and resolve. She had to keep reminding herself that the curtain was still up and she, the lone actor, was center-stage. She spent several hours on the Internet before the memorial reception searching for literary tragedies with heroines that faced great loss. While not wanting to over-dramatize things, she did discover one consistent theme; the fictional widow, in spite of the greatest challenges the author could muster, would suffer, rise to her challenge and persevere. It was the expectation of the human condition.

 As Michael walked through the front doors of the Puget Golf and Country Club he was immediately struck by the furnishings, even though he'd seen them before. This was, after all, his dad's club. There were large, overstuffed leather chairs scattered around fine antique tables with ornate lamps. Along one wall was a row of pictures of past club presidents going back to 1892, the year the club was formed. The top floor contained the formal and casual dining areas, the men's lounge for after-golf drinks and round replays, as well as the 'game room' in which non-golfers usually played cards. Downstairs, outside the men's locker room was a similar row of pictures of the top flight club annual golf champions, including several pictures of his father. Michael knew he had to head down to that level, since that's where the large reception room was. But he avoided 'victory row' as it had come to be called. The pictures of his beaming father would be where they always had been.

 Since the club house was high atop a hill overlooking the golf course, the back wall of the reception room, usually used for wedding or business receptions, was all glass with several sliding doors leading out to a patio outlined by a brick wall. When the room was used for celebratory occasions, the ability to venture out onto the patio, with, drink in hand, in order to admire the plush landscape below, was one of its key features. Today, it being a memorial reception, heavy, dark floor-to-ceiling curtains blocked the view.

 As Michael made his way down the stairs, he could hear muffled conversation and even the odd laugh. It made the room sound full, which, as he discovered, it was, primarily of expensively dressed men. Clearly Seattle's branch of Wall Street investment bankers had come en masse, just as Jennifer had predicted, to offer their condolences to the young widow and offering to help - anything at all, she just needed to ask.

Watching from across the room, he could see that many were leaving their business cards, in a way that reminded Michael of some sort of sales meeting. A gap appeared in the line of well-wishers as the next-in-line had turned his head to the person behind him to finish a story. For that brief moment, until the next in-line realized he was holding things up, Michael caught his first view of the widow, and caught his breath. If he had been expecting to see someone nondescript with eyes red from weeping, he had been barking up the wrong tree because she was petite and lovely with thick black hair beautifully arranged in a stylish chignon, and wearing perfectly applied makeup that accentuated her high cheek bones. Most surprising of all, she looked perfectly composed. Whoever this woman was, or wherever she came from, she was handling this room full of high-powered money merchants and the sudden tragic death of her young husband with aplomb.

They say that if you stare at someone from across the room, their eyes will eventually find yours. Michael couldn't tell how long he'd been gazing but just at that moment, the widow's eyes met his. They exchanged looks for what seemed like an awkwardly long time and just as the next in line moved forward to block Michael's view, the widow smiled and then quickly looked away to greet the next banker type and his wife.

Michael looked away, as well. He had completed the first task Jennifer had assigned him, that of making some sort of contact. A waiter in a starched white vest and black bow, carrying a silver tray of glasses of red and white wine stopped in front of Michael, but although he could certainly have used a drink, now was not the time. The reception line was starting to dwindle and Michael's hands were perspiring. What he really wanted to do was leave, now, before it was too late. When the last of the well-wishers had paid their respects, the widow would be alone, and it was then that Michael knew he would have to act. Maybe if he just stood still, he could tell Jennifer that he never got a chance to speak with his intended contact. But Jennifer had portrayed the movement of people at the reception as if she had scripted it, right down to the ceremonial handing out of business cards. She would not accept any excuses on his part, and Michael knew he couldn't risk that scenario. He thought again about the wine but knew that, while it would no doubt calm his nerves, he needed to be on his game. For his sake, his delivery had to be spot on.

The widow tolerated all of the well-wishers, one of whom had called her Alice. There was little point in embarrassing the man or anyone else in the room, the vast majority of whom she had never seen or heard of before. Her husband had never been interested in sharing stories about his work. When the reception was over and she was home again she would dump all of their business cards into her shredder.

Except for perhaps one. There was a man across the room looking at her who was somehow different. His was the only brown suit in the room and, for some reason he wasn't part of the receiving line. When their eyes met, Angela's first impression was that this was a very attractive man indeed. She naturally smiled as she would for any man like that who appeared to have an interest in her - through her eyes anyway. But she quickly reminded herself where she was and why she was here. Smiling, for any reason, would be considered completely inappropriate.

But she was intrigued. As the last well-wisher finished expressing his condolences, she looked across the room and saw that her brown suit-in-armor had not moved. Instead, he appeared to be anxiously looking around - anywhere but in her direction. Was he shy or just terribly uncomfortable when it came to death? There were only two couples left in the receiving line. He should have moved her way by now. Why hadn't he? For some reason, it was important for her to know.

As Michael watched the line grow shorter, his anxiety grew. Soon, ready or not, it would be time for him to act. He thought of an old war movie he had seen, one in which trainee paratroopers, preparing to make their first jump, had stood nervously in line while somewhere in the background the voice of the commanding officer could be heard shouting, GO! GO! GO! Only the voice he heard was Jennifer's. He had to get out of here before she, like the officer in the film, gave him a push.

The interesting man was going to leave! Angela could not let that happen - not without learning more first. Someone had discovered that behind the curtains were sliding glass doors and the majority of well-wishers were now sipping wine on the patio, talking about the markets and their latest deals. But the mystery guest was still there and on impulse she approached her shy caller.

Michael had been looking around as if to find the closest fire exit when he turned to see the widow halfway across the room, walking directly towards him. He had an urge to run, but even if that had been socially acceptable, she was on him before he could do so much as move away.

"Hello," she said. "I'm Angela. Thank you so much for coming. I've been overwhelmed by the response to my husband's death. But you - you seem different than all of these investment banker types. I'm embarrassed to ask, but my husband didn't share much with me about his work. Tell me - how did you know him?"

Like it or not, Michael was out of the plane and his chute was open.

"Yes, hello Mrs. Messina." Michael strained to remember the lines he and Jennifer had practiced. "My name is Michael Franklin. First of all, I just wanted to express my deepest sympathy for your loss. I know this must be a terribly difficult time for you and, to be honest, I considered not coming. How did I know your late husband? John and I went to school together - seems like ages ago now, but we were best friends at the time. Princeton has a rich history of creating friendships that last a lifetime."

From the information in the obituary and a few hours using search engines, Michael had learned quite a bit about the deceased. There was no way she, or probably anyone else here at the reception if it came to that, could question the veracity of this particular claim.

"Anyway, let me get to the point. John contacted me several months ago. While he went into a career of investment banking, I went into financial planning. Without you knowing it, he and I have been working on a plan for the two of you."

Michael stopped. The fact that both he and the deceased attended the same school was meant to foster an element of trust. As Jennifer instructed, it was time to measure the initial reaction.

"Forgive me," he said in the pause that followed. "At your time of trial I'm talking business. We can do this some other time."

Seeing that there were two glasses of wine on the tray of the waiter who was just passing, Angela took both and offered one to Michael.

"Don't apologize, Mr. Franklin," she said, taking a sip. "It *is* a difficult day for me but I am interested in whatever you have to say. If nothing else, it will take my mind off all this. Will you join me?"

There was something about this man. She wanted to hear what he had to say, because the sound of his voice was... well, very pleasant.

Michael accepted the glass gratefully. If the widow was drinking, then it was certainly OK for him to.

"So please," she said, "continue."

Michael searched his mind for what was supposed to come next in his presentation.

"Like I said," he continued, "your husband approached me a few months ago. He said he wanted a financial plan for you in case he..." Michael stopped himself. "In case something happened to him. He told me he was planning on taking out a rather large life insurance policy - and why not? They're very inexpensive these days and for a man in his position the cost would be inconsequential. I don't know if he ever did that or not. But he wanted to talk to me because he was concerned that you weren't that familiar with how to manage a large sum of money and he was hoping that my firm could step in to help - if that day ever came. We only had a few meetings but once he heard my presentation, he told me my firm was the one. We never got around to putting anything in writing - I guess he got busy on some sort of deal - but I just wanted to let you know that if you think it appropriate or even necessary, my firm is here to help."

Angela considered this man. Up close she could see the clean-shaven face, the smooth skin and solid black eyebrows. There were no marks on his fingers to indicate that he wore a ring although, of course, these days that wasn't as reliable an indicator as it used to be, but still. She thought about her husband. Would a man who almost killed her really have been worried about her financial future? Had her late partner suddenly grown a conscience? Or was there more to this than met the eye? She couldn't be sure so she decided to just play along - for now.

"Well, Mr. Franklin, you are correct," she said. "John never told me anything about this plan."

Michael was ready for that.

"I do remember him saying that he wanted to surprise you. He said he'd been working so hard that he felt guilty that he had neglected some very important things. He said his plan would at least look after you. To be honest, he was quite advanced in his thinking. He was going to set it up such that the life insurance proceeds, which are, of course, tax free, would be invested in an offshore account - which is also tax-free - the investment selection to be run by my firm."

Jennifer had told Michael not to come away without knowing if there was a life insurance policy and, if there was, how much. But he couldn't very well come right out and ask this woman that. Not now, at least.

Angela found herself wondering how much she should tell this man who, up until ten minutes ago, had been a perfect stranger. Apparently he had gone to the same university as John and he knew that there was a life insurance policy. Her natural sense of cynicism made her cautious but... she wasn't going to be single forever and here was this very attractive man offering to help her. She'd be able to determine the legitimacy of his story soon enough. If she brushed him away now it might be the last time she'd see him. And that would be a shame. Besides, she had a perfect excuse for future meetings with this Michael Franklin - business, all business.

"Well actually Mr. Franklin, as it turns out, my late husband did manage to take out a life insurance policy. Of course I don't have any of it yet. There's quite a bit of paperwork involved in dying it seems. It is a large sum of money and I don't have the first clue how to deal with it."

Michael checked another box in his head.

"Oh, I am so glad to hear that there is a policy Mrs. Messina. That must take a huge load off. Of course, it creates a new set of pressures. But listen."

Jennifer had explained to him that the proper approach, once he had learned that the target was worthwhile, was to appear hat-in-hand.

"I don't want to presume anything. I did make presentations to your late husband and he apparently was satisfied with the investment expertise of my firm. But you know nothing of this.

I would be immensely gratified if you would even give me the opportunity to explain our capabilities. If you decide to go with another firm, then so be it."

Angela was impressed by his show of sincerity.

"I would be more than interested in hearing about what you have to offer," she told him. "Please give me your business card, and when things settle down, I will most definitely call you and arrange a meeting. If nothing else, I had a tremendous amount of respect for my husband's knowledge about money matters, and if he thought your firm was the one, then that means a lot to me."

She took his card and put it in a pocket far away from the others. As they shook hands, she leaned forward and whispered into his ear. Her smell was sweet, like a bloom of flowers.

"By the way, you didn't ask me - another sign that I can trust you, I'd say - but it's six million, my husband's insurance I mean. I will definitely need help with that."

Angela was too busy watching Michael's departure to notice that a man was standing beside one of the pillars, taking notes in a small, rather tattered notebook.

## Chapter 30

There was one more shoe to drop for Angela, and that was payment for services rendered. The man to whom she had spoken on the phone had told her to wait until things died down a bit before contacting him. When she asked how long that would be, he'd laughed and said she would know.

The next weeks did, in fact, go quickly for her. The man at the funeral home put her in touch with the trust company that helped her with the 'final accounting.' Armed with a list of things to look for and no longer fearing the repercussions, she went through her dead husband's papers - every single one. In the desk she discovered a key to a safe-deposit box and, in there, a will. The realization that she was named his sole beneficiary made her pause. At one point, this man had actually worried about providing for her future should something happen to him.

She frequently shook her head of late at the irony of life. He had a bank account with close to $100,000 in it. The $200,000 mortgage on their home had its own policy and was paid in full upon his death. There were tax-free savings accounts totaling close to $500,000. And the life insurance company came through as advertised - $6 million. They even offered to replace his BMW.

No matter. She would see to that later. The paperwork was done. She had totaled the assets. Like the man on the phone had warned her, it was time to settle up. Truth was, she wanted to be done with that dirty part of this business and move on.

It was now mid-winter in Seattle with day after day of misty, rainy weather that seemed to reach into your bones to suck out the heat. She found her heaviest coat and boots and headed out to the park, hoping that the pay phone was still working.

The raspy voice on the phone answered promptly. The instructions were clear. $50,000 cash, withdrawn five thousand at a time so as not to draw attention, was to be put into a bag and delivered on a certain date to a bus station locker.

"Now gelato girl, you got all this?" he demanded. "If you got any questions, you ask 'em now."

She stopped by the bank on her way home to make her first withdrawal. She considered where she would hide the money and realized that her husband's old gym bag, which still smelled of him, reminding her of her fortunate loss, would work fine. When she got home, she put the kettle on to try to deal with the goose bumps on her arms and legs. She wondered if that was just the cold or something else perhaps because change was definitely in the air. All this was hers now, the shabby house that she had wanted to redecorate for so long, everything. She could do anything she wanted. All that was needed was to decide what that was. This must, she realized, be what it felt like to win the lottery.

When someone knocked on the door, she was surprised to find that two police officers were standing there, one of them Officer King from the highway patrol whom, of course, she recognized. She showed them into the living room where Officer King introduced Sergeant-Detective O'Lafferty from the Seattle accident investigation team.

"The group has now had the opportunity to fully review your husband's accident and they still have a few outstanding issues," Officer King told her. "Our focus is on trying to recreate what actually happened and, to be absolutely honest we haven't been able to do that yet. To that end, Detective O'Lafferty would like to ask you a few questions."

"Mrs. Messina," Officer O'Lafferty said, "I'm a busy person and I'm sure so are you so let me get to the point. There are a few disturbing facts we have been able to determine that leave us unable to rule out foul play. To begin with, near the accident scene there were no obvious signs of braking and the skid marks and the distance of the wreckage suggest the car was travelling at a very high rate of speed, perhaps over 100 miles per hour. This scenario could have been caused by the obvious, but it also could have been a result of a massive failure in the braking system. In addition, it is apparent that the air bags did not deploy, which would have contributed to the trauma inflicted on your husband. We could write either one of those things off to chance. The existence of both however is too much of a coincidence. So tell me, did your husband have any enemies? Was there anyone who might have wished to see him come to harm? The investment banking business is, after all highly competitive."

Angela could think of only one person, who was, of course, herself. Some tears would likely be appropriate at this point, but a full-blown melt down would not. She covered her face with her handkerchief and gave a little sob.

"No," she said when she had recovered her composure, "I'm sorry, I can't think of anyone."

"Let me ask you something else if you don't mind," the officer went on. "In circumstances such as this we, uh, become concerned for the well-being of the surviving family members - that is until we sort things out. If your late husband had enemies that would go to this extreme, they might come after you as well. So, we've had officers watching... the neighborhood, and as a result, I received a report that you walked to the park this morning to use the pay phone. That seemed a bit unusual to us."

Angela felt as though someone had punched her in the stomach.

"What!" she gasped. "You mean to say that you've been watching me? You have no right to do that? That's against the law. Surely to God you don't think I've done anything."

The officer, judging by his face, didn't share her concern.

"We placed extra officers on patrol out of regard for your well-being. The park is public property. We aren't watching you, but our officers saw you. So tell me, Mrs. Messina, why go out in the freezing cold to make a phone call at a public pay phone when you could have used your own in the comfort of your home?"

The officer's explanation gave her racing mind critical time to recover.

"Well, if you must know," she said, "my telephone is on the fritz. Sometimes, right in the middle of a call it just loses the line and you get a dial tone. I haven't had a chance to get it fixed. Besides, it's not that cold out and I thought the fresh air would do me some good. I haven't had a decent sleep since..."

She buried her face in her handkerchief again.

"So you've told the phone company about your problem?"

She could now tell that the officer was asking questions about her in particular and not the accident. Her voice became lower and her eyes narrowed slightly, becoming laser beams on to his.

"Officer, have you ever asked the phone company for help?" she demanded. "If you must know, that was who I called. They told me since my husband bought a cheap phone at Radio Shack instead of one of theirs, it wasn't their problem. The phone was a piece of junk to begin with and the other day it fell on the floor. It's garbage and needs to be thrown out. Did you really come all this way to ask me about my telephone?"

If her change of tone took him by surprise, he did not show it. But Angela could tell that he still had his suspicions.

"All right then, Mrs. Messina, I've taken up enough of your time. Here's my card. Please let me know immediately if you think of anything or someone tries to contact you."

Angela followed the two policemen to the door.

"Officer," she said, "I have a question for you. My husband went to a bar that night and he had been drinking. Why has no one mentioned that?"

Officer King's eyes widened. The autopsy of what was left of the body had found no traces of excess alcohol. A quick survey of the local taverns located the one that John Messina had attended that night. Perhaps because bartenders didn't like to finger their customers since they were responsible for the damage caused by a client that was over-served, he had been told that the deceased had consumed two beers over three hours and had said that wanted to go home early to surprise his wife. Apparently there had been some sort of argument.

More interestingly, the officer realized that at no point in their questioning had they said the deceased was suspected of DUI. As they left, neither of them noticed that her eyes had narrowed again. And this time there was no handkerchief in sight.

## Chapter 31

Angela just wanted it all to be over. After Officer King and the detective came to her door and asked all those questions - they were watching *her*? She realized that she would have to give all this some more thought. One thing was certain. The thought that it would take ten weeks to gather and deliver the money was just unacceptable. The voice on the phone hadn't warned her about what might happen after the accident. Had she known that there was a chance that she would be investigated, would she still have gone ahead with it? She sighed. What choice had she had?

But ten weeks was too long. She couldn't sleep knowing there was one more scene in the play before it was over. She reasoned that with the police out there somewhere, suspecting something, her going to the bank and withdrawing the remaining $45,000, even in increments, was just too dangerous. Why would anyone need that kind of cash for anything? She had come up with the idea that, if ever questioned about the cash withdrawals, she could say she was planning on having some work done on the house - a fairly extensive home renovation - and everyone knew those people charged less if you paid in cash. But still, she couldn't bear to think of this travesty being played out over nine more weeks.

She settled for four weeks - $10,000 for the next three and $15,000 on the final. Then off she would be to the bus station and the start of her new life. As of yet, she hadn't even been able to rejoice in the fact that she was single again - and rich - and could do anything and go anywhere she liked.

For safety's sake, she drove a different route to the bank each time. She couldn't imagine that the police would be watching her that closely but, like her dad used to say on the farm, an ounce of prevention was worth a pound of cure. Maybe she would go back to the farm, apologetic, hat in hand, and start her life over. She doubted the police would be watching her milk cows.

When the day of the final withdrawal came, she didn't waste any time. Although she had dressed in her normal outfit to go to the bank, she came home and changed into blue jeans and the darkest top she could find. She had driven by the address the voice on the phone had given her several times and the bus station, the walls of which had turned yellow after years of soot and grimy exhaust, wasn't in a great part of town. She parked very close to the front door and waited until it began to get dark, around five. As she entered the building, she headed for the long wall of stainless steel doors, clutching her husband's gym bag tight and placed it in one of the lockers. After locking it, she slid the key - the key that must not be lost - in her jacket pocket before going to the bank of pay phones in the corner and dialing the by now familiar number for what she hoped was the last time.

"Gelato girl, is that you? I told you, don't call me until you was ready."

"Well, I just wanted to get this over with is all," she told him. "I couldn't stand waiting so long. I want to be done with this and get on with my life. So you can send someone to pick up the key to the locker. I'm in the bus station right now."

"Yeah well, I got to call a guy. Tomorrow. Same time."

Angela exhaled deeply. Finally there was some hint of a resolution. There would be some closure to the nightmare. Then, she remembered that she had meant to tell him something.

"Oh, you should know, or at least I think you should know, that the police came to see me - again, asking a bunch of questions. I think they're watching my home. They asked me why I went to the park to make a phone call."

There was a long pause, too long for comfort before he said that he had to call a guy and that she was to call him back in fifteen minutes.

Before Angela had a chance to protest, the line went dead. She sat back down on the blue-green hard plastic bowling alley seats and waited for fifteen long minutes that seemed like hours. He picked up the phone on the first ring.

"Gelato girl, my guy wants to know something. Are you starting to panic? Your husband dies in a fiery blaze and you wake up with a few million. You think they ain't going to ask any questions?"

Angela's hands started to shake. She had not expected this degree of confrontation. After all, she had the money ready for him, money that he must want to get his hands on as soon as possible.

"Well, how am I to know? It's not like I've ever been through something like this before. You made it sound like everything would be fine. You never said the police would come."

Once again there was a long, frightening pause. And when he spoke again, his voice had taken on what she could only characterize as a solemn tone.

"OK, you lissen up, and lissen good," he told her "because I'm only sayin' this once. I didn't think you had no guts but it don't matter. The police ain't done with you yet. They thinks they might got a murder on their hands and they ain't goin' to stop until they find the bad guy. So, them asking you questions could go on for *years*. Ya got that? Ya better learns to suck it up and live with it. You taking the money out of the bank so fast waves a big flag to them so that ain't too smart. I got some boys watching too, you know? Look here little girl. You're in this for the rest of your life. Even if the police go away, and they will sooner or later, you won't ever be done with this."

As the realization of what the man was saying started to sink in, Angela's entire body started to shake and she wiped tears from both of her eyes.

"Hey, what the hell," he was saying now. "You gots lots of money now and you won't be needing to ice your face no more. Tino says he's going to miss you. So, maybe leave town - it doesn't matter. Not many people gets a clean slate. But look here, ice cream girl! You don't never ever say nothin' about our business. You don't know me. We ain't never talked. Understood? We ain't very nice people - that's why we do what we do. We know where you from, a farm in Iowa. Your parents still run it. If you put the heat on us because you can't keep your trap shut, well, it would be, what do you call it? Unfortunate."

Angela had known fear before, thanks to her husband, but she had never experienced outright terror.

"Now, in five minutes a guy, wearing a red shirt and a Seahawks hat, is going to come in to the waiting area where you are," the man told her. "He's going to buy a newspaper and sit down right next to you. You see to it that the key to the locker falls out of your pocket and is on your seat. You get up, walk away and don't look back. You got it? Ever."

He did not have to tell her twice.

## Chapter 32

Angela couldn't stop thinking about the man from the reception; the way his lips formed his words when he spoke to her, his modest, almost apologetic approach as he explained his and her late husband's financial plan for her. He was gracious and kind; his voice and his eyes were soft. She had lived with her husband's jealousy and rage for so long that she had thought a man like this was a very rare find - or perhaps they didn't exist at all. But life happens in strange ways sometimes. Who would ever have thought that a conversation with Mr. Carrantino would ultimately lead her to Michael?

She knew she was allowing her thoughts to get ahead of - to get ahead of what? This wasn't a romance. A person couldn't become so attracted to someone that quickly. Could they? She had clearly moved too fast with her first attempt at finding lifelong love and it was a miracle, really, that she lived through it. Slow down, Angela, she told herself. You know nothing about this man. But, as hard as she tried, she knew she had this side to her. She just wanted to be in love, married and raising a litter of children. It was all she had ever really wanted, after all. She must restrain herself, do her homework, and get to know what kind of man this one really was.

Angela had waited for it to be five-thirty all day. She didn't know what kind of hours investment managers worked or, for that matter, since he owned his own firm, whether Michael went to an office at all. But it was an appropriate time to call. She had wanted to clear things up with the raspy voice on the phone before talking with Michael again. But that was now done and it was time to move on. She held his business card gingerly in her right hand as she dialed the phone.

Jennifer had bought a new desktop cell phone just prior to printing their business cards and since then, it had sat patiently, quietly like a newborn baby yet to exercise its lungs for the very first time. It had seemed like a long time since Michael had given the widow his business card. Jennifer was starting to wonder if the phone actually worked or, perhaps Michael had lied to her about how well the first meeting went. They had placed it at the small desk area often built into kitchens and had nicknamed it the Bat Phone.

When it rang, finally, for the first time, she was so startled that she actually jumped. It was the widow. It had to be; she was the only one who had the number. As she waited three rings, she cleared her throat. She wanted to sound as professional as she could.

"Model-Op Investment Associates," she said. "How may I direct your call?"

Jennifer had chosen the name because it highlighted the 'science' of their approach. Their strategic advantage, the critical factor that set them apart from all of the other firms providing investment management services, was her proprietary model. Her program optimized the weighting of the three different investment valuation theories at just the right time. It was her purported New York experience that had given her the idea to create the model, which had been rigorously back-tested through every type of market environment imaginable - even the Great Wall Street market crash of 1929.

Michael's first reaction was that her model couldn't work, but she had kept pressing him and now he seemed to believe that it might. He hadn't even asked for a demonstration of the so-called back-testing, which would have ended the debate. There was no such thing, of course but it was too great a risk for him to ask. It was brilliant of her, really she thought. He had come to equate his faith in her abilities as a condition for continuing their relationship. Deny one and he would lose the other. He had no choice, really. He wanted her so much it made him accept anything necessary to achieve that goal. Such were the vulnerabilities of the gullible.

Angela's eyes widened at the sound of the very feminine sounding voice answering the phone. She wasn't thinking about there being a woman involved. Later, she laughed to herself - Michael was running a highly successful company - that was how he and her former husband came to begin their talks. The man she couldn't seem to take her mind off clearly wouldn't be working alone. There would have to be support staff for goodness sake.

"Oh yes, hello," she said. "Could I speak with Michael, uh Mr. Franklin?"

Jennifer didn't miss a beat.

"May I say who is calling, please?"

For some reason, the thought of giving her name, of exposing who she really was, gave her pause. She quickly realized the silliness of it all. This was a business transaction - for now at least. Of course she had to give her name.

"Yes, sorry, my name is Angela Messina."

As was her way, Jennifer made instantaneous mental notes. The woman was clearly nervous, repeating herself and almost stammering. Why? Was she always like this or was there something about making this phone call that made her nervous? Michael had said she seemed more confident than he had expected, given the situation. She would quiz him again. Even the smallest detail was important.

"Thank you, Ms. Messina," she said. "If you wouldn't mind holding for just a second, let me see if he is available."

She put the phone on hold and checked the built-in timer. She would make their first prospective client wait about thirty seconds. Michael was in the shower but she wouldn't let him talk to this Angela girl directly yet until Jennifer had reviewed the script with him one more time. She clicked the 'connect' button.

"I'm so sorry Ms. Messina but Mr. Franklin is still on a conference call with Australia researching some potential mining-company investments. He motioned to me that he's very eager to speak with you and asked me to find a time that would be most convenient for him to return your call. I don't think he'll be too much longer but I see that it is getting late in the day. Can he call you, say, in the next thirty minutes? Or would you prefer something tomorrow?"

Angela was already wearing her favorite dress, one that she hadn't worn in quite some time because her husband, with his usual delicacy, had told her that it made her look like a slut. She was relieved to find that it still somehow seemed to cling in just the right places and had already decided that a cocktail at Bamboo, a quiet bar with booths at the back where they could speak more privately, would be an appropriate next step.

"No, I would like to meet with him tonight," she said quietly but firmly. "Please have him call me as soon as he can."

Jennifer smiled.

"Go put on a suit," Jennifer told Michael when he came into the kitchen where she was busy making notes on a yellow legal pad. "You're meeting the widow at the bar in thirty minutes. It looks like we've got a nibble."

Angela arrived at Bamboo first. It was that special place that she and her late husband used to go to, earlier in their relationship when there was still a semblance of love and caring. Most importantly for Angela, they could sit in a back booth where the likelihood of her being seen with another man was minimized. She didn't know how much time was supposed to pass before people would consider it appropriate but she wasn't going to wait. She had found a man, or at least he had found her, and she was intrigued. She had received a check for $6 million from the insurance company and she had no idea what to do with such a large amount of money so, if nothing else, a business meeting between her and her future financial advisor was 'appropriate.'

As Michael walked into The Bamboo Bar and Grill, he immediately noticed the island theme, often described by its clientele as being decked out like Don Ho's rec room. He was replaying Jennifer's instructions to the effect that, since the widow had taken the initiative and called him, it probably meant that the money had landed and that she was starting to get nervous. But the timing - after dinner - and the venue - in a small, cozy bar, made Jennifer's radar go up just a bit higher. 'Be aware of her signals,' she had coached him. He was, after all, not only a good-looking guy but someone who, as far as the widow was concerned, represented both companionship and security. She concluded by telling him to keep it professional to begin with but that, if her eyes, body language or the conversation started to drift, he was to play along.

Angela flashed a broad smile as Michael walked towards the back of the bar where the booths were made of bamboo with Hawaiian leis hung on the posts, and there were flowered foam cushions to sit on.

"What will you have to drink?" she asked Michael when the waiter arrived.

"Oh, I don't know," he said. "A ginger ale would be fine."

"Ginger ale!" she said. "It's after dark, I've had a long day and I hate drinking alone. Come on, Michael, you can do better than that."

Michael cringed inside. He had made a mistake and knew that Jennifer, had she been present, would not have been pleased.

"Oh, all right then - twist my arm. I'll have a glass of chardonnay."

"Make it a bottle," she said to the waiter, and then to Michael, "This is a business meeting and we have a lot to discuss."

When the wine was poured, she swirled hers expertly and watched as the small streams of it flowed slowly like lava down the insides of the glass, giving herself time to think about where to begin.

"First of all thank you so much for agreeing to see me on such short notice," she said. "My life has been a whirlwind since my husband passed away and I find myself having to act almost on the spur of the moment. I have so many things going through my head that I feel like I have to deal with the issue du jour right away, lest it fall through the cracks somewhere."

"Not at all Mrs. Messina," Michael said. "I am at your service."

"Good," she replied. "I like an attitude where client service is important. But the first order of business is for you to please call me Angela. Other than being less formal - and I hope I don't sound too crass here - the fact of the matter is that, due to my husband's untimely death, I am no longer Mrs. anything."

Michael wanted to either remind or explain to this woman that referring to her as Mrs. Messina for at least some period of time after her loss was nothing more than a show of respect. He made a note to tell Jennifer about her apparent willingness to jettison her former last name. It might have some significance.

"Now, secondly, before I give you the right to handle my money," she went on, "I want to know a bit more about you and your firm, of course. I am assuming that yours is a small shop, perhaps consisting of just you and your, uh, secretary."

Before she went much farther down this path, Angela wanted to know all of the players in the game. She was particularly interested in the identity of the soft voice that answered the phone - and whether Michael was sleeping with whoever it was.

"But let's start with you," she continued.

Michael, having been schooled by Jennifer, characterized his upbringing as one in which, thanks to his father, his fascination with the stock market had begun at an early age - it was in his blood. Like any son, he explained, he didn't want to follow exactly in his father's footsteps. That realization had come home to roost when, in his position as a retail salesman, he would often shun the opinions offered by his firm's research department. Instead, he would do his own analysis both from the perspective of the merit of the investment in question, but also, in terms of the appropriateness of the recommendation for the needs and circumstances of each client. Most, if not all of the other brokers would just take the latest BUY opinion, don their headsets and start pushing buttons on their keypads. They called it, he confided in her, 'dialing for dollars.'

Angela felt as if she would fall asleep but she *had* asked.

As Jennifer had instructed, Michael didn't bring up his termination even though it was highly unlikely that this woman would know anything about something that would only have appeared as a small item on the business page, if at all.

"Isn't that fascinating?" she said, taking the liberty of refilling his half empty glass. "I'm impressed that you were so committed that you branched out on your own." Commitment and a willingness to follow his dreams! This man was becoming more compelling with each passing minute. But, Angela reminded herself; she still needed to conduct herself as if she was indeed in a business meeting.

"Enough about you," she said briskly. "At the reception, you mentioned to me that your firm had developed a unique way to manage money. I'm not very sophisticated about this sort of thing so I am sorry but I need you to explain that to me."

Jennifer had told Michael to keep an ear open for language that was sheepish and apologetic. She had studied, at great length, the personalities they were looking for that would indicate a greater level of gullibility. This first target, Angela - nicknamed Bashful - should be genuinely embarrassed about her lack of knowledge and thus more willing to accept his somewhat technical explanation. She cautioned him against being too technical. If she really didn't understand anything and he tried too hard to impress her with his expertise, he might very well scare her away. As a result, Michael had come up with an analogy that he thought would work very well.

"Well, Angela, let me explain it to you like this," he said. "There are three widely-accepted ways to go about picking stocks. The problem is they aren't all equally effective all the time. For years, people have been trying to predict which will work the best and when, but haven't been successful. Suppose there were three ways to drive into work in downtown Seattle during rush hour. You might have your favorite way but, since your objective is to get to work on time, you'd like to know the fastest route before you take the wrong one and get mired in a sea of honking, crawling cars. I, and my partner, have teamed up to be able to do just that. We don't believe anyone else had succeeded in this - and we have."

The wine was making Angela's eyes start to droop but she perked up when she heard the word 'partner.'

"Ah, yes, that was another question I wanted to ask," she said. "Tell me about your 'team.' Surely you can't do all of this money management work on your own."

Jennifer had made it clear that in a Ponzi scheme, the clients would never meet more than the original contact person, while at the same time believing that there was a well-established infrastructure supporting that individual. Michael remembered suggesting that he say they were a smaller firm right now but that as word of their investment success spread growth was assured.

He particularly remembered Jennifer's shrill laugh before she said, "Oh my god, you must be joking! Let's be real clear about this. While you just joined the firm full time several months ago, the investment management business was actually started in the Cayman Islands five years ago and we have audited financial statements that support the achievement of vastly superior investment returns. We currently have $400 million in assets under management and our goal is to grow that to $1 billion over the next two years. The only thing new is our launch into the Western United States. You and one of our valued portfolio managers have agreed to relocate to the Northwest area to help grow the business."

"Would you give your money to a start up?" she asked and Michael had to agree.

"So," Michael finished answering Angela's question, "while we are a small group in the Seattle area at the moment, our firm is international in both size and geographic expertise."

Angela listened carefully. It all sounded good but he still hadn't touched on the question she had in mind, one she really needed to know the answer to.

"That sounds very professional," she told him. "But I won't need to see those financial statements you mentioned. I trust you Michael... and your wife. That was who answered the phone I presume?"

Jennifer had prepared Michael for this, too, although at the time Michael had thought that his future fiancée was being paranoid - that the means to assure Angela about the expertise of their firm should remain at a professional level. Personal information would not, and should not, enter the fray. But Jennifer understood how some women think in such times, she had told him. Michael, being a man, wouldn't. He *must* not suggest there was any person of importance in his life. By preparing him with the answer, she was not only removing one more barrier separating them from winning the widow's money but, perhaps more importantly, identifying a new line of approach that would be more powerful and with a much greater chance of success than any presentation she could create.

"Oh, that was just my secretary," Michael answered.

Angela tried not to smile too broadly.

"Yes, of course, I knew that. I was asking about the business partner you said you worked with. Is it just the three of you here in Seattle area? How do you and he or she allocate the responsibilities?"

Jennifer, as usual, had been right. He would have underestimated the depth of the question raised by this woman but he guessed that $6 million was $6 million.

"There is the administrative staff of course, which will grow as our list of local clients increases," he told her. "For the portfolio management expertise, we have two people on the ground here, Jennifer Salem and me. She relocated from the New York City area at the same time I returned from the Cayman Islands. Understand, it isn't really just the two of us. We participate in our global conference call every morning at seven, six days a week."

Angela did her best to express interest but what she really wanted to ask was, "What kind of girl is she? What does she look like?" But, instinct told her that she would have to just accept what she'd been given. Since the woman had just moved from New York and he from the islands, the chances that a romantic relationship had started to form were reduced. She imagined they'd been too busy for something like that to start. But, still, she wanted to - she had to - dig a bit further.

"And what do the two of you actually do?"

Michael thought it was uncanny that Jennifer had been able to predict the widow's concerns so well. He repeated the answer Jen had given him.

"Actually, while we are a 'team' per se, we don't usually work that closely together. I spend most of my time on individual security analysis while she is the quantitative expert - otherwise known as the 'geek.' She does her thing and I do mine and we compare notes when it is time to make a transaction."

Angela smiled again. 'Geek.' She liked the sound of that.

"Oh, OK, I get it now. I'm sorry for all of the questions but, you know, I just want to be sure. So then, Michael, just to make sure I understand, if I give my money to your firm to manage, I can expect to deal with you, on a one-to-one basis. You see, I have some very, well, personal things to share. I think it is critical that the person who looks after me gets to know me on a very private level."

She knew she was going far beyond what was appropriate for this meeting, but he hadn't recoiled yet and the longer he didn't, the more intrigued she became.

"Do you think we see eye-to-eye on that? It's very important to me."

Michael was becoming increasingly concerned. It was as though this woman was coming on to him - and he had no interest in that. But Jennifer had predicted it, and she couldn't have been clearer in her instructions. Get the money in hand first and then they'd worry about the details.

"Yes, Angela, we are totally on the same page," he said. "I will personally look after you - your account."

She brushed her hand across the top of the table.

"Well then Mr. Franklin," she said, "on that basis, I will absolutely give your proposal my full consideration. I have to warn you, I am a deliberate person and I will likely have more questions. Hope you're OK with meeting me again, maybe more than once, before I make my decision."

## Chapter 33

Michael virtually skipped through the door, humming a tune, and calling out, "I'm home!" louder than necessary.

Jennifer was still sitting at the kitchen table where Michael had left her, drawing some sort of flow chart. She looked at him, somewhat quizzically.

"What did she say?" she asked.

Michael's grin spread across his face. On his way home from the bar, he had reminded himself that he still wasn't 100% sure about the ethics of funding the startup of their new business but, it was exciting that he had almost secured his first client.

"She said she would absolutely consider my proposal!"

Michael did a little dance across the kitchen floor and pretended to shoot a basketball across the room.

Jennifer looked at him, somewhat amused, but at the same time, annoyed. "What do you mean consider? That's not the same as having the money. Exactly what did she say?"

This was not the sort of homecoming Michael had envisioned, and his shoulders slumped. Why couldn't someone - just once - congratulate him for doing a good job? "I'm sure she's going to give us her money," he said defensively. "That's what you sent me out to do, and I did it!"

"Really?" Jennifer snapped. "How do you know that? If you're so sure, when do we get it, and how much? The whole $6 million? How is she going to get it to us? Money order? Wire transfer?"

"Well, she didn't say all that stuff," he admitted. "She just said that she would consider it and she might want to meet with me again before she decides, that's all."

Jennifer wiped her forehead with the palm of her hand. Reminders of Michael's naiveté could come crashing back at any time.

"Michael, until we actually *have* the money, we don't have any money," she told him. "Do you understand that? Tell me about your conversation, and don't leave out one word. Then I'll figure out what we need to do next."

Michael tried as hard as he could to remember their dialogue, although some parts were a bit blurred. During his recitation, Jennifer kept interrupting him to ask about the widow's body language, facial expressions and tone of voice.

"Are you serious, Jen?" he said finally. "I can't remember all of that stuff."

"Well *try* Michael. Every single bit of information is important. If you overlook or misread even the slightest signal, it could mean the difference between success and failure."

Michael leaned back in his chair. He had been expecting a light-hearted conversation, accompanied by high fives, but instead he felt like he was being interrogated. As he strained to recall every ounce of information, Jennifer looked deeply into his eyes, jotting down a short note from time to time, but still interrupting him occasionally.

"What was she wearing, Michael?"

"What? I don't know. I wasn't ..."

"MICHAEL!"

He held up his hands in surrender.

"OK, OK." He scrunched his eyes to try to recreate the scene in his mind.

"It was a dress of some sort, one of those ones with little thin straps. Kind of a nice dress, I guess. Now that you think about it, it was pretty fancy for a bar."

"And she wanted to know who you worked with, and whether the woman who answered the phone was your girlfriend or your wife?"

Michael wasn't sure what all this had to do with anything, but he answered as best he could.

"Really try to remember," Jennifer pressured him. "She said that if she was going to give her money to your firm to manage, she expected personal, one-on-one service just from you, right? She said she had some personal things to share and that it was critical that the person that looks after her got to know her on a very private level. She said it was very important to her, right? And it was on the basis of that promise, after you'd killed a bottle of wine that she said she would seriously consider your proposal?"

Michael nodded again. He didn't understand why it was so important to go over every detail like this.

"And you said to me earlier, Michael, that towards the end of the meeting you were starting to feel a bit uncomfortable because... what was it you said? You thought maybe she was coming on to you a bit?"

"Yes, Jen I did, but I swear I didn't say or do anything to provoke that," he protested. "She was pretty normal at first but by the time we finished the wine, she was leaning over the table towards me, putting her hands on top of mine. It was getting a bit awkward."

Jennifer waved him off.

"Awkward? Not in the least. Have you been paying attention? In order to make this work we have to get inside each of our targets' heads."

She laughed, stood up at the table and leaned over towards him.

"Did she do it like this Michael? Did you get a good look down her dress? What color was her bra - if she was even wearing one?"

Michael's face turned beet red. He started to stammer an answer but Jennifer raised her hand to stop him. Her grin spread from ear to ear.

"That's all the information I need," she told him. "This woman absolutely has things on her mind other than who's going to look after her money, and you're her target. Tomorrow you are going to call the widow and invite her out to one of the finest restaurants in the area. You will bring her flowers. And the unspoken purpose of the meeting will be to show her what we, or rather you, mean by personal service. You'll say something like 'I saw these flowers on the way here and I thought they were beautiful - so I brought them for you.' Got it?"

Even after having her husband killed, his presence still haunted Angela's thoughts. After getting back from meeting Michael she sat on her bed in her nightie, knees pulled up between her arms, and closed her eyes. There were so many things to think about, decisions to make; it was like a pack of flies around her head that she couldn't shoo away. On the way home in the taxi, she'd realized she had just agreed to a 'deal' without really understanding what it was or, really, who she was dealing with. Even her former husband would have called that into question and he would have been right.

Before going up to her bedroom, she went through his files again. She reasoned that her former husband, having been an investment banker type, would have at least started a file of his 'plan' for her future with some background information about Model-Op Investment Associates. But there was nothing - not a single piece of paper. What did that mean? Was it just an oversight on his part? Did he have some files at work? She'd assumed that anything done at the office would be considered proprietary and unavailable. Was he just keeping the information from her? It certainly wouldn't have been the first time he had misled her in some way.

Equally troubling was the fact that she searched the name of the firm on the Internet and found nothing, not even the phone number on the business card Michael had given her. There was obviously an explanation for that but still, if someone was trying to grow their business, wouldn't there at least be some sort of attempt at marketing? Or maybe this was one of those companies available only for the mega-rich. Everything was done word of mouth and if you had to ask, you couldn't afford it. She'd have to ask Michael about that.

She sighed. For all of his faults, her husband would have known what to do.

Michael. He was an entirely different can of worms. It was too early to enter into another relationship but then again, who was it that made those rules? More importantly, was he interested in her? She'd looked for all of the 'clues' by watching his body language in the bar. At the table, he faced her directly and never seemed to lose eye contact. He was dressed in an expensive business suit - she didn't know if he had worn that because it was their first 'business' meeting or was trying to impress her. He hadn't flinched in the slightest when she put her hands on top of his. And whenever she spoke, he seemed to be interested in every word. She shook her head. Come on, Angela, you're completely off your rocker. But still - things happened for a reason, didn't they? Her abusive husband, now gone, had led to her having money and being available. Michael could help her on both fronts - a lot. The money was a complexity. If he became as attracted to her as she was to him, then she would have to give it to him to invest. But if he suspected there was any hint of distrust or skepticism on her part that would be the end of the relationship before it even started. The more she thought, the warmer her face became. This was the frustrating part. It was sort of like some Catch-22.

Taking the framed picture of her and her husband on their honeymoon out of the bedside table drawer, she stared at it, wondering how long that sense of bliss lasted; likely it had been longer for her than him. The more she stared at the picture, the grimmer she found herself feeling. All of this, all the pressures and uncertainty, was because of the bastard who had said he would honor, love and cherish her for life. How could she have misread things so badly? And if she had gotten the read of her first relationship so wrong, what was to say she wouldn't do it again? Did she have some sort of internal flaw, a self-destruct mechanism waiting to ignite?

Dammit! This wasn't her fault. Look what this smiling bastard had done to her life. She alone - again because of him - had to go through all of those stupid feelings like she was a teenager because he had stripped her of any self-confidence. And now all that money was hanging over her head like an axe. She didn't want to have anything to do with it but she also knew she couldn't live without it.

She threw the picture across the room, yelling "You BASTARD." It shattered into several pieces, glass flying everywhere. Leaning forward, she put her face in her hands and reminded herself - breathe Angela, just breathe. There was Michael Franklin, a new man and perhaps - she prayed - a new beginning. She would see where it went. If, by some grace of God, a relationship between them started to take shape, she was fully ready to give him all the love that she had.

But what did she *know* about this man? Couldn't he be just as terrible as the last? She looked up from her hands at the now broken picture frame on the floor. You couldn't live your life constantly worried about the ogres under the bridge. But, if the unthinkable happened again, as horrible a thought as that was, she knew that she could fend for herself.

If nothing else, she had learned to take matters into her own hands.

So really Angela, there was no risk in starting a relationship with this Michael Franklin, none whatsoever.

## Chapter 34

"My late husband and I used to eat here now and then."

Michael and Angela were sitting in the Space Needle restaurant. She had asked that they arrive before sunset so they could enjoy the view. In less than a minute, the scene moved from Puget Sound to the snow-capped Mt. Rainier. Float planes landed below them on Lake Union as the ferries, cruise liners and cargo ships crossed Elliott Bay. The city streets always seemed to be busy. It reminded Michael of the activity around an anthill.

Instead of wine, Angela had suggested champagne because, after all, this was a celebration. She saw the look on Michael's face at the mention of her dead husband and reached her hand to touch his. At her request, they were sitting next to each other - so they could both enjoy the view.

"Oh dear Michael," she said. "I didn't mean to make you uneasy. This is all so new to me. I don't know whether to talk about him or not. I mean, I have no problem with it now. I am over him or at least I think I am. But, when I bring it up, people get all uncomfortable, which makes me look like, what? I don't know. Am I a bad person for wanting to get on with my life? He's dead. There, I said it. The whole story is horrible. But it's in the past, right?"

She moved closer to him, her head almost resting on his shoulder as, sipping their champagne, they watched the sunset in silence. "I want to start my life again," she told him when the beautiful show was over. "And I think you can help me in more ways than you know. But I want you to promise that you won't judge me. Just accept me and my situation for what it is. Will you promise me that?"

She was so close to him now that he could smell a faint hint of some perfume that was unlike anything he'd ever smelled before. Even in the somber restaurant lighting he noticed a scar, just above her left eye. But he had been coached - drilled really - by Jennifer, to let this woman take the dinner wherever she wanted it to go.

"Oh - you noticed my scar," she said, pushing away from him. "I tried very hard to cover it up but I just can't seem to get it right. I guess I'll have to go the plastic surgery route at some point."

Michael didn't realize he'd been staring. He imagined if Jennifer were here, she'd be furious.

"Oh, no, Angela," he said, trying to make a quick recovery. "I didn't notice anything? Do you have a scar?"

"A woman sees everything in a man's eyes," she told him playfully. "Yes, you did notice my scar and now you're trying to deny it. You're also wondering how I got it. Well, my husband was quite the athletic type. I'm OK at sports but never at his level. Anyway, one day, he decided that we should try rollerblading. So we went to one of those outdoor hockey rinks in the summer after the ice was all gone. While he was breezing around the thing, I was just trying to hang on. Finally, I tripped and struck my head on the boards. What a mess. I was bleeding like a stuck pig. The young kid who was in charge of playing the music called 911. I was thoroughly embarrassed. It was awful. And now I look like a prize fighter after losing a big fight."

Angela was pleased with herself for coming up with a cover story so quickly. Actually, her husband had come home drunker than usual and had thrown the TV remote control at her. She hadn't reacted fast enough and it had hit her, just missing her eye. The blood everywhere part of the story was true but not the urgent medical attention. Instead, he had told her to put a Band-Aid on it and come to bed.

Michael found himself wondering why she was going to such pains to explain what was, after all, a simple scar. Something about her reaction made him feel uncomfortable.

"Angela, I'm so sorry," he said, determined to say the sort of thing that would make Jennifer proud. "You can't really see it. I just, well you are such a beautiful woman. It's only the smallest 'imperfection' on an otherwise perfect face."

"Thank you Michael, thank you very much," she told him, clearly pleased. "It's been a long time since anyone has spoken to me like that." She paused. "Would you like to touch it? No, it's all right. Give me your hand. I want you to touch it. There. See. It's not so bad, is it?"

The first compliment had gone over so well that Michael tried for another one. But she beat him to it.

"And you, Mr. Franklin have hands like a baby's bottom."

She reached for her champagne.

"But I think we should order dinner. I mean, this is a business meeting... isn't it?"

The first bottle of champagne didn't last long because Angela didn't wait for the waiter to refill their glasses, so she quickly ordered another. With each sip, her confidence that maybe, just maybe, this could turn into a genuine - they lived happily ever after - relationship grew. She laughed at every joke, appeared mesmerized when Michael described his background and basically used every trick in her book to let this man know that she was interested. The more she drank, the more she thought about his soft hands.

Michael's thoughts were starting to drift. It was impressive really. Here was this woman who'd had her whole life turned upside down, her future dreams and plans washed away like footprints on a sandy beach. And here she was, despite having been dealt such a hard blow, seemingly very positive about her future. Whatever difficulties Michael had to face, including being deserted by his mother, and finding out that his father wasn't really who he thought he was, paled in comparison to what this woman had endured. Michael wasn't sure that, given the same circumstances, he would do nearly as well as she.

Maybe it was the bubbly but Michael noticed something else. This Angela was a strikingly attractive woman. She likely would have no problem finding a new mate especially once they learned about her wealth. But he was in love with Jennifer - he reminded himself. He had to admit it would be easier if she had a job and contributed a bit towards the expenses. Then, maybe, they wouldn't have to be in such a hurry to raise money relying on… what? Even a white lie was still a lie. He had agreed to go along with the 'arrangement' for a while, but he wanted everything to be on the up and up as soon as possible. There was no way he would sit still for taking a widow's money under false pretenses, for long.

The courses came and went and they shared a piece of key lime pie, after which Angela ordered them both a small glass of brandy to go with their coffees. If nothing else, Michael thought, this woman could hold her liquor. When the bill came, Angela reached for it but Michael quickly took it away knowing that, otherwise, Jennifer would have his head on a platter.

"I like a man who fights for what he wants," Angela said, laughing. "But really Michael, I'm the rich widow, remember?"

When she said that, Michael remembered that they hadn't even discussed when she would transfer the money and how much she intended to let him handle. Jennifer had said that he wasn't to come back without that information. But the dinner had just flown by. They talked about everything *but* her money.

Although it would appear awkward, Michael didn't dare go home without at least asking the question.

"Oh, right Angela, you just reminded me," he said. "May I ask when you plan on transferring the money to us and how much you will ask us to manage for you? We need to know to, uh, prepare."

Angela leaned over the table towards him with a teasing frown on her face.

"After such a lovely dinner you still want to talk business? Well, certainly not here. If you want to talk about my personal affairs then we'll need a much more private place... like my home. After all that bubbly, neither one of us should drive. So share a cab with me back to my place. I'll be more comfortable there. We can speak openly and, anyway, it still freaks me out a bit to come into an empty home at night."

Although Michael didn't want to go back anywhere with this woman, she held all the cards. He didn't want to face Jennifer either, without getting the required information. Worse, she hadn't coached him about this scenario.

In the cab, Michael soon realized that they were in Phinney Ridge, an upscale neighborhood in the Seattle area where wealthy investment bankers lived. "Ah, here we are," she said, after fumbling in her bag for her keys. "I'm not sure how clean everything is but I wasn't expecting guests tonight. Oh!" she added, turning to face him, "Where are my manners. I forgot to thank you for dinner."

Her mouth was on his and her arms around his neck before he knew what had happened. Her lips were warm and moist and moving gently in a circular pattern, pressing and easing. His first instinct was to push away - but he didn't - and they stood on the doorway for what seemed like minutes.

"There," she said finally. "I've wanted to do that all night Michael, and to be honest, I really don't want to talk business with you tonight. But I do want you to come in and let me show you how appreciative I can be for everything you've done and are going to do for me. What do you say? You're single and so am I. We're both adults. I think you can feel something happening between us or at least I hope you can."

When she grabbed his hand and started to lead him over the threshold, his mild curiosity about what was going to happen next turned to panic. Jennifer had told him to play along with the widow if she became 'friendly' but it seemed pretty clear what was going to happen next. Cheating on the woman he loved was not part of any scenario he was interested in - and he was pretty sure Jennifer would agree.

"Oh, God, no, I mean I don't think it would be such a good idea, Angela," he said, releasing himself. "Uh, yes, this is, was supposed to be a business meeting and, well, you know what they say. Never mix business with pleasure."

Angela looked at him, up and down. It wasn't her nature to throw herself at a man - she wasn't sure she'd ever done it before. And here, having found the courage to do something she'd never done in her life, she was being rejected. Suddenly, she felt like a piece of two-bit trash.

"Michael, you're kidding me right?" she exclaimed. "You're turning me down?"

As he started to walk down her steps, he turned to face her. "No, don't get me wrong. I'm not doing anything. I just… I just need to go home. Thank you for such a pleasant evening."

She stood at the top of the steps, arms folded, the realization of what had just happened really beginning to sink in. Her face was burning from a combination of embarrassment and anger. She started to say that he should come inside to let her call him a cab; the nearest busy street where he was likely to find one at this time of night was a good ten minute walk away. But she stopped herself. Let the bastard walk. She hoped he got mugged.

It was after eleven but Jennifer was waiting up for him. When he came through the door, she was sitting up in bed, reading. "Well, well," she said, smiling, "the cat out on the town finally comes home. It must have been a successful night indeed. Come sit down here, Don Juan and tell me all about it. How much is she going to give us and, more importantly, when?"

Michael sat down but when she saw the look on his face, hers disappeared.

"What is it Michael? Don't tell me you didn't ask her."

She was, he knew, prepared to be angry with him, but when he explained, everything would be all right.

"No, Jen," he said. "I was going to but I didn't get the chance."

Jennifer listened quietly as Michael recounted the events during their meal, the after dinner drinks and then the invitation back home. As he spoke, Jennifer was nodding her head in approval.

"Yes, yes - go on. This all seems to be going well."

Michael paused to gather his thoughts.

"And then, when we got to her front door - listen Jen, I swear I didn't do or say anything to provoke this - well, she grabbed me around my neck with her arms and started kissing me - hard. Then, I can't remember exactly what she said. Everything was happening so fast. But when she started to pull me into her house, it was pretty clear that all she wanted to do was have sex with me - right then and there."

"WHAT?" Jennifer exclaimed.

"Yeah, that's what I said. I know you told me not to tell her about us, so I didn't. But she was going too far, too fast so I just high-tailed it out of there."

Jennifer's eyes seemed to be burning into Michael's.

"Michael!"

"I know, I know, Jen. I'm sorry. I promise I didn't do anything. It just happened."

Jennifer was now breathing short, sharp breaths through her nose.

"Holy shit!" she exclaimed. "I can't believe it. You were that close to landing her. She opens her kimono wide and you walked away?! Are you stupid?"

Michael heard her words but had to replay them in his head before they made sense.

"Jen, what are you saying?" he protested. "I didn't think you would appreciate me cheating on you just because she has money."

She looked the other way and slammed her hand down onto the bed. She couldn't believe the naiveté of this fool.

"Michael, for Christ's sake!" she cried. "This is BUSINESS. It has nothing to do with us. I don't care if you spent all night with her if that's what it takes to get her money. Tomorrow, you understand, tomorrow you call and apologize. Say you want to make it up to her. You were nervous or tired or whatever. Think with your dick. That's what guys do. And if it means you have to hop in the sack with her, well you do it and you do it well! Fuck her brains out if you have to. Do you understand?"

Michael looked at his future fiancée, with his mouth open. He started to say that his sleeping with another woman, regardless of the justification, could be very, very bad for any future they had ahead of them. But, the look on her face kept him from arguing.

And all that he found he could respond with was, "Yes, Jen. Anything you say."

## Chapter 35

Angela had acted like a teenage girl.
It had been a long time, longer than she could remember since she had been so embarrassed by her behavior. She had basically thrown herself at Michael, right at the front door and he turned her down. Turned her down! Was she that out of practice at this sort of thing? These days, if you found a man, you sure as hell had to go after him. And this wasn't just a man, he was a beautiful man, kind, soft spoken, someone who had probably never hurt a fly - or most certainly never hit a woman. And he understood money. Her inheritance was hanging over her like a curse.

She had scared him away. He wasn't ready for the passion that had been building up inside her since she first saw him at the memorial reception. She kept trying to remind herself - it was all too early and too fast. But she couldn't deny that her feelings were real. All of this, the money, her being single again; it was all meant to be.

How should she feel? It was like being back in high school again, worried about which boy liked which girl. Should she be angry that he had literally left her standing at her doorstep when she was feeling that, once inside, her clothes would be quickly on the floor and they never would have made it to the bedroom? Or should she be apologetic that she had let herself be carried away by her emotions? This was, after all, a business relationship and she wasn't thinking or acting in a very business-like manner. She had picked up the phone three times to call and say she was sorry and then put it back down. What would she say? And what kind of man walks away from a situation like that? She couldn't have made it more obvious what was waiting behind her front door. She looked in her full-length mirror and ran her eyes up and down her body. She was still a very attractive package.

Maybe it was her scar.

Or maybe there was more of a relationship between Michael and his female partner than he owned up to. Perhaps he was playing her, making it look like he was attracted to her just to get her money. But he hadn't really done that; he hadn't come on to her at all.

Perhaps he just wasn't interested. Or, she shuddered, gay. Whatever the reason for his response, she had resolved that she should just leave well-enough alone for now, give it all some time for the immediateness of what had happened to wear away. He had to come back to her at some point if he wanted to invest her money. She could just say that she didn't drink much and, she'd been lonely since her husband's death. She was very sorry and it would never happen again.

But for God's sake, it would happen again. It had to. This man could be her destiny and she'd never forgive herself if she didn't find out. She desperately wanted a good man in her life.

Her thoughts were interrupted by the phone. Seeing from the call display that it was Michael's company, she found herself in a dilemma. She wasn't ready for this call yet. She let it ring... four times. Should she pick it up? What did he want? Finally, she couldn't stand it.

"Hello," she said, "Angela speaking."

It was a bit unnerving for Michael to have had to make this call in the first place, but with Jennifer sitting across the table from him, listening to every word, he felt like he'd never been so nervous.

"Ah yes, good morning Angela," he said. "It's Michael Franklin. How are you? It looks like we'll actually get some sun at some point today - hardly ever seems to happen in the Seattle area this time of year."

"Hi Michael," she replied hesitantly. "I'm sorry I couldn't get to the phone sooner. I was in the shower."

Jennifer could neither hear nor see the thoughts in Michael's mind about what Angela might look like wet and naked.

"Oh, I'm sorry about that. Is this a bad time? Should I call back later?"

He looked up to see Jennifer's angry expression, as she mouthed the word "no."

"This is fine," Angela assured him. "What's on your mind?"

Michael was now watching Jennifer for any positive or negative feedback as he spoke.

"I just wanted to thank you for meeting with me yesterday," he said. "We are very encouraged that you are considering our firm to manage your money. Frankly, I think the deliberate, pragmatic approach you are taking with deciding who you will use is entirely appropriate. Six million dollars is a lot of money. You should be, and we want you to be completely confident about our capabilities. In respect of that, the purpose of this call is to see if you have any questions you'd like me to deal with."

Jennifer was nodding her head. Apparently, he was following the script well.

"Any questions?" Angela exclaimed, laughing. "I don't normally have that much to drink. I think that there's been so much on my plate, all the stress. I appreciate your bringing me home. Everything's a bit fuzzy after that."

This was so awkward. There was an elephant in the room that neither wanted to notice. Jennifer was motioning with her hand that she wanted Michael to get on with it - to get to the point.

"Oh, right," he said, "about last night."

Both Jennifer and Angela sat up straighter.

"Well look, there is no easy way to say this so I'll just come right out. I wanted you to know two things. First, if I offended you in any way whatsoever, I am terribly sorry. It's just; you know, I've always been taught never to mix business with pleasure. And I didn't want you to think that I was acting in anything but a professional manner. We very much would like the privilege of managing your inheritance for you and I didn't want you to think… Wow this isn't easy is it? There's a right way and a wrong way and I never wanted to put myself in a position where you might second-guess my integrity. There are a lot of unscrupulous people in this business, Angela, and I am not one of them."

Angela was now twirling one strand of her hair around her index finger.

"Oh well that's good!" she said. "I thought maybe I'd had too much garlic, or my makeup had gone bad or some other wardrobe malfunction."

Michael looked at Jennifer again. It was as if she could hear across the table. But she knew the topic would come up. They had gone over his answer several times. She was softly tapping her index finger on the table.

"Angela, nothing could be further from the truth," Michael went on. "If I am not being out of line, let me say that you are an extremely attractive woman. It was, ah, very difficult for me to leave you standing there. But, you know, that other side of my brain kicked in." He laughed. "At least you know I'm ethical."

"So, there's no other woman Michael? I was afraid I was turning myself into a home wrecker."

"No Angela, there is no other woman. I promise you."

He glanced at Jennifer when he said this, and was reassured by the look in her eyes. He was, apparently, doing it right for a change.

"What's that," he said as Angela issued an invitation. "Friday night at your house for dinner? Fine. Seven-thirty it is. You're going to get tired of seeing me. Yes, I'll bring all the material you need to see."

Jennifer punched her fist into the air.

When Michael rang the doorbell at Angela's house, his hands were shaking so much that the petals of the roses he was carrying were in danger of falling off. He kept trying to remind himself that, no matter what happened, this was just a business call, nothing more. On his way out the door from home, he remembered Jennifer's last effort to make him relax. "Hey, look at it this way," she had told him. "There aren't many girls who would order their partner to go out and get laid by another woman. Enjoy it. But make sure she has a good time. I don't want you coming back without the money."

He had been able to swallow that, but when she had asked him if he needed any pointers about how to sexually satisfy a woman, his anger and embarrassment had made him leave the room.

He wasn't sure what to expect. Jennifer had said it was unusual for her to want him to come over on such short notice because, as it was, she would have to make sure the house was immaculate, and cook a fine meal, all in less than a day. He imagined finding a somewhat haggard but smiling widow, brushing hair off her face, telling him to have a seat on the couch, that she had something on the stove that needed immediate attention.

But that wasn't the case.

The door was opened to the smell of garlic and butter and the sound of soft music playing. "Michael," she said softly smiling, "thank you so much for coming."

Now, in the light of the front hall, he could see her hair shimmering down to her shoulders. She wore a very light blouse and he could clearly see the outline of a black bra underneath. Her matching black skirt was slit nearly up to her hip on one side, and a loose gold chain encircled her waist.

While Michael lost himself for a minute, it was like Jen was in his head, watching, coaching and evaluating.

"You look fantastic, Angela," he said, handing her the flowers, "really fantastic!"

He started to explain that they were simply an expression of gratitude for allowing his firm to present their credentials when she cut him off. Although her voice was low pitched, it sounded to him like the rumble of faraway thunder, a warning of sorts.

"It's been a long time since a man brought me flowers. Have a seat on the couch while I put these in water."

She disappeared into the kitchen but quickly returned and sat down next to him.

"I really do appreciate you coming over. I know this is a business meeting but I feel like it is the first time I can relax in months. It's far more comfortable talking like this. Don't you agree?"

Michael started to agree when the kitchen door opened and a man in a starched white shirt and vest, black bow tie and white gloves emerged carrying a vase full of Michael's flowers. He efficiently set them down on the coffee table in front of them.

"Oh Michael, this is Arthur. He is going to look after us tonight. I thought, with our having so much to discuss it would be better this way."

Michael tried hard not to show his amazement. Was it really possible that she had engaged someone who appeared to be a professional caterer to wait on them?

"Could I offer you something to drink, sir?" Arthur asked.

Michael had thought, on the way over that it probably wasn't a good idea to drink too much, but knowing that Angela wouldn't let him pass, he asked for a glass of white wine.

"Yes sir, of course. I have a lovely California chardonnay that was stored in oak barrels before bottling that I've been allowing to breath for an hour or so. Would that be acceptable?"

"Good choice, Michael," Angela said when Arthur was gone. "I selected this wine myself. I hope you enjoy it. I find the oak flavor leaves a wonderful, lingering taste on my tongue."

"Oh, are you one of those wine aficionados?" he asked her. "Once the conversation gets past red and white I am usually lost."

"Well, when I was married, my husband didn't believe that a wife should work. So I had quite a bit of time on my hands. I like a nice glass of wine. I have for a very long time. So I decided to learn more about it. The more I started reading, the more my fascination grew. I'll take you to the next big wine tasting event. Every summer the California vintners bring their best wines up to this area to show them off. I hear it's a fantastic outing."

Arthur finally announced that dinner was ready. The meal was like nothing he had ever had before, starting with a melted camembert with truffle and cream sauce appetizer - served with another glass of the chardonnay, followed by a small plate of sorbet to cleanse the palate. A ten year old bottle of Napa Valley cabernet sauvignon was opened and decanted, and served with sliced beef tenderloin swimming in a mushroom-wine sauce, fresh baby asparagus spears roasted with garlic and thyme and roasted baby potatoes. The service was neither too slow nor too fast. When they had finished, they returned to the living room where coffee was served.

"OK," Angela said, "now it's time for the most important decision of the evening. Arthur has brought some lovely pastries for dessert or, we could have my all-time favorite. What will it be, Michael?"

He laughed.

"I learned a long time ago never to get between a woman and her favorite dessert."

As it turned out, Angela's favorite was a flaming dish of bananas foster which Arthur set on the coffee table and, after waiting for the flames to die down, started to serve.

"Just leave it like it is, Arthur," Angela said. "We'll share. Oh, and that will be all for this evening. I'll clean up tomorrow. But let me congratulate you. Your culinary skills are second to none."

Angela accompanied Arthur to the door, and as it closed behind him, he heard the sound of the deadbolt clicking into place. 'Oh, to be a fly on the wall in that home tonight', he thought.

As Angela returned, Michael sat up straighter. The first thing that came to his mind was Jennifer's instructions. But was he supposed to be the aggressor? Or should he wait for his hostess to initiate whatever it was she had in mind? She had kissed him deeply on the front steps the last time they were together and later said that was because she'd had too much to drink. But tonight Michael had lost count of the glasses of wine. He could feel his heart pounding.

After rejoining him on the sofa, Angela, cut off a piece of banana dripping in cognac sauce and, using her hand as a napkin reached the fork over towards Michael's mouth.

"Open up," she said. "You're going to like this."

It was like the meal that had preceded it - unbelievable, the warm banana melting on his tongue. Sauce had dripped onto Angela's fingers. She slowly put each of them into her mouth, one by one, making a sucking sound as she did so. Chills ran up and down Michael's spine. "Now, we must get down to business," she told him when they had finished. "This has been a lovely meal Michael, and I greatly appreciate you spending your Friday evening with me - talk about working overtime! - but I wanted to meet with you to tell you, I am sorry to say, that a problem has come to my attention - a very important problem - and without some sort of resolution to what appears to be an awkward situation really, I won't be able to hire your firm to manage my money."

It was as if, with the wave of a wand, what remained of Michael's sense of wellbeing disappeared. Once again he thought of Jennifer and what her reaction would certainly be were he to return home empty handed.

"I'm sorry to hear that, Angela," he said. "Please tell me what it is. I'm sure we can work something out."

"Actually, I suspect we can," she told him. "At least I very much hope so. Now, just sit back and let me explain. After that, well, it will be up to you to decide how you want to resolve the issue." She reached down for a sip of coffee although the cup was clearly empty.

"Here goes. The other night Michael, when we met in the bar and you explained to me all about your new money management firm, do you know what I was feeling? It was pride. I was so proud of you for following your dreams. And I remembered, the first time I met you at my husband's memorial reception - our eyes met all the way across the room. Do you remember? I have replayed that moment in my mind a hundred times. Now I know that in today's society, I am supposed to spend my time grieving, working through the loss and having girls from the club come visit me with coffee cake for tea. But that's rubbish, Michael. If there is one thing my husband's tragic death taught me it's that we only have one life to live and it is an unthinkable sin to waste any of it."

She paused and patted a napkin to her forehead as she slowly undid the top button of her blouse.

"Is it me or is it hot in here?" she said. "Anyway, Michael, let me get to the point. The other night when you took me home and I kissed you, I said it was because I had had too much to drink. That isn't the truth. The fact is, the entire time at the bar, I was imagining what it would be like to…well, feel your lips on mine. They - they look so soft. And they were, Michael. I don't know what this is - is there such a thing as love at first sight? But the fact is, I haven't been able to stop thinking of you. I know you don't feel the same way about me, or at least you don't yet. But here's my dilemma. You said we shouldn't mix business with pleasure - a very noble stance indeed. But the thought of you having my money to manage, and that's all, would just be too much for me to bear. So, this is the way it's going to have to be. I'll let you manage my money, but in exchange, I want you to give it, give us a chance. We're both adults and neither one has a serious partner. And I know there are all kinds of awkward, emotional things that could happen but I don't care. If it doesn't work, maybe I'll become so frustrated and hurt that I'll decide to take all my money back. Who knows? But what do you say, Michael? You get my money in exchange for a rich, attractive - you said so, remember - and young widow. There are a lot of guys that would jump at that opportunity."

Michael could not stop thinking of Jennifer and her suggestions, which, he knew, were more like commands. She had told him to take full advantage of this woman, using sex to create a relationship that didn't exist, in exchange for her money. Was he that kind of person? He didn't think so - even if the money would someday be given back. Now that he was close, this close to pulling the trigger, as Jen had called it he realized his hesitation had nothing to do with Angela. Having sex with her would be the same thing as cheating in a marriage or at least the marriage he dreamed of one day having with Jen. A night with Angela wouldn't just destroy his sense of self-esteem it would forever tarnish whatever he and Jen might someday have. Did Jen understand that? Did it bother her? What about that part about forsaking all others?

Michael knew he couldn't bail out now. He had to accept her offer.

"Angela," he said, after taking a deep breath, "you are a very powerful woman, and attractive, bright, vibrant - how am I doing so far? On behalf of my firm, I accept the terms and conditions of your business proposal."

When he extended his hand to shake on the deal, however, Angela took it and started to lead him toward the stairs.

"Excellent choice Mr. Franklin," she said, clearly delighted. "You're a shrewd negotiator. Now if you will come upstairs with me please, I think it is time that we consummated our new relationship."

Michael had no choice but to go along with her, even though he tried to find a way out by muttering that he really should be going and that this wasn't a good time, whatever that meant. But Angela was quick to cut him off. "You and I just made a business deal," she reminded him, "and now it's time for you to hold up your end of the bargain. Don't tell me you're going to renege so quickly."

As they went into her bedroom, the smell of flowers caressed him, like he was walking in a field after a fresh rain.

"While I'm in the bathroom," she told him, switching on a single, rose-shaded light, "I suggest that you undress and slide under the covers and think about me. We're going to see if you can manage my heart rate - and other things - as well as you manage money."

When she was gone, Michael sat on the edge of the bed and looked around him. The bedspread was some sort of white, with lace around the sides, and was covered with oversized pillows of various shapes and sizes. The room, with its soft, white carpet, felt warm and safe, like a cocoon. He imagined that, once under the covers, you could stay for days and never come out. His thoughts were interrupted by the light under the bathroom door going out, and the slow sound of the turning handle. The widow emerged with a white silk bathrobe, her hair gently brushing her shoulders. He could see the smile on her face.

"Ready or not..." She stopped abruptly. "Michael, you haven't moved. What's wrong? Are you feeling all right?"

Sitting down next to him, she started stroking his leg.

"Oh, don't tell me," she said. "I get it. You're one of those shy guys that want the woman to take the first step."

She stood in front of him, took off her bathrobe and threw it on the bed, revealing a see through nightie that just came to the top of a white bikini bottom. After his first startled glimpse of her, Michael made a point of only looking at her face. To get aroused now would send the wrong signal and then things might clearly get out of control. He did not stand to face her and could see that her smile was slowly fading like a setting sun.

"Michael, aren't you attracted to me?"

As she moved closer to him, Michael could feel she was starting to have her desired impact, and knew that he had to get out of there. He stood, brushed to one side of her and stood by the bedroom door.

"Listen Angela, I'm sorry but I just can't do this," he said, "not now anyway. Everything is going... too fast. That's it. You said we would give our relationship a try and I agreed. But not just in one night."

She sat on the bed and folded her arms.

"Michael, I'm not going to beg you," she told him.

"No, Angela, I can't. Someday, hopefully you'll understand. I need to go."

"It's that other woman isn't it!" she cried. "You said you were business partners! Why the hell did you come over here if you're seeing another woman? Oh SHIT. I know why. You just want my God damn money!"

"No Angela, nothing like that," he protested. "I would never do something like that."

"GET OUT. Get out of my house and don't ever come back. You bastard! I thought you were different but you men are all the same."

That was it, she told herself as he hurried down the stairs and out of the house. There *was* another woman and Michael was closer to her than he was to Angela. It was probably that other woman that was pushing him - to get her money. He clearly didn't want to do it. Well, at least the man had integrity. But, Jennifer whatever your last name is, Michael Franklin had more than integrity. He had beautiful soft lips, eyes the color of a robin's egg and he was caring. His hands were gentle - the man had clearly never been in a fight. No, this was the man she was going to have. If she had to fight the other woman, then so be it.

But, Angela Messina wasn't a quitter. If she could deal with her abusive, life-threatening husband, she could deal with another woman.

The next morning, Jennifer awakened wondering what time Michael would come home. She was eager to hear his story. It was amusing, really. You send a guy out to do what guys like to do best and still wonder if he had sealed the deal, and if the widow had been pleased. She reminded herself that most women just learned to put up with guys' inexperience and lack of skill in bed. It was one of the challenges of being a woman.

Only then did she realize that Michael was curled up beside her.

"Michael? Michael!" she yelled, shaking him hard. "What the hell. Wake up."

"Whoa, damn Jen," he mumbled. "Let me sleep. It's Saturday morning."

Let him sleep when their entire future depended on how he'd performed last night? Was the man a fool!

"Why are you here? You should have slept at her house. Tell me you didn't mess this up last night. That would be impossible. What happened? Did something go wrong? Did you somehow get into a fight? Did she change her mind? Come on Michael, what the HELL..."

Michael pulled himself to a sitting position.

"Yeah, that's OK. I didn't need any sleep anyway. Why am I here? You might remember Jen, I live here."

Jennifer grabbed her pillow and held it tightly over her face as she screamed. She pulled it away.

"Michael... tell me you didn't... your instructions were clear. Even you couldn't have screwed this up."

He'd been thinking about how to tell her because it wasn't just about Angela - in fact not at all. It was about *them*. He knew that Angela would likely be a bit surprised at him not agreeing to sleep with her. His mission was to get the money, not necessarily have sex with her. They'd had the nice dinner. Everything had gone well. But that was all there was to it. This wasn't some sort of budding romance. He'd agreed to go through with it only because Jen said it was necessary. Angela had said that if he'd agreed to 'see where their relationship went,' she'd give him her money. So, job done.

"Look Jen, I did what you told me to, OK?" he said, rubbing his eyes. "She agreed to give us her money. And, by the way, if you haven't noticed, you are the one I love, not the widow, not ever. I was never going to sleep with her because of what that would mean for the two of us. Don't you see that Jen? So, maybe she was a little surprised that I didn't go to bed with her. So what? That is the reality of the situation. It never was going to be anything different."

Jennifer was trying to contain her rage. She didn't want to frighten him. She asked for more details and when Michael replayed them, her anger boiled over.

"YOU... FUCKING... IDIOT!" she cried. "I CAN'T BELIEVE IT. YOU LEFT HER STANDING THERE HALF NAKED? PLEASE DON'T TELL ME YOU DID THAT!"

Jennifer's nostrils actually flared as she continued, speaking slowly, enunciating each word.

"Michael, what in God's name were you thinking?! Are you completely clueless? You've made things worse, not better. This woman goes to all the trouble to entice you into her home, makes you a nice dinner, takes you up to her bed and wants to give you everything she's got. And you say no? You know what she's probably saying now? How about 'I'm a fool' or 'I've never been so embarrassed in my life?'"

Michael thought that, as much as he knew she wouldn't want to talk about it, it was time.

"Look Jen, maybe you're right. But if I'd slept with her, she'd think this was the beginning of some sort of romance, which it isn't. I thought it would be better not to go down that path because it would just be more difficult later. But look, that isn't the point. I love you Jen. I want to marry you. You just don't go off sleeping around even if it is for business. The thought of me with another woman, of violating your trust, it turns my stomach. I'm not going to do that Jen."

This was the tricky part. She still needed Michael to believe that they would someday live happily ever after. She imagined that, in the real world, a woman would be thrilled by Michael's honesty, to get that close to the forbidden fruit and not take it. But this wasn't the real world. She had to play along by pretending that fidelity mattered.

"OK, Michael, I see your point," she told him. "I guess that, for me, there are two kinds of sex: casual and when you're in love. Yes, we have a future together but we're not married yet. I guess maybe I thought you could think of it as you sowing your wild oats. But I get it. I put you in a tough position. I'm sorry."

She kissed his forehead.

"We'll figure out another way to deal with the widow."

## Chapter 36

Any chance of bringing in the widow's money was now gone.

But Jennifer had worked far too hard and for too long to let her plans go off track. She'd spent her whole life, it seemed, dealing with setbacks. She would overcome this one as well.

As much as she hated the press - they had almost ruined her life - it was time to go to plan 'B' - the reporter. As she heard Michael come towards the kitchen, she quickly gathered up the newspaper and pretended to be reading.

"Hey Michael," she called out. "You know what? I was just rereading this article that Andrew guy wrote about you. The focus was to put those pricks at Fifty States in their place - he obviously has an axe to grind - but I'm thinking maybe we can use this guy to help raise the money we need. Let's have a meeting with him to tell him about our new business and see where it goes. With luck, he could really help us get off the ground. I'm sure he was happy with his last piece - it did sort of tug at the heartstrings a bit. Now though we - I mean you - need to contact him and get him working on another article. He can call it 'life after death' or something like that."

Michael scrunched up his face and frowned.

"Jen, be serious. You don't tell a reporter what to write. There are editors and to some extent they don't have control. Besides, he wanted to interview me for the first article because he obviously hates Fifty States. Why would he care about our new business venture?"

"You're both right and wrong, honey. It does take a while for a story concept to be approved, for the reporter to do the research and the writing and to get it into print. Since the article we want him to write won't be timely or news-breaking, it could get shuttled until there is a slow day. But that all takes time - time we don't have. We want the world to know about our new business as soon as possible and such an article might be just the thing. I think you're wrong and that he'll care about our new initiative - a lot. He clearly is a human-interest kind of guy and here you are, fired and blacklisted trying to make a comeback. He'll be on it like a dog on a bone."

She sipped her coffee, long-since cold.

"Jen, I really don't think this will work," Michael said.

Jen looked at him, frowning and shook her head.

"Michael," she said, "let me remind you, the reason we are having this conversation at all is because one of us completely fucked-up a $6 million lay-up. You know what? I don't really give a shit what you think. You will do this because I am telling you to. You owe me. Now, we will practice what you will say and you will call him this afternoon. Got it?"

Michael cleared his throat and sat up straighter.

"What is your opening line?" she demanded.

Michael scratched his head. He had no idea. But he'd seen this look from her before and now was not the time to fool around.

"Hi Andrew, it's me, Michael Franklin," he suggested. "Do you have a minute? I have a potentially exciting business opportunity to tell you about."

Jennifer closed her eyes and exhaled. "Oh my God, Michael, that's horrible," she told him. "You couldn't sell beer in a bar like that. Let's try a more direct approach. How about you saying

'The bastards are trying to continue to hurt me, Andrew, to keep me from ever trying to work again. But I won't let them and they will be sorry. I need to meet you ASAP to explain how.'"

She waved her hands in a flourish, as if having just finished a magic trick.

"You see. You have to grab him by the nuts," she explained. "He'll feel both angry and guilty about the fact that you've been blacklisted because you agreed to help him with his story. After you tell him the story and get him all excited, you say, 'But I need your help, Andrew. Help me show Fifty States that they don't have all the power over the little guy. Help me show them that they are messing with the wrong man.'"

"But Jen," Michael protested, "that was something Ivan said. We have no idea if he was telling the truth - that Skip Williams ever said he'd make sure I couldn't find a job in this town again."

"Doesn't matter, does it? He told you very specifically that Skip said you'd have to move to a new city to find work. Why should you doubt that it is the truth? You have no way of knowing and you don't have the time or resources to find out. You're desperate, Michael. Your severance money is running out and what did you do to deserve this? You have just been going to work, minding your business. You can say that your plans to ask me to marry you have been put on hold as well. You really have to play this up as much as you can."

Michael wanted, very much, to say that the phone call from Ivan wasn't the reason his plans for marriage had been delayed. He had tried to raise the discussion many times with Jen only to be met by vague references to her mysterious, traumatic past, which prevented her from being ready. 'Don't ask me until I tell you to, Michael,' she always said, 'because I will turn you down. Marriage isn't like looking for a job where you just keep knocking on doors until you find something. When the time is right, I'll let you know.'

Now was not the time or place for that discussion.

She continued to coach him for the next hour and, when the pitch started to sound good enough, she gave him the green light. With Jen sitting across the table from him, he dialed Andrew's number and was surprised to find that he was at his desk, with time to talk.

"Yeah, hi there, Michael," he said. "How have you been? I think about you now and then. You never told me what you thought about my article."

"Oh, man," Michael replied. "Sorry Andrew, I meant to call you. I've just been so busy. It was a great article even though it was weird to be reading a story about a disenfranchised employee only to realize that it was me you were talking about. You made me, and hopefully the rest of Seattle, realize what a terrible thing they've done to me and how it's going to take quite a bit of effort or maybe just plain luck for me to get back on my feet again."

He paused as Jennifer, who had been scribbling something on the yellow lawyer's pad, pushed it in front of him. He read, *DESCRIBE first and THEN drop the bomb!* Michael understood where she was coming from. He had negotiated with Jen to let him present his plans as two-fold; the first being to find another shop that would take him on. He was not going to willingly give up on that option. It was what he had wanted to do for as long as he could remember. He would also present the second choice, the start-up of their new investment management firm. Jen had willingly agreed to him discussing both options with the reporter, notwithstanding that she knew the first one would never happen. Once Michael disclosed that he had been blacklisted, the investment management option would gain a large amount of credibility since, by definition, it was his only choice. She wondered how it was that Michael couldn't see that scenario as inevitability. Maybe it was a guy thing. She knew that a good chess player always looked three moves ahead.

As the conversation went on, it appeared that Andrew was becoming interested.

"So, explain that investment management strategy to me again, Michael," he said. "Instead of picking one investment analytical approach, you're going to use three - fundamental, technical and quant. And you've figured out some way to weight the relevance of the signal each gives you so that, in all markets, you will be able to outperform. Have I got that right?"

Michael was smiling now. "Yes, Andrew, that's how it works. I'd like to meet with you to explain it in more detail."

Jennifer was pleased. He was following the script well. She had drawn a picture of an airplane with bombs dropping from its belly and was ready to push it under Michael's nose.

Andrew had stopped talking. Michael could hear the clicking of computer keyboards in the background and the sound of ringing phones disrupting the low hum of several conversations interrupted, at times, by loud bursts of laughter.

"Yeah, um Michael, that investment management thing sounds like... well, interesting I guess. I have to tell you though that I know a lot of people that have run money for their entire careers. If there were such a thing as a magic box, someone would have discovered it by now. Correct me if I'm wrong but you've never been a research analyst or done any work picking stocks or creating portfolios before - at least I don't think so. I hate to rain on your parade but, well, without a track record under your belt, you're not likely to attract any clients. People don't want to give their money to an investor in training if you know what I mean. You know the old saying. If it sounds too good to be true, it probably is."

Jennifer had not coached Michael on the prospect that Andrew would do anything other than accept their new business plan with open arms. Seeing Michael's bewildered expression, Jennifer leaned forward.

"Yes, but, Andrew," he protested, "they blacklisted me!"

Jennifer rolled her eyes. Something was going wrong and Michael was panicking. It was far too early to play that card. She snapped her fingers to get his attention, but he simply held up one hand to indicate that he could handle it. Jennifer, however, was not convinced. Was it possible that he was fucking this up, too? Couldn't he do anything right? As Michael started to tell the story of Ivan's phone call, Jennifer's eyes widened and she reached again for her yellow pad, writing furiously in large letters.

"GET BACK ONTO THE NEW BUSINESS!!!!" which caused Michael to stop in mid-sentence.

"No, but look Andrew, we can talk about that later," he said. "I don't think I explained our new investment management technique well enough. I hear what you're saying about there being nothing new under the sun, but this really is different. It's been thoroughly back-tested and it works! We were hoping you'd write an article about it to, you know, help us get going."

Jennifer now held her face in her hands. He was completely butchering it, absolutely forgetting everything they had practiced. It was all going backwards.

"Michael, look, you know I'd like to help you any way that I can," Andrew was saying. "And I do want to hear more about you being blacklisted; that's a very disturbing accusation. But I have to say that this new investment management business sounds more like a pipe dream than anything else. Even if you back-tested your black box going back several years, there's no proof that it would work in real life. If I write an article promoting something that isn't proven and it ends up not working, we'll both look bad."

Michael was quiet for a few seconds, not sure what to say since Jennifer had apparently given up trying to direct the conversation, one half of which she couldn't hear. Then it came to him.

"Actually Andrew, you're sort of right about me," he said. "I've never worked as a research analyst but I *have* taken a lot of courses and I don't pass on any recommendations from our own research guys until I've done a complete review myself, you know, to make sure it is appropriate for the client. But I didn't create the model. My new... partner, Jennifer Salem did. I'm sure it has been both thoroughly back-tested and has a real life performance track record."

As he spoke, Jennifer was waving her arms frantically for him to stop. She had *told* him not to mention her name, not yet, not until it was absolutely necessary.

Michael sighed. This woman had been beating up on him all morning to sell their new business plan, one that was entirely created by her. And then, when it came time for him to call upon her to answer questions that he clearly couldn't, she'd freaked out on him.

"Look Michael, I can't talk any more right now," Andrew said. "I've got a deadline. What do you say we meet at Starbucks and you - and Jennifer - can tell me all about it?"

As Michael hung up the phone, Jennifer, arms crossed and apparently unable to find the words she wanted, just stared.

## Chapter 37

As much as she didn't want to, Jen knew she had no choice.

Michael's complete ineptitude at dealing with the reporter meant that, as had happened so many times in her life, she would be forced to take over. It would be easy to be furious with him or just dump him completely and carry out the scam herself but, she now realized, she almost felt like she owed him a debt of gratitude. She had been beaten in New York, taken down by the spineless analyst, David Heart, who got a promotion while she was run out of town. Most disturbing was the fact that she had under-estimated him. The one thing that she had relied on her entire life was the uncanny ability to read situations with the smallest of clues. Everything she was good at had failed her and she had almost gone to jail as a result. That was just plain and simply unacceptable. In hindsight, though, perhaps it wasn't that bad. She did, in fact, get herself out of an impossible situation that any other operator would have failed at. It was the Russian that was taken down and deported, not her. True she was no longer allowed to work in the securities industry but that was OK too. There were people, like those two guys from the SEC, who spent all their time trying to catch people like her. It was hard enough trying to gain inside information from unsuspecting donors without having to watch your back all the time.

No, this was a better plan. Without even beginning to realize it, Michael was forcing her out of hiding. She had licked her wounds and analyzed and re-analyzed her New York episode long enough. It was time to get back in the game. She was in a new city, with a new name and face and promoting a new way to take advantage of the system that had done nothing but let her down her entire life. Sandy Allen was back - as Jennifer Salem. It was a new dawn.

As she and Michael walked towards the coffee shop, she wondered if he had even noticed her precautions, which included wearing a drab, dark dress that went almost to her knees and showed no cleavage. She'd also put her hair up in a tight bun, scrubbed her face clean of makeup and worn the thick black rimmed glasses she had used when she was twelve. The prescription wasn't exactly right any longer but it was close enough. To the greatest extent possible, she wanted the reporter to focus on Michael. There was nothing to gain by promoting herself at this point.

"Now Michael, when we are sitting with the reporter, it is very important that you take the reins," she warned him. "You want to be seen as the brains behind our new investment management business, not me. I will only be there to prop you up if you need it, OK? Whatever I say, any descriptions or logic I might use, even if you don't understand, just go with it. I'll explain later."

As they approached the door, she stopped him and grabbing both of his shoulders turned him to face her.

"You got it?" she demanded. "If you aren't sure, tell me now. Are you ready?"

Michael tried to smile but it was clear that Jen was nervous, very nervous. He'd never seen her act like this and she looked pale. He wiped his hands on his trousers and nodded his head.

"All right then Mr. Franklin," she said, "let's do this."

Andrew had already secured a table at the back, as far away from others as possible. Michael Franklin and his what? Assistant?

Girlfriend? Not that it mattered. What did matter was that they were going to try to sell him on some new and unproven investment management technique. It would be inappropriate for some member of the unsuspecting public to hear before he'd had a chance to separate the facts from the opinions.

As the coffee was ordered and delivered, Jen assessed the situation. Andrew the reporter had barely looked up when they arrived at the table; he was totally immersed in some important message on his smartphone. He was a little, black haired man wearing a casual sports jacket with frayed cuffs, and gold wire-rim glasses. "Sorry," he said, "I just have to... I've got this editor from hell, and a deadline."

As he spoke, his fingers furiously typed on the small keyboard. Finally, he held the device away from him and considered it, and apparently satisfied that he had put out that fire for now anyway, turned to Michael and Jennifer, shook both of their hands and introduced himself.

Jen was the first to speak, which immediately threw Michael off since the entire way over she had said she would stay in the background as much as possible.

This reporter was busy and there wouldn't be enough time for Michael to spell out his monotonous and methodical approach to the markets. She had decided that it was up to her to set the hook as quickly as possible.

"Andrew, thank you so much for taking the time to see us," she said. "I know you're pressed for time and so are we. Our entire day is filled with meetings with prospective clients. Word of Michael's amazing discovery is apparently getting out and our phone is ringing off the hook."

Listening to the lies slipping effortlessly from her lips, Michael reminded himself to smile and look as enthusiastic as she sounded. "The reason we, well Michael really, wanted to meet you is because we think there is an opportunity, a mutually-beneficial possibility that only someone like yourself can make happen. It was his idea and came as a result of the article you recently wrote called 'What Price Progress?' which, by the way, was one fine piece of journalism."

Good, Jennifer, Michael thought. Win him over to our side.

"And, let's be clear Andrew, we're not here for the reason you might suspect. We aren't asking you to promote our new business venture for us. We're not having any problems in that regard and, in fact I think we're pretty quickly getting to the point where we'll have to turn people away."

Michael just kept smiling, even though he was, by now, completely confused. They weren't meeting with the reporter to promote Jen's scheme? Then why were they there? He was interested in the answer as well.

"No, let's be honest here," she went on. "It would be easy for Michael to be bitter and vengeful for the way he was treated. There may have been some things that were done and said to him that are just flat out illegal. He's consulting a lawyer about that."

As she spoke, she was drawing imaginary circles on the table, deep in thought about what she was going to say. She could see that both of them were listening intently and that was exactly what she was determined to maintain.

"We've talked about this a lot," she continued. "Part of us just wants to say, 'Oh well, bad things happen to good people. Let's just drive on and do the best we can.' Frankly that's exactly what Michael *has* done. It's impressive and overwhelmingly inspiring. But there's another way to look at this. What they did to Michael was wrong and, apparently they do it all the time. We could only guess at how many lives they've ruined, families they've shattered, all in the name of higher profits. Reading your article, it seemed pretty clear that you see things the same way. Am I right about that?"

"Well, actually, not many people know it," he said, laughing, "but my first job was as a junior analyst. I didn't last very long. It's a different world they operate in on Wall Street. Basic human civility, caring about things like health, career progression and personal wellbeing are all cast aside to make way for the money machine. Don't get in its way. It stops for no man."

He paused for a moment, and Jennifer had the good sense not to jump in. Who knows how she might be able to use a bit of personal info?

"But a writer has to be careful not to be seen as having a bias," he went on. "That's why I don't tell anyone I was fired. Besides, I am still very interested in the stock market and the industry. That's why I write about it so often. I have met many high quality people in that business who are genuinely interested in helping others."

Andrew had been fired. Excellent! Jennifer had discovered the key.

"Oh Andrew, we are so totally on the same page," she exclaimed. "We don't want to launch some vendetta against the big, ugly money machine either. Besides, what power do we have? After your last article, Michael didn't even say anything and now he's blacklisted. Can they do that? Isn't it illegal? Haven't they hurt him enough?"

She didn't even have to pose the question.

"Jennifer, like I said, I completely understand."

She turned and looked at Michael and put her hand on his arm.

"Here's the point I guess and, we're pretty sure that someone in your position is the only way to help. There are lots of people who find themselves in Michael's spot, and it is a very lonely experience. All we were hoping is that you could help spread the message that being run over by the Wall Street bus isn't necessarily the end of the world and here's one guy who's a survivor. People can form their own opinions about what they think of Fifty States' actions. But that line you had in your article - 'a voice cries in the wildernesses' - that's Michael, Andrew. We want to tell people hey, he's still here, bruised but not beaten."

She watched Andrew's face as she spoke. She could tell he was interested but not yet convinced.

"Yeah, I get it. I think I could write an article like that. And I think you're right, it might help some people. Oh, but man, look at the time!" he exclaimed as his PDA vibrated.

"Listen, before I leave, one of the reasons I came here was because I have some concerns. I wanted to hear about this new money management technique you're using. I, uh, may be able to help you to… avoid making a mistake."

It was time for Jennifer to pass the baton.

"Michael is the brains behind the operation," she said. "I'm just a computer geek."

Jennifer smiled as Michael followed his script perfectly. Andrew was leaning forward towards him now trying to screen out any background noise in the room. When Michael had finished, Andrew started to fold up his weathered notebook.

"Look guys, that sounds very interesting," he said. "I agree that you've identified the three most common valuation models, fundamental, technical and quantitative. And I totally agree that depending on the market environment, one will work and the others won't. But you don't know that until after the fact. What you say you can do, a lot of very smart people have tried before and failed. The fact is you can't predict human emotion and that is, at the end of the day, what drives share prices. The market is driven by greed and fear and always will be. No one, even the most sophisticated computer model ever made, can predict it. You'd have a far greater chance with the weather."

He started to get up.

"Do yourself a favor. Pick one of the three. Get very good at it and drive on. That's what the other guys do. You'll be wrong some of the time. Assets will flow in and out like the tide. But you can still make a good living."

Jennifer took him by the arm as he started to rise, anxious for him not to leave yet.

"That's it! You've just hit on the secret. Everyone goes about this the wrong way. Think about it. We know full well that some or all of the models will be wrong some or all of the time. You're right. You don't know that until after the fact. But listen to this. Let's say we have a portfolio invested in stocks that have been picked, a third using fundamental analysis, another third technical and the rest quantitative. At the end of the month, we look and see how our three disciplines have done. We identify the stocks that have outperformed and determine which methodology was used to pick them. If the fundamental technique is 'beating' the other two, next month we'll go to 40% fundamental and 30% technical and quant. We do that because we know the quant and tech models aren't working as well in this market. Yes they *have* been inferior and in a perfect world it would have been better if we hadn't owned any stocks using those disciplines. But that's the point, don't you see? We do what the market tells us to do. We are absolutely wrong some of the time. That feedback is critical to our re-balancing. By steadily under-weighting the technique that isn't working and overweighting the one that is, we are wrong far less often than we are right. It's all done using a sophisticated linear regression model. I won't go into any more detail - it would put you to sleep - but I will say that the numbers don't lie."

Andrew leaned back in his chair and thought. Brilliance was always so simple and obvious when someone else discovered it.

"You... you can do that?"

Jennifer smiled and patted Michael's forearm.

"It was Michael's idea and he has been working on it for several years. I just crunch the numbers."

Moving as close to the newsman as she could, she said, "We have $50 million in client assets so far," she said in a low voice.

"And the money is coming in at the rate of about $10 million per month. Last month our portfolio returned 1.84%. That's over a 20% annualized return."

Andrew let out a low whistle.

"Wow," he mouthed silently.

Jennifer smiled. As far as Andrew was concerned, she knew the article was all but written.

## Chapter 38

# THE SEATTLE REPORTER
### *"A Phoenix Rising."*

By Andrew Millcroft
—— *Staff* ——

Often considered an important part of Egyptian legend, the Phoenix is a sacred bird of fire found in the mythologies of the Arabians, Persians, Greeks, Romans and Chinese to name a few. The bird was known to have a colorful plumage with a tail of gold or scarlet and was said to live between 500 to 1,000 years. When it came to the end of its life, it would build a nest of small twigs and sticks, which would then catch fire reducing both nest and bird to a pile of ashes. From the ashes, a new young bird would emerge, restarting the entire process. This symbol of rebirth, dating from thousands of years ago, has been used by authors and philosophers to depict man's ability to recover from the ravages of life. Phoenix, the capital city of Arizona was so-named because it was built on the ruins of the Hohokam civilization that existed on the site hundreds of years earlier. The bird became the official symbol of Atlanta, Georgia in 1888 after it was burned down and then rebuilt in the American Civil War.

# The Ponzi

*Why has mythology crept into my reporting of local Seattle news? Because we have at hand before us a wonderful example of adversity having been overcome with a rebirth. Readers might recall an article published several months ago just following the acquisition of MOGI by Fifty States Investments. In the piece entitled "What price progress?" I asked that we remember during times of thirst for lower costs and higher profits that some people are left behind. These are people with lives, families, hopes and dreams. I reminded readers that all of us are always looking forward and, by doing so, do not stop long enough to consider from whence we came. And I asked the question what if, heaven forbid, that someone might be you? The article was more than philosophical because, as a result of the merger I was able to interview, on a confidential basis, one individual who suddenly and without warning found himself on the outside. To make matters worse, as a consequence of the transaction, father was pitted against son in a terrible conflict of interest.*

*Recently, I had the privilege of meeting with the unnamed protagonist in my story - to see how he was getting along - and I am happy to report that, not only is he surviving, but a Phoenix is rising in our midst. My subject is now happy to be named because he is seeking clients for his new business venture; his name is Michael Franklin Junior, son of Michael Franklin Senior, one of Seattle's most successful and respected financial consultants, with a long history of contributions to our city. While the father is not the topic of my article today, no doubt in his rise to success he had to face adversity and recover from setbacks. It appears the son has inherited some of those noble qualities. In my interview with the son, and his comely business partner, I learned that not only had he opted not to spend the last few months wallowing in self-pity, railing at the slings and arrows of outrageous fortune, he instead was excited to tell me about a new business venture, which ironically could not have been born unless Fifty States had* let him go shortly after the merger was announced. *As they say, things do happen for a reason.*

It seems like Michael Franklin Junior has been a student of the market for many years, having earned his Chartered Financial Analyst designation soon after joining the business. People in the securities industry who earn their CFA are widely recognized as having one of, if not the finest educations from which to try to solve the riddle of the markets. In Michael's words, he tried to use his learned techniques with customers but was often faced with the struggle for acceptance of anything new by them and management alike. He was told, in his words, to advise his clients 'like it has always been done.'

Now, out from under the oppressive thinking of the old regime, Michael has developed and refined an approach to money management that this reporter has never heard of before. When Mr. Franklin explained the foundations of his investment methodology to me the simplicity and logic were almost overwhelming, and my immediate thought was why someone hadn't thought of this before. His new model has been back-tested using historical market results dating to the early 1900's. Let me be clear, this article is not an endorsement or a thinly veiled piece of advertising for Michael and his new firm, a private company for high-net-worth clients only. I have always said that if something sounds too good to be true, it most likely is. I encourage readers to satisfy themselves if they have any interest at all. Caveat Emptor.

Having said that, Michael revealed last month's results and, if sustainable, his approach is out-performing traditional money management techniques by a wide margin. Rumor has it that investor money is pouring in and, in Michael's words they are forced to defer taking some. "Too much money too fast might impact our ability to achieve superior investment returns."

Too much money too fast! The Phoenix has indeed risen.

When Skip finished reading the article, he threw it on his desk.

"My God," he said, "someone has to be kidding."

He shouted to his secretary.

"Get me that idiot reporter Andrew Millcroft on the phone!"

There was no way he was going to sit idly by and not challenge this garbage.

## Chapter 39

Angela thought her anger might suffocate her.

After finishing reading the 'Phoenix Rising' article, she felt as though she was lost in a nightmare of her own making. Michael had *lied* to her. He wasn't from the Caymans. It was all right there. He'd been fired. Why had he failed to mention that? He had come off as so calm and confident but he was nothing more than a scared young man worried about finding work. OK, so it seemed like he did have some education. The reporter called him a 'student of the market for many years,' and he seemed to have come up with some sort of new idea for managing people's money.

But if he had lied to her about his past, how else had he deceived her? Was he not really her husband's classmate working on her financial plan? If not, what the hell had he been doing at the memorial reception?

The nerve! She was falling in love with this man and he treated her like she was an idiot. Thank GOD she hadn't slept with him.

She started to search her house, hunting for any trace of Michael's presence. The silk bed sheets, bought for just his occasion, had been stripped and thrown into the garbage. All leftovers, including a half-full bottle of expensive wine had been poured down the drain. She started with the dirty wine glasses, shattering both into the sink, following them with the dessert plates, all the time muttering to herself, "Do that to me will you? Well, you've messed with the wrong girl. And you want my fucking money! Hah!"

Finally, she sat down on her couch, and wondered what was wrong with her.

"There is nothing wrong with me," she said aloud. "You son of a bitch, you *will* be sorry."

Jumping up, she headed towards her late husband's den. She had been trying to find a way to check out Michael without him knowing. It was, after all, a fortune they were talking about. But she hadn't wanted to risk him learning that she didn't fully trust him. Now, who cared? The reporter would know whether this whole thing was some sort of fairy tale. She started to dial the newspaper's telephone number and hung up.

It dawned on her, if Michael was legitimate, if perhaps he lied from embarrassment more than anything else, she could blow their relationship sky high before it even got going. She needed to calm down. Maybe this was just their first fight. That was OK; couples fought all the time. She was in a Catch-22. If she denied him the opportunity to manage her money, or was seen to be blatantly questioning his integrity, any chance of their romance would disappear into the wind. But if she freely gave him everything, she could end up without him or her money.

And why wouldn't he sleep with her?

She had to make the call. She just needed to be careful what she said. She was relieved and disturbed when the receptionist put her right through and he answered on the first ring.

"Andrew Millcroft speaking."

Angela could hear all of the keyboards and conversations in the background and knew immediately that this was a very busy man that she had disturbed. It took her a second to re-collect her composure.

"Oh yes, good morning, Mr. Millcroft. My name is Angela Messina. You don't know me and I am terribly sorry to disturb you but I wanted to speak to you about your article today about Michael Franklin."

Andrew had received enough of these calls in the past to know that an early exit was his best move.

"I'm sorry ma'am but it's policy that any complaints be directed to the editor. I'll forward your call."

"No, no, this isn't a complaint, not at all. I'm just, well, looking for your advice. In your article, you talked about Michael - Mr. Franklin running a new investment firm. I'm about to give Mr. Franklin's company some of my inheritance but to be honest I really don't know what I'm doing. I've heard about unscrupulous people in the businesses who steal your money. I mean, don't get me wrong, Michael is a lovely man, it's just... how do I know whether he's on the up and up?"

Andrew's face lit up. He knew that Michael and his partner Jennifer would never disclose the names of any of their clients to him and here, out of the blue, one appeared. He needed to keep her talking to see what he could learn but, at the same time, be very careful what he said, lest he had to say it again in front of a judge someday.

"Well Ms. Messina, I'll talk to you but I need to warn you up front that I can't give you investment advice of any kind. Nor can I recommend Michael's new firm - or not. Tell me, how did you find out about him? Was it just reading my article?"

The widow explained that she first met Michael, of all places at her husband's memorial reception, but she left out the part about their eyes meeting from across the room. Andrew couldn't write fast enough.

"You say you had never met him before? He just showed up there?"

Angela continued. John, her late husband had contacted Michael several months ago. They were supposedly buddies at

Princeton and the two of them had been working on a financial plan for her and her husband. It was supposed to be some sort of surprise. John was trying to look after her financial future. Well, as it turned out, he did but not in the way he or anybody else expected.

She remembered to add a sniff from restrained tears to her conversation.

Andrew took a deep breath. He had talked to Michael several times now and there'd never been any mention of Princeton.

"Oh right, I remember now. Your husband, he's the one that died in that awful car crash. Please accept my condolences, Mrs. Messina."

"Thank you, Mr. Millcroft. I'm doing OK, you know, taking it one day at a time. But the fact is I haven't had much time to grieve. My husband had a life insurance policy and left me with quite a large sum of money. Before I give it to this Michael fellow, I just want to, you know, make sure everything is OK."

It did seem like quite a coincidence, he told himself, that she had actually been approached by a broker at the memorial reception. He'd heard of more brazen approaches by scam operators but, on the other hand, there was nothing to suggest that there was really anything wrong. After all, this was the son of one of the most respected men in the Seattle area.

"Tell me, Mrs. Messina," he said, "what exactly did Mr. Franklin say to you about his money management capabilities?"

"He didn't say anything right there at the reception. I mean, he wasn't pushy or anything. I liked that. He seemed to genuinely want to help me. He just gave me his card and left it up to me to call him if I wanted to. We met several times. I think he has been very good at disclosing everything I needed to know, and answering all my questions."

Andrew continued exploring this opportunity even though he couldn't assess a value to her story yet. He did want to ask her why, if Michael had been so good at answering her questions, did she call him?

"Could you maybe be a bit more specific? Like, what were your questions exactly?"

Angela easily replayed the scenes in her mind because, up until this morning, it was a movie she had never wanted to stop watching.

"Well, let's see. I asked him about his background. He told me about his upbringing and how his father got him interested in the stock market. I'm not sure he mentioned the part about being let go by that new company. I guess maybe he was embarrassed. Then he started to go into his bit about there being three widely-accepted ways to pick stocks but that was about the time he started making my head spin, so I told him to stop, that I didn't need to know about all that stuff. That was what I was going to hire him for, right? He told me he had a partner. He called her a 'geek,' who helped him manage the money. I don't remember much more than that."

Andrew was checking off the list in his head as she spoke. The 'geek' must have been Jennifer. That was, he thought, one fine looking geek.

"Well, Mrs. Messina, that all sounds like what he has told me so at least his story is consistent. Anything else you can think of?"

"Yes, the last thing he said was that it was against the law to guarantee any sort of percentage return, but then he said he was certain that his new investment technique would beat everybody else and it didn't matter if the market was going up or down."

Andrew wondered about the difference, legally, between not guaranteeing something and using the word "certain," instead.

"He's right about the guarantee part," he told her. "And I guess time will tell whether his certainty is justified. But Mrs. Messina, while I have you on the phone, could you tell me about your late husband? Where did you meet him? You said that Michael said the two of them were friends at Princeton was it? Did your husband ever mention Michael Franklin to you, even in passing?"

Angela was starting to realize that she had let her emotions get the better of her when she had made this call. Had she forgotten her own recent past? The last thing she, of all people, should be doing was talking to the press. She was starting to feel like she was the one being interviewed, not the other way around. She considered saying that it was too difficult to discuss her husband so soon but then realized that she had brought him up in the first place.

"Oh my goodness, look at the time," she said instead. "I have to jump, Mr. Millcroft. Thank you so much. You've been very helpful. Just to be clear, everything we've talked about is between us, right? I wouldn't want it to get back to Michael that I was questioning his honesty?"

And why not, Andrew thought, because isn't that why you called? But all he said was, "Yes, of course," and after telling him to have a nice day, she hung up.

Andrew looked at the receiver. He'd been at this reporting business for a long time and, over the years had learned to trust his instincts. And right now those instincts told him that there was more to this story - he could taste it. Why did everything need to be 'between us?' What was she worried about? And most importantly, why didn't she want to talk about her husband?

## Chapter 40

The 'Phoenix Rising' article had more impact than they could have dreamed of and the money was starting to pour in.

As Jennifer predicted, interested investors would come from some of the most unlikely sources. So when Michael fired up his computer, he was and wasn't surprised to see a message from his former boss, Harry Van Buren, wanting to talk to him about the potential for the newest, hottest money management firm in the Seattle area.

Jennifer laughed out loud when Michael told her about the message.

"I *told* you, the sheep are going to come marching right into the pen. That's the beauty of starting up our business this way." And then, seeing the concern on Michael's face, she added, "Relax, honey. Nothing has changed. We're still just borrowing money until we get enough assets to launch the model. And the way things are going that won't be much longer now. By the way, just because Harry wants to talk to you, doesn't mean he'll jump in. He still needs to be sold and we still have to customize our pitch to him. I feel like I sort of know this guy but tell me all about him - everything you can think of. Don't leave anything out."

Michael went through as much as he could remember, about how Harry was like the dog whose bark was far worse than his bite. About how he'd made a decision at some point in his career to go into management and, as a result, never made the big bucks that a really successful broker would have. Most importantly, Harry was a 'lifer.'

After about fifteen minutes, Jennifer held up her hand.

"OK, got it, or I should say got him. Remember when we first prospected the widow, I told you we could categorize most of our clients into sort of a seven dwarfs kind of scenario? Well, we're going to say that Harry is the 'Happy' dwarf. You say you never really knew if he was your boss or your buddy, walking around the office, always smiling, pumping people's tires. Perfect. When faced with a difficult decision, these types of people don't want to ask the tough questions. The conflict makes them uneasy. They tend to jump to conclusions early without having all the facts. When you're ready to push them over the edge, they'll worry about what might happen if they reject you, rather than whether it's a good decision or not. So, your strategy here is to plant the seed that you will be hurt if he doesn't sign up. This guy's whole thing is he wants to be your friend and that leads to a fear of rejection. In this case, it's even better because he already feels terrible about firing you when he didn't want to. I'm thinking Harry's a bit bitter about the fact that they only kept him long enough to chop all the heads, so he'll see giving you his money as some sort of revenge."

Jennifer had been ticking off boxes on her yellow pad as she spoke.

"Go get him partner" she was when she was finished. "This fish is all but in the boat."

"Harry, its Michael Franklin. How are you old friend?"

Jennifer had suggested calling him 'old friend' because that was how guys his age referred to each other. It also would remove any worries on the target's part that Michael bore any grudge, since it was Harry who did the actual termination. More importantly, Harry, as a 'happy dwarf' would respond best to someone in that frame of mind. Conflict, either expressed or implied, made him uncomfortable

"Ah, Michael, it is wonderful to hear from you," Harry said. "I've thought about you - a lot. How have you been? How is life on the outside?"

Harry's voice on the phone sounded different than Michael remembered it, almost frail, as if he was just getting over a bad cold. It used to be warm and deep, even when his old boss was trying to scold him for some misdeed. They all used to joke about it. Being taken to task by Harry Van Buren was like being licked to death by a puppy.

"Well, Harry, I've been thinking about you and the guys back in the office. I miss you all."

The fact was that when he was working there Michael often kept to himself and there were some people he couldn't stand - especially that arrogant bastard Ivan. But he was following Jen's scripting to the letter. After the exchange of a few more complimentary remarks, Harry brought the meeting to order.

"Thank you for returning my call, Michael. I want to talk to you about something personal. I need to get some things off my chest. First, I have to tell you that I couldn't be prouder of the way you've handled yourself after, well, you know. You've gone and started up your own company and, look at you. You're a money manager! You know what your old man was like. We'd just sling the latest opinions that came out of the research department on our unsuspecting clients but you - you actually make your own buy and sell decisions. Based on that article the other day - Phoenix Rising, you're good at it! Why hell man, you're a star! I'd love to be a fly on the wall of Mr. Skippy. I bet he wishes he'd thought things through just a bit more before jumping the gun. But who cares about him? Man, you must giggle yourself to sleep at night."

Take every opportunity to be friendly, Jennifer had said. No hard feelings towards anyone.

"You know what Harry?" Michael said. "When one door closes, another one opens. In a way I owe Skip a debt of gratitude because if it hadn't been for him, I never would have gotten to where I am. I'm not bitter and I never really was. He had his job to do. Life's hard enough without carrying grudges."

But, Jennifer had said don't let any mutual tummy rub go on too long. If it went down that path, he was to bring the conversation back to the business at hand as fast as he could.

"But Harry, you called me," he said. "What can I do for you?"

"Yes Michael I did. You're obviously busier than I am so I'll get to the point. When I read the article and realized the kinds of things you were doing, it was like an answer to my prayers. You might not be aware of it, but I've been managing my own retirement fund for years. I don't know why because, judging by the returns, I'm not very good at it. I've said more times than I can remember that I really should get someone else to do it but then I always get stopped when I think that I don't really know the person I'd be giving my money to. There has to be a lot of trust you know? This is my retirement we're talking about here, which as you know has happened sooner than planned - at least based on the lack of responses I'm getting after sending out my resume."

That was another thing Jennifer had accurately predicted, Michael realized. This man's retirement funds were important now. Before the takeover, Harry could have looked forward to getting a watch at age of sixty-five, but now with Skip running things, that scenario had gone right out the window.

"But see, Michael?" Harry was saying. "I know you and I trust you and now that you actually manage money, you're the answer I've been looking for, for years."

Michael wanted to hang up. This was Harry, not some stranger. He didn't want to have to lie to someone who was almost more of a father than his own. But Jennifer had written the script. He knew he had to follow it to the letter.

"Harry," he said, "I'll do everything in my power to help you. Just let me know."

He could hear Harry shift in his squeaky office chair although he knew he wasn't in his office any longer. Maybe they had given him that chair as a retirement present. The familiar sound told him that Harry had leaned forward to 'get down to business' with the person on the other side of his desk, or in this case, the telephone.

"Well, I do need to ask you some questions, if that's all right," Harry began. "I don't mean to offend you but you have to admit that this whole thing of yours pretty much sprang up out of nowhere."

When Harry asked if it was 'all right,' Michael could hear the concern in the older man's voice. Jennifer had been right again. People like Harry worried about being rejected by anyone he might have offended and it was his hot button. Damn, she was good at this. And damn he hated to lie to this man. But, reminding himself that it was only temporary, Michael explained the apparent appearance of his new company 'out of nowhere' by revealing that he had been working on his investment idea, in private for some time. He explained first meeting Jennifer and outlined the experience she had brought to the table. Once they realized the opportunity that was in front of them, all that had been required was the back testing that covered a few generations. The results were irrefutable. The model worked in every market environment known to man. Michael then started to get into more details, about the three different disciplines and about the model's capability, using linear regression to shift the weights of each one based on the performance. Michael knew that Harry was unfamiliar with modern portfolio theory and wouldn't know a linear regression if he tripped over it. As a result, he was likely to skim over this part.

People like Harry tended to jump to conclusions without having all the facts.

"Yeah, well thank you for explaining all that to me, son," Harry said when he was finished. "I'm going to admit that I'm an old school guy. I don't know much about all of that scientific stuff but then I don't need to, do I?" He laughed. "That's why I'm hiring you, isn't it?"

When faced with a difficult decision, these types of people don't want to ask the tough questions, Jennifer had explained, because the conflict makes them uneasy. But Michael had heard something that Jennifer had told him to be on the lookout for. Harry had said, 'That's why I *am* hiring you,' not 'that's why I *might* hire you.'

This deal was done.

## Chapter 41

"OK, Michael," Jennifer called out, "this is the fun part. This is how we both keep the fish in the boat and encourage new ones to jump in."

Jennifer had the financial section of the newspaper spread out on the kitchen table and her laptop open and connected to the Internet. Michael watched with interest, not really sure what to expect as he watched her put a red check mark next to certain names in the 'New Highs' and 'New Lows' section.

"OK, here's one," she said. "ABC Mines, up 23% in the last month alone. That was a good one to own."

Sometimes, Michael wondered about his new business partner. How was finding out which stocks went higher after the fact going to help them pick solid investments going forward? Just because a company's share price went up didn't mean it was going to keep going up.

"Jen, that's interesting but we don't own this stock and, more importantly we didn't own it last month while the price was increasing by 23%."

But Jen had moved her attention to her laptop where she was expertly typing away.

"Ah, here's another one," she said. "XYZ Securities share prices rises to all time high on rumors of a takeover bid. Perfect."

She stopped reading for a moment and looked up.

"What was that you were saying Michael?"

Michael looked at the ceiling and sighed.

"I was saying that, whatever it is you are doing, finding stocks that went up already is a waste of time because we don't own them now and didn't own them while they were going up."

She smiled at him.

"You see, honey, that's where you are wrong," she told him. "The secret to all of this is to tell people what they want to hear. We want them to believe that we *did* own this stock and the reason we owned it was because our technical research indicator was showing a very positive correlation with the stock price movement. I think you understand that the best thing technical analysis does is monitor 'investor sentiment' as measured by the stock price move. All stocks tend to trade in a pattern and when they deviate, for example, if a stock starts to rise faster than normal, it could mean that something is going on. In takeover bids, there are so many people involved; lawyers, accountants, investment bankers - from both sides - that news always leaks. So, while we didn't know why this stock was running, our models just showed us that it was and we bought it. We found out the 'why' later, after we bought it and after we made over 20%."

The frown on Michael's face made Jen burst out laughing.

"JEN! That is nonsense. We can't lie to people like that. Someone will eventually figure it out and then, my God, who knows how many laws we would have broken."

But Jen was back busily checking off names.

"Ooh, here's another one. The share price of PQR Company rose on the back of a series of analyst recommendation upgrades. Let me find this one on the net. Yep, there is it. The stock was trading below book value, which caused all of the deep value fundamental analysts to get interested. While the business isn't great and neither apparently is company management, this stock price got so low that a merchant banker could buy the whole thing, break it up and sell off the pieces and make money. So, clearly, our fundamental analysis model scoped this out and knew the Wall Street analysts would discover it at some point."

"Jennifer, STOP IT. Stop it right now!" he exclaimed. "This isn't some sort of game. We can't make this stuff up. We are dealing with people's money here. What if someone finds out? We'll get blown out of the water before we even get started. For crying out loud, the stock market went down last month. We are still in the middle of a bear market. If we tell people that we're making all kinds of money buying things that we didn't really buy, don't you think people are going to start asking questions? And then where will we be?"

Pausing, she looked at him, clearly formulating a response. She knew she couldn't lay it all out on the table, not yet. He knew that they were pretending to invest the money they had received but he was still under the impression that, once their assets reached a certain level, they would start managing the money using a fairy-tale computer model that couldn't and didn't exist. So, she had to respond to his immediate concern without revealing the whole truth, not that there was any now or ever would be.

"OK, Michael" she said, rubbing the bridge of her nose with her thumb and forefinger. "Sure, let's stop. Let's just forget about the fact that our clients are going to want to hear from us each and every quarter, just like they did when they had their investments with one of the bigger firms. They've given us their money and now they want to know they've made a good decision. They are greedy. Thanks to the newspaper article, they believe that we have discovered the mother-load of investing and have something that will turn the money-management world on its ass. But I told you, our model won't work until we get $100 million in the door. And it's coming in fast. Nobody wants to miss the boat and they are clamoring to get on board. We have huge momentum now. What do you think would happen if we told them, 'Oh by the way, we haven't actually invested one penny of your money yet.' Our bubble would burst so fast they'd be scraping our little balloon and us with it off the sidewalk."

She pushed the newspaper towards him.

"So, Michael, if you've got a better way, fine. The report is due in five days. If you're so smart, you figure out what we're going to say to them. But you're right about one thing, Junior. We *are* lying to them. We've been lying to them all along. You and I both know why. But there's one thing about a lie, particularly a big one like ours. Once you tell it, you can't just change your mind mid-stream. You have to follow it through or you'll be worse off than if you never told it in the first place. You know the end-game to this - I'm not going to explain it again. So, what do you want to do? It's your call. You obviously don't think I know what I'm doing so, over to you."

Michael could feel his face flush. He loved this woman. But there was one thing about their relationship that he really didn't like - resented actually. It reminded him of the way his father had always talked to him - all those belittling and sarcastic remarks. Jennifer knew full well that he hated being called Junior but, whenever they got into some sort of debate, she always dropped that bomb into her delivery. He really didn't like it when she just walked away and threw whatever it was in his face. That wasn't how partners worked together. True cohorts would have a healthy debate and then come to a reasonable compromise - but not this woman. It seemed like her favorite point of view was 'my way or the highway.'

Although he could never tell her, he looked forward to the day when he could stand up to her and prove that he was, in fact, a force to be reckoned with in this relationship. That day would come and while he wouldn't push her face into it like she would with him, he would savor it.

"All right Jen," he said as she rose from the table, "don't walk away. We'll do it your way this time. I think I have a legitimate point but we apparently don't have the time to consider another approach."

She'd known he would fold, like he always did. But they needed to get this done. Sitting down again, she gave him the paper and the red pen.

"Yeah sure Michael," she said wearily. "Whatever. Now it's your turn. We need to find six winners for our report and we only have three so far. So, find one."

## Chapter 42

Andrew's phone rang as he sat at his desk, wearing a headset to block out the combined noises of computer keystrokes, printers and conversations, which permeated the room like a morning ground fog. Without even looking at the button, he pushed *accept call* as he read the draft of his next article with a cup of coffee in the other hand.

"Andrew Millcroft speaking," he muttered.

"Yes, good morning Mr. Millcroft, it's Mr. Williams' office calling from Fifty States Investments. Please hold and I will connect you."

The line went quiet and Andrew imagined what was happening on the other end. These corporate big shots didn't even make their own phone calls. The secretary would have just informed Williams that she had "reached Mr. Millcroft." The corporate executive would keep Andrew waiting for about fifteen seconds, whether he was busy or not, just to remind the reporter of the hierarchy in their relationship. Andrew always wanted to hang up when he got these calls just to mess with the head of the caller. But Andrew had been expecting this call; he was surprised it hadn't come after the first article was published.

The line came back on with a crisp "Mr. Williams will speak with you now," and he heard Skip say, "Good morning, my friend.

Thanks for taking my call. Life is so busy these days, isn't it? It's hard to get someone on the phone. Anyway, how's it going?"

My friend? How's it going?

Andrew knew that Williams would never want to be his friend and could care less about how it was going. He was intrigued to learn the real reason for the call.

"Everything is good here, Mr. Williams," he replied. "You know how it is. The news just never seems to stop so there is something for me to do every day. It's hard to keep up."

Williams smirked. The reporter was so busy, was he? Go get a real job, like his. Then he'd learn what 'busy' meant.

"Please, Andrew, call me Skip," he said. "I want to respect your time so I will get right to the point. I'm calling about the articles you have written about the recent takeover of MOGI by Fifty States. As you can imagine, I have people on the watch because, in our business, we are in the court of public opinion every day. You, of course, have a great influence in that regard."

Andrew thought it was absurd that this senior manager big shot had people read the paper for him.

"Now, that first article you wrote, just after the acquisition," Skip went on, "I guess I didn't disagree philosophically; when people get displaced it's the corporation's responsibility to help them get back on their feet. That's why our policy is to offer fair and reasonable severance packages as well as outplacement services, which, of course, we did in this case. I thought you could have cut us a bit of slack. In these types of acquisitions, often times hundreds of people are let go. In our case, it was just a few and, frankly one of them was an employee that should have been terminated some time ago."

It amused Andrew that Skip couldn't use the word 'fired.' 'Displaced' and 'let go' sounded so much more humane.

"Well, Skip" he said, "We can talk about the first article if you want. But I have a feeling that isn't why you're calling."

Skip looked around his office. He wasn't used to having the pace of his conversations dictated by the other person on the line. He had a point to make and then he'd be done with it.

"Andrew, I don't say things to hear myself talk and, yes, we can discuss that first article and maybe we will. Frankly, the point of that discussion would be for me to educate you a bit in regard to corporate acquisitions. If you had the experience I have, you'd see that we really are best in class. But, never mind that. I wanted to speak with you about this morning's article. I believe it was called 'Phoenix Rising.'"

Andrew could hear a newspaper being picked up and then dropped on the desk. He was quickly growing tired of this man's attitude. He didn't need any education, thank you. The number of people terminated had nothing to do with his point.

"Yes, Skip," he replied. "It was great to be able to write something positive that came out of a negative situation. Michael Franklin appears to have found something better than what he had before. In his words, it was a godsend that he was let go because he never would have ventured down this path otherwise. Surely you can't have a problem with that."

They both knew what Skip's problem was. For Michael to go off and publically rebound in such an apparently strong position would suggest that Skip had made an error firing him. The point of this call was to sow the seeds of uncertainty in the reporter's mind so that Skip didn't have to face a stream of articles about how successful the faltering broker had become.

"No, of course not," he said. "I'm happy to hear that it appears he has rebounded so well. But look, Andrew, can I be honest with you? I think you've been used."

"Really! Do tell Skip. How am I being used? That suggests I don't know what I'm doing, doesn't it?"

Skip didn't want to alienate the reporter, which might likely lead to a whole other series of disturbing articles. So, he decided that he would take the time and walk through this with him.

"I am not trying to insult your intelligence - not at all. But give me the benefit of the doubt for a minute if you will. I'm not making a comment about your knowledge or background but I will argue that, after twenty years in the industry, I've learned a thing or two. The reason for my call - and you may want to thank me at some point in the future - is to warn you that this scenario with Michael Franklin may not turn out the way you've been led to believe. Are we OK so far?"

It was these people's air of superiority that bothered Andrew the most. It didn't matter what the situation, they would always present themselves as being more experienced and knowledgeable about whatever the topic at hand was. It would serve him right if Andrew just hung up now.

"Yeah, fine Skip," he said. "But I'm busy and I have a deadline I have to meet. What is your point?"

Forget alienating the reporter, Skip thought. Now he wanted to strangle him.

"Andrew, doesn't it seem odd to you that, all of a sudden, Michael Franklin has become an expert money manager? The people I know that do this for a living spend twenty, thirty or forty years working at it and never quite come up with a way to beat the market. And no one does - ever. So how, after a few short months, does Michael Franklin figure it all out?"

This is what Andrew had been expecting - jealousy.

"Well, Skip, if your people had read the article carefully you would know that Michael has created a new approach, one that I've never heard of and one that appears to be very effective. It has been back-tested for up to 100 years and, most importantly - this is the part that you'll appreciate - client assets are streaming in through the door."

Skip leaned back in his stuffed leather office chair. He knew that some of those assets were coming from his recently acquired firm.

"Andrew, come on," he retorted. "Haven't you heard the expression that if something seems too good to be true, it probably is? How is it that this person has by-passed years and years of experience?"

Andrew looked at his clock. They'd been talking for twenty minutes - and for what?

"Look, Skip," he said. "I have to go. He has a new approach. Only time will tell if it works or not. There's risk in everything right? Thanks for the call and your comments."

"But Andrew, if this guy crashes and burns, as I fully expect him to, he's going to take your reputation with him."

Andrew clicked the disconnect button without saying goodbye.

Skip punched the intercom button on his phone. There was one more call to make, insurance really, just in case the rookie really *had* discovered something.

"Get me Michael Franklin on the phone," he told his secretary. "Junior not Senior."

Jennifer had gone out for a run and Michael was sitting at the kitchen table, now called his 'office,' reading material that she had downloaded and printed off about gullible people and how to deal with them. They still hadn't heard back from the widow, but Jen was preparing him for the next pitch. And since he wasn't expecting a call, he literally jumped when the phone rang.

"Uh, hello?" Michael said tentatively.

"That's no way for Seattle's new star money manager to answer the phone," Skip told him. "Does your firm have a name yet? When are you going public? I want to buy shares."

Michael was, at least momentarily, speechless. This was a voice that he never wanted to hear again but likely would also never forget.

"Hi Skip," he said finally.

"Well it's great to hear from you, too! I was actually thinking about you the other day, asking your friend Ivan how you were getting along. He said he wasn't too sure but then, wham, this article comes out and I wanted to be the first to call and congratulate you. You have obviously been using your free time and relocation package very well. There's an old saying that, when someone leaves a firm, they are 'between successes' and that certainly seems to be true in your case. I might ask you to come in a do a presentation to our HR people about how to manage the transition."

Skip wanted to be sure that his approach was warm, supportive and caring because he needed Michael to disclose as much as possible before he dropped the bomb.

Michael was torn between anger and surprise. Here was the bastard who had him fired, who clearly didn't know a thing about him, a man who actually thought that he and Ivan were friends - calling and pretending to be his best buddy. What was that about? He should just hang up now.

"Well, thanks I guess."

"No really, Michael. When I read the article I couldn't help thinking how inspiring this is. Our business is nasty, most of the time and, well I'm sure you'll never believe this, but sometimes I get put into awful positions where I have to make gut-wrenching decisions - like with you. I didn't feel very good about myself after that - and I still don't - which is why I am so excited for you. Please, Michael, tell me all about it. I'm serious. I may want to put some money in, either for you to invest for me or to buy a piece of ownership - if you're selling, that is. I'm not sure I would be if I were you."

Michael was frowning. Part of him wanted to believe what Skip was saying but... he wished Jennifer was here. Still, he reasoned, Fifty States was a public company and Skip was an influential guy in the Seattle area now so what could the harm be? The conversation quickly got into the mechanics of the new investment management process.

"And you've somehow come up with an optimizer model that re-balances the weighting of each of the three major disciplines based on how well it is predicting the market?" Skip exclaimed. "That's so damn simple, it's ingenious. And, you back-tested it for close to 100 years? That's brilliant, too. Not only did you come up with a revolutionary idea but also you proved that it would have worked already. Managers spend their whole career trying to gain credibility based on their actual results, but you.ve figured out a way to circumvent that whole process. Brilliant!"

Michael desperately wished that Jennifer would come home. He wasn't comfortable talking about the back-testing because he'd had nothing to do with that - Jen had done that all in New York, before she came out to Seattle.

"Yeah, it's working out OK for us."

"But Michael, 100 years of data, on each stock and testing how each valuation philosophy performed would have required a huge amount of computing power?"

Skip still seriously doubted whether the rookie had truly discovered what he was saying he had. He might believe it but, going forward, no computer, not even a super computer could outthink the markets. Still, thanks to the bonehead newspaper reporter, the kid had gained the momentum he needed to make a killing. Skip wasn't 100% sure what he was dealing with yet but he knew it was in his own best interest to try to slow things down. There was still the matter of Junior and Senior, not to mention former clients, and he wanted to avoid any possible leakages.

As for Michael, he didn't want to answer questions about computers and accumulating data because he didn't know the answers. But since it was a key part of the selling story, the question couldn't be ignored. One thing he was sure of, however. Jennifer wanted to be kept in the background and would flip out if he told Skip the truth. Michael didn't know that much about computers and, in fact had no idea how someone would go about back-testing a theory. But he figured that Skip didn't know that much either.

"Well, you know, we have, or I should say had computers at work."

He quickly realized that he could be getting himself into hot water or, at least validating Skip's decision to let him go.

"After the market closed, when everyone had gone home of course, I did the back-testing then. It isn't that hard. It just took a lot of time."

Skip had been listening for some sign of a slip-up and he had just heard it. Michael had paused and his voice had changed a bit - a true indication that he was now lying. Either he hadn't back-tested the model at all and was just flat-out strewing bullshit - Skip doubted that because the kid was honest to a fault - or someone else had done it for him. Either way, Michael had given him the opening he'd been looking for.

"Of course," he said. "That makes sense. Good for you to do it on your own time and not when you were supposed to be dealing with clients. Of course you must have got legal to sign a release for that, right? I don't recall seeing anything go by my desk."

Michael sat up straighter. A release? From legal? For what? He cleared his throat - twice.

"I'm not sure what you mean, Skip. What does a release have to do with me?"

Skip knew he had him by the short hairs now.

"Oh you know that legal mumbo jumbo. When you left the firm, you signed a form attesting to the fact that you weren't taking anything that was the property of the firm with you."

Michael continued to frown. They had made him sign a lot of forms but he hadn't read any of them closely. Still he knew he was OK. He hadn't so much as taken a pencil with him.

"Well, that's fine Skip. I didn't take anything with me. There is no problem there."

"But Michael, you just told me that you did the back-testing for your optimization model using the company's computers."

Michael's palms were starting to moisten. If only Jennifer would come walking through that door.

"Yeah but remember Skip, I said I did that on my own time. Besides, who cares about the computers?"

Skip was smiling now. This was fun. He made a point to lower his voice and to speak in a slower, more deliberate tone.

"Who cares about the...? Michael, you know about these lawyer types. All they do is complicate our lives. Technically, legally, any work that you did using the company's computers, whether after hours or not, is the product of the firm. There have been all sorts of court cases about it in which employees have said that, because it was something they did, the product belonged to them. The courts don't see it that way. But, hey we're reasonable people here and we don't want to spend money on legal fees any more than you do. So that's why we came up with the release form. All a departing employee has to do is tell us about what they'd created while they were here. We then sign a release saying we no longer have any rights to the product or service that was developed using company resources. I'm sure I have never turned one down."

Michael was now frantically looking around the room. Skip relished the sound of silence on the other end of the line.

"You did get a signed release, didn't you Michael?"

Andrew knew that being a reporter was sometimes a gift and other times a curse.

First the widow had called him, and then Skip Williams, and all they managed to do was to make him question his judgment. He kept reminding himself that objectivity and logic must rule the day. He had an obligation to the community he served. To allow his personal emotions to invade his writing was the kiss of death, or worse. It was, he decided, time to tally up the facts.

Skip Williams came from a cutthroat capitalistic background where the only measurement of any value was money. He had jettisoned Michael Franklin Junior immediately after the merger was announced, with little care for the life or lives he would harm. Michael's new firm was starting to attract assets away from Fifty States, which would be very troubling since the whole point of a merger was to make more money. In Skip's world, an actual decline in profits would be a disgrace that he couldn't afford, something that he would do anything to avoid. In spite of Andrew's intense dislike of Skip and all those like him, it was his responsibility to consider, at the very least, the allegations levied against Michael. When he did so, he came away with more questions than answers, which meant that he had to give Skip's points some serious consideration. Lord knows how he'd got it, but Skip had faxed Andrew a copy of a quarterly report with some of the 'facts' circled. Had Michael's new model for picking stocks really come up with what seemed like the only winners in an otherwise poor quarter for markets? Unlike a report you might receive from a mutual fund company, just the names of the companies Michael had bought, and not the number of shares owned, were revealed. This made it impossible to even estimate the financial possibility of the supposed returns.

Then there was the matter of Jennifer. She had a mysterious past, which she didn't seem comfortable discussing. How did that fit into the picture?

He had to consider his reputation. Here he had written a glowing article about the beauty of someone picking themselves up when they were down; about facing and overcoming their adversities. By creating the story, he had - like it or not - endorsed Michael's new firm. For him to write an article questioning the validity of the same firm so soon after the laudatory one might do irreparable damage to his reputation, not to mention giving rise to the threat of a lawsuit. After all, what evidence did he have that he'd been taken for a ride? Fifty States had its nose out of joint because it was losing assets to Michael's new firm. So what? That's what competition was all about, right?

Andrew was glancing through the day's edition as he usually did, to make certain that his own contributions were properly positioned, when he came across the article in the Society section entitled, *Local Investment Manager Steals the Show at Charity Auction.* Apparently Michael Franklin and his 'partner' had attended a recent charity auction, entered the winning bid - $10,000 - for the most expensive piece of art and immediately donated it to a local Seattle art museum. Mr. Franklin was quoted as saying "The Seattle community has contributed more to my personal wellbeing than could be repaid in a hundred lifetimes. This gift is a small token of my appreciation." While Michael might have had some difficulty in his role of a young stockbroker attending to his father's clients, he was clearly having no trouble following in his father's footsteps as a man about town in Seattle society. And his new money management business was clearly doing well for him to be able to drop ten big ones on a painting, only to give it away - probably because with all the money coming his way now, he needed the tax deduction.

The article went on to list the other dignitaries and their wives. The picture of Michael and Jennifer reminded Andrew that something was nagging at him. He prided himself on never forgetting a face, and ever since he first saw her in the coffee shop with Michael, he couldn't escape the thought that he had seen her somewhere before. Compounding his anxiety was the lack of any information about Jennifer's background. He considered walking down the floor to speak with the Society page reporter but he knew what the answer would be. There was likely little or no history provided and, at any rate, the story was about the Franklins, as it had been for many years. The woman's role was clearly secondary and not worthy of mention.

Although it was driving him a bit crazy, he put the page down and started on the article he was writing for tomorrow. Or, at least, he tried. But he found that he couldn't help glancing at Jennifer's picture, hoping for the epiphany that would give him the "aha" moment. Finally, he couldn't stand it any longer. He walked alongside the row of desks to that of the Society author. When Andrew started to speak with her it dawned on him that this might be the first time. A newsroom was a busy place. No one had time to socialize. But still, it was a bit embarrassing when she shook Andrew's hand and said that it was nice to meet him at last. I mean, she had been sitting not fifty feet from him for weeks. Furthermore, when Andrew asked her about Jennifer, her answer was clear and definitive.

"Oh yes, I remember her," she told him. "I tried two or three times to get something about her, but she acted so shy that finally I just came out and asked what her role was in the new business venture. She just said she was Michael's 'partner.' Those were the only words that came out of her mouth. So, that's all I put into the piece."

Andrew thanked her and said they should go for coffee sometime. Back at his desk, he had learned nothing and was annoyed with the woman for not having dug harder as an experienced reporter like him would have done - because something didn't add up. When he had met with Michael and Jennifer, she'd referred to herself as the 'geek' meaning she crunched a lot of numbers. When asked by the society page reporter, she tried to position herself as little more than Michael's eye candy.

Andrew knew that whenever someone told two different stories about the same topic to different people, a warning light should go on. And he *had* seen her before. He was sure of that.

He'd tried to explore the Internet, using all of the leading search engines and the names Jennifer Salem, J. Salem and just Salem but none of the people he found matched anything close to her description. Whoever this Jennifer was, she'd apparently done nothing noteworthy in her life.

Now, well behind schedule to meet his deadline, he folded the paper and put it into his desk drawer.

But, he promised himself, he would come back to it. No really good reporter let questions like his go unanswered.

## Chapter 43

Saturday morning was Andrew's time off, since he didn't go to print with anything until Monday. Like most Saturdays, he sat in his comfort place, a large overstuffed, cracked brown leather behemoth that clearly didn't belong with any of the other furniture in his modest apartment. He couldn't begin to know how many hours he'd spent reading and writing, with his laptop on the worn wooden board that stretched across the arm rests, relishing the sunlight that came through the window. Like a bus driver who religiously took a bus trip on his holiday, Saturday morning was his time to read every word of the big weekend edition of his newspaper because he believed in the power of being informed - even about things that at first blush might not seem interesting. He liked experiencing events through the words of other authors and taking notice of how they structured their articles to achieve maximum effect. And, as always, he finished with the puzzles page, often going well into the afternoon to finish the weekend crossword, the toughest test of the week.

When he got to the Society page, he was surprised - or perhaps he wasn't - there was a picture of Michael Franklin and Jennifer Salem, this time attending the annual fund raiser/silent auction for Multiple Sclerosis. Whatever Michael did or didn't know about managing money, he had really taken to heart his father's uncanny ability to be in the eye of the public. At last night's event, Michael had won the bid for season's tickets, fifty yard line seats, to all Seattle Seahawks home football games, which he had immediately donated to a foster home for street kids who would have the chance of a lifetime to see their heroes live.

Putting the paper down, Andrew considered that fact that, if Michael's charitable giving activity was any testament to the health of his new business venture then, clearly he was raking it in. But Jennifer Salem was still a mystery woman. Putting that section aside for further consideration, he turned to the articles on recent crimes.

Andrew had never kept track but his gut feel was that the rate of crime was pretty steady in the Seattle area. That was a good thing because the city had grown impressively over the years but still tried to keep that small-town, everyone knows your name atmosphere. This morning, he read with interest about a woman, married for twenty-two years, who had received a call from a stranger. The voice on the other end of the line claimed that she was the child of her husband. After the birth mother had passed away three years ago, the stranger, who never knew her real father, set out to find him. And now, she claimed, she had. Her father, the voice alleged, had moved to Seattle and changed his identity to avoid the responsibility of the child he had created.

Andrew chuckled to himself. What a mess that was going to be! DNA testing. Lawsuits. How would the woman, who'd thought she'd been happily married for twenty-two years, handle this new information? "What a tangled web we weave, when first we practice to deceive," Andrew said out loud. It was one of his favorite sayings.

He started to deposit the newspaper section onto the 'finished' pile and stopped, thinking about the man in the story who had allegedly been trying to escape a tarnished past by changing his name and assuming a new identity. Was it, he wondered, really that easy to become a new person in another city and leave your baggage behind? And then it came to him. Pulling himself slowly out of his chair and going to his computer, he set about trying the new face-recognition feature offered by the leading Internet search engine. He knew that the FBI had such a tool with the ability to check people's driver's license pictures or even mug shots. These, of course, were not available to him nor should they be. There were already enough circumstances of privacy invasions for people to deal with. However, this company claimed to have downloaded digital copies of every picture of someone's face that had appeared in the newspaper over the last five years, from every reasonably-sized publication in the world. Their software apparently compared things like eye and hair color, nose structure and size and other geometric measurements.

What the hell? Nothing ventured, nothing gained. Calling up the on-line version of today's paper, he went to the society page, and made a digital copy of the smiling couple from their latest charity event appearance. After eliminating Michael's picture with the photo editor program, he was left with a homemade mug shot of Jennifer Salem which, after calling up the facial recognition program, he dragged into the search box and clicked the run command. Almost immediately, he received a message, which read *Beginning search. This operation could take an extended period of time. Estimated time to completion four hours and fifteen minutes.*

Four hours? Andrew doubted that this program was going to be very successful in terms of selling access to the database to the general public. As a reporter he had access to just about every information source known to man - and some not so well known. But people on the Internet these days were spoiled. They wanted everything in seconds. Andrew imagined how many pictures there were in the firm's database and figured that there must be billions.

So, if it took four hours, it took four hours. After all, he had the time and the patience. Settling himself in his comfort chair again, he turned to sports.

When the computer beeped from across the room, it awakened him from his Saturday morning nap in the sun, the half-finished crossword having slipped from his lap to the floor. He had no idea how long he'd been asleep but that was also what Saturdays were for. It had been a busy week and his batteries needed a recharge. Only then did he remember the computer search he had started that morning.

He launched himself out of his chair, study board and puzzle sent flying as he raced over to the desktop computer. Moving the mouse, he roused the machine out of sleep mode, and read, *Search complete. Click here for results.* When Andrew did, he saw that the program had returned seven pictures. Seven? He imagined there'd have been a hundred or so. Either the database of this program wasn't as large as advertised or the search engine itself wasn't as precise as claimed. Or, he thought, maybe it was quite precise, saving the operator countless hours of further search.

He quickly clicked on the first picture. Below it was the name of the person, the date and title of the article and which paper it had appeared in. In addition, there was some sort of rating, or score that the program assessed to describe the quality of the match. The first picture, with a match score of 100%, was that from today's paper. At least the program could find a perfect resemblance. Andrew thought that was a design flaw until he realized that the picture used for the search didn't necessarily have to come from a recent newspaper article and, in fact would be more likely to come from a personal camera. That, of course was the point of the search - to locate private people that had appeared in a public arena. To the side of the picture was the byline attached to the story in which the picture had appeared, with an option to click on the full article.

Andrew eagerly went down the column of seven pictures, clicking 'print full story' for each one. While the matches weren't perfect, he could see why the computer suggested a resemblance.

The seventh picture on the list was the least accurate, with a matching score of only 48%. The woman had black hair and Jennifer Salem was clearly a blonde. The article was from the *New York Times* and the byline read, *Wall Street Salesman Barred for Life in Insider Trading Scandal.* Andrew almost deleted it on the grounds that the story was written about someone living on the other side of the country. As the article's text appeared on his screen, he noticed the black-haired woman's name; Sandy Allen. That wasn't a match either.

But still, he thought. This person named Sandy Allen, who lived in the wrong city and had the wrong name and hair color, did work in the right industry. He wouldn't delete her just yet.

## Chapter 44

When Michael heard Ivan's voice on the answering machine, he turned to Jennifer and said, "No way. I don't know what he's calling about, but he absolutely doesn't want to give us a dime. He's a sneaky, manipulative prick and I don't trust him. I don't want his money even if he were to give it to us."

"He said something about a business arrangement," Jennifer told him, "so not so fast there, partner. We're not in a position to turn anyone's money away - and probably never will be. Tell me again about this guy, especially about that lunch when he tried to get you to give him your dad's book of business."

As usual, Jennifer had her head down, listening intently and scribbling notes on her yellow pad. It was like she was solving a puzzle each time a new potential client contacted them. After twenty minutes, she sat up straight and slapped her pencil on her notepad.

"OK, got it," she announced. "We're going to call this dwarf 'Grumpy.' Ivan is grumpy, Michael because he is jealous. He didn't like it when you had your dad's accounts and was happy as hell when he got some of them after they canned you. But for these people, that's always a temporary high. He's envious again because you have found something he doesn't have - the ability to actually manage money. It's your smiling face in the newspaper, not his. Now he's worried that he is going to lose his new accounts back to you. With Skip walking the carpet, giving everyone a daily report card, that wouldn't be good at all. That's another thing. You don't have a Skip hanging over your head anymore and he would desperately like that. Everyone there knows that Skip has the hatchet ready at all times and isn't afraid to use it."

She bent over Michael and massaged his shoulders.

"We most certainly want Ivan on board, both him and all of his clients," she continued. "But playing him will be a bit more complicated. Here's how we'll do it. Since Ivan thinks he's such a big deal in the business, you can explain our management style to him in such a way that he will accept it because he doesn't want to admit that it is over his head. Since he's jealous of your success, he wants 'in' in some way and these types of people will believe in something even if it lacks in supporting evidence. He'll probably want to offer you some sort of deal in exchange for bringing his accounts over. Play hard to get, at first. Say that, with the business going the way it is, the accounts will probably join us with or without him. He'll get all excited and say no way - they trust him or some other sort of bullshit. Finally, you'll 'give in.' Since he still works at Fifty States, you can tell him that we'll pay him a monthly retainer, a percentage of assets, for the business he steers your way. If he starts talking about joining our firm, or entering into some sort of partnership, the answer is no. If he presses, tell him to take it or leave it. I can promise you that he'll fold like a cheap suit."

When Michael got Ivan on the phone, he tried very hard to be both pleasant and professional. As soon as Ivan realized who it was on the other end of the line, he lowered his voice to a whisper. Michael imagined he was leaning forward on his desk, looking side to side as if someone actually cared whom he was speaking with.

"Yo, Michael, my MAN," he said. "Thanks, brother, for getting back to me so soon. I saw you in the paper. Wow buddy, congrats. We really got to do lunch right away so you can give me the whole story."

Michael pulled the handset away from his ear for a moment. He wondered if Ivan had any idea what an idiot he sounded like. The only thing he could think of was that the money management business wasn't that good if it meant you had to deal with fools like this just because they had money and you wanted it. But he'd rather deal with Ivan over Jennifer so Michael didn't even object when Ivan insisted they go to the same restaurant where Michael had walked out on him. Either he had forgotten about that episode or thought Michael had.

When Michael walked in to the restaurant, there was Ivan sitting at his regular table, chatting with the same ditsy hostess with a tight blouse pulled taut over oversized breasts who, if he remembered correctly, was named Kitty. He found himself wondering if she serviced Ivan after hours, too. Once Michael was seated, she grabbed the pencil that she had stuck into her hair and started her service routine.

"So, what will it be boys?" she demanded, chewing gum frantically. "How about something to calm the nerves? You stock market guys need that, right?"

"Sorry Kitty," Ivan told her, "this is a working lunch. We'll just have beer."

Michael had agreed to listen to Ivan's proposal, but not to have a drink with him like some old buddy catching up on old times.

"Just ginger ale for me, thanks," he said.

Kitty put on a fake pout but, when she saw the look on Michael's face, she just turned and clicked off in her high-heeled shoes towards the bar.

"You know what they say, Michael," Ivan remarked, grinning. "You can't trust somebody that doesn't drink."

Michael wanted to say, "Well, I guess if you don't trust me then why the hell are we sitting here?" but he just smiled. "I have to run some complex calculations on the model this afternoon and need a clear mind. You know how it is."

As Ivan nodded his head in approval, Michael knew that, in fact, he clearly didn't know how it was at all.

After lunch was ordered, Michael agreed to listen to Ivan's proposal.

"So, Ivan, what can I do for you?" he began, stifling his amusement as he recalled the fact that Grumpy was Jennifer's name for his envious former colleague. He might have picked up Michael's father's accounts but now he was concerned that, with Michael's newfound skill, he could lose them again. And Skip, the hatchet man would look at him like a vulture assessing fresh kill. But Michael had not forgotten Jennifer's warning; 'playing' Ivan would be more complicated than Harry, who just fell into the boat.

"Well, Michael," Ivan said, "thanks muchly for coming out to see me. I know how busy you must be - guys like us get that, you know what I mean?"

What an arrogant fool, Michael thought. The sooner he could get away from him, the better.

"Yeah, so anyway, I'll get straight to the point. I believe that there is a very lucrative business opportunity just shouting at both of us. You have a young money management company that is taking the world by storm and I have assets. Sounds like a perfect marriage, don't you think? Even though there are some logistical hurdles to our potential relationship - I'll get to that in a minute - I think it would work famously. You interested?"

"Absolutely, Ivan. Keep talking. I'm all ears."

The food arrived and, even though there were only two of them - and Michael had ordered an oriental salad - Kitty had to ask who had the burger with extra cheese. Within seconds, there was ketchup all over Ivan's plate and soon, the side of his mouth. As he chewed on a bite, he continued to speak.

"Excellent, Michael, you always were a good businessman. But look, before we go any further, I need to ask you a few questions - do my due diligence on behalf of my clients. They rely on me for that, you know."

Ivan was a 'legend in his own mind' as Jen had called him so, even though he was the one who called this meeting, he would still need to appear to be sold. Jennifer said to go through the description of their management style, certain, given what Michael had told her, that it would be well over Ivan's head. He might ask a couple of irrelevant questions but ultimately he would accept it because he wouldn't want to admit that he didn't have the first clue. Jennifer had said to watch Ivan's eyes widen a bit when he heard Michael use the term 'linear regression.' When they did, Michael had to cough into his napkin to hide his laugh.

Ivan now put on his most serious look.

"I have to tell you Michael, I've been in this business a long time and that is far and away the most amazing thing about managing money I have ever heard. But, here are a few things that concern me. Can your model be used in other markets around the world? What if I wanted one of my clients to have exposure to, say a Canadian gold mining stock?"

Jennifer had coached Michael to be firm if this topic came up.

"Well Ivan, with the money you entrust to us, it wouldn't be possible for you to recommend specific stocks. All of our clients are required to give us 100% discretion to invest in what we want, when we want, according to what the model tells us."

Ivan screwed up his face a bit.

"Hmm, Padre, that might be an issue. All of my clients look to me to tell them what to do. If they thought I had nothing to do with managing their money any longer well then where would I be?"

Jennifer had coached Michael on this, as well.

"Look, Ivan," he explained, "hedge funds are well known these days and these money managers are like us - if you aren't willing to let us do what we know how to - then keep your money. I don't want to tell you how to run your business but you could tell your clients that you want to diversify their asset mix and, after exhaustive research, you have selected my firm. It's no different than buying a stock really, and every quarter we disclose in a newsletter what we've bought and sold during the previous period. So, it's not like you won't know what we've been doing with the money; you just won't have any input. If you want to retain the ability to buy Canadian gold stocks, then don't give us all of your client's money. Keep some in a separate account that you look after."

"Ah, right. Brilliant!"

Michael could see that there was something else on Ivan's mind.

"Of course the only problem left would be getting your company approved by our compliance department as an accredited money management firm. I've never actually had to do that before but what do you think? Would that be OK? I guess the only other alternative would just be to move the money out of my client book, into yours. But that, too, has some... challenges. As you may or may not know, most of my clients' assets are in mutual funds and the fund management companies pay me a monthly retainer fee as long as the assets stay with their firm. If I move my business to you, that income disappears. Are you guys thinking about paying a retainer fee to brokers that bring in money?"

The clear conflict of interest in mutual fund trailer fees was why Michael had never sold one fund as a broker even though that practice had probably contributed to his demise. As he formulated his response, he realized everything Jennifer had told him to say was working perfectly. In fact there was no way they were going to subject their investment management process to the scrutiny of Fifty States' compliance department. If Ivan was worried that the loss of assets would reflect poorly on his own income statement, Jennifer told Michael to say, 'I don't know. We've never done that before' and, after Ivan sold him on what a great deal this would be for all concerned, to 'give in' - to make sure Ivan felt he had won. Michael would pay Ivan a monthly retainer, a percentage of assets, for the business he steered their way. This would more than make up for any income loss.

So much for thinking about the client's needs first, Michael thought.

"Ivan, let me put it to you this way. First, as far as bending over backwards to get on your firm's approved list, we'll pass. I doubt old Skip would allow it anyway because it might make him look bad. If he likes what I have to offer now, why did he get rid of me in the first place? He could have saved the firm the severance money. More importantly, we think - no, we *know* - that we have discovered something unprecedented in the money management industry. So, we are secretive. Hopefully you can understand why. Obviously then, there has to be a level of trust. If you need more assurances than my word, we aren't going to be able to work together."

Michael pushed his unfinished salad to one side. The dressing was so full of cream that the lettuce was completely flaccid.

"And as far as giving you a retainer fee of some kind," he continued firmly, "I guess the question I'd put back to you is why? With the way our business is going now, your clients are going to sell their mutual funds with or without your blessing and give their money to us. I hate to be harsh but, frankly, we don't need you."

Ivan finished his beer, grabbed the red cloth napkin, and threw it on the table. Michael had surprised even himself by the force of his reply. It was going to make his capitulation more genuine.

"Well, Michael, I don't mean to be harsh either but, hell, this is money we're talking about, right? So I guess the gloves have to come off a bit. First off, I'm going to tell you that you have under-estimated the strength of the relationship I have built with my clients. My assets have grown steadily, year after year and not one client - not one - has decided to move their business somewhere else. Secondly, and I guess this is the hard part, a meaningful portion of my book of assets used to be your dad's. You inherited them and then they came to me after you left. I want to remind you, Michael, that, right or wrong, they weren't very happy with you when you left the firm. At some point, if I tell them to move their money into your hands, I am going to have to identify the principals of the new firm. They won't have forgotten your name, my friend. In fact, it will take some convincing on my part to get them to agree. I'm pretty sure I can or I wouldn't be here wasting your time or mine."

Michael made the appearance of considering Ivan's argument.

"OK, Ivan. That isn't the most pleasant way I've had to be convinced of something but I'm going to agree that you have a legitimate point. You bring us documentation on what you are receiving from the mutual fund companies and we'll match it - for as long as the assets are with us, right?"

Ivan smiled and stuck his hand across the table to seal the deal.

"Like I said, Michael, you are a smart guy," he said, cocky as usual. "The assets are as good as yours."

## Chapter 45

At Jen's suggestion, they had employed an outsourced phone answering service, which was set up in such a way as to make it appear that the woman who answered was their receptionist, a ploy of many businesses that wanted to appear larger and busier than they really were. And since they were just taking the money, not actually doing anything with it yet - like investing - it left Michael with plenty of time on his hands. He was therefore excited when the answering service called to say that Andrew had left a message. After waiting the obligatory thirty minutes, which Jen said would be the minimum period of time that should pass before any call was returned Michael found that it was a pleasure to hear the reporter's voice.

"I've been thinking about you guys, quietly going about your business while you grow leaps and bounds," he said. "How's it going? I can't imagine how exciting this must be for you. Are you too busy to talk right now?"

"I'm always busy these days," Michael told him. "Right now IBM just reported their earnings so there's some excitement about that."

Michael had learned to always keep his Bloomberg website up and running so that he could drop the latest business development as evidence that he was in a room full of people glued to their computer screens.

"Oh, right. I guess that would be important. And I thought reporters were busy people. Look Michael, I won't take up much of your time. I was hoping that you and Jennifer could steal another hour for me over coffee. Your story has truly been one of the most interesting and inspiring that I've come across in years and I know my readers feel the same way. I keep getting calls asking me how you're doing. So, I'd really like to give them an update if I could. I promise - no more than an hour. Is that possible? You tell me when and I'll clear my calendar."

Michael was really starting to enjoy this. He and Jennifer had beaten the system and now everyone wanted to know them, to spend time with them and, hopefully, give them their money. Thanks to Jennifer, he had never felt more successful.

"We'd be honored, Andrew. Jennifer isn't available right now and I need to check her schedule. As soon as I speak with her I will call you personally to book the time. I can't tell you how much we have both appreciated your support."

Jennifer had taught him to compliment at will, anyone that had the potential to be useful.

"That's wonderful Michael. Please do make sure that Jennifer can make it. This is clearly a team effort and I want to see the team."

As Andrew hung up, he hoped he hadn't been too obvious about wanting Jennifer at the meeting, but even if he had, there was no way Michael could suspect the question marks swirling in his head. It was like coming home after a vacation and being met by a bad smell in your house, one demanding an immediate investigation. Maybe it was nothing - but a search was required none-the-less. He had to see Jennifer's face, up close and in person because he had to be sure before he started pointing fingers.

When Jennifer returned, her hair was disheveled and her face still red from yoga class. "Whoa," she said, "if you want me, I've moved to the shower - permanently!"

"Hey, guess what?" Michael said. "That reporter, Andrew Millcroft wants to meet with us again."

Jennifer stopped and wiped her face with the white towel draped across her shoulders.

"The reporter," Jennifer demanded. "Why?"

Michael understood her reaction. She didn't like the unexpected, and he knew she didn't trust his judgment. But he also knew that he was truly starting to 'get' how this business worked and was enjoying every minute of it. She'd come to recognize that in him over time.

"He said he wanted to do a follow up article because the one on us was one of the best stories he'd done in years and he has all kinds of readers calling him and asking how we're doing."

Jennifer scratched her head. "OK, that makes sense I guess. But he doesn't need both of us there to do that. You can handle that one by yourself, right?"

Jennifer didn't know why or how it happened, nor could she explain the circumstances that led up to it, but she had learned over the years to never, ever ignore your instincts, and right now the hairs on her arm were standing up. As a rule, she avoided publicity - it certainly had never done her any favors.

"Well no, he specifically said he wanted us both there. He said this was a team effort and he wanted to meet with the team. Come on, it's only for an hour. Let's go show him how it's done."

Michael's newfound confidence, she told herself, was becoming irritating and troublesome. He wouldn't see danger if it hit him in the face. Still, though, she was probably overreacting. Theirs was a good story and, as a reporter Andrew would rightfully want to milk it for all it was worth.

And so, putting instinct aside, she agreed.

Andrew had found a quiet table off the corner of the coffee shop that was often occupied by writers who needed a place in which to be creative or by people just wanting a quiet time with their favorite novel. It was around the corner without a view of the front door or the 'baristas,' as they called themselves, standing behind the counter ready to prepare the coffee of your dreams in a coded language that only regulars truly understood. As Jennifer and Michael approached, she did a quick scan of the room and was somewhat relieved.

Andrew greeted them like old friends. When he took Jennifer's hand, she started to have that feeling she'd had so many times before when a man's touch lingered longer than necessary, particularly when that was accompanied by his looking at her too closely. She was about to pull her hand away when Andrew released her and pointed towards the coffee line-up.

"Thank you both so much for coming. What can I get you?"

They hadn't rehearsed this so Jennifer stepped in to manage the length of the meeting.

"Thanks," she said, "but we've already been in several meetings. If I have any more coffee they'll have to take me out of here in a straitjacket."

Andrew repeated the offer to Michael who, having picked up on Jennifer's lead, refused as well. Instead, he reached into a worn leather satchel sitting on the floor and pulled out his spiral notepad.

"Right," he said. "You folks are busy and they say the stuff isn't good for you anyway. Let's get at it, shall we?"

Jennifer's eyes narrowed at the sight of the notebook. They'd already had one interview. Surely Michael hadn't told him he could have another. When Andrew explained that he just wanted to have the answers to the questions people were asking him when they called, she relaxed. But soon after Andrew started, it became immediately apparent that he wanted to know far more than that.

"Andrew, if I might interrupt you," Jennifer said, "the questions you are asking seem pretty technical. Are you sure this is what your readers want to know, or are we here to satisfy your own curiosity? You want to know details about how we are achieving our performance, don't you?"

Andrew was starting to annoy her by looking at her too closely, almost as though he were romantically interested in her - not that it hadn't happened before. The reporter certainly wasn't the first man who had tried to undress her with his eyes. It was the downside of being beautiful. At least his eyes hadn't ventured down to her tits yet.

"Well," he was saying, "I - I mean my readers would like to learn more if possible. I know your investment style is proprietary and I'm not trying to get you to tell any tales out of school, but the reality is that you do have something very unique. That's why the world is beating a path to your door. People are enamored but they want some sort of reinforcement, something to confirm for them that this truly is one of the greatest discoveries in the science of investment management in a very long time, perhaps ever. How did you come up with it? Jennifer, I have this feeling that you're one of those unselfish people that doesn't want any credit when it's clearly due but you've had a lot more to do with this than you're letting on."

Michael seized on the opportunity to respond before Jen had a chance.

"Jennifer used to work on Wall Street," he said proudly. "She's knows more about the markets than I ever could."

Andrew's gaze became even more penetrating and she was feeling the moisture gather in her armpits. Damn! Why had she agreed to do this interview? She tried to hide the New York part of her life as much as she could, but Michael just blew that out of the water. But even if Andrew tried to do an Internet search for Jennifer Salem from New York, he'd come up empty. Thank goodness she'd changed her name. Still, she decided, it would be best if she took control of the conversation.

"Michael, stop it," she said with assumed modesty. "It's never good to represent something in a way that overstates its true value. And Andrew, you're quite right that there's only so much we can or will tell you. You can say this. I *do* have a background on Wall Street but only in computers. Michael is the numbers guy. But we have been able to put our heads together and marry experience and understanding with technology. The key to our technique - and Michael gets all the credit for this part - is what I will call the 'feedback' mechanism. Our program monitors what each of the three disciplines we told you about predicts in terms of which stocks should do well compared to their actual price performance. I won't tell you how often it checks, because it took many, many months of testing to find the optimal time period, but when it sees that one discipline is starting not to predict as well as it was, we start to underweight the use of that methodology and shift assets into one or both of the other two."

Andrew, who had been jotting down notes, paused and stared at her.

"In other words," she continued, "we just listen to what the market is telling us."

Andrew wasn't 100% convinced.

"But, as you say, none of those disciplines works all of the time. What do you do if none of them are working?"

Jennifer started reaching for her purse. This meeting was coming to a close.

"Then we just go 100% cash - until our models tell us we should start buying again."

Andrew looked around the room as he digested her words.

"I have to tell you, Jennifer, there are some people who would say having such a model is a pipe dream. Can't you give me any more than that?"

Her furrowed forehead was an unmistakable sign that he had gone too far.

"Look, I know that you're just doing your job" she told him, "but why do I feel like you don't believe a word I've said."

"No, no Jennifer. Don't take my questions the wrong way. But you have to admit..."

Jennifer stood.

"I don't have to admit anything. You know what? Go ahead and be skeptical. I really don't care. In our business it's the money that counts. And, guess what? We have over fifty million reasons to think there are plenty of people who believe in what we do and those are the people who deserve our time and attention. Come on Michael, we have a client meeting back at the office. And there's one rule you don't need either a computer or a financial analysis background to understand. *Never* keep a client waiting."

As they went on their separate ways, Andrew had to restrain himself from running back to his desk, to re-read the articles from his search and look at the pictures again. Judging by the way he had raised his eyebrows, Michael, her supposed partner was as surprised as he was at the size of the asset pool. Over fifty million dollars? Furthermore Jennifer - if that was really her name - had been clearly uncomfortable when Michael brought up her New York background. And last but not least, the part in her hair had disclosed dark roots. Had she, he wondered, always been a bleached blond? Skip Williams' words echoed in his ears.

"If something seems too good to be true, it probably is."

## Chapter 46

As Jennifer and Michael were continuing their discussion about how they could use the characters in the Seven Dwarfs to help bring in new assets, the sound of an incoming email message came from Michael's computer.

"What does it say?" Jennifer demanded when she heard him moan.

"I guess it was inevitable he would hear about all this when he came back from Santa Fe," he said. "The e-mail is from my father saying he wants a dinner with me ASAP, to discuss my new business venture and perhaps manage some of his money. No way are we doing this, Jen. I don't want his money, borrowed our otherwise."

"Sorry Michael, we can't pick and choose. He's probably mad at you because you didn't call him about it. Don't worry. You and he have a history, which makes it seem as if he's a bigger issue than he really is. He's just a person like everyone else, easily classified, and there will be little difficulty getting his money on board. In fact, I've been thinking about him - I had a feeling this call was coming - and you know what? There's a dwarf that describes him, too and it's 'Doc.' In the story, Doc is the smart one - the expert. Your dad was a big swinging dick in his career and he knows everyone in the business. They meet and talk about the markets all the time. When you look at the psychological profile of a person like this, the likelihood that a smart person can be tricked increases when he is part of a group - like his investment club. You tell him that in exchange for taking on his money, you want to make a presentation to his club. When you do, he'll be proud as hell. Your presentation will include all kinds of facts and figures and, even if he is a bit suspicious, he won't admit it because it would look bad on him. These types of people, while they might have strong preordained beliefs about how to make money in the market, will change the facts or ignore obvious questions in order to support your story. I'm telling you Michael, this will be the easiest one of all."

Michael watched her lips as she spoke and didn't miss a word. But he also frowned.

"I hear what you're saying and it's probably all true" he told her, "but, all my life I have lived in this guy's shadow. He has second-guessed everything I've ever done and, while your theory may be right, this is Michael Franklin Senior we're talking about. He doesn't really want to give us his money. He's a slime ball, and he knows that I won't return his call if he didn't at least hold out the prospect that he might. All he really wants to do is have me show up to meet him and then rip apart our pitch to make him feel superior. No Jen, this one won't work or at least it won't work coming from me. You may think you've got him all sorted out but I have to pass."

"OK Michael, I see your point. You don't have to face him. We're a team and I will go after this one. Five bucks says I bring him in."

Michael laughed and shook her hand. "Easiest five bucks I ever made."

"We'll see about that, Michael," she warned him. "I can be very persuasive when I need to be."

## Chapter 47

Andrew was out of breath when he got back to his desk. Amidst the din of the newspaper room, he sat motionless, considering what to do next. There was something wrong about that woman and he couldn't let it go.

Finally, calling up the Society page article with Jennifer and Michael's picture and, using his photo editor software, he drew a circle around Jennifer and 'cut' her part of the picture out. Since all he had was a print version, he called up his second program that converted print photographs into digital. The program had to 'look' at each pixel, decide what color it was, like blue or green or some shade in-between, and then record it in the correct position. There was a secondary option to 'improve the quality of your digital picture.' A dark red pixel couldn't be directly 'touching' a white one - there would need to be several shades of pink for the transition to be real. When the software was done working its magic, he saved the file and compared the computer-generated digital photo to that in the newspaper article.

If anything, it was better and clearer.

For the next step, he typed in to his search engine *See what you'd look like with a different hair color.*

He laughed out loud. There were pages of different programs. He picked one and uploaded his newly created digital photograph of Jennifer Salem, a blonde. He had to 'tell' the program where her hair was by outlining it with his mouse pointer and indicate what color he was changing it to. Finally, the software, which was clearly targeted towards teenage girls, offered the command 'Click here to see the new, sexy you!' and Andrew did. He was mesmerized as the program changed each color dot from a yellowish light color to black. Line by line, he watched as the black shade systematically 'marched' across Jennifer's head. When it was finished, he sat back and considered her. She was a fine looking brunette, very beautiful and elegant.

There was still one more step.

He saved the picture and called up the photo search engine. Since his search would be narrowed now down to just one picture, it shouldn't take long. It was the *New York Times* article he was interested in, the one that had returned a 'similarity rating' of only 48%. He dragged the picture from the article onto one side of the program and then the black-haired picture he had created to the other and clicked 'compare.' He waited for the software to run. The answer was returned in less than one minute.

The similarity rating had risen to 95%.

Andrew leaned forward, and moved the mouse to read the full article, which, at only a 48% rating, he hadn't bothered to before. It was like reading a dime-store novel that he couldn't put down. Sandy Allen, an institutional salesman working for a boutique off-Wall Street investment firm had been involved in a multi-million dollar insider trading scandal. In exchange for testifying against a Russian president of a drug development company, she had avoided going to jail and instead was barred from working in the securities industry for life.

On the way home, Andrew's thoughts were in turmoil. He'd found something very important - or had he? If he had, what could he do with it? He thought about going to his editor saying that, although, he wasn't sure, but based on the research he'd done, he thought he might be on to something. But that was risky. Either his boss would scold him for wasting his and the paper's time on a wild goose chase, or perhaps even worse, he would become totally enamored with the story and tell him to drop everything to continue his investigation. The second reaction concerned Andrew more because it would mean a loss of control. He would then have to go full out when, in all likelihood some judgment, understanding and perhaps even compassion were called for.

He knew that, if he approached anyone, it would have to be Michael first. What would he say? Hey Mike, your partner is a hardened criminal who avoided a long stay behind bars by the skin of her teeth. How could he approach him without her knowing? If it were true, she'd no doubt be on the lookout for someone who might blow her cover. If Andrew told Michael that he'd like to meet him alone, he, in turn would no doubt tell Jennifer. Then she'd become highly suspicious and there was no telling what she might do or say. He couldn't possibly confront Jennifer directly. Therefore, he'd have to do this over the phone - not his preferred course in the slightest - but given the circumstances, he could see no other way.

If she was, in fact the disgraced Sandy Allen from New York, then her behavior would seem to fit as a piece to this puzzle. But, if Jennifer was Sandy so what? Perhaps she'd made a mistake and was trying to rebuild her life. The problems in New York had centered on an insider trading scandal. The newspaper report said that the person convicted - and ultimately deported - was an illegal Russian immigrant. She would have been tainted by association since, apparently, he was her client. That wasn't always entirely fair. Sometimes, these law enforcement officials got carried away.

The fact was that Sandy Allen had been barred from working in the securities industry for life - but not convicted of any crimes. What did that mean? Didn't she deserve the right to make a new start? Wasn't that what Michael Franklin was trying to do? Weren't they each, in their own way, a phoenix rising?

That was if Jennifer really was Sandy Allen. There was no hard proof of that, either.

He went through his mental checklist, item by item. Jennifer had admitted that she was from New York and that she'd worked in the investment business in computers. If the adjusted picture told the true tale, she was lying. She hadn't offered any reason why she had left New York and come to Seattle but then Andrew hadn't really pushed that question either.

The problem was that he couldn't gather any more evidence without strongly inferring accusations.

Maybe he should just leave it alone. If there was something amiss, it would show up sooner or later. But he couldn't shake what Skip had said to him about something sounding too good to be true, and this new dynamic-duo were taking in people's money. If Jennifer was a fugitive from New York with a criminal past, didn't he have a duty to the public to expose her? She was the one who seemed to get uncomfortable when he probed about their 'unique' investment management technique. What if it was a sham? It wouldn't be the first time.

There was a name for it, one that appeared in various papers every six months or so. Andrew could have inadvertently stumbled onto a $50 million - and growing - Ponzi scheme. He would never forgive himself if, having the knowledge and resources to prevent people from being hurt - perhaps more than they already were - he simply stood by the sidelines. Ponzi schemes were, sadly, not that uncommon. People just couldn't seem to manage their own greed and thus, were easy targets - like bugs attracted to an electric bug zapper.

He couldn't sit back and do nothing but he couldn't actually do or say what he wanted.

He decided to do more research on Ponzi schemes. After a few expert keystrokes, on his screen appeared the now famous black and white picture of Charles Ponzi, the smiling swindling Italian immigrant, whose name became the symbol for financial sleight of hand.

It was at that moment that an idea came to him. While he couldn't yet write anything that might call into question Michael Franklin's new firm, he could help make the general public aware of the danger. Readers might not be able to put two and two together, but it was better than doing nothing. He started to type a headline on his laptop.

*Charles Ponzi and the History of Financial Management Imposters.*

Andrew allowed himself one assumption. If Jennifer Salem *was* Sandy Allen, Michael didn't know because she wouldn't want him to. Given that, Andrew had no choice but to make the call. He was home now and, it being after hours, he connected with the answering service and left a message that he would like to ask some questions about Michael's father's career and how that helped Michael in his own learning process. He hoped that Jennifer, if Michael told her about the request, would be bored, leave the room and let the two of them speak alone.

Although he left his home telephone number, he was surprised when his phone rang twenty minutes later.

Michael had been sitting at the kitchen table, scanning the Internet for hot investment stories when the automated message came in. He thought it would be good to show Andrew how late they worked in order to achieve investment excellence. Jennifer was out again - he wasn't sure where. As their asset pool had increased, she seemed to be going out more. "Prospecting for new business, partner," she'd say with a wink and a wave of her hand as she went out the door.

"You guys are burning the midnight oil, aren't you?" Andrew greeted him. "I guess it's harder to sneak home earlier without the boss noticing when you are the boss, huh?"

"Well, you know what they say," Michael told him. "Got to make hay when the sun is shining. I thought I better call right away because your message said something about my dad. What's up?"

Andrew hesitated. He chose his words carefully.

"I just wanted to get more background information for the story, that's all. But we can certainly do it later if you and Jennifer are busy."

"Now's fine," he said. "Jennifer's out so I'm all yours. What's on your mind?"

Having passed the first hurdle, Andrew breathed a bit easier.

"I'm planning on doing a follow up article on the circumstances that led to your current success" he explained. "Readers like to know that sort of thing because they want to think in terms of how they might be able to achieve as much as you have. I think I'm pretty well up to date on what happened to you after the takeover but I'm thinking there were two other influences in the background that you managed to use to your benefit. In my mind, one had to be your father. Can you talk to me a bit about how your relationship with him, and what I would guess was a life growing up as a broker-brat, impacted your ability to go ahead on your own?"

Michael thought for a minute and started to recount the history with his father, careful to leave out any negatives. If his comments to Andrew were going to appear in the paper, it was in his best interest to have a positive spin to them. People out there who remembered and admired his dad would transfer some of that positive vibe to his son and, hopefully, bring in more money.

Andrew listened but took no notes as Michael rambled on for more than fifteen minutes. He was worried that Jennifer would come home before he'd had a chance to raise the topic that was the real reason for the call.

"That's great background about your dad," he said when Michael started to wind down. "I think it speaks to the point I've been trying to make about what really happens when big Wall Street firms come in and make all sorts of changes without the slightest effort at getting to know the people. Clearly the working relationship between you and your dad is an asset they just chose to piss away."

Andrew took a deep breath and exhaled. It was now or never.

"The other influential person I wanted to discuss was Jennifer. I know she is a critical part of your team but I don't feel as if I know her that well. What can you tell me?"

"Uh, what would you like to know?" Michael said after a long pause.

Andrew heard the unmistakable change in Michael's voice. He started his sentence with the word 'uh' and he answered a question with a question. Discussing Jennifer's history made him uncomfortable, probably either because he'd been instructed not to talk about it, or he didn't know the truth.

"Well, maybe you could start with a bit more about her background," Andrew prompted him. "I know she worked on Wall Street but when and for how long? She said she was in 'computers' but what kind? Was she one of those IT people?"

There was an awkward silence again as Michael realized he had to be extremely careful. Jen would flip out if Andrew wrote something in the paper she didn't want to see. At least Andrew wasn't asking details about how their investment techniques worked.

"I'm not so sure I am going to be able to give you the level of detail about Jennifer like I did my father," he said. "I mean I've lived with him all my life. I only met Jennifer two years ago."

Another piece of the puzzle fell into place! *The New York Times* article was dated three years ago. That would have given her plenty of time to relocate to the Seattle area.

"Believe me, I don't mean to pry," he assured Michael. "I hope she isn't still mad at me for asking so many questions about your newfound secret to success. I apologize for that - please pass that on. It's just my nature as a reporter."

Michael was nervous. He knew that Jennifer didn't want him to reveal anything personal about her.

"Andrew, can I tell you something that *has* to be off the record?" he said. "If you print this, she will kill us both."

Andrew pressed the handset closer to his ear.

"Sure Michael, off the record - all the way."

"The truth is I don't know much more about Jennifer's history in New York because she doesn't want to discuss it. She'll only tell me that something very bad happened and her trust was betrayed. She's still quite upset and felt that she had no other choice but to leave. She said she had to get as far away as possible and basically restart her life."

This was getting better and better, Andrew thought.

"Wow, Michael. Yeah I can see how that would be tough for you. How about this? How did you guys meet?"

Michael relaxed a bit. Surely Jennifer wouldn't mind him discussing this.

"Actually Andrew our meeting was serendipity. I was at the Y for a swim and all of the sudden the most beautiful girl I'd ever seen in my life just gets out of the pool - I mean it was like that Bo Derek scene in the movie *10* - and we started talking. She told me she was new in town and we just hit it off."

Andrew knew it would take less than a few minutes for someone handy on a computer to learn that the name Franklin was a big deal in the Seattle area and that the old man had a son, but all he said was, "Yeah, Michael. How lucky was that."

He was past the point of no return now. He likely wouldn't get another chance.

"Michael, tell me, did Jennifer change her hair color after you met her?"

Michael narrowed his eyes. Where the hell had *that* come from?

"What kind of question is that?" he demanded, on the defensive now. "Of course not and what the hell would that have to do with anything even if she did?"

But Andrew had opened Pandora's Box. He had to keep going.

"Are you at your computer?" he said "Will you give me your email address so I can send you an article I found? It isn't long. Please read it while I have you on the phone. I'll wait."

Michael couldn't believe what he was reading.

"Holy shit, Andrew!" he exclaimed. "I can't believe this. What are you suggesting? Have you lost your mind?"

Andrew had his speech prepared because he knew he would only be able to deliver it once.

"Michael, please listen to me. It might be very important to you. You know way more about the stock market than I ever will but give me some credit for being a reporter. One of the most important parts of our jobs is to investigate. Don't take my questions personally but do understand that this is what I do. You now have something over $50 million in assets and your partner is a woman who, by your own admission, has a mysterious background from New York. That's a bit of a puzzle Michael so I've tried to solve it. I'm not saying that your Jennifer is in any way related to this woman from New York - Sandy Allen but," he paused to choose his words carefully, "I am saying that some sort of connection, based on what I've found, can't be ruled out."

Michael stared blankly across the room before responding.

"Well, aren't you the clever reporter," he said finally. "It must be slow around there so now you're making up your stories. You should write some fiction. Oh, and by the way, Sherlock Holmes, you seem to have missed an important clue! The woman in your article has black hair. Maybe you didn't notice but Jennifer is blonde. You might want to check your facts before you go off half-cocked making accusations."

"Michael I have something else to show you. I just sent it attached to an email. Please open it and tell me what you see."

Michael opened the email and sighed. He didn't know why this Andrew had decided to chase down some sort of fantasy story, but he needed to nip this in the bud.

"Come on, Andrew. I have to say you're really starting to piss me off," he snapped. "You clipped the picture of the woman in the *New York Times* article and sent it to me. Why? Do you think there is some sort of resemblance to Jennifer? Is that why you're asking me about her changing her hair color? I've had enough of this."

"Michael WAIT. Don't hang up. That picture I just sent you is *not* from the article. It is Jennifer, taken from the picture of the two of you at that charity auction you two attended recently. I used the computer to change her hair color."

Michael felt as though someone had struck him in the stomach - hard.

"And Michael," Andrew continued, "it was you that said the picture I sent you was taken from the *Times* article, not me."

Michael could feel moisture on the back of his neck. The realization of what was happening was overwhelming. Had this reporter really been able to find out something about Jennifer's background that she'd refused to disclose? Every time the subject came up, he'd always accepted her explanation and her desire for privacy. As he started reading the article again, he knew this was clearly not something he was prepared to discuss with anyone but Jennifer. He would have to push her a bit more now.

"I'm not going to talk to you about your little witch hunt any longer," he told Andrew. "For that matter, don't call me again. Here you come in like some white knight after I was fired. Looking out for the little guy, were you? Now we see the real you, don't we? It's sad, really. I thought I could trust you. I guess these days you can't trust anyone. You're just another one of those scum-sucking pond creatures that sticks its head out of the mud every now and then. I'm just mad at myself that you fooled me. Goodbye, Andrew. Don't bother to call again."

"OK. Fine, Michael. You do what you want. I called to warn you that you might be into something way over your head. You'd better read the article again, very carefully. This Sandy Allen was part of a felony and, as a result, was barred from working in the securities industry for life. Apparently she was able to plea bargain her way out of going to jail. Somewhere in the world, she is a free woman, and women change their hair color all the time. So put it all into your computer model and figure it out - for your own good."

And with that, the line went dead.

## CHAPTER 48

Jennifer came through the kitchen door just as Michael hung up the phone from the reporter.

"Uh oh, the cat's away and the mouse is in play," she joked. "Who was that, partner?"

Michael could feel his face starting to burn, and knew that she wouldn't miss it - because she never missed anything - which made it burn even more.

She stopped, folded her arms and considered him. He was, she could see, trying to hide something from her because her radar was humming. Sometimes she thought that this guy was more trouble than he was worth.

"Who was on the phone?" she demanded.

Michael didn't know where to look. He hadn't had time to process Andrew's remarks, to replay them, to analyze the source and understand the underlying motivations. He didn't have time to make up a lie. Jennifer would expose him for sure and then the other issue would be why had he lied, what was he trying to hide and what else had he lied about? This would be added tension for no reason. But, he couldn't very well tell her the truth.

"Really Jen, it was no one, or at least, no one important."

"If it was no one important, then why don't you want to tell me? Come on, Michael, fuck off, I don't have time for your bullshit. Who was it? If we are supposed to be a team, then true partners don't keep secrets from each other. Tell me now."

So, he thought, true partners don't keep secrets from one another. Talk about the pot calling the kettle black.

"If you have to know," he said, "it was Andrew, the reporter."

"Holy shit Michael," Jennifer said, sinking onto a kitchen chair facing him. "I told you not to call him. We've gotten what we wanted out of him and now we just leave that alone. For Christ sake's, Junior, can't you follow the simplest of instructions without screwing it up? Why the hell did you call him? What did you talk about?"

As she spoke, Michael had started leaning forward on the table, eyes locked on to hers. He had, she realized, never looked at her that way before. What the hell was going on?

"Well, I'm certainly glad to hear that partners don't keep secrets," he said. "That's a big relief. And I didn't call Andrew. He called me."

He paused and pushed his glasses up the rim of his nose.

"And don't call me Junior. I don't like it and you know that. So don't do it again - ever."

For Jennifer, it was like that scene from the horror movie in which Dr. Jekyll was turning into Mr. Hyde right before her eyes. As for not calling him Junior, she'd call him whatever the hell she wanted, whenever she wanted and no wet-behind-the-ear punk was going to tell her otherwise. But rather than rip him to shreds, she stayed with the line she was on because, as she well knew, Michael had this overwhelming need to prove himself - no matter what the cost. And it was imperative that she know what he'd done this time.

"Why did he call you?" she asked as calmly as possible.

Now he sat up straighter because, for the first time really, he was in control. Jen or Sandy or whomever it was he was talking to, was going to have to dance to his tune for once because she had a secret, or at least he thought she did, and he knew what it was.

"He called to warn me - about you," he told her. "He said that I may be into something way over my head, without realizing it. He'd been doing some Photoshop work on the picture of you and me at the last charity auction. And you know what? He apparently changed your hair color and ended up with an almost perfect match of your picture with that of a woman who was also in the paper a few years ago named Sandy Allen. This woman, who lived and worked in New York was charged as being a part of an insider trading felony and, as a result was barred from working in the securities industry for life. Apparently she was able to plea bargain her way out of going to jail. Somewhere in the world, she's a free woman."

Jennifer registered bewilderment, while thinking of how to best buy time. She would, she knew, get only one shot at this. Think on your feet girl, she told herself. It's what you do best. The best approach was to answer the question that he hadn't actually asked by asking a question, about him, thus temporarily turning the tables.

"That's an interesting story, Michael," she observed, "but you didn't finish it."

Michael could now feel his entire body radiating warmth because he had crossed a line he had never dreamed of crossing before.

"What... what do you mean? Yes I did."

"No, you didn't. What you haven't told me is how you responded. We've lived together for two years but after a few minutes talking to the reporter you apparently agreed - without even talking to me - that I am a fugitive felon. When he made that accusation, did you even think to defend me Michael? I'd be interested to know."

It was happening again. Every single time he tried to express his point of view, she would somehow turn it on him so that, in the end he felt like he was wrong for even having an opinion, let alone articulating it. But he wasn't going to give up that easily, not this time.

"Well, as a matter of fact, I said to him that I wasn't going to listen to his witch hunt any longer. I told him to never call me again. I said he was a fraud pretending to be helping me when in fact he was trying to dig up dirt. I think I called him a scum-sucking pond creature."

There it was. There was her opening. Thank you, Michael. She was back in complete control now. She buried her face into her hands and spoke through her fingers.

"Oh, God DAMN it Michael. What the hell? Are you a complete idiot? We *need* the press. Here was the one guy who was helping us. How much money did we take in after his article about your new beginning? Well, not now. You managed to piss away the greatest asset we had."

She could see that her arrow had found her mark. He looked like a little boy being scolded for breaking a toy. Now was the time she'd been waiting for, and there wouldn't likely be one better, for her to reveal her 'past' in a way that best suited her purpose.

"I suppose this Andrew fellow has done one valuable thing," she said reflectively. "I've been waiting for the right time to tell you my whole story. You see, behind my brave and pushy front Michael is a scared girl. I had to leave everything I knew behind. It was my sole source of safekeeping, what little it was. Now I only have you. You seemed to come from such a stable secure background that I thought you might think less of me if I was completely honest with you and that it would affect our relationship. I couldn't risk that, Michael, I just couldn't."

Now was the time to introduce the idea that she was fighting back tears. She'd learned, over the years, that if she visualized herself, in her room sobbing as she had all too often done as a child, she could actually start crying. Now, closing her eyes, she dredged up memories about her mother and father, about the yelling, dishes smashing against the wall - the sound of a fist hitting human flesh and the anguished screams.

Michael wasn't prepared for this, having never seen her so vulnerable before. He leaned over to hug her saying "Oh man Jen, I'm sorry," but she pushed him away.

"NO! I can do this," she told him, assuming a brave expression. "I have to do this - for us. Now, don't interrupt me. I'm not sure I can say it more than once."

Michael leaned forward over the table so as not to miss a word. He felt helpless, because he clearly couldn't do anything to help her, and fascinated, because he'd been waiting to hear this story for a long time.

"My childhood was a nightmare," she told him, wiping her eyes. "My parents fought all the time and my father hit my mother. I used to go into my room and wedge a chair under my door thinking that would somehow protect me. I'd put a pillow over my face trying to drown out the noise and, I can tell you that, on more than one occasion, I wondered if I held it against my face hard enough, maybe I would suffocate and die - and never have to listen to it again. But I learned something from that - to survive in this world, you have to be strong and ultimately rely only on yourself. I guess that's why you'd say I'm a tough bitch. I had to become that way - to stay alive."

Michael started to say that he hadn't known and that he was sorry, but she made a stop sign with one hand. In her mind, this was a great performance.

"So, I start working on the trading desk in institutional sales," she went on. "I won't even talk about the challenges of a woman working alongside a bunch of testostcrone driven males because you, as a man, could never understand. They gave me the shittiest accounts, never talked to me and clearly didn't want me there. I figure I was the token woman to keep the people in HR happy. But you know what, Michael? I would rather have died than let them win and before they knew it, the shit accounts they gave me were doing more business than any others. The token chick on the desk had become the number one sales person.

The head trader - his name was Blackie - hated my guts and I'm sure in his own mind vowed that he would get me off his desk if it killed him. But I never let my guard down so, while it wasn't the most positive experience of my life, I was winning and making money and I was happy."

Michael was hardly breathing.

"That was my big mistake. Never underestimate your enemy. I didn't know they were conspiring against me. Some rookie analyst was hired - his name was David Heart - and they used him to set me up for a fall. First, Blackie went after him and would literally rip the poor guy a new asshole every day. So, I started sticking up for him. What else could I do? Next thing I know, David starts telling me about how this Russian president of one of his companies he does research on is beating him up, too. I say I will help him. I go meet the guy. Well, I'll make a long-story short. The next thing I know, the SEC is investigating me for insider trading! How the hell did that happen? Blackie was smart. He planted evidence everywhere to make them think it was my doing. It took everything I had to keep them from busting the wrong person. It was my work that led them to the Russian, who they ended up kicking out of the country. What did I get for my troubles? I get my name and reputation ruined in the paper. And, are you ready for this? I am barred from working in the securities industry for life. I will never forget the smile on Blackie's face when I packed up my things. In the end, the bastard had won."

Jennifer had practiced this story many times, since, other than the names, it had little factual basis. But she had almost memorized the *New York Times* article about her leaving. Her story would have to stand up to the facts presented in the paper and, in order to refute them, Michael would have to actually travel to New York and speak to the parties involved. She knew that would never happen.

"So I left New York with my tail between my legs," she concluded. "I was so thoroughly humiliated that I changed both my name and my hair color. I chose Seattle because I wanted to be as far away from my past as I could. And then, just when I was at my lowest, something magical happened to me. I met you and I thought, 'My God, there *are* angels after all.' I'm not sure what I would have done without you, Michael."

She was able to quickly turn on the tears again and this time she allowed Michael to hug her and make comforting noises that would, thankfully, preclude him from asking any more questions.

The thought that he could have brought someone so innocent such pain without even realizing it made Michael burst into tears as well. The two of them, sitting at the kitchen table sobbed in each other's arms.

Well played, Sandy Allen, Jennifer thought. Well played.

## Chapter 49

Jennifer arranged the dinner where she would ask Michael Franklin Senior if he would be interested in them managing his money. Even though Michael had said he would have nothing to do with prospecting his father's wealth, now that he knew the truth about Jen's background, he changed his mind. It would be thoughtless to force her to face his father alone.

They were both surprised when they arrived at the restaurant, to find Senior waiting by the front door for them. In all the years that Michael had eaten with his father, this was a first. In the past, when he arrived, his father was already sitting at the table, as if to say, 'OK, I am here now. The process of having dinner with me has begun and I am waiting.' It never mattered what time Michael had showed up, his father always gave him the look that said, 'I've been here for hours. What took you so long?'

Tonight, as they entered the lobby Senior kissed Jennifer on the cheek and then shook Michael's hand with both of his.

"Thank you so much for coming," he said. "It's been so long. We have so much to catch up on. Please come in. Our table is waiting."

They both picked up on the nuance. 'His' table had become 'our' table. When Senior turned to walk into the restaurant, Michael looked at Jennifer, bewildered, and saw her wink.

He still didn't believe that Senior would give them any of his money to manage, but Michael wasn't going to try to collect his $5.00 bet when he was proven right. They sat in their usual positions, Jen having moved her chair closer to Dad. The waiter came quickly and left with drink orders. In an attempt to break past patterns, Michael tried his best to wear a smile and appear interested in what his father was saying.

"Now, before we get started with the business at hand, I do have a bone to pick with the two of you," he announced. "Here I am, Michael, your first contact with the business of managing people's money, not to mention being your mentor for all these years, and I learn about your new, exciting business venture by reading it in the *Seattle Reporter*. I've had more than one call from my friends asking me for details and, I have had to tell them that all I know is what was in the paper."

The hairs rising on the back of his neck was a familiar feeling for Michael. Jen saw his smile turn to a grimace and immediately jumped into the conversation.

"You were in Santa Fe, sir," she reminded him, "and Michael has been totally immersed in running our master portfolio. And since the money has literally been pouring in, he's hardly had time to come up for air. My job is, or was supposed to be, to handle all relations with clients either current or future. I guess I figured that you know so much about the business that our investment management style required no explanation to you. You can't imagine how much time I've been spending with people going over the basics. I called you to arrange this dinner as soon as you came back. There was certainly no disrespect intended."

Senior grunted and arranged his cutlery into a straighter, more symmetrical position. The apology would have been better coming from Michael but this would do. The waiter reappeared and their dinner orders were placed.

"All right then," he said. "Apology accepted. The second thing I wanted to discuss was your so-called investment management style. I've been in this business my whole adult life, and I've seen brokers, clients and investment managers come and go like the seasons. The only thing predictable is that there is nothing new under the sun. You say that you have 'discovered' a new technique but I know there is no such thing. I, for one am completely skeptical and I would like an explanation."

Jen started to respond but this time Michael interrupted her.

"No Jen, I will handle this one," he said. "You fill in anything I leave out. Listen, Dad, when I was working at MOGI, you and everyone else wasted no time telling me that my thinking about the markets was wrong, that there was a right way - the old way - that was tried and true and forever would be. While we didn't see eye-to-eye on that, and probably never will, I think the one thing we would agree on is that the market and stock prices are nothing more than a reflection of human emotion or, stated more simply, greed and fear."

"Yes but that's not..."

"Dad, please let me finish. I completely understand your apprehension and I believe I can explain this to you in a way that makes perfect sense. I think you will also agree with me, that given the fact that it is greed and fear that drives markets and, given that we all have different personalities and our own unique ways of dealing with uncertainty, that each of us 'adopts' - I guess is the right word - a philosophy of understanding and measuring what is going on. So, you are a fundamental analysis kind of guy. You've spent your career reading analysts' reports that predict corporate earnings, and buying those stocks that look like they will have the best earnings growth because you and others like you believe that positive earnings growth will drive the stock price higher. Am I right?"

Senior nodded his head, clearly taken-aback by Michael's newly acquired confidence.

"But, you also have to agree with me that there have been times, lots of times, when the company came through on its part in terms of increasing its earnings but the stock price didn't respond like it would have been expected to. Am I right again?"

"Yes, of course, that is the way of the markets. But I still don't..."

Michael interjected with a force that surprised both he and Jennifer.

"Please, Dad, you have to let me finish. I'll get to my point, I promise."

Jennifer, although just as bemused by Michael's aggressive stance as his father appeared to be, maintained a frozen smile and hoped for the best.

"I know you think that there is nothing new under the sun," Michael continued. "But, you have to admit that discoveries about human behavior have been happening for years. You are 100% right that the emotional aspect of investing has not changed and never will. You also just said that when your approach wasn't working it was due to the 'way of the markets.' What if I told you that there was a method of measuring that apparent 'mysterious aberration,' in other words to tell which one of the three major techniques was the most accurate predictor of stock prices at any given point in time? What if you knew that, for the time being and for whatever reason, following earnings reports was *not* a good way to predict share prices? Don't you think that would be a very powerful tool?"

"Well, yes of course. But such a tool doesn't exist."

Their meals were served, interrupting the conversation for a moment. Jennifer looked at Michael with the pride that a teacher feels for a young pupil who has learned his lesson well. He had set up the conversation perfectly and was ready to deliver the crushing blow.

"Ah, Dad, that's the point. It *does* exist and it is called regression analysis. This is a technique that years ago could only be performed by super computers. Today, with the cost of technology continually getting cheaper, anyone who knows how can use it. But listen, even that isn't news. What is different, and what Jen and I bring to the table, is the application of the new technology to the old ways of the market. It works, Dad. It works so freaking well that the returns are astounding. It isn't just some black box. In a way, the market has always been telling us that there is a better way to manage stocks. We just didn't have the ability to listen. Now, we do."

Jen had coached Michael that now was the time for him to pause. When people who believe they are well informed on a subject are faced with new information that they don't understand, they're likely to accept it because to challenge it raises the specter that they don't really know as much as they thought. Inside, of course they knew that. What they feared most, she'd explained, was that others would realize that they didn't understand and respect them less. Michael knew that his father probably couldn't even spell the word regression much less know what it meant. It was at this point that he would have to give in. For effect, he pushed his warm plate of angel hair pasta in oyster sauce to one side.

"Michael, my God, I'm astounded. It's been sitting there right in front of us all these years and you discovered it. Congratulations - and you too Jennifer. That is very exciting indeed."

He continued to talk but Michael was no longer listening. His father stopped in mid-sentence when he noticed his son looking across the room.

"Are we not interesting enough for you Michael? What are you looking at?"

He turned to face his father, his faced flushed. In that instant, all three heads turned toward the general direction that Michael had been looking. But the apparition was gone.

"Uh, nothing, no one. I just thought I saw someone I recognized. One of our clients! But, apparently not."

But he *had* seen her. She was standing at the far side of the restaurant looking, watching them at their table. As soon as she realized that Michael saw her, she disappeared behind a partition. It was the widow. He was sure of it.

"All right then," his father was saying, "let's eat our meal before it gets cold. There are a couple of other issues we need to discuss, but we'll do that over coffee." He smiled. "You haven't got my money yet! And Michael, I would appreciate it if, when I am addressing you that you not let your eyes wander off halfway across the room. If I am going to become a client, I believe I deserve more respect than that."

After a dessert of fresh berries and sorbet, followed by cappuccino and brandy, Senior decided it was time to start the negotiations again.

"Now, getting back to the business of my money, there are two more things we need to discuss. The first, while I will admit this has nothing to do with managing money, is still a concern. You two say you are managing this business like a partnership," the older man said. "It appears that you have taken the investment management role and Jennifer you, the marketing and sales side. I would say both positions suit your backgrounds. In the small businesses I have seen during my time, one of the big first mistakes is the lack of a clear definition of who is going to do what. The two of you appear to have avoided such an error. That's very good. You might not realize how good it is."

He hadn't gotten the roles right - in fact completely backwards Jen thought - but if that was the way he wanted to perceive things and it made him happy, she wasn't going to argue.

"But did you hear what I said? *The two of you.* In a small partnership, at the beginning at least, there is no one else to do the work and you have no idea how much work is to come. The success of the business literally depends on the strength of the partnership. I don't want to entrust my hard-earned money to you unless you can focus all of your energy on your work, not thinking about some fight you had last night or how one of you discovered that, at the end of the day you don't really like the other.

Disharmony on the home front is stressful and requires a great deal of time and energy, which, if you spend it, is a resource not devoted to my money."

Jennifer wanted to throw her coffee at him. Every time he used the word 'money' in a sentence, it was so heavily emphasized that you'd think he was the only one in the world that possessed the sacred stuff.

"I've watched you both for what, two years now? The relationship you had early on appears to be just about the same one you have now. That concerns me. A stagnant relationship is an unhealthy relationship."

He leaned back in his chair and swirled his brandy, apparently certain that he didn't need to say anything more. Michael hadn't thought about it that way before or, maybe he had and just didn't want to admit it. But one thing was consistent. Leave it to Senior to bring up the most awkward thing he could think of just to obliterate, as completely as possible, any sense of enjoyment anyone might have been having. But this *was* a problem and the issue was Jennifer.

Jennifer, however, didn't miss a beat. Reaching across the table, she took Michael's hand. "Well," she cooed, "we didn't want to bring it up here - this *is* a business dinner after all, and the subject is you, Mr. Franklin, not Michael and I, but, since you asked, we have our own announcement that I think will allay your concerns about the two of us being compatible enough to run and grow our business."

It felt to Michael as though the entire restaurant had gone silent, waiting to hear what Jennifer had to say. And then she said it.

"Michael and I are engaged!"

Flute glasses of champagne were quickly ordered and consumed. Senior asked when and where this had all happened and Jennifer said just before they had left for dinner and right at the kitchen table. No they hadn't set a date but they did want to make sure that Senior was the first to find out. Michael did his best to let Jennifer do the talking and to smile when she did.

Finally, his father pushed himself away from the table.

"Well, I'll tell you kids, I need to go home before I put my face on the table and spend the night right here."

"But Mr. Franklin," Jennifer said, "you said you had something else you wanted to discuss. Shouldn't we do that before we go?"

Senior smiled, put his hand on top of hers and turned towards Michael.

"There, you see, Michael?" he said, patting her hand. "You've selected both your life and business partner very well. She's still trying to close the deal. But there's no way I'm going to tarnish this joyous event with a discussion about my business issues. Call me in the morning, son, and we'll talk. It was something that is, or now I guess I should say *was*, between you and me. Actually, don't call me; come over. What I need to say to you should be said in person."

As Jennifer and her fiancé walked arm-in-arm out of the restaurant, Michael's head was reeling. They were engaged? When the hell did she decide that?

And what was Angela doing in the restaurant?

## CHAPTER 50

Michael felt a sense of irony as he approached the house he grew up in. Last night, his 'father' had behaved like any normal man would, proud of his son entering marriage and thrilled to have a new daughter in-law. But, since Michael now knew his whole life was based on a lie, it was impossible for him to share in the old man's apparent elation.

Besides, even the so-called engagement could just be one of Jennifer's moves to close the deal.

He sighed. It seemed like everywhere he turned was a deception.

In the past, Michael would be careful not to disturb the iconic figure. Now he knocked on the door loudly. This whole episode was starting to make him queasy. Whatever the old man had to tell him, he just wanted to get it over with as quickly as possible.

He was taken aback by the speed with which the door was opened, by a man who actually looked glad to see him.

"Ah, Michael, good morning!" his father said. "It's a beautiful day, isn't it? Come out back on the patio. I have coffee and fresh croissants waiting for us."

Coffee? Croissants? What had happened to this man?

His father served him coffee and offered the basket of fresh pastries. Michael took one and immediately bit into it. It was soft, very fresh. When, he wondered, had he bought these?

"All right then, Michael," his father said, taking a seat. "Thank you very much for coming over. I've been awake for hours, sitting out here, and thinking. I've been trying to solve a riddle, a complete and utter mystery. Here I am, sixty-eight years old and what do I have to show for it? I've got no wife. That's a difficult thing to live with but there's something worse. I've been a bastard to you for as long as I can remember. I suppose I could blame your mother but, really there's no excuse. I've been treating you as if you were a complete failure at virtually everything you've tried and that's not only heartless, it's wrong. When I gave you my book of business, that wasn't for your benefit; it was for mine. So many of my clients have been my friends for so long, they wouldn't have understood if I'd just dropped them by selling their accounts to a perfect stranger. So, I used you and I put you in a most difficult position. As they have been drifting away, you're the one who has been taking the blame. I've been acting like I could have done better when the truth is, Michael, what we've been going through, and still are for that matter is the worst bear market since the great depression. No one, even me, can escape the bear."

He took a sip of coffee, dabbed his lips with a napkin and put it back down on the table. It was quiet on the patio, as if the birds and animals were as surprised as Michael by what they were hearing.

"So the first thing I wanted to do this morning is ask for your forgiveness," his father went on. "I don't know how long I might have to make it up to you but I promise you that I will try."

Michael was at a loss for words. It was as if his dad were speaking another language, one that he didn't know too well, and it was taking him time to translate.

"Uh, no, I mean, yeah," he said finally when he realized that his father was waiting for a reply. "It's OK, Dad. But, ah, why?"

"There's no easy way to do this so I will just come right out and say it. I'm dying Michael. I have an inoperable tumor in my brain. They don't know how long it's been there but I went to see the doctor about headaches and blurry vision and this was their answer. I said that I was going to Santa Fe on vacation, but actually I went to see the folks at the Mayo clinic and they confirmed it. I might have three months, maybe up to a year. But no longer."

Michael suddenly felt as if he were in a dream. This wasn't really happening. It was like a scene from *Alice in Wonderland*.

"Oh, my God, Dad, no. That can't be true. We'll go find another doctor. Get you some treatment. We can..."

Senior smiled and held up his hand.

"Michael, if you know anything about me, you know that I do my homework. I have researched every article, talked to all the doctors, made all the phone calls and done all the tests. The answer is the same so don't waste your time. If you want to do anything, just help me enjoy my remaining days."

Michael had so many conflicting emotions he closed his eyes to hold back the tears. They talked for a while longer about details of his trip, the nice people at the Mayo, all seemingly unimportant now. But, as his father kept speaking, Michael realized there was one question he had wanted to ask for as long as he could remember. Perhaps now was the time. Maybe it would be one of his few remaining chances.

"You know, Dad when I was growing up, I would look at other kids, listen to their stories. For years I wondered. Where were you? Why didn't you teach me to catch a baseball or ride a bike? Where were you on Saturdays, when I was playing soccer? You were never there, not at a game or even a tournament. You told me the story that you had to work on weekends but I would overhear you talking about playing golf with your buddies. I felt like there was something wrong with me. Why didn't you like me? Why did you ignore me?"

Now it was his father's turn to look away.

"Michael, this is going to sound like a weak excuse and I suppose it is. But I have asked myself that very question many times. I have thought and thought and, I don't know. Maybe the idea that you weren't really my son just kept eating at me. I suppose your mother having an affair and then leaving me with the responsibility to raise you caused a tremendous amount of resentment on my part. I didn't resent *you*. How could I? You were a wonderful boy. But, I guess sometimes life throws you a massive curve ball and the measure of a person is how well they handle it. I didn't measure up too well, Michael. That's my fault certainly, not yours. I can't change the past. I should beg for your forgiveness. But I realize you won't."

When Michael returned home, he recounted his father's story, having to stop a couple of times to fight back the tears. Imagine, a man who lived his life in an awful lie learning that he was dying. He decides to make a deathbed confession to let him live whatever time he had left with a clear conscience. Jen just sat motionless and silent. Finally, when Michael was done, she spoke up.

"Life's full of surprises, isn't it?" she said. "You were probably torn between smashing the guy in the face and giving him a hug. He made you live with a lie but he didn't dump you in a home. I guess, since his days are numbered, you have to cut him some slack. But what did he say about the money?"

Michael's head snapped up. The money? Was she kidding? After the story he'd just told her! Michael was starting to realize that this woman had developed some pretty thick skin, probably as a result of her experience on Wall Street. If she did have any compassion it came second to a seemingly insatiable desire to bring money into their business.

"Well, I was getting to that. After he dropped the bomb on me, he also said we're not going to get any of his money. He told me that since our business was running so well, he was leaving all of it to the golf club. Apparently they are going to build a new lounge for golfers to have a drink and a sandwich after their rounds, and just socialize. They're going to call it the Michael Franklin Lounge and any money left over will be used to redo the sand traps. And that's OK because I told him we didn't want his money. It would just be a hassle when he passes when we have to deal with his will and probate - that kind of thing. I guess I was a little surprised that he wasn't leaving me anything but then I had never given his death a thought, and now that I know the true story, I understand."

"You're kidding me, right? You didn't actually say that to him did you?"

Michael frowned. No, he wasn't kidding. They had lots of money and didn't need his father's. He wasn't his real father. They weren't related at all. Why would there be any expectation of an inheritance?

"No, I'm not kidding. The man is dying, Jennifer. If we take his money it will just make things more complicated. What if he passes and it is an inconvenient time for us to give it back? The directors at the club already know that they are the sole beneficiaries of his estate. I realize that we are trying to grow our business and everything, but this is just one of those times when we have to pass."

Jen imagined a dump truck full of white sand dropping its load into a crater in the ground. Not fucking likely.

"Michael, you know, you're a funny guy. Just when I think you are starting to get it, you start talking crap again. We need *every* dollar we can get our hands on, understand? It doesn't matter from whom or what the background story is. The man who brought you up, even though he never told you the truth about your relationship is going to die anyway so what do you care? And throw the money into sand pits - have you lost your mind?"

Michael sighed. It wasn't always about the money.

"Well, Jen, look at it this way. To begin with, it isn't our money and if Michael Franklin Senior wants to build sand traps with it, then that is his prerogative. Remember, this 'imposter' raised me as a single parent. His dying wish is to give the money to the club because he told me it was the one place where he felt at peace. The best thing for us to do is not get in the way."

"Michael, stop it! You said that you were in this with me and you're not bailing on me now. I couldn't care less about some guy's dying wish. We take the money when and where we can get it. You don't know when the next opportunity might come to build the pool to the right size. For Christ's sake, Michael, all I've ever heard you say about your phony father was that you hated him, didn't like the pressure he put on you, etc. Come on. Get with the program. Either you call him up right now and try to sell it to him, to say that the golf club will get even more money if he lets us manage it until he dies, or I will!"

Michael couldn't believe that she'd say something like that. Who was this woman? Money, money, money. She'd just learned his father was dying and it made her rub her hands together. How could anyone be so cold? He loved her but he was starting to wonder. She seemed to lie about everything. She said she loved Michael but it was *too early* to get married. How convenient when she wanted to convince his father that their partnership was secure, that they were suddenly engaged. That was probably a lie too. And she had been training him, day after day, how to trick people into giving up their money by telling them what they wanted to hear.

He was getting concerned. Was he becoming like her?

Worse, he wondered whether he might be just another one of her 'targets.'

His mind quickly flashed back to seeing Angela in the restaurant. He wished he could confide in her. In fact, he wished he could talk to her about a lot of things.

## Chapter 51

The game was on and business had never been better. It seemed as though, once a core group of 'investors' from various parts of the brokerage community came in, word started to spread like a forest fire through the California mountains and Michael no longer needed to do any prospecting because so many people were calling to say that they wanted to invest their life's savings. Brokers begged him to take the assets of their entire client list. Day traders, hedge funds, charitable organizations, they all couldn't wait for a piece of the discovery that had changed investing forever.

Ironically enough, Michael had never felt worse in his life.

This morning when he woke, he found Jennifer, staring at him speculatively, something that always made him uncomfortable, particularly since she'd been doing that a lot lately.

"It's about time you woke up," she told him, her face close to his on the pillow. "I want to tell you about our party."

A party? Was this another type of prospecting technique, the next phase of building their assets to the 'magic number' level?

"OK, I give up. Surprise me."

He had been faking being excited for a long time, and Jennifer knew it, even when more and more money came in. If that didn't thrill him now then the road ahead would be extremely difficult. She thought he might also have been a bit disillusioned by the way she'd approached his dying step-dad. She guessed she could have pretended to be a bit more compassionate. It was just so damn exhilarating to see everything going so well. She'd thought about it and decided to create a bit of a diversion and to have some fun. He needed to see the benefits of her scheme. He was still far more valuable onside than not.

"Well," she said slowly, "we are going to have a hundo party."

Michael supported his head using his hand and elbow.

"All right, now I know for sure that you've lost it," he said, looking down at her. "I've been wondering if the stress of all this has been getting to you. What in the world is a hundo party?"

"Figure it out," she told him, grinning. "As of last night, the total assets of our little firm reached $100 million." She split the phrase up into pieces, savoring each word - 'one - hundred - million - dollars.'

It took a moment for the words to sink in. That was 'critical mass.' That meant they could start using her investment technique, if one actually existed. Was there a chance they would no longer have to live a lie?

"Wow, Jen!" he exclaimed. "I can't believe it. That's incredible. I mean, you said we'd get there but it is so much money. I was never really sure."

"I was always sure. You see now you should believe me when I say I'm going to do something? Your life would be a lot easier if you did. Whatever, we did it Michael. Now we're going to have our party. You, my friend, are a very rich man. This poor little girl is very attracted to that."

She threw off the covers revealing her nakedness and then she was straddling him, unbuttoning his pajama top, kissing his neck, moving her hips from side to side and softly singing the Beatles' song, "Yes we're goin' to a party, party."

When they were done, Jen moved over to her side of the bed, both of them recovering their breath as they reveled in the sweet after effect of endorphins flooding their systems.

Michael spoke first.

"So, where did the final money come in from?"

Jennifer knew she had to be careful about this. He would never understand. She had simply granted a dying man one of his last wishes - in exchange for his money. She knew she was very good at the efficient use of sex, like she had just had with Michael.

"That's where I went yesterday when I said I was going out to do an errand," she told him. "I went over to see Senior. I suggested to him that, after all the lies and the aggression, he had an opportunity to set things right by entrusting us with his money and allowing our business to really take off. I said that, using our system, his money would double in a few years anyway. I said we would honor his wishes to build a restaurant and fix the sand traps at the golf club but, after that he should just leave the rest with us."

Michael sat up absolutely straight, his face a mask of astonishment.

"Really? You said that to him? Did he go crazy?"

Jennifer just smiled.

"Oh, he took a bit of convincing but eventually I got my way. I usually do."

Michael decided not to ask any more questions about how Jen got Senior's money.

"Now Michael, please get dressed. Any good party has some surprises and so will ours. You're going to take me out to breakfast."

Michael did as he was told. If nothing else, Jen appeared to be happier than he had seen her in months. Just as they were about to go through the front door, she stopped him.

"OK, Michael. Here is your first surprise. Close your eyes."

He could hear her unlock the deadbolt and open the door, letting in a puff of fresh air.

"Now open your eyes and look," she told him. In the driveway was a yellow BMW convertible. The top was down and there was a small red bow tied to the driver's side door handle.

"What?" he exclaimed. "Jen, is that... ours?"

She smiled, hugged him and kissed him on the neck.

"No, Michael, it's yours. You've put up with me being such a bitch for all these months; you deserve it. I just hope you'll let me ride in it now and then. Now, please, IHOP waits."

As he walked slowly towards the car, it was the shine that captured him. What was it about new cars that made them look like that? The new leather fragrance hit him before he touched the door. As he started untying the bow, a troubling realization came to him.

"Wait a minute, Jen," he said. "How did you pay for this? You said we were just borrowing people's money until we got up to critical mass - which we just did, right?"

"Michael, don't be silly. As money managers, we are entitled to a management fee. Even at 1% per year, that's $1 million. You're going to have to get used to what we can afford now."

Michael wanted to argue that, before they were entitled to a management fee, they were supposed to have done something to earn it, which as far as he knew, hadn't happened yet. But this was a side of Jennifer he'd never seen. It was as if she'd been holding back - everything. He didn't want to tarnish the mood. They could discuss what it took to earn a fee later.

When they arrived at the IHOP, Michael noticed that theirs was the only convertible BMW in the lot so he parked as far away from any other cars as he could. Jennifer laughed as they got out.

"Hey, call me a cab, will you? I'm having breakfast way over there."

As they settled into their booth, Michael, who had a swimmer's build and, most days would have a fruit smoothie for breakfast, decided to go 'all in.' Soon a plate full of buttermilk pancakes, with a side of eggs over easy and English sausages appeared. He ate like he hadn't in days.

When they walked back to the car, he said, "Ugh, I need to go home and crawl back into bed. I'm stuffed."

"Yeah, well, Michael. Not yet. I have another surprise for you. For this one, I have to drive."

As they travelled along the interstate, Jennifer relished the fact that the BMW attracted a lot of attention. She knew that Michael was watching her and the road, trying to figure out where they were going. But this was her time. And this was what a BMW did best, cruising along the highway, with its stereo system playing her favorite song from *Genesis*. And she knew she was looking good with her hair being tossed by the wind. No wonder people were looking at them. So this was how the other half lived. It almost seemed unfair. Soon, she knew, Michael would come to understand.

She was startled, annoyed really, at the presence of the detour sign. The route she had meticulously planned was closed. Jesus, what now? She'd taken this way to make sure that Michael couldn't realize where they were going until the last second. She followed with the other cars, bumper to bumper, on the exit ramp. She'd never been down this way before. The open air highway sun was quickly yielding to dark buildings stained by years of grime. A bus stop cubicle with a picture of a model had a red gang insignia painted over it. The smooth highway skin was replaced by a pockmarked mixture of concrete and repair asphalt. As she came to the stop light, a man, unshaven and dressed in filthy clothes was pushing a shopping cart filled with random cans and bottles. He had just finished adding to his collection from a nearby garbage bin.

"Jen, where are we going?" Michael asked. "Is part of the surprise getting mugged?"

"Hang in there," she told him. "I'll get us out of here. There's nothing to get nervous about."

But Jen was growing more frustrated by the second. She didn't *like* it when her plans didn't go the right way. This bullshit of working on the highways when people wanted to drive on them was just that. Bullshit. The light turned green and she roared into the intersection, only to brake to a sudden stop because the cars had not cleared on the other side. She looked from side to side at the cars waiting for their own turn and realized that she was completely blocking them. When her green light turned yellow, she pounded the steering wheel with her fist.

"Jesus, dammit, MOVE!" she shouted.

"What are you doing? We're in the middle of the intersection."

"MICHAEL, just shut up, OK? You're not helping matters."

Her light turned red. She leaned on her horn.

"Come on, you bastard, get your fucking car out of the way!"

At that, the man in the car in front of her gave her the finger, and the drivers of the cars on either side started honking in unison. Some rich bitch with a flashy car and a dopey looking boyfriend was right in the middle of the intersection, blocking their green light, and they were taking full advantage of it.

People were staring at her and the noise was maddening. Seeing an opening on a side street, she jerked her car into reverse, and pulled the steering wheel until it whined. Cramming the wheel the other way, she pressed on the gas until her tires squealed with white smoke. All the drivers were now honking but who cared. She was away. The street she was on was clear.

"Jen, look out!"

She looked up a moment too late. It almost seemed like the homeless man had thrown his cart in front of her car and then fallen to the pavement. The sound of metal scraping metal, like fingernails on a blackboard, filled the air and the cart bounced up from the front grill and came to rest against the windshield. Cans clanged down the street and bottles splattered when they hit the pavement. Had she hit him? How had he got over here so fast? She jumped out of the car, door open, and engine running and ran around to the front, almost tripping over the garbage now strewn on the street. As she bent over the man, she was almost overwhelmed by the smell of wine, grease and urine. His black hair was matted with dirt and his grizzled beard was full of flecks of food. Michael was still in his seat, belt on, yelling "Do you want me to call 911?"

"Shit man, are you OK? You should look where you're going."

The man stared at her and smiled, revealing crooked, yellowed teeth, one missing in the front. Was he crazy, delirious? Had she really hit him? She looked up, around the deserted street, for help. Then she saw them, a group of men, young, wearing black leather jackets and red bandanas, their faces the color of the grime in the metal barred street level windows.

"Uh, Jen, get back in the car," Michael shouted. "Now, OK?"

One of the bandanas was standing next to the car, caressing it with his hand.

"Who-wee bitch! Now this is what I'm talking about. This is some fine ride."

The other gang members were leaning over into the car, the apparent lead continuing his introduction.

"What's this you got here, girl, some weak, white thing? Come on now, you knows it, sugar, what you need is a real man. Let's hop in the back seat and I give you what you been dreamin' of. Boyfriend don't need to watch," he laughed. "But he can if he wants. Maybe he learns somethin'."

"Hey, asshole," Jennifer shouted as he jumped into the back seat. "You don't know who you're fucking with but you better get your greasy ass out of my car before I kick it down the street. NOW!"

Michael said nothing. He looked, she thought, as though he might pass out. The smile left the bandana's face. He looked at his partners, one of whom had let out a long slow whistle.

"Well, what do you know? Lady's got some attitude. Where I come from, I think you'd call that downright rude the way you just talked to me. What say, boys? We need to teach the bitch some manners?"

Jennifer saw that Michael was leaning as far forward in his seat as he could. She knew he was weak but, she hadn't realized how weak. She was on her own.

"You come so close as to even touch me and I will feed your balls down your throat. Do you understand?" she hissed. "Take your little group and crawl back into whatever hole you came out of. And take the wino with you."

She looked again for the man lying in the street who was now sitting on the curb, watching and smiling.

The man in the back seat pretended to admire the interior of the car and titled his head to one side.

"Like I said, this is a fine looking ride. Thing is, it needs a bit of customizing."

He slowly reached into his jacket pocket and the unmistakable click of a switchblade echoed off the city walls.

"Maybe I start with some of this fine leather and then maybe I do a little work on you."

"You touch my fucking car you're going to be one sorry motherfucker!" Jennifer shouted.

Suddenly, one of the gang members whistled and the back seat guest retracted the blade, and as a siren sounded, hopped out of the car, and ran down the street.

"OK lady, what's going on?" the officer demanded. "Why'd you run over Louey's cart?"

Jennifer was furious. The fucking road was closed and then some punks had pulled a knife on her.

The policeman watched her and tried to listen to her rant. What in the hell was this woman, driving a car like this, doing in this neighborhood?

"Lady, stop talking," he said. "You do not swear at an officer of the law and I do not like your attitude. Those were some serious dudes you were messing with there. If someone hadn't called this in, you'd be heading to the hospital instead of the police station... which is where you're going if you don't smarten up."

She stared at him, eyes narrowed.

"Have you been drinking, lady?"

Her eyebrows shot up.

"You come this way to buy some drugs?"

"Officer, this wasn't my fault! We were forced off the highway. Look what that shopping cart did to my car."

For the first time, she'd noticed the scratches running up the car hood, like rain streaks on a window. As she spoke, the officer was taking notes.

"OK, lady, I don't know who you and your friend are, or where you came from, but you're either stupid or have a lot of balls coming into this part of town. I suggest you give Louey $20 for his troubles, help him get his cart off the car, put your top up, get in, lock the doors and drive your white asses out of here."

"What" Jennifer exclaimed! "What are you saying? I'm not giving that bum any money. He ran in front of my car."

The cop, arms folded, shook his head.

"Well then, you're going to help him clean up all this trash - every last bottle and can. There's a law against littering and besides, you just knocked over Louey's dinner money. He's probably been working all morning for that."

Jennifer turned to Michael who had been cowering in the passenger seat and told him to give the man twenty dollars.

Michael had been sitting quietly, mouth open, still stunned by the previous scene. The guy had pulled a *knife!* He looked again in the back seat as if the intruder was still there and, seeing it was safe, took his wallet out of his back pocket.

"I'm sorry Jen," he said. "All I have is a fifty."

The officer smiled for the first time. "Oh, I'm sure Louey will take that," he said.

"Look officer," Jen started. "This is ridiculous. We're not giving that man $50."

"No, YOU look lady. You got a list of charges against you already; speeding, dangerous driving and hitting a pedestrian. That move you pulled back in the intersection made the 911 call center light up like a Christmas tree. There are lots of witnesses. If I wasn't coming to the end of my shift, both of you'd be in the back of my car right now on your way to jail. So, you listen and listen good. Get in your car and go down this street to that traffic light - slowly. Turn left and stay on that road."

Louey was now standing alongside her, awaiting his settlement. Michael gave him the $50 bill as Jennifer glared at the officer. She considered taking his badge number and threatening to see him in court but decided that it was probably better just to leave. She got into the car and pushed the button for the automatic roof. As all parts clicked to a close, her four windows automatically rose as well. The officer stood by the driver's side door and monitored the progress as she readjusted her rear view mirror and put the car into drive.

"Seat belt not fastened," he yelled, pounding on the window. "That's another moving violation. You better get out of here now… and do have a nice day."

They drove in silence for the first few minutes. Michael looked into the distance like he'd seen a ghost. Finally, he turned towards her.

"Jen, what were you doing back there? You could have got us killed."

"Those were kids Michael, just little punks," she said in a disgusted voice. "And, I do have a black belt - Tae Kwon Do. It comes in handy some days. That kid with the mouth is lucky the cop came by or he'd still be picking up his teeth."

It was another revelation. What he knew about this woman, he was coming to realize, was only the tip of an iceberg.

"Jen, the car, look what they've done to the car!"

"Michael, shut up! Who cares about the car? I'll go get another one."

With the top and windows up and doors locked, Michael felt like he could breathe again, but he could see that Jennifer's knuckles were white as she gripped the steering wheel. She didn't seem afraid though. It was something else.

They soon found the entrance ramp onto the freeway, on the other side of the construction. As they moved onto the ramp, she seemed to relax a bit.

"OK, Michael," she said. "Sorry about that. Our little detour was most definitely not part of the program. We do have another stop. This is the biggest gift from your hundo party."

The paint on the hood of their brand new BMW had been ruined, they had been threatened by a gang, and Jen had almost killed a homeless person. Now, it was as if none of that had happened. They were in a party again. The woman was never short on surprises. Without warning, Jen took the upcoming exit. Michael saw a small sign reading 'Marina District.'

Now that they were back into the sunlight, his fear melted into curiosity.

"Where are we going, Jen? What in the world is my surprise?"

She was smiling again as she said, "Oh, just wait, Michael. Just wait!"

There were a number of boats from smaller Boston Whalers to large two-mast sailboats in the marina, and the air was fresh with the taste of salt, the sound of seagulls and the smell of fish. The sailboats' rigging clicked against their aluminum masts in the wind. Michael had now figured out that Jen had rented a boat and they were going for a cruise somewhere. Or, more likely, she had hired a small crew who would escort them on a tour of Puget Sound. As they walked down the dock, Jen held his hand, the breeze playing with her hair. Strolling alongside the increasingly larger boats, Michael enjoyed reading the clever titles the owners had created and painted on the sterns. When he came to one that read *For Love of Money*, he thought that was pretty arrogant.

"OK, here we are" Jennifer said. "Hop in Michael."

He looked around and was immediately struck by the contrast of the white silky smooth hull against the stained wood floor.

There was a steering wheel at sea level and another on a small second floor used for deep-sea fishing. Every corner of the boat was polished, clean and sparkling. Michael hadn't spent much time on boats but he thought this one to be the most beautiful he'd ever seen.

"Wow Jen, you do know how to throw a party!" he exclaimed. "What a gorgeous boat. Where are we going? Is there a captain? I don't have a license. Do you? I don't even want to know how much this cost to rent."

"We're not going anywhere. You're right, neither one of us can drive but soon we will. It doesn't take much time. No, this morning we're just going to sit here for a while. I simply wanted you to see it."

If today was unusual, it had now turned strange. This morning she went from sensual to excited to threatening to carefree in a matter of a few hours. But he didn't want to get her riled up again. She'd obviously gone to a lot of trouble, expecting Michael to be thrilled to go sit on a docked boat. He could see her watching him as he looked around the cabin.

"You still don't get it, do you?" she asked finally, as she playfully twisted her upholstered chair from side-to-side.

"Come on, Jen. Your surprise is that we are going out for a day on the Sound. It's a wonderful gift, really. It will be so much..."

"Michael, this boat is yours. You own it."

It took a while for her words to sink in.

"The boat is yours, Michael," she repeated. "You are now managing $100 million. It is entirely appropriate for you to own something like this. Clients will expect that a man of your means entertains this way. It is a necessary part of the program. This boat, by itself will bring in tens of millions of new money. Think of it as an investment."

Michael was shaking his head. Something was very wrong.

"Jen," he said, "hold on a second. I didn't want to say anything about the car this morning because the truth of the matter is we haven't done anything to earn any fees. So, it's like you borrowed our salary in advance. I think that is wrong but I am, or I was, willing to go with it. This boat must cost ten times the car. We can't just start spending money like this. If anyone found out, they'd take their money out so fast it would make your head spin."

Jen patted the captain's chair next to her.

"Michael, sit down," she said. "We need to talk."

He lowered himself into the white leather swivel chair, which was as comfortable as anything he'd ever sat in, but he was far from being pleased. He'd always given Jen the benefit of the doubt but this time, she'd gone too far. He sat, turned the chair to face her, and waited.

"Before you get started, I have to get something off my chest," he told her. "This whole plan of yours, raising money by lying is really starting to worry me. You said over and over that we were borrowing people's money until we got a large enough pool of cash for your new investment program to work. I have never been comfortable with that, the whole deception thing. I think you know that. But, I've just gone with what you said because you know more about it than I do. Then you threw me my hundo party with a new car and boat. Where did the money for *that* come from? Don't answer that, I already know. We are at the point now of being able to launch, which is wonderful because we can stop living a lie. I want to do that as soon as we can. At the very least, we'd better not take a salary for a long time."

She looked at him and rubbed her armrests. How long before she revealed everything?

"Michael, let me put it to you this way. I don't actually know how big our asset pool has to get before we, as you put it, launch. I am watching the markets and, when we get there I'll know. We only get one shot at this. Once we engage my new system, we can't go back and if our returns don't come in as advertised, the money will leave and fast. Do you understand what we are doing here? It takes years for money managers just starting out to get their business up and running and, often times they never get there. All I am doing is circumventing that process. My model will only work in a market environment that has a lot of liquidity and volatility. You know what it's like out there; we've been in this bear for what, two years now? There's no volume and prices just drift lower. It's like pushing on a string."

She was, he realized, changing her story.

"What? Jen, you said to me that $100 million was the target - that's why the party."

Jen sighed deeply.

"Michael, you say you trust me but what you're saying now doesn't support that. If you aren't nice, I won't take you with me."

Michael's face contorted.

"What do you mean? Where are you going?"

"Look sweetie," she said, "Seattle is a dump and it rains all the time. After we launch, we're driving this baby to a place called Turks & Caicos. It's my favorite place. The whole country is something like forty islands and cays. We're going to find the littlest one we can and start working on our tan. No clothing required."

"What? You never said anything about that. All our clients are here. We can't just move away from them."

Jennifer laughed and rubbed her hands together.

"Of course we can, Michael. Have you ever heard of the Internet? Airplanes? We'll come back once a quarter for update meetings."

She was thinking out loud now. None of that was ever going to happen, of course.

"By the way, there's no income tax down there, did you know that? Hey, we might even invite our best clients down for a few days, our treat. Who knows? We'll have to see how big this whole thing gets."

Michael's eyes narrowed. Not only had she not answered his direct question, she had introduced a scenario they had never discussed before.

"I'm still waiting for the answer to one simple question," he reminded her. "You just keep dancing around it, but I want to know, right now. When are we going legitimate?"

Jennifer was not accustomed to having anyone speak to her in that tone of voice and she didn't like it.

"Michael, who do you think you're talking to? Dancing around... fuck off, OK? The answer does not keep changing. GET MORE ASSETS! By the way, your only job has been to get the widow's money. I haven't seen it yet, have you? So don't stand there all high and mighty and lecture me."

So there was Angela again. There was no way he was going to allow her to put her money in to whatever this scheme was Jennifer had cooked up.

"Forget it Jen," he said. "I won't take her money. It's all she has. I've put up with all of this, but this is where I draw the line."

Jennifer smiled. For the first time, he was getting aggressive with her.

"Really Michael, you're getting tough with me? That's cute."

Of course she had known that this moment would come at some point. Michael was a pretty bright guy and would figure things out eventually. The weeks and months of preparation had finally come to fruition. This was absolutely the right time and place to pull Michael over the threshold and to introduce him to his new life, one she was sure he never imagined but, she was also sure, could not turn away from.

"Michael, you told me before that you 'knew' about Ponzi, but do you really appreciate the magnificence of a true Ponzi scheme?"

"Jen, you're scaring me a bit here. What does a Ponzi scheme have to do with this conversation? They are illegal. That's all I need to know."

She decided to fully explain it just to make sure he could appreciate the beauty of the plan. The legendary Charles Ponzi was a visionary and the genius of the scheme was its simplicity. All that was required was people with money who, either driven by greed, fear or some other combination of emotions, would happily entrust it to someone else. If they gave you one dollar, you simply gave them back twenty cents of their own money and declared that you, using your new and improved technique, had earned 20% for them. Then they would give you another dollar and soon tell their friends who would rush to get 'in' as well. As long as the money flowed in, there would be more than enough cash to pay out. And soon, you'd offer a re-investment plan where, rather than pay out cash, you offered the 'client' the opportunity to just purchase more units. Maybe you'd tell them that, using the efficiency of offshore tax-free havens like Bermuda or the Cayman Islands, they would only pay tax on cash received. Meanwhile clients would watch their investment grow, unaware that the entire operation was a sham, and wake up one day realizing their assets were long gone. She and Michael would be rich beyond their dreams. The only decision was when to stop bringing in the cash and, instead to cut and run.

Michael's head was spinning as, bit by bit, he began to realize that he had become an unwitting party to a huge financial crime in the making.

"Jen, no, this is really wrong." he protested when she had finished. "You said we were just building up the assets. That we were just telling, sort of a white lie."

She laughed. "Well, I don't know what qualifies as a white lie but, yes, you're right. We've been telling a lie."

"But you said that once we got to $100 million, we'd start using your new technique to manage money."

"Yep, that was a lie too."

"So there is no new technique for managing money?"

"Nope," she replied, grinning. "But you have to admit I made it sound pretty good."

"And $100 million was not ever a goal of some kind?"

Jennifer had built in a couple of 'safety valves' to make sure Michael stayed committed to the 'cause.'

"Actually Michael, there is something significant to that number. At that level of assets, should you ever be caught, you most certainly would go to jail for life, without parole. I wanted to make sure there was enough money here to make it impossible for you to leave the table."

"But the people, their money, this isn't right!"

"Oh Michael, it is *so* right. And you've been amazing at it. You learned the lesson of the seven dwarfs so fast. I've really been so impressed."

He got up from the chair as if it was on fire.

"NO!" he shouted. "We have to give all the money back and the car and this boat. All of it! This is awful. What the HELL have you done Jen?"

"Michael, we can't give the money back," she told him calmly. "We've gone too far. Maybe you want to go to jail but I don't."

Now the full realization about the woman he had thought he loved, wanted to marry and spend his life with came crashing into the ground, as if smashed by an enormous wrecking ball.

"YOU! You did all this. You've ruined everything. I will turn you in. I am going to the police right now!"

"I think you'd better sit down again, Michael," she told him. "Did you happen to notice that every single piece of paper, 100% of all communication with clients has your name on it? Not mine, yours. So, if you want to fall on the sword, feel free. But you'll be doing that without me."

"OH MY GOD!" he cried. "What have you done to me?"

He jumped out of the boat and started walking quickly down the dock. She let him go. It would take him awhile to understand that he had no other options and, like it or not, accept his new life. Besides, the direction he was walking down the dock was a dead end.

He'd be back.

She caressed the leather arms of her chair. It really was a lovely boat. "Thank you, Michael," she murmured to herself. "Thank you very much indeed."

## Chapter 52

The nightmare was unlike any he had ever had before, involving a vicious dog attacking a little girl standing by the edge of a cliff. He lunged to save her and, at the last second managed to push the dog plunging over the edge, barely managing to keep himself from the fall.

He felt the jostling on his shoulder as if he had hit the ground.

"Michael, wake up!" It was Jennifer's voice. "Are you OK?"

He shielded his eyes from the bright overhead light. "What the hell?" she demanded. "You were screaming and grunting like a caged animal."

He gathered himself as best he could. He wanted to yell that he had never been sicker and to never talk to him again. To think he had actually been more than ready to marry this... whatever kind of person she was.

But Jennifer knew how revealing dreams could be, and she convinced Michael he'd feel better talking about it. And this one was easy to interpret. The little girl was the widow. The vicious dog? Nice analogy, partner, but clearly that was her. Actually, she didn't mind the characterization at all. And Michael was Michael. The dream, like most of them were, was very close to real life or the scenario he had imagined. The widow, standing at the top of the cliff not only survived unharmed, but also was saved by Michael from the evil Jennifer. In his dream, Michael risked sacrificing everything to save this Angela girl. He had fallen for her and he probably didn't even realize it yet.

But the dream, she knew even if he did not, had been misleading. She would not be the one falling through the sky - straight into a jail cell. She would be sipping a cool drink on a beach.

The knock on their door interrupted the argument that had begun over breakfast. Jennifer had been trying to explain that he should no longer fight it, that they were both in up to their necks and, given that he had no idea what he was doing, he really had no choice but to trust her. She decided to leave the topic of the widow alone for the moment. He deserved to be forced to understand that a real man would have had as much sex and made as many promises as necessary to get her money on board. But Jen now realized, the real reason he hadn't was that he was in love with her to the point where he wanted to protect her at all costs. That would make it trickier to get her money, but she wasn't going to give up yet.

They both turned to face the sound. When Michael opened the door, any discussion about the future of their mutual crime was quickly terminated.

"Good morning Mr. Franklin," one of the police officers said. "I'm Detective Tomkins and this is my partner Detective O'Leary. We're from Seattle homicide and wonder if you'd mind chatting with us for a few moments."

Michael grabbed the door with the other hand to support his knees, which were about to buckle. The police! Their scheme had already been discovered.

"Of course, officer," Michael managed to say. "What did you want to talk about?"

Officer Tomkins looked at his partner and smiled.

"Do you think maybe we could come in and sit down?"

Michael felt an immediate sense of panic but then relief. Jen would know how to handle this. But when he opened the door wider to let them in and started to introduce them to her at the kitchen table, she was gone.

Officer O'Leary made a mental note. Mr. Franklin appeared to have been sitting by himself, doing what? There was no newspaper, no coffee cup, nothing. As they sat down, Michael thought he should offer them water or coffee but his shaking hands would make for an awful, if not incriminating display of nerves.

"Everyone is busy these days so I'm going to get right to the point," the detective said. "We have been working on a situation for a while now. We don't have all of our facts lined up yet, but we have reason to believe that you might be able to help us a bit. We'd like to ask you a few questions if you don't mind. You don't have to talk to us if you don't want to. We haven't felt the need to get a subpoena at this point."

Michael was ready for him. Wherever Jen had disappeared to, he was thanking her for the hours of training she had put him through.

"Officer, I know our investment style, and our results are nothing short of remarkable and to some may appear too good to be true," he said, clearing his throat. "But I can assure you that our back-testing process is as scientifically valid as anything you've ever seen. We can..."

He stopped short as Officer Tomkins held up his hand.

"Yes, Mr. Franklin, I'm sure that's very interesting but we're from homicide. We didn't come here to talk about investments."

Michael could feel the blood rush to his face.

"This won't take long," the officer said. "Like I said, we just wanted you to answer a couple of questions. You don't mind do you?"

Michael, silent, nodded his head.

"OK, great. First off, Mr. Franklin, do you know a woman by the name of Angela Messina?"

Michael tried to keep his face expressionless, but he knew from the way the two men looked at him that he had failed.

"Uh, yes, we've met."

"You're aware then that she is a recent widow?"

*That* was it. They were coming after him for trying to steal the widow's money. Maybe she had figured out the scheme and was still mad and turned him in. Jen should be thanking him now for not being as efficient a thief as she wanted.

"Yes, I am aware of that. Apparently her husband died in some horrible car accident."

"That's right Mr. Franklin. Seemingly, it was an accident. We're here to try to make sure of that. Our forensics guys did quite a bit of work on the car, or at least what was left of it. They came up with evidence that suggests, perhaps, the crash wasn't accidental at all. It appears that someone very skilled and knowledgeable about cars might have tampered with the brakes and the air bags. That would explain the very high rate of speed just before the crash and the trauma to the victim inside the car. Tell me, Mr. Franklin, how well do you know Mrs. Messina?"

Michael shook his head. What on earth were they getting at? They didn't think he had had anything to do with that, did they?

"Not so much," he told them. "She's a, uh, potential client of mine. But, I can't imagine she's involved in anything. She's one of the sweetest people I've ever met."

Officer Tomkins nodded his head in agreement.

"Yes, I imagine she must have taken it very hard. She's probably dealing with a very long period of grieving, do you think so?"

Michael didn't think before he answered. It was likely best to just agree with everything the officer said.

"Oh yes, I can't imagine how upset she must be."

The officer was now tapping the eraser of the pencil on the table.

"Well actually Mr. Franklin, we were thinking that maybe you could imagine. See, once we learned that the husband's death could be a homicide, we started checking out a number of things, one of which was to watch the funeral reception. That's where we saw you. You aren't related to her in any way, are you, Mr. Franklin? If not, could we ask why you were there at such an intimate, personal gathering?"

Michael kept his hands under the table.

"Well... the former Mr. Messina was working with me on a financial plan for him and his wife. He wanted to surprise her. I guess I figured it would be appropriate for me to at least offer my services if she wanted to continue with her husband's wishes, especially now that she would have an inheritance to look after. It was pretty awkward, I can tell you."

Michael breathed easier as he was talking, realizing there would be no way to verify whether he had ever spoken to the late husband or not.

"Yes, Mr. Franklin. That's very neighborly of you," the officer said. "As you probably know, the widow has inherited $6 million. That's a tidy sum, don't you think?"

Officer Tomkins reminded himself that he was here to talk about a potential murder, not bust a low-life ambulance chaser.

Michael was nodding his head in agreement but was surprised that the police knew the exact sum of money. What else did they know, he wondered?

"Did she talk about the money right there at the reception Mr. Franklin? That would be interesting don't you think? There's a widow all full of grief who is still quite ready to talk about her financial future."

Michael had never considered that before. It was a valid point.

"Well, I don't know. I guess some people handle their grief different than others."

"OK, let's move on," the officer said briskly. "We have reason to believe you've had additional conversations with Mrs. Messina after the reception. When you talked, did she ever mention her relationship with her husband?"

She hadn't. He was telling the truth.

"Mr. Franklin, I want you to think very hard. Is there anything she has said to you, however seemingly small, that you think we should know? You aren't under oath, but you could be sometime in the future. I strongly suggest you leave nothing out."

It never occurred to Michael that in his and Jennifer's quest to gather as much money as possible, there could be a risk in where that money came from. Thank God that part of the scheme had fallen through.

He was relieved when the officers gave him their business cards.

"All right then, Mr. Franklin," one of them said "if you do think of anything, you be sure to call one of us, any time, day or night."

As he started to put away his notepad, he stopped and smiled, immediately making Michael uncomfortable.

"Mr. Franklin, do you know the story about the black widow spider?" he said. "After the female mates with the male, she kills and eats him. It might be something to keep in mind."

## Chapter 53

When the police left, Michael went to the window to make sure they really had gone, grabbed the portable telephone handset and locked the bathroom door behind him. He didn't care what Jen thought. Angela was in trouble and he had to warn her.

Jen, who had been hiding around the corner listening to every word, heard him run upstairs and the click of the bathroom door and seeing the 'in use' light on the phone's base station, knew who he was calling. It was at that moment she realized that she wasn't the only liar in this relationship. This was not a very street-smart man. She thought she had made it quite clear, just a few days ago, that she had him by the balls and, if she chose, could put him away for life. And now that he'd learned that the widow was a suspect in a murder, he was preparing to run into her arms. Either route was a dead end. She wanted to quietly pick up another handset but it wasn't necessary. She knew what they would talk about.

"Angela, hi it's Michael."

"Michael? Oh, Michael! Can you speak up a bit? I can barely hear you."

Michael had one hand covering his mouth over the handset's microphone.

"Actually, no I can't. I have to keep my voice down."

Angela's first thought was that he didn't want to be caught phoning her. There was definitely something going on between him and his so-called business partner. She had been an idiot not to suspect it sooner. That explained why he wouldn't go to bed with her. The reporter was right - there was something fishy about these two, especially the woman. But dammit, that Jennifer wasn't right for him. Still, there was little point of going any further with this if there wasn't at least some form of a spark. She might as well test him and be done with it.

"So Mr. big finance guy, are you calling to apologize?" she asked.

Apologize, for what? He was calling to warn her that the police were after her. Then it dawned on him. Jen was right. Angela was still bitterly angry. He sighed and shook his head. How had he gotten himself into this position? He would never take her money now, given what Jennifer had revealed on the boat. She couldn't see that he was protecting her from something that would ruin her life. He desperately wanted to tell her how Jennifer had set him up. But he couldn't. He was guilty, and to tell her the whole truth would mean the end of his miserable life. He'd been thinking about the 'nothing happened' night every day. The weight in his chest came from the terrible realization of the opportunity he had likely squandered. He'd never met a woman like Angela before - so beautiful, kind, caring. There was a lot Jen could learn from her, that was for sure. When he and Jen first met, she had seemed to be the most fascinating woman he had ever encountered, and he had wanted to spend the rest of his life with her. Now, she represented nothing but pure evil.

"Well, ah, yes. I am calling to say I'm sorry. I'm so very sorry, Angela. I am coming to regret more than you will ever know. I really don't know what else to say."

He didn't sound good, at all. As much as she was mad at him, she realized that it had nothing to do with him passing on her. It could have been the most wonderful, beautiful night of her life. She had fallen for him. This was the type of man she deserved. She was angry because he hadn't seen that in her. And she wasn't ready to give up. It was worth one more try.

"Well, a real man, determined to offer a proper apology would be standing at my doorstep with an arm load of flowers," she said.

Michael ran his fingers through his hair and let out a deep sigh.

"Angela, you're right. I'll be over as soon as I can."

Jen had repositioned her laptop on the kitchen table and was trying to look focused on her work when Michael came into the room, jacket in hand.

"Oh there you are," she said casually. "What did the cops want? Are you going out?"

Michael wanted to grill her as to why, as soon as the police showed up, she had disappeared but he probably knew the answer, perhaps not completely, but close enough. He couldn't be sure what, if anything she'd heard, not that it mattered.

"The cops were looking for witnesses," he said, not looking at her. "Apparently some guy's car down the street got broken into. I said we couldn't help."

"So, where are you going then?"

"I've been thinking a lot about what you said. So, we're in a Ponzi scheme, fine. That isn't the way I wanted to do things but I guess I really have no choice but to go along with it. You're right. I'm a man and the widow is holding out everything for me to take from her on a platter. I'm going to go get it. I just called her to say I'm on my way over."

Jen looked at her watch and smiled.

"Ooh, a little afternoon delight. Good for you Michael. She'll appreciate that."

She knew that wasn't the reason for his visit. Regardless, it was time to layer in a bit of insurance.

"Michael, let me remind you of something. If anyone - and I mean anyone - finds out about our little arrangement before we are good and ready to get our asses out of town, we will both be going to jail until we die. So you go have a nice conjugal visit with the widow. But keep your mouth shut for both of our sakes. You got that?"

As he drove along in his new yellow BMW, Michael kept replaying scenarios in his mind, like clips from a movie. Jen's version would have him lie to Angela, take her money and give her all the signs that he was very interested in her. Or, he could just warn her that the police were asking questions about her, let the money thing alone, and leave.

But the police wouldn't come to his door without some reason. He had to ask her, but how? What he really wanted to do was tell her the whole truth, about Jen and what she'd done to him - reveal the entire Ponzi scheme. Then she'd truly understand why the last thing she should want was for him to take her money. She'd likely never see it again and then where would her life be? But he couldn't risk her reaction. To reveal the truth to her could easily mean, as Jen had so quickly pointed out, that he would spend the rest of his life in jail.

He sighed. Given his father and mother, Jen, Angela and now him, it seemed like everyone in the world was living a lie.

He realized he was about to miss his exit and had to quickly cut across two lanes. Another driver, who had to swerve to avoid him, leaned on his horn.

Angela was waiting for him in her front yard. So he was driving a new car, a BMW no less. What was that all about? And he did not bring flowers.

"Nice wheels, Michael," she said. "I know I said I wanted an apology but, really flowers would have been more than enough."

Aw shit, the flowers! He couldn't get anything right. He hurried up the steps and kissed her on the cheek.

"I'm sorry Angie. Can we go inside and sit down. We really need to talk."

Angie. Her father used to call her Angie. And Michael looked pale, like he was sick. Ushering him inside, she went into the kitchen and filled up a glass with cold water. He hadn't asked but he quickly took the drink and held it to his forehead.

"Michael, honey, you look awful. I know I said I wanted an apology but I'm just kidding. I'm mad, more disappointed really, but I won't bite you."

She leaned toward him and stroked his arm.

"I'm glad you came to see me again."

He opened his eyes, looked at her and then looked away. His confession had to come now or never and he knew it.

"Well, maybe you won't be so glad in a minute."

Her bottom lip started to quiver. This was it. He was coming to tell her he was engaged to that bitch partner of his. He couldn't even look her in the eye. Please God, no!

"Michael, what are you saying?"

"Angela, I'm not really sure what to tell you. I was sitting at my kitchen table this morning and there was a knock on my door. It was the police. They came to see me, to talk to me... about you."

Angela had been listening for the words 'have to tell you about Jennifer' or 'we need to keep this professional.' Now her head snapped up at the sound of the word 'police.' Her breath was gone. It reminded her of the feeling after each time her husband had struck her, of her body trying to brace itself for the next blow.

"The police? Oh dear Michael. They came to see you... about me?"

He could barely make out her last words. She was whispering, looking off into the distance, seemingly bewildered. He wondered if she was playing him or did she really not have any idea. If she didn't, and it certainly sounded that way, then maybe the officers were wrong.

"They came to ask me about you and your late husband. Apparently they think, well, maybe his car crash wasn't an accident."

Angela's body started to shake, which she realized could be viewed by him as full incrimination. She had to deflect. She put her face in her hands.

"These awful policemen" she cried, "they're HORRIBLE. They came to my house to tell me the most devastating news of my life and then they start asking me these questions, like I could possibly have had something to do with it. And now they are bothering you? I am so sorry Michael. I wish I could do something about them but I can't. But wait a minute. Why in the world would they want to talk to you? Why would they even know you exist?"

"They saw me at your husband's funeral reception," he told her. "They asked me why I was there and how much I knew about you and your past. I think they are watching me Angela, because they think you might have had something to do with the accident. Why would they say that?"

"Michael, not you, too," she said, looking into his eyes. "Why are you asking me questions?"

He thought he could now detect her entire body quivering and realized that her husband's death was still fresh on her mind. He felt like he had kicked a puppy.

"Ah, Angie, I'm not, I'm really not at all. I guess I was surprised and I came over because I thought you'd want to know about everything they'd said and asked."

"There's more?" she gasped. "Michael, please tell me. I need to know what these... people are saying about me."

He wanted to ask her if she was sure of that, but this was the reason he came over - one of them anyway. He needed to know if there was any possibility of the police being on to something. He repeated everything the officer had said.

Angela watched his face as he spoke. His eyes were so beautiful and his voice so soft. But his words were like arrows into the core of her heart. She bowed her head and he could hear her whisper, "Dear Jesus, forgive me for my sins." The tears and the wails burst from her like a violent thunderstorm, as she threw herself into his arms.

"MY HUSBAND WAS GOING TO KILL ME. YOU HAVE TO BELIEVE ME. HE ALMOST DID. I HAD TO SAVE MYSELF SOMEHOW."

He just held her now, her words having melted into something unintelligible. There was nothing for him to say anyway so he put his arms as far around her as they would go. Sometimes a person just needed to be embraced, momentarily sheltered from the harsh realities of life. He wished there had been someone like that for him.

When Angela had recovered, she pushed him away again and told her story. Her makeup had streamed down her face, her eyes were dark red and she wiped her nose with her sleeve. She recounted everything; even the wedding night when she thought her husband was being overly aggressive in bed. If only she could have imagined that this was a warning sign of terrible, painful things to come. What had seemed like a dream come true had turned into a nightmare. She had tried, she had really tried to make things right. She knew what she did was terribly wrong but, in the end, she had to save her own life.

When she had finished, she was breathless, but clearly relieved.

"Michael, let me go clean up a bit and maybe you'll drive me down to the police station so that I can turn myself in. After all, I am guilty. It's the right thing to do."

She started to get up, but he pulled her back down beside him on the couch. Her story had left him so full of disbelief and shock that he could hardly speak

"No Angie, wait. Let me think."

"Michael, you don't understand. I'm tired of this hanging over me. Do you know what it's like to live a lie like this? Every waking hour, even in your dreams, it's there, staring at you, wondering when you are going to do the right thing. I've had enough. The police are probably going to come get me anyway."

The guilt was like a lava flow, cascading down his arms, chest, legs, burning any sense of self-respect he might have thought he still had. Here was a woman, a real person who was ready to face the consequences of her actions. He of course wasn't. He needed to tell her, right here and now, that she was the bravest person he had ever met - and she made him feel small, like a cowering dog. The words were out of his mouth before he thought any further.

"No Angela, *you* don't understand. All you did was defend yourself. And now you want to just tell the truth and face any consequences. You're honest... and brave... and beautiful. I too have a terrible secret that I've been living with, but unlike you I haven't had the guts to admit it. Well, now I am. You've told me your story - here's mine."

He grabbed her hands with his and leaned towards her.

"There's a reason I've been stalling you… about a few things… but it isn't what you think."

She watched every feature of his face as he spoke. He started with his being fired, about being desperately in love with the woman he thought Jen was. He was blind and didn't see what she was leading him into. Now everything was completely out of his control. He was a criminal too.

"Wow," she said, "one hundred million dollars? The car? The boat? And it's all make believe?"

It was such a relief to have said it. Michael had no idea what would come next, but at least he, too, had told the truth.

"There is no new system. Even if I wanted to, I couldn't give the money back. Everyone will want to see those great 20% returns we promised them. The only way we can pay that is to trick new people. It's as though we're rats on a running wheel. We can run as hard as we want but we can never get off."

Angela was frowning.

"I'm so sorry Angie. I wanted to tell you but I couldn't."

"No, Michael," she told him, "it's not that. It's the reporter. After you left me in my bedroom, well I was still pretty upset the next day. I saw his article about your new company in the paper so, I called him. I asked him some questions. He seemed suspicious Michael. I hope I didn't make it worse. He might not be the police but if he writes the wrong article, and people start asking for their money back, you're in serious trouble, aren't you?"

Michael felt as though someone had struck him in the stomach. How could he have forgotten about Andrew?

"So that's why he called me to warn me about Jen. He told me and I didn't believe him. Her real name is Sandy Allen, and she has a criminal record from New York."

He took both of her hands into his.

"You know what Angie? We're both going down. There's nothing we can do to stop it."

The tears started to quietly flow down her cheeks. The thought of prison didn't frighten her as much as the realization that now she had finally found a wonderful man, there was no way for her to have him.

"Why, Michael?" she cried. "Why can't we have each other? It just isn't fair."

He reached over and gently wiped the moisture off her cheek.

"We can't see each other anymore. The reporter could come out with his story any day now. If people see that you had been spending a lot of time with me, they might assume that you were part of this thing. The police may be watching your house right now. If they see..."

"That Michael Franklin helped me kill my husband to collect his life insurance money... Why else would you have known to come to my funeral reception?"

She breathed in deeply as if she could suck in the awful situation and never let it go. They sat together quietly for what seemed like hours, trying to think of something to say when there wasn't, trying to create a magic solution that didn't exist. Finally, she flashed a crooked smile.

"Michael, I knew the first time I saw you that you were special, different from any man I've ever met. And I will admit I've been trying every way I could think of to make you more interested in me."

Michael started to shake his head. She took his hands and continued.

"That night we were supposed to make love, I was so hurt. Now I see you've been protecting me. But, it's funny, you know? Things happen for a reason. If that girl hadn't coaxed you to come to my husband's funeral reception to steal my money, we never would have met. Now, we will never know what you and I might have become."

He looked up the stairs towards her bedroom door. Without a word, she took his hand and led him up the steps. After she closed the door behind them, she had his belt on the floor and his shirt unbuttoned. She pushed him back onto the bed. As the sheets rustled, she tried to never lose sight of his face, or miss the sound of his breathing. His caresses were making her entire body ache... until he touched her stomach. She inhaled sharply. Michael stopped.

"Angela?"

She pulled the sheets down to her waist, disclosing the scars her husband had left on her abdomen.

"Jesus. No!" Michael cried. "He didn't. He couldn't. The coward! The bastard!"

"It's all right Michael. I don't have to worry about it anymore, do I?"

He leaned over and lightly kissed the area. She could hear the change in Michael's breathing. Slowly, carefully he moved his body on to hers.

## Chapter 54

Michael and Angela made love several times that afternoon and evening and finally, exhausted, fell asleep into each other's arms. The next morning, over breakfast, both of them were somber.

"OK, so this is what we promise each other, right Angie?" Michael said finally, kissing her lovingly one last time. "You're not going to try to see me because it can only hurt you. And as much as I want to, I'm never going to call or try to get in touch with you again. Maybe someday, someone will wave a magic wand and this will sort itself out. But until that happens, we can't see one another."

As Michael was driving back home, he thought maybe he should look around to see if he was being watched. But he didn't care anymore. Come get him. He wouldn't put up a fight. When he walked through the door, Jen was sitting in her usual spot.

"Decide to come up for air, did you?" she said. "Talk about taking one for the team. I don't need or want to hear any dirty details. Just tell me, when does the money come in?"

Michael looked at this woman who he had thought he loved, now like she was a leper. Her jokes weren't funny and she was the most heartless person he had ever met.

"I don't want to talk about that. Haven't we ruined enough lives? I'm going to bed."

She laughed after him as he walked up the stairs.

"Ha, stud duty over and the bull has to catch his breath. Good for you Michael. I think you've done the firm very proud."

He wasn't tired, at all. He just couldn't stand to be in the same room as her. He wouldn't allow her to debase the beautiful passion he and the widow shared into some disgusting sexual analogy.

One day passed then two and then a week. Jen would be sitting at her normal position, typing away into her laptop, sometimes humming a tune. At one point she asked him if he would like to help her write the monthly statement. He said no and left the room to watch TV. He would have nothing more to do with the scheme. He refused to try to raise any more funds. He simply sat and waited for the knock on the door, which would collapse their house of cards once and for all.

Jen watched and waited. He had fallen full on for the widow simply because he'd had sex with her. The normally cheery, upbeat guy who was always eager to help had turned into a sullen, dour face. She'd never seen him behave like this before. Even though she knew he hadn't tried to contact the widow in any way, she also knew she would have to take additional precautions. Finally, her patience expired.

"Michael, for the record, your fuck-fest was over a week ago and I still haven't seen a dime. We could use some fresh coin because a few of our clients want a distribution this month. What do you suppose is the problem?"

The filth that came out of this woman's mouth was made a thousand times worse when she applied it to the woman he could never have. He had heard enough.

"Jen, you know what? I really don't want to talk to you. I'm going to the Y."

He had to get out, away. He felt like he was watching a movie where the images just kept coming, faster and faster to the point of making him dizzy: his father, Jen, Angela, the police, all at the same time. It was like an earthquake and he was living amidst the aftershocks.

For as long as Michael could remember, the swimming pool was the place he could go for solitude. He'd put on his goggles and earplugs and be lost in the serenity of his movements through the water. His arms and legs were in perfect harmony with his breathing, extending left, then right. For those moments, he became deaf and blind to the realities of the outside world. His father could never understand his love for swimming, saying it was something children did. It wasn't really a sport, like football or hockey. Michael would swim until his muscles ached and begged him to stop. He never counted laps or time. Thinking about what Senior said, he had to agree. For Michael, it wasn't a sport at all. It was a form of contemplation. Just swim, Michael. That is the first step. Then go through your mental Rolodex, one at a time, systematically, slowly. A solution of some kind would come to you like it had so many times in your life before.

Today, he wanted to swim until his every last ounce of strength was spent. It seemed like the pressure was coming from all sides now. He thought back to Andrew, the reporter's warning, that he was 'way in over your head.' He'd hung up on him. Why hadn't he listened? He was now the main figure in a full-fledged Ponzi scheme that was growing by leaps and bounds. There was no way to stop it. To give everyone's money back - if he even could since Jennifer controlled all the accounts - would be an admission of guilt. To let it keep going would mean that he was knowingly stealing money from innocent people. If he weren't guilty before he certainly would be going forward. His choices were to accept a life of crime or go to jail.

After all, he had been no different than the victims of the Ponzi scam. He had been one of Jennifer's seven dwarfs. But, dammit! He knew right from wrong, and he would do the right thing. Jennifer had to be stopped. To do so required full self-incrimination but he refused to go to jail for a crime he didn't commit. He would stop her *and* find a way to give everyone their money back. Thank God he had never taken Angela's.

But how? He was trapped in a terrible maze, from which there was no escape.

He stopped suddenly and looked around him in the water.

*Escape...* That was it! Perhaps there *was* a way.

He started swimming again, the solution coming to him in waves he could barely navigate. Like turning the pages of a book, a story - his story was unfolding. As his plan fully crystallized in his mind, like the sun rising over the horizon, he realized the hardest part concerned Angela. Would she ever accept what he did? But he couldn't worry about that now.

For the first time in his life, he felt in total control.

## Chapter 55

On the boat, *For Love of Money*, for the last time, Michael looked at the stars as he slowly motored out of the harbor into Puget Sound. Turning back, what few lights were on at 4:15 a.m. grew smaller. He didn't think he'd been seen or heard, as he kept the engines at their lowest speed, but it didn't really matter anymore. He looked around the inside of the beautiful, brand new pleasure craft and realized that he could have gotten used to this. Whatever Jennifer/Sandy's real name was, and wherever she was from, she had good taste.

He turned again to the shore and could see that he was far enough away now. He throttled the boat back to idle and, a small glass of whiskey in hand, re-read the letter.

> *You know, I never understood what she was doing until it was too late. I had no idea it would get like this. I started out clean. I never intended to be part of anything that would take all of these people's money. I was going to do it the old fashioned way, just like dear old dad said I should. He gave me his accounts, like he was doing me a favor. He knew what would happen. All it did was cover his ass. Now he says he's dying. Sorry to hear that but I guess we all do, right?*
>
> *But just because I am doing... this, I'm not a quitter. Jennifer thinks she's got me in a corner but I've figured out a way to set everything right.*

# The Ponzi

*I have to laugh. Franklin Senior, I showed him... and everyone else for that matter. They couldn't believe it. I had more money in my hands than they ever dreamed of. They all thought that I was some sort of prodigy, a mind that comes along once in a generation. Senior bragged about me to all his friends and even helped us take their money. He won't be bragging much after he reads this.*

*We are running a full out Ponzi scheme. The whole thing was created by Jennifer Salem aka Sandy Allen. She tricked me into believing that we were just building a business and then threatened me when I finally figured out what she was doing. She said she had set it up so that nothing would stick to her. All the accounts are in my name, any correspondence everything even this frigging boat. It wasn't me - it was all her. I'm not lying. Have a look at her computer. You'll see - it's all there.*

*The thing I don't get is why did everyone including me, accept such complete bullshit? None of it was true, ever. But it seems like people just want to believe. They want to know that there is an easy way to get rich.*

*The thing has gotten too big now anyway. It's out of control. I don't know how to shut it off or, at least I didn't. Now, I do. Party's over folks. Like cracks in the Hoover Dam - there's one big flood coming. I hope by writing this letter people will get most of their money back. Jennifer/Sandy will have to face the consequences of her actions. For me, let's just say that I'm not going to jail for something I didn't do. I've made sure of that.*

*For all the people I have hurt, I am truly sorry. My only wish is that someday you might forgive me. But, I guess I will never know.*

He started to refill his glass just as the boat shifted from a sideways wave, spilling the whiskey on him and the deck. But that didn't matter now. He drank what made it into his glass and felt the burning in the back of his throat. He then took a piece of rope out of his jacket pocket and carefully tied the steering wheel so the boat would slowly travel in circles until it was found. He hoped they could sell it and give more of the clients' money back.

Finally, he secured the letter with tape to the laptop to make sure it couldn't blow away and looked over the side into the blackness. He prepared himself for the initial shock; the water was bitter cold at all times and an unprotected person would last only minutes before hypothermia made them succumb.

He slipped into the water and watched as the boat gently pulled away.

## Chapter 56

Lying in bed and listening intently for sounds that would tell her what was going on in the house was a skill Jen had learned when she was very young. Were her mother and father fighting? Was her father slurping on his Cheerios before leaving for the day? Was there anyone home at all? This morning when she opened her eyes and saw that Michael wasn't there, she quickly turned to the bedside clock. 6:00 a.m. She lay still, listening until she was certain that she was alone.

She jumped out of bed, grabbed her bathrobe and ran down to the kitchen and found that, although her computer was still there, his was not. Hitting the ON button, she tapped her fingers nervously on the table.

"Come on, dammit, come on!"

When the laptop had finally powered up, she opened the program that ran the hidden outdoor security camera and started to laugh. He had left at 3:00 a.m. What a fool. The first rule was to *never* underestimate your adversary. She quickly ran through the list of bank accounts, and was relieved to see that none of the money had been disturbed. She had started seeing Michael's signs of withdrawal, both from her and the business. There he was, in his pitiful way telling her that he wanted out. Was that his idea, the widow's or both? It didn't matter really. The only thing of any consequence now was to avoid any awkward situations he had inadvertently created for her. Or maybe they wouldn't be unintentional. He had been starting to act pretty high and mighty lately, perhaps because he had some sort of realization or, perhaps, since the widow wanted to have him for her own, she might have thought implicating Jennifer might help their own cause. There was no telling what the fool might do. It didn't matter. Jennifer would soon have all the insurance she needed.

She reached into the cutlery drawer, grabbed the black memory stick that was taped to the underside of the plastic tray and jammed it into the USB port. Racing against the clock, she quickly went through, file by file, transferring those that could be useful, erasing those that might seem incriminating and smiling finally as the laptop was clean and all the important files reclaimed. She removed the memory stick and put it into a cushioned envelope sent to her private post office address and drove to the nearest collection box. As the metal lid banged shut, she breathed a sigh of relief. She couldn't yet know what Michael was up to but, whatever it was, she would be OK.

It was just before noon when she heard the knock on the door. She quickly tussled up her hair, and rubbed her fingers in her eyes to redden them a bit. Michael hadn't come home yet. Where in heaven's name could he be? When she opened the door a crack, she saw the familiar badge worn by Seattle's finest.

"Oh thank God you're here," she gasped. "I am so worried. I was just about to call you. My Michael isn't here. He disappeared sometime in the night. He hasn't called me. I'm afraid something terrible has happened to him."

The officer introduced himself as Sanderson as she showed him to the kitchen table. She almost offered him coffee or water but then thought better of it. A distraught woman wouldn't think in those terms at a time like this.

"Ah, yes Ms. Salem is it? I'm here as part of an investigation and I need to ask you a few questions."

"Yes, ask me anything. Is Michael OK?"

"That's what we're trying to determine. Does your husband own a luxury yacht?"

"Uh, yes, he just bought it. Our business has been going so well, he decided to treat himself. He's not my husband, at least not yet. I keep asking him and he keeps putting me off."

The officer looked back at his notepad.

"And was the inscription on the yacht *For Love of Money*?"

"Yes. I told Michael that was a bit over the top, but he insisted."

"You say Michael Franklin disappeared sometime during the night?"

She closed her eyes and sighed deeply.

"He must have. We went to bed together and he wasn't there when I woke up."

"Did he mention to you that he was planning on going out in the boat in the middle of the night? Did he seem upset when you went to bed? Did you and he have some sort of argument?"

"No!" Jennifer exclaimed. "Why? What's happened?"

It was clear from the officer's expression that he did not relish saying what had to come next.

"Well, I am sorry to inform you that the Coast Guard was called to investigate a yacht that was drifting a few miles off shore in the Puget Sound. They called ahoy and, receiving no response, boarded the vessel only to find it unmanned. The harbor master confirmed that it left the dock around four this morning."

Jennifer thought Michael's plan was starting to take shape, but she needed to maintain the appearance of complete bewilderment.

"Officer, you're not making any sense. Why would Michael decide to go out on his boat, in the dark when there was nothing to see?"

"There's more, Ms. Salem. The Coast Guard found other things on board. There was evidence of alcohol consumption and…"

"The WIDOW!" Jennifer cried. "I should have known that she has something to do with this. She's been after Michael ever since she met him. We're engaged, if you didn't know. Now she's taken him out to get him drunk and try to seduce him. I bet they were on board all right - and the Coast Guard caught them in the act so they had to keep quiet. Wait until I get my hands on him, the bastard."

Engaged? Based on what officer Sanderson had read in the note left on the vessel, that seemed unlikely.

"Ms. Salem, I can assure you that the yacht was thoroughly searched and there was no one on board. In fact, the steering wheel had been tied so that the boat would just run in circles - so it wouldn't drift too far out to sea. It was as if someone, presumably Michael Franklin wanted to make sure it was found."

Jennifer assumed an expression of horror and disbelief.

"But, Ms. Salem, there's more," the officer went on. "There was a note. Our lab is looking at it to confirm its legitimacy but, on the surface, it looks as if... your fiancé has taken his life."

Aha! What a brilliant idea. The only way to get out of the scheme without implicating himself was to completely disappear. He'd left a note, had he? Jennifer knew what was coming next. But she'd just found out that her fiancé had committed suicide. She had to go through with it as if this was the worst day of her life. She put her hands over her face, wailing "NO! NO! NO!" before falling into the officer's arms and burying her face into his uniform. When enough time had passed, she allowed herself to recover ever so slightly, speaking in broken tones and gasping for breath.

"I just ... can't ... believe it. No, officer, there's *got* to be some kind of mistake. I mean, I know he was upset lately. He got some horrible news that his father was not only very ill, but he wasn't even his real father. We've been working very hard but, no officer, I can't accept this. There must be another answer."

Officer Sanderson was taking notes. His father wasn't his father? There apparently had been no mention of that in the note. This case just kept getting screwier.

"Well, actually, Ms. Salem, I'm here to see you today on two official pieces of business. The first was to inform you about Michael Franklin's apparent suicide. The second however will require that you come to the precinct with me. In his note, Mr. Franklin has made some very damaging allegations against you, claiming that you lured him into a massive financial fraud, without his knowledge or consent. He said he couldn't live with himself and the sense of guilt over stealing so much money from so many people. In his note, he said he would rather die than go to jail for a crime he didn't commit. He said that, if it was the last thing he did, and apparently it was, he would see you brought to justice."

The cards had been played. She had to hand it to Michael. This was a better scheme than she thought he could create. But, it wouldn't be good enough. Before they got anywhere near the police station, and she lost control of the agenda, she had some of her own facts to reveal.

"Officer, now I understand what is happening here. I am horrified to say it, but my fiancé and the widow are having an affair before we even got married. Thank God I learned about it before it was too late."

The officer just shook his head.

"Ms. Salem, I think we need to go downtown. This is getting very perplexing."

She agreed to go with him - anywhere he liked - and help in any way she could, even offering her computer to assist in their investigation. She had her own cards to play, including the ace of trumps. The timing of that however would be critical.

## Chapter 57

It had been only two weeks but they felt as if they had lived there forever.
Their maid and housekeeper, Margarita, applied the finishing touches to massaging Michael, lying naked underneath the protective palms of the coconut trees that lined the soft sand beach. They could go days without seeing another person and, even if you did no one seemed to care. Once Michael had laid out his plan, Belize had been Angela's idea. With 9,000 square miles and only 350,000 citizens, it was the perfect place for them to get away, to never see a single person that they knew or, more importantly, anyone who could recognize them. Their 4,200 square foot beachfront home on Costa del Sol with four bedrooms and four baths was just the right size for the honeymooning couple, and the 1,400 square foot patio was really where they spent most of their time. The house came with a staff of four, including a full time chef and security guard. They rented of course, for cash. They had lots of cash. No one asked any questions. This was a perfect place to live.

Michael had just given Margarita his order for lunch, stewed fish with rice and beans, as Angela, in her pink bikini top and gym shorts, sauntered towards the massage table.

"You're going to have the tannest ass in the entire world, Michael. But you need to get dressed. The water taxi will be here in an hour or so and I'm starving. I really can't wait for the trip through the jungle."

They went up towards the patio, Michael wearing nothing now but his cut off jean shorts that he had hung on a piece of frayed palm tree bark. He put his arm around his young bride and kissed the side of her neck. They weren't really married, of course; they just told everyone they were. He had never been happier than he was right now. It truly was like a rebirth. All of his worries, anxiety and stress seemed to melt out of his pores as he emerged from the airport. He had never seen Angela happier either. She too had been granted a new life. And they were rich.

Michael had wrestled with that decision for a long time. He didn't need to keep any of the Ponzi money. With Angela freely offering the use of her full inheritance, they could have lived a very comfortable if not simple life together. He thought about taking an amount equal to his father's inheritance but that money, like all of it, didn't belong to him. Besides, had he taken a penny, how could he look himself in the mirror and think he was any better than the people he had escaped from? He had given all of the necessary information in his suicide note and the computer. He hoped his former clients would eventually get most of their money back - which was better than the result in many other Ponzi schemes he'd heard of.

He did owe Sandy one debt of gratitude. Without her cynical outlook, he would never have met the true love of his life. Angela was the answer to his dreams. They needed each other since she was a fugitive and he was dead. Neither one could ever go home again.

He thought about Jen. She had planned for him to take the fall for her crime. But, maybe for the first time in her life, she had underestimated someone. He wished he could have been a fly on the wall when the police showed up at their house. She'd got him into this dirty business. She, by all rights should be the one that paid the price - while he worked on his tan.

The meals were promptly served, as always. Angela had ordered escabeche, an onion broth with chicken and chaya tamales and, as had become their custom since they arrived, they washed down their lunch with Champagne. As they ate, they talked about their plans for the rest of the day. They were taking a private car and driver through the jungle where they hoped to find howler monkeys and, if they were lucky, perhaps a jaguar sunning himself in a tree. The driver would drop them off at one of the many ancient Mayan temples for some exploring. If they had time, they would come back home and swim out toward the reef to snorkel amongst the dolphins and multi-colored fish. But, if the sun started to set before they got everything done, well, there was always tomorrow.

## Chapter 58

Sandy had been in a room like this before.
She supposed they were all the same - bare white walls and a cold, tile floor. In the middle sat a rectangular table surrounded by four metal-framed chairs with yellowed vinyl seats. On one side of the room was a mirror, which she knew to be two-way so there could be witnesses to the answers given during the interrogation. At the very least, the police psychologist could monitor the body language of the person answering the questions in order to identify when the lies had likely been told. She was led in and allowed to sit alone and unobserved, or so she was supposed to think, for about ten minutes. Sometimes valuable clues could be picked up when the accused thought they were completely alone. Sandy looked at the mirror and wondered how many people were on the other side. Finally the two officers entered the room, Sanderson and his partner.

"I'm Mueller, with the white collar crime division. First of all, is it Ms. Salem, or Ms. Allen, what would you like us to call you?"

Sandy didn't hesitate. She was not intimidated by this man or any other.

"You can call me anything you like, but my name is Sandy."

The officer cleared his throat.

"OK, *Sandy*, let's get on with it, shall we? You are here because you've been asked to help us understand a disturbing situation.

Mr. Michael Franklin, your apparent former fiancé is missing and presumed drowned somewhere in the Puget Sound. When Officer Sanderson told you this at your home, you seemed shocked and saddened, as would be expected. Unfortunately, there is more for us to discuss. In his suicide note, which was found on the vessel named *For Love of Money* the deceased implicated you in a very serious crime. Specifically, Mr. Michael Franklin admitted to the two of you running a massive Ponzi scheme, cheating your victims out of an estimated $100 million. He alleged that the idea was entirely yours. He accused you of operating under a false name and said you tricked him into believing that the two of you were just building a business. He said that you threatened him when he finally figured out what you were doing, and that you had purposely put his name on everything instead of yours; meaning he would have been set up to take the fall should your scheme ever be discovered. Apparently, his only avenue for escape was to end his life. It's a terrible story at best."

Officer Mueller looked up from the paper he had been reading and removed his glasses.

"Let me be clear. You have not been charged nor arrested based on the statement from someone who was clearly disturbed and, perhaps under the influence of alcohol. Still, there are a number of troublesome accusations that Mr. Franklin has made that we at least need to discuss and, if nothing else, hear your side of the story. You are here speaking with us on your own free will and we are recording this meeting on videotape. With that in mind, I must inform you of your rights. You don't have to answer any of the questions that we ask you and, for that matter you have the right to remain completely silent. At any point in our conversation you can choose to have an attorney present."

After the officer had finished with the Miranda rights, he paused and looked up at her.

"Now Sandy, before we proceed, do you have any questions?"

Locking her eyes onto his and clenching her teeth, she decided that the direct approach was probably best. Officer Mueller continued.

"All right then, the first thing we need to do is establish, for the record, your true identity. Are you Sandy Allen, formerly of New York City…"

Sandy interrupted him.

"…who was framed, as I am being here, in that case, for insider trading? While I was never formally charged with any crime, I was barred from employment in the securities industry for life. I was thoroughly devastated and embarrassed and decided to get as far away from there as I could. I assumed a new name and even changed my hair color so no one would recognize me."

Mueller raised his eyebrows.

"Yes, that's me."

The two officers on the other side of the table were staring at her. She flicked a strand of her hair back over one of her shoulders.

"I met up with Michael Franklin just as I did with a crazy Russian president of a drug company in New York. Both men turned out to be disasters for me. I guess I'm just not very lucky in love."

Sanderson rubbed his upper lip with his index finger.

"You already know all of this. I thought I would just save us some time."

They glanced at each other briefly and Officer Mueller looked back to his notes.

"Of course, Sandy, we're all interested in saving time. Now…"

"And before we go any further with your questions, I would like my laptop computer back. I need to show you a few things that will have a material impact on your investigation that you might not have noticed."

Sanderson left the room and returned with the machine in a few moments. Feeling the warm underside, she could tell it had been running for some time. When it was set up, Officer Mueller continued.

"Then, Sandy, as I was saying, did you have any idea that Mr. Franklin was planning to take his own life? Did you have any discussions with him that might suggest anything in his letter was true? Did you have some sort of lovers' quarrel that might have left him quite upset?"

She kept her eyes trained on his, although it was becoming increasingly difficult. But she knew that the people behind the mirror would be taking note of signs of discomfort.

"I haven't seen this letter," she said. "It sounds like some of what he said is true, but certainly not all of it. It wasn't the two of us running a Ponzi scheme; it was Michael. He knew that, based on my circumstances when I left New York, he only needed to drag me into his arrangement a little and then he could make me do anything he wanted. I can't tell you how many times he's threatened to 'turn me in.' He knows no one would believe my side of the story. He's a ruthless bastard who is bitter towards anyone who has been more successful than he, especially his father. He bragged to me that he tricked the widow out of her inheritance. You know who I'm talking about because you came to our house to warn Michael that she might have murdered her husband. You should have a chat with her, the whore. I'll bet she has lots to say."

"Yes, Sandy we might well do that, but please carry on."

She barely paused at the interruption.

"He even took all of his own *father's* money *after* the man revealed he had a terminal illness. You said that he said the idea was entirely mine. Are you kidding? After what I went through in New York I even stop my car at yellow lights now. Yes, I have been operating under a false name but that isn't a crime. All of the accounts are in his name because I tricked *him*? Come on officers, does that make sense to you? You *know* why all of the accounts are in his name."

The two men were writing feverishly as she spoke. Finally, Officer Mueller raised his head.

"So then, you are saying you had nothing to do with handling the money?"

"Not a thing."

Sandy reached across the table and positioned the laptop in front of her.

"Actually Officer Mueller, if you pay attention to what I am about to show you, the *circumstances*, as I think you referred to them are not what they seem."

Officer Mueller was becoming a bit annoyed at the cockiness of this woman who was facing a far more dire future than she realized. He nodded for her to continue.

Sandy expertly manipulated some of the keys as she spoke.

"Well officer, it's like this. After my little New York experience, I decided no one would ever take advantage of me again. So, I put in some safeguards. They sell these mini wireless surveillance cameras everywhere now. They're small, not easily noticed and send a signal right to your computer. Ah, here it is. On the night that the despondent Michael Franklin supposedly disappeared from this earth, look at what my video camera came up with, right outside our door."

She turned the screen so the officers could see it. In the upper right hand corner, a clock was slowly ticking. At 3:04 a.m. a male figure could clearly be seen walking towards the BMW. Before he reached the door, the figure stopped and turned to look back at the house. At that moment, Sandy froze the frame, clearly revealing the face of Michael Franklin. Under his arm, he appeared to be carrying a laptop computer. He got in quickly, fastened his seat belt and sped off.

"So, gentlemen, let me ask you a question. Who fastens their seat belt on their way to commit suicide? And why would you take your laptop with you? I don't think there is any email in heaven."

The officers' eyes quickly moved up towards the mirror and then back to the table. Sandy stifled her smile as she imagined the people behind the mirror frantically wondering why they didn't have this evidence.

"Well Sandy, that is intriguing material but I have to say, inconclusive. Seat belts are an unconscious habit for most of us now. And perhaps we'll have a better understanding of the lap top's significance in a minute."

Sandy slowly turned her head from side to side.

"There's more, Officer Mueller. The other thing I did to protect myself was to install a tracking device onto both of our computers. With all of the thefts these days, you can never be too careful. So, let's have a look at how Michael's laptop fared during his final ordeal. I haven't had a chance to download the movements, but I can tell you, the reason he took it with him, and it is very significant indeed, is it gives him access to all the money, account numbers, passwords, the whole thing. Find that laptop and you've found not only your man but all of the money he stole."

Officer Mueller looked up from his notes.

"I thought you said you had little knowledge of any of the workings of this apparent fraud," Mueller said. "How then would you know what information was on that laptop Mr. Franklin was carrying?"

She sat up straighter and turned her head to one side. It was her first mistake. Everyone in the room and behind the mirrors noticed the posture change.

"Well… he used to brag about it. He said all the information for his whole scheme was on that laptop but that… I was too stupid to ever be able to get past the passwords."

The officers turned their eyes to her screen. Officer Mueller motioned to it as he looked up.

"Sandy, this surveillance work you've done, did it ever occur to you that it's a complete invasion of privacy? Why would you install a tracking device on his computer?"

"I was just protecting... myself. He kept saying he had all kinds of incriminating evidence about me on there. I had no idea what but I didn't want it to fall into the wrong hands."

Officer Mueller continued to shake his head. That was the second time she pleaded ignorance. The trap had been set. She only needed to spring it.

"This is ridiculous," he said. "If Michael Franklin isn't dead, where is he? From where the boat was found, he couldn't have swum to shore. That water is frigid. He wouldn't have lasted more than just a few minutes."

"I guess you guys didn't know that he is an expert swimmer, best of his team in college and he considered trying out for the Olympics but his father squashed that. Put a wetsuit on Michael, give him flippers, a mask and a snorkel, maybe even a floatation device of some sort and he could have swam for twenty miles."

The two officers looked at each other. She was really grasping at straws now. Besides, even if Michael Franklin was alive, they had all the evidence they needed, including most of the money. The FBI was on its way. This woman would not escape again.

"We found a BMW at the dock. Did he purchase that using the proceeds of the scam?"

Sandy slapped the table.

"NOW you're starting to get it. And he bought the stupid boat too."

Officer Mueller rubbed his hand over his forehead.

"Right, so then, I guess what you are saying is whomever made those purchases is likely the person we should be talking to since they had to know where the money was and how to access it?"

"ABSOLUTELY!"

She had, of course erased any evidence of the transactions.

"All right then, you said you had some sort of tracer built into the laptop he took with him but you hadn't had a chance to run it. Could you do that for us now?"

Sandy punched a few keys and then turned the screen to face them.

"By all means, I think you will find that the computer Michael took with him decided to take a plane trip out of the country. Just watch and learn."

The screen clicked on revealing a typical computer-generated map, with the name of the street off to one side. A small blinking yellow light indicated the current location of the sensor. The time on the screen was 3:04 am. As the time clock advanced, the light could be seen moving down the street.

"Watch this. There, the computer is moving as he got on the highway. See, he is taking the exit towards the marina. He turned down to the dock area... and the car has now stopped."

Sandy stopped talking as she continued to watch the blinking light that was no longer moving. She decided to fast forward the recording to the point where it was on the move again. Michael clearly could have left the lap top in the car, set up the boat scenario to draw attention away from him and then swam back to shore.

But, as she started to press the keys, Officer Mueller stopped her.

"Not so fast there, Sandy. I don't want to miss anything."

Something was wrong. Officer Mueller decided to take over the narration.

"That computer appears to be stationary, so he or it must have spent a fair bit of time at the dock. Ah, here we go. The laptop is on the move again. There, it looks like it is heading ever so slowly towards, wait a minute, that's the water. The laptop has either learned to swim or Michael took it on the boat with him."

Sandy frowned. There was no way even Michael would be so stupid as to blow their plan and not take at least some of the money with him. Unless he really did... Could he, just to seek revenge? Had he lost his mind?

She whispered.

"That can't be."

"Well, Sandy, how else did the laptop get on board if Michael didn't carry it with him?"

What was happening?

"What do you mean, *on board?*"

"That's where the Coast Guard found it when they picked up the boat. And, you know, your friend Michael was a solid business partner. He knew how important the information was on those computers. Somehow you lost a ton of information on your computer here, but when we compared the one you have in front of you to the one we found on the boat, we could see that Michael did a full backup of every single file, right down to the invoices for the car and the boat."

Sandy's mind raced, trying to find a new line.

"I have no control over what he did to the computers."

"Perhaps not, but somebody very early this morning erased a significant number of files from the laptop you had in your possession. If that wasn't you Sandy, who was it? We know, using your very own videotape, that it couldn't have been Michael. If it was you, why did you do it? Don't answer me yet. That's leads me to another point. A minute ago, you agreed with me that whoever bought the boat and the BMW is likely the person in charge of the scheme and the one we should be after."

He reached into a leather folder and pulled out two pieces of paper.

"Here are copies of the agreements taken from the computer on the boat. It shows very clearly that they were purchased by one Jennifer Salem. And you won't believe what else we found. You even applied for a boating license. Were you planning a trip in your new boat, Sandy?"

Sandy closed her eyes and shook her head. She'd seen all kinds, fought against the best and brightest and always, always landed on her feet. But Michael was a kamikaze. He had taken his own life to end hers.

## Chapter 59

"Guess what I found on the Internet today, Michael?" Angela loved playing this game with him. He would always respond, "Who cares? We live in another world now." But she would persevere. It was she who first found the article about the abandoned boat at sea, which was discovered by the Coast Guard. After an intense seventy-two hour search, Mr. Michael Franklin was declared 'missing and presumed drowned.' While the press wasn't supposed to either learn about or disclose key facts about an investigation, at one point the line *a source close to the investigation revealed the discovery of a suicide note found onboard the vessel* really closed the books that the world would never see one Michael Franklin Junior again. It had been a simple-enough matter for Angela to get a fake driver's license and passports for both of them. She rented a car, paying cash of course, and picked Michael up on the other side of the sound. They went straight to the airport, after ditching his wetsuit in a trash dumpster and took the first flight out of the country. Long before the 72 hour search for Michael's body was called off, they were in their new country.

Michael's suicide led to the long, sorry article Andrew wrote how about capitalism can literally destroy lives. It was like the reporter delivered the final sermon on the tragic tale of the son of Michael Franklin Senior. Actually, Michael appreciated the closure Andrew had provided. As time went on, his would become a fading memory. He wished he could thank the reporter someday.

It was Angela that found her own story. According to the sheriff's department, the inquiry into the tragic death of John Messina had now turned into a full-scale murder investigation and, a warrant had been issued for the popular Wall Street banker's ex-wife. When the police raided her home, however, the woman, Angela Messina had apparently moved out with no notice to anyone who knew her. Any persons with knowledge of her whereabouts were instructed to contact the Seattle homicide division immediately.

Angela could live with the fact that she would always be a fugitive. They would never find her here.

Michael really didn't want to play the game but he knew that she did so he went along with it.

"OK, you found an article about Ponzi schemes."

She twirled her Champagne glass and smiled.

"Nope… try again."

Michael leaned back in his chair. He combed his fingers through his hair and thought. There had been plenty written about him and Angela. There was even a quote from Skip Williams that his firm was launching its own internal investigation to ensure that this former employee, a *terminated* employee he added for effect, had not somehow compromised the compliance policies and procedures of his firm. He had been quoted as saying "We, at Fifty States Investments, take the fiscal responsibility of our clients' assets very seriously."

"OK, you found another article about Jennifer or Sandy's conviction."

"Oh please Michael that is such old news. What was it she got, twelve consecutive life terms?"

Michael nodded his head and smiled. Sandy Allen was where she belonged.

"All right then, I give up, what is it?"

She turned the laptop to face him.

"Let me just put it to you this way, lover. I found a *very* interesting headline. The story doesn't even matter. What's important is, finally the world seems to be catching on."

## *Case of woman acquitted of hiring hit man to kill abusive spouse goes to top court*

*Washington - The Supreme Court will hear arguments this week on whether the battered woman's defense can include the hiring of a hit man to kill an abusive spouse.*

Michael didn't need to read any further. Angela leaned forward, put her hands on top of his and, grinning, whispered,

"you better treat me right, boy."

– *The End* –

Made in the USA
Middletown, DE
25 March 2017